D0594424

About the Author

BERNARD CORNWELL is the author of the acclaimed and bestselling Saxon Tales, which include *The Last Kingdom*, *The Pale Horseman*, *Lords of the North*, and *Sword Song*, as well as the Richard Sharpe novels, the Grail Quest series, the Nathaniel Starbuck Chronicles, the Warlord Chronicles, and many other novels, including *Stonehenge* and *Gallows Thief*. He lives with his wife on Cape Cod.

WILDTRACK

Books by Bernard Cornwell

The Saxon Tales

THE LAST KINGDOM*
THE PALE HORSEMAN*
LORDS OF THE NORTH*
SWORD SONG*

The Sharpe Novels (in chronological order)

SHARPE'S TIGER*
Richard Sharpe and the Siege of Seringapatam, 1799

SHARPE'S TRIUMPH*
Richard Sharpe and the Battle of Assaye, September 1803

SHARPE'S FORTRESS*
Richard Sharpe and the Siege of Gawilghur, December 1803

SHARPE'S TRAFALGAR*
Richard Sharpe and the Battle of Trafalgar, 21 October 1805

SHARPE'S PREY*
Richard Sharpe and the Expedition to Copenhagen, 1807

SHARPE'S RIFLES
Richard Sharpe and the French Invasion of Galicia, January 1809

SHARPE'S HAVOC*
Richard Sharpe and the Campaign in Northern Portugal, Spring 1809

SHARPE'S EAGLE
Richard Sharpe and the Talavera Campaign, July 1809

SHARPE'S GOLD
Richard Sharpe and the Destruction of Almeida, August 1810

SHARPE'S ESCAPE*
Richard Sharpe and the Bussaco Campaign, 1810

SHARPE'S FURY*
Richard Sharpe and the Battle of Barrosa, March 1811

SHARPE'S BATTLE*
Richard Sharpe and the Battle of Fuentes de Onoro, May 1811

SHARPE'S COMPANY
Richard Sharpe and the Siege of Badajoz, January to April 1812

SHARPE'S SWORD
Richard Sharpe and the Salamanca Campaign, June and July 1812

SHARPE'S ENEMY
Richard Sharpe and the Defense of Portugal, Christmas 1812

SHARPE'S HONOUR
Richard Sharpe and the Vitoria Campaign, February to June 1813

SHARPE'S REGIMENT
Richard Sharpe and the Invasion of France, June to November 1813

SHARPE'S SIEGE
Richard Sharpe and the Winter Campaign, 1814

SHARPE'S REVENGE
Richard Sharpe and the Peace of 1814

SHARPE'S WATERLOO
Richard Sharpe and the Waterloo Campaign, 15 June to 18 June 1815

SHARPE'S DEVIL*
Richard Sharpe and the Emperor, 1820–21

The Grail Quest Series
THE ARCHER'S TALE*
VAGABOND*
HERETIC*

The Nathaniel Starbuck Chronicles
REBEL*
COPPERHEAD*
BATTLE FLAG*
THE BLOODY GROUND*

The Warlord Chronicles
THE WINTER KING
ENEMY OF GOD
EXCALIBUR

The Sailing Trillers
STORMCHILD*
SCOUNDREL*
WILDTRACK*
CREAKDOWN*

Other Novels
STONEHENGE, 2000 B.C.: A NOVEL*
GALLOWS THIEF*
A CROWNING MERCY*
THE FALLEN ANGELS*
REDCOAT*

* Published by HarperCollins*Publishers*.

WILDTRACK

A Novel of Suspense

BERNARD CORNWELL

HARPER

NEW YORK . LONDON . TORONTO . SYDNEY

HARPER

It is inevitable that some boat names in *Wildtrack* will coincide with the names of real boats. Nevertheless every vessel in the book, like every character, is entirely fictional.

First published in Great Britain in 1988 by Michael Joseph. A paperback edition was published in Great Britain in 1993 by Penguin Books.

FIRST HARPER PAPERBACK PUBLISHED 2008.

Library of Congress Cataloging-in-Publication Data is available upon request.

ISBN 978-0-06-146264-1

HB 02.21.2020

Wildtrack is dedicated
to the memory of
David Watt

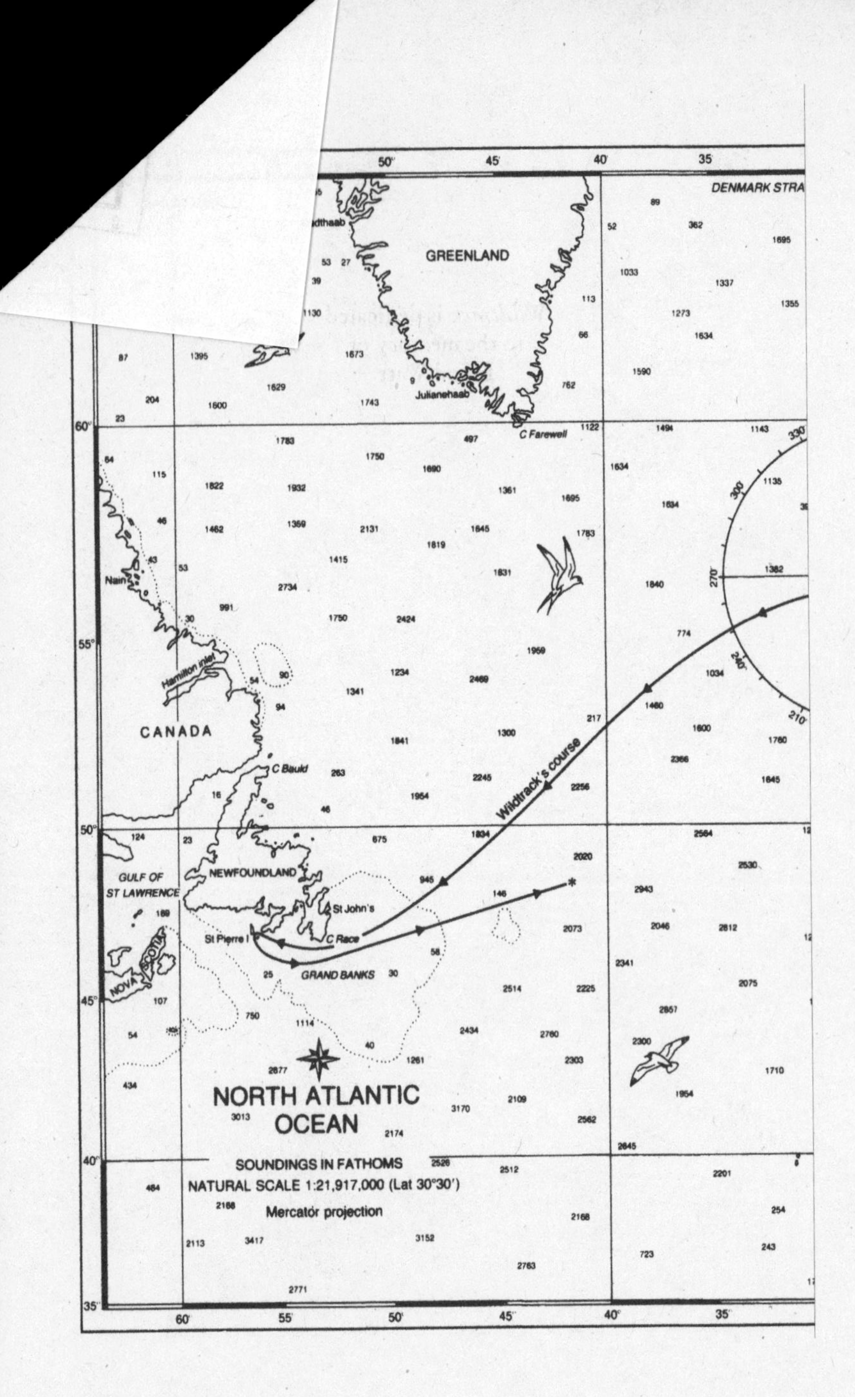

DENMARK STRA
GREENLAND
Julianehaab
C Farewell
Nain
Hamilton inlet
CANADA
C Bauld
NEWFOUNDLAND
GULF OF
ST LAWRENCE
St John's
St Pierre I
C Race
GRAND BANKS
NOVA SCOTIA
Wildtrack's course
NORTH ATLANTIC
OCEAN
SOUNDINGS IN FATHOMS
NATURAL SCALE 1:21,917,000 (Lat 30°30')
Mercatór projection

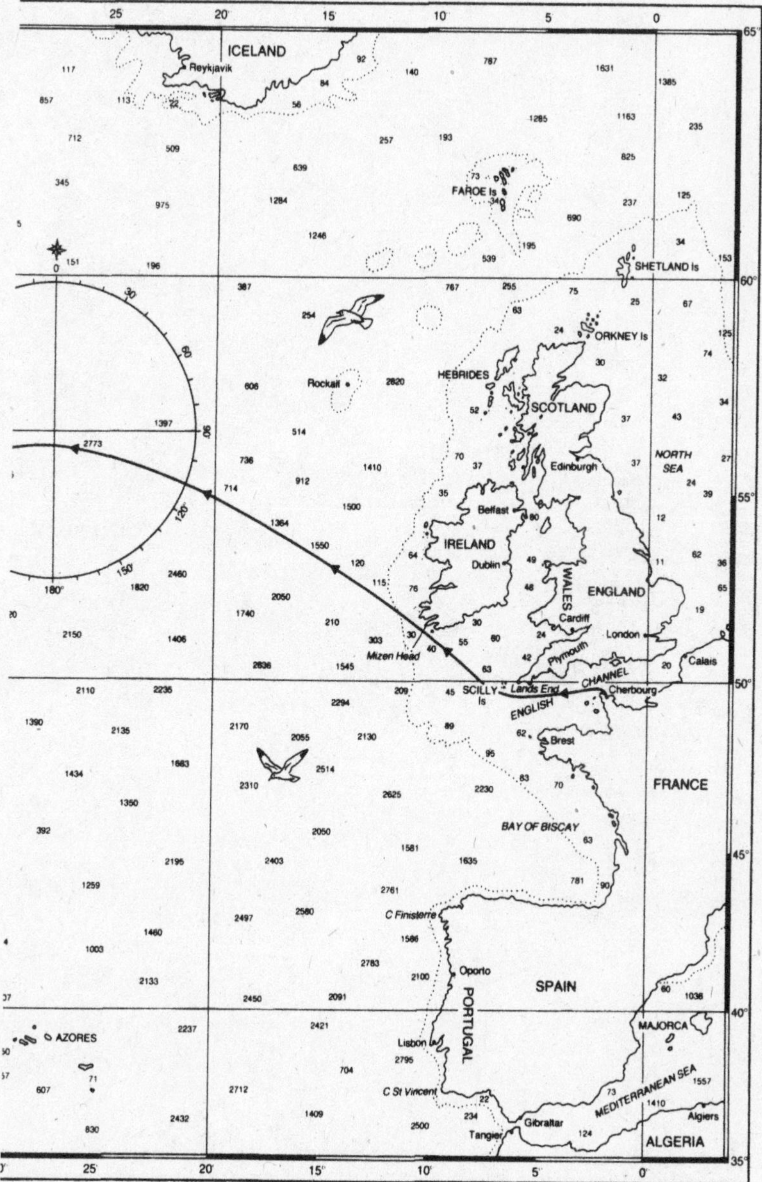

ICELAND
Reykjavik
FAROE Is
SHETLAND Is
ORKNEY Is
HEBRIDES
Rockall
SCOTLAND
Edinburgh
NORTH SEA
Belfast
IRELAND
Dublin
WALES
ENGLAND
Cardiff
London
Plymouth
Calais
Mizen Head
SCILLY Is
Lands End
ENGLISH CHANNEL
Cherbourg
Brest
FRANCE
BAY OF BISCAY
C Finisterre
Oporto
SPAIN
PORTUGAL
MAJORCA
Lisbon
C St Vincent
MEDITERRANEAN SEA
Gibraltar
Tangier
Algiers
ALGERIA
AZORES

PROLOGUE

They said I'd never walk again.

They said I'd be in a wheelchair till they lifted me into the box and screwed down my lid. I should learn a trade, they said. Something cripple-friendly, like computers.

They'd had me for damn nearly a year. They'd put a metal rod into my right thigh, and grafted skin where my thighs and arse had been burned. They did a mixture of rough carpentry and micro-surgery on my spine and, when it half worked – which meant I could twitch the toes on my left foot – they opened me up again and did a bit more. It had all taken months and still I could not walk.

You must get used to it, they said, because you're never going to walk again. You're never going to sail again. You're a paraplegic now, Nick, so kiss it all goodbye. I told them to get stuffed.

"That's not the spirit, Nick!" Doctor Maitland said in his no-nonsense voice. "There's no stigma involved, you know. Quite the opposite!" He flipped the pages of a yachting magazine that lay on a pile of similar magazines beside my bed. "And you'll be afloat again. You can go sailing this very spring!"

It was the first sign of hope he'd given me, and I responded eagerly. "Can I?"

"My dear Nick, of course you can. There's a motor sailor on the Solent that's specially adapted for your sort of case."

My eagerness ebbed. "My sort of case?"

"Ramps for the chairs and a trained volunteer staff on board." Maitland always spoke of these things in a matter-of-fact voice, as if everyone in the real world went around on wheels with tubes sticking into their bladders. "And perhaps you'd let the press go along?" he added hopefully. "They all want to interview you."

"Tell them to go to hell. No press. That's the rule, remember? I don't want to see a bloody reporter."

"No press, then." Maitland could not hide his disappointment. He loved publicity for his paraplegic paradise. "Perhaps I'll come along. It's been many a long year since I went sailing."

"You can go on your own," I said sullenly.

"That isn't the right spirit, Nick." He twitched at my curtains, which didn't need twitching.

I closed my eyes. "I'm going to walk out of this bloody place on my own two feet."

"That won't stop you going sailing in the spring, will it now?" Maitland, like all his staff, specialized in that bright interrogatory inflection at the end of statements; an inflection designed to elicit our agreement. Once they had us accepting that we were doomed, then half their battle was won. "Will it?" he asked again.

I opened my eyes. "The last time I went sailing, Doc, I was in a friend's forty-footer coming back from Iceland. She was knocked down near the Faeroes and lost all her mast above the spreaders. We hacked off the broken stuff, rigged jury hounds, and brought her into North Uist five days later. That was a neat piece of work, Doc." I didn't add that the friend had broken his arm when the boat had broached, or that it had happened in the depths of a bloody awful night. What mattered was that we took on that bitch of a northern sea and brought our boat home.

Maitland had listened very patiently. "That was before, Nick, wasn't it?"

"So there's no bloody way, Doc, that I'm going to sit on your cripple barge and watch the pretty boats go by." I knew I was being churlish and ungrateful, but I didn't care. I was going to walk again.

"If you insist, Nick, if you insist." Maitland's voice intimated that I was my own worst enemy. He went to the door, then stopped to glance back into my room. A look of utter astonishment dawned on his round pink face. "You haven't got a television!"

"I hate bloody television."

"We find it an extremely effective instrument for therapy, Nick."

"I don't need bloody therapy. I want a pair of walking shoes."

"You really don't want a television?" Maitland asked in utter disbelief.

"I don't want a television."

So that afternoon they sent the new psychiatrist to see me.

"Hello, Mr Sandman," she said brightly. "I'm Doctor Janet Plant. I've just joined the orientation staff."

She had a nice voice, but I couldn't see her because I had my back to the door. "You're the new shrink?"

"I'm the new orientation therapist," she agreed. "What are you doing?"

I was holding on to the bedrail with my right hand and edging my right foot down to the floor. "I'm teaching myself to walk."

"I thought we had a physio department to do that?"

"They only want to teach me how to pee in a wheelchair. They promise me that if I'm a good boy we'll go on to number two in the spring." I flinched from the excruciating pain. Even to put a small amount of pressure on my leg was enough to twist a fleshhook in the small of my back. I supposed the psychiatrist would say I was a masochist because, as soon as the pain struck, I put more weight on the leg.

God, I was weak. My right leg was shaking. The nerves of the leg were supposed to be severed, but I'd discovered that if I locked the knee with my hands it would stay locked. So now I thrust the knee down and very gingerly pushed myself away from the bed. I was still holding on to the rail. My left leg took some of the weight, and the pain slid down those tendons like fire. I had no balance and no strength, but I forced myself away from the bed until I was standing half bent, with my right hand gripped so hard about the bedrail that my knuckles were white. I could not breathe. Literally. The pain was so bad that my body could not find the breathing instructions. The pain coursed up into my chest, my neck, then flared red in my skull.

I fell backwards on to the bed. The pain began to ebb out of me as my breath came back, but I kept my eyes closed so the tears would not show. "The first thing I have to do" – I tried to sound nonchalant – "is learn to straighten up. Then how to put one foot in front of the other. The rest will come easily." I wished I had not spoken, for the words came out as sobs.

I heard Doctor Plant draw up the chair and sit down. I'd noted that she'd made no attempt to help me, which was all part of the hospital's treatment. We had to fail in order to discover our new limits, which we would then meekly accept. "Tell me about your boat," she said in the statutory matter-of-fact voice. It was the same voice she would have used if I'd claimed to be Napoleon Bonaparte. "Tell me how you won the battle of Austerlitz, Your Imperial Highness?"

"It's a boat," I said sullenly. My breathing was easier now, but my eyes were still closed.

"We sail a Contessa 32," Doctor Plant said.

I opened my eyes and saw a sensible, short-haired and motherly woman. "Where's your Contessa moored?" I asked.

"Itchenor."

I smiled. "I once went aground on the East Pole sands."

"Careless."

"It was at night," I defended myself, "and there was a blizzard blowing so I couldn't see the marks. And a dirty great flood tide. I was only fifteen. I shouldn't have tried to make the Channel, but I thought my old man would tan the hide off me if I stayed out all night."

"Would he have done?" she asked.

"Probably not. He didn't like using the cane. I deserved it often enough, but he's a soft bugger really."

She smiled, as if to indicate that I was at last entering a territory she could understand; a channel well marked by the perches and buoys of the clinical studies of parenthood. "Your mother had left you by the time you were fifteen. Isn't that so?"

"I'm a right bloody monkeypuzzle tree for you, aren't I?"

"Is that what you think?" she asked.

"What I think," I said, "is that I hate it when bloody shrinks ask me what I think. My father's a grease-coated crook, my mother did a bolt, my brother's a prick, my sister's worse, and my wife has left me and married a bloody MP. But I'm not here for any of that, Doctor. I'm here because I got a bullet in my back and the National Health Service has undertaken to put me together again. Doing that does not, repeat not, involve poking about in my doubtlessly addled brain." I stared up at the ceiling. I'd spent nearly a year staring at that bloody ceiling. It was cream-coloured and it had a hairline crack that looked something like the silhouette of a naked woman seen from behind. At least, it looked like that to me, but I thought I'd better not say as much to Doctor Plant or else I'd be strapped on to a couch with the electrodes glued to my scalp. "I delivered a Contessa 32 to Holland once," I said. "Nice boats."

"They are," she said enthusiastically. "Tell me about your boat."

I suppose it was because she was a sailor herself that I told her. The trick of surviving the National Torture Service is to have one dream they can't meddle with, one thing that gives you hope, and mine was *Sycorax*.

"She's called *Sycorax*," I said. "Thirty-eight feet, mahogany on oak, with teak decks. Built in 1922 as a gaff-rigged ketch. She was built for a rich man, so no expense was spared. Her usual rig is jib, staysail, main, topsail and mizzen; all heavy cotton. She's got brass scuttles, gimballed oil-lamps in the cabin." My eyes were closed again. "And the prettiest lines this side of paradise. She's dark blue, with white sails. She's got a long keel, is built like a Sherman tank, and can be as cantankerous as the bloody witch she's named after." I smiled, remembering *Sycorax*'s stiffness in a freshening wind.

"The witch Sycorax." Doctor Plant frowned with the effort of placing the name. "From Shakespeare?"

"From *The Tempest*. Sycorax was Caliban's mother and she imprisoned her enemies in timber. It's a joke, you see, because a timber boat imprisons you with debts."

Doctor Plant offered a dutiful smile. "I hope you've had her ashore since you've been in here?"

I shook my head. "I wasn't given time to take her out of the water, but she's sheathed in copper and berthed on a private wharf. She's been battered about a bit, but I can repair her."

"You're a carpenter?" There was a touch of surprise in her voice.

I rolled my head to look at her. "Just because I was an Army officer, Doctor Plant, doesn't mean I'm totally bloody useless."

"You're good at carpentry?" she insisted.

I held up my hands that were calloused from the exercises I did, but, though the callouses were hard, the fingertips were white and soft. "I used to be. And I was a good mechanic."

"So you see yourself as a practical man, do you?" she asked with the professional inflection.

"You're meddling again," I warned her. "You've come here to sing Doctor Maitland's song. Get a skill, Nick. Learn to be an accountant or a computer programmer. Talk to the newspapers, Nick. They'll pay you for the interview and you can buy a nice little electrically-driven wheelchair with the cash. In short, give up, Nick, surrender. But if I'd wanted to do that, Doctor, I'd have stayed in the Army. They offered me a desk job."

She stood and went to the window. A cold wind drove spits of winter rain against the glass. "You're a very stubborn man, Mr Sandman."

"It's true."

"But how will your stubbornness cope when you discover that you can't walk?" She turned from the window with a quizzical look on her motherly face. "When you discover that you'll never sail your *Sycorax* again?"

"Next year" – I ignored her blunt questions – "I'm going to take her south. I'm going to New Zealand. There's no particular reason for New Zealand, so don't ask." At least, there was no particular reason I could think of. I knew no one in New Zealand, had never been there, but somehow the place had become my Promised Land. I knew they played good rugby and cricket, had splendid sailing waters, and it seemed like a place where an honest man could spend honest days unencumbered by the pomposities of self-important fools. Doubtless, if I ever reached New Zealand, I would discover I'd deceived myself, but that disappointment could wait till my boat made its far landfall. "I'll sail to the Azores first," I went on dreamily, "then across to Barbados, south to Panama, across to the Marquesas . . ."

"Not round the Horn?" Doctor Plant interrupted sharply.

I gave her a warning look. "More meddling?"

"It isn't an unfair question."

"You think I don't want to go to the South Atlantic again?"

She paused. "That thought did cross my mind, yes."

"I don't have nightmares, Doctor, only dreams." That wasn't true. I still woke up shivering and thinking of an island in the South Atlantic, but that was my business, not hers.

Doctor Plant smiled. "Dreams can come true, Nick."

"Don't patronize me, Doctor."

She laughed and suddenly sounded much more like a sailor than a psychiatrist. "You really are a stubborn bastard, aren't you?"

I was, and two weeks later, though I told no one, I managed to hobble, hop and shuffle as far as the window. It took three minutes, much pain, and my breath was rasping like glasspaper in my throat when I finally clutched the sill and rested my forehead against the cold glass. It was a cloudless winter night and there was a full moon over the hospital grounds where the bare trees were frosting black and silver. A car turned a corner in the neighbouring housing estate and its headlights dazzled me for an instant, then were gone. When my night vision returned I searched for Aldebaran among the stars. There had been a time when I would bring that far sun sweetly down to the dawn's horizon, mastering it with the miracle of a sextant's mirror. Now I was a shivering cripple, but somewhere far to the west and south my boat waited. She would be plucking at her warps, rubbing her rope fenders against the stone quay, and waiting, like me, to be released to the long long winds under Aldebaran's cold light.

Because one day, whatever the bloody doctors said, *Sycorax* would take me to New Zealand. Just the two of us in great waters, sailing south, and free.

PART ONE

I walked out of the hospital fourteen months later.

I knew Doctor Maitland would have told the press that I was leaving, so I discharged myself two days early. I didn't want any fuss. I just wanted to get back to Devon and walk into the pub and pretend I'd been away for a week or two, nothing more.

So I limped down the hospital drive and told myself that the pain in my back was bearable, and that the hobbling walk was not too grotesque. I caught a bus at the hospital gate, then a train to Totnes, and another bus that twisted its way into the steep river-cut hills of the South Hams. It was winter's end and there were snowdrops in the hedgerows. I wanted to cry, which was why I'd told no one that I was coming home, for I had known just how glad I would be to see the hills of Devon.

I asked the bus-driver to drop me at the top of Ferry Lane. He watched me limp down the vehicle's steps and heard me gasp with the effort of the last, deep drop to the road. "Are you all right, mate?"

"I'm fine," I lied. "I just want to walk."

The door hissed shut and the bus grumbled away towards the village while I went haltingly down the lane which led to the old ferry slip. From there I would be able to stare across the river at *Sycorax*.

To stare at my home, for, however battered she might be by the winter's ice and gales, *Sycorax* was home. She was the only home I had, or wanted any more, and it had been thoughts of her that had steered me through the long months to this moment when I walked towards her.

Or rather limped. It hurt to walk, but I knew it would hurt for the rest of my life. I'd simply have to live with the pain, and I'd decided that the best way to do that was to forget it, and that the best way to forget it was to think of something else.

That was suddenly easy, for, as I turned the steep corner halfway to the river, a watery sunlight reflected with surprising brilliance from the windows of my father's old house which stood high on the far bank.

I stopped. The new owner of the house had extended the river façade, making a great sweep of plate glass that looked down the wide expanse of sloping lawns to the water. The towering mast my father had put on the terrace still stood complete with its crosstree, shrouds and angled yard. No flag hung from the mast, suggesting that the house was empty. To me, as I gazed across the river, the house seemed like a foreign place for which my visa had long been cancelled.

I picked up my small bag and hobbled on. In summer this lane was busy with dinghy-sailors who trailed their craft to the water's edge, but now, in the wake of winter's cold, there was just one car parked at the head of the old slip. It was a big shooting-brake filled with paint and tools and warps and all the other gear needed to ready a boat for the season. A middle-aged man was stowing cans and brushes into a bag. "Morning! It's a bright one, isn't it?"

"It is," I agreed. There were a dozen boats moored out – only a handful compared to the scores that would use the anchorage in summer, but just enough to hide *Sycorax* from me. She was on the wharf by the deep cut that led to my father's old boathouse on the far bank.

The tide was ebbing. I hoped the middle-aged man would ignore me now, for this was the moment that had kept me alive through all the months of hospital and pain. This was the dream; to see the boat that would sail me to New Zealand. I was prepared for the worst, expecting to see her topsides shabby and her hull clawed by the ice of two winters. Jimmy Nicholls had written in the autumn and said she needed work, and I'd read between the lines that it would be a lot of work, but I had persuaded myself that it would be a pleasure to mend *Sycorax* as the days lengthened and as my own strength seeped back.

Now, like a child wanting to prolong a treat, I did not look up as I limped to the slip's end. Only when my shoes were almost touching the swirl of falling water did I at last raise my eyes. I was holding my breath. I had come home.

And *Sycorax* was gone.

"Is something wrong?"

My right leg was shaking uncontrollably. *Sycorax* was gone. In her place, tied to the ancient wall that was my private berth, was a box-like houseboat.

"Excuse me?" It was the middle-aged man who had approached me on soft-soled sea-boots. He was embarrassed by needing to ask the question. "Are you all right?"

"Yes." I said it abruptly, not wanting to betray the dismay I felt. I looked into the big upstream pool where another handful of boats was moored, but *Sycorax* was not there. I looked downstream towards the bend which hid the village, but no boats were moored in the reach. She was gone.

I turned round. The middle-aged man had gone back to loading his inflatable dinghy with supplies. "Were you moored out through the winter?" I asked.

" 'Fraid so." He said it sheepishly, as though I was accusing him of maltreating his boat.

"You don't know what's happened to *Sycorax*, do you?"

"*Sycorax*?" He straightened up, puzzled, then clicked his fingers as he remembered the name. "Tommy Sandman's old boat?"

"Yes." It was hardly the moment to say that my father had long ago sold me the yacht.

"Sad," he said. "Shame, really. She's up there." He pointed across the river; I turned, and at last saw her.

She had not disappeared, but rather had been dragged on her flank up the wooded hill to the south of the boathouse. I could just see her stern in the undergrowth. A deep-keeled hull like *Sycorax*'s should be propped on a cradle or held by sheer-legs if she's out of the water, but whoever had beached my boat had simply hauled her like dead meat and abandoned her in the undergrowth.

"A bloody shame," the man said ruefully. "She was a pretty thing."

"Can you take me across?" I asked.

He hesitated. "Isn't it private?"

"Not the woods, I think." I was sure, but I did not want to betray my connections with this stretch of river. I wanted to be anonymous. I wanted no one to share my feelings this day, because, even if the dream was broken, it was still my private dream.

The man did not want to help, but the freemasonry of the river would not let him turn me down. He watched my awkward manoeuvres that were necessary because I could not simply step down into the dinghy, but instead had to sit on the stones at the slip's edge and transfer myself as though I was going from bed to wheelchair.

"What happened?" he asked.

"Car accident. Front tyre blew out."

"Bad luck." He handed down the bags of paint and brushes, then climbed in himself and pulled the outboard into noisy life. He told me he was a dentist with a practice in Devizes. His wife hated the sea. He pointed out his boat, a Westerly Fulmar, and said he thought he was getting too old for it, which probably meant his wife's nagging was wearing him down. In a season or two, he said, he would put his Westerly on the market and spend the rest of his life regretting it.

"Don't do it," I said.

"She wants to see Disneyworld."

We fell into companionable gloom. I looked up at *Sycorax*. The gold lettering on her transom caught a shaft of sunlight and winked at me. "Who beached her?" I asked.

"Lord knows. It isn't the sort of thing Bannister would do."

"Bannister?" I asked.

"Tony Bannister." He saw with some astonishment that I did not immediately place the name. "Tony Bannister? *The* Tony Bannister? He owns the property now. He keeps his boat down in the town marina."

It was my turn to be astonished. Anthony Bannister was a television presenter who had become the darling of the British public, though his fame had spread far beyond the glow of the idiot box. His face appeared on magazine covers and his endorsement was sought for products as diverse as cars and sun-tan lotions. He was also a yachtsman, one of the gilded amateurs whose big boats grace the world's most expensive regattas. But Bannister, I recalled, had also known the sea's horror; his wife had died the previous year in an accident at sea while Bannister had been on course to win the St Pierre trophy. The tragedy had prompted nationwide sympathy, for Bannister was a true celebrity. So much of a celebrity, indeed, that I felt oddly complimented that he now lived in my father's old house.

"Perhaps it's an unlucky house, eh?" The dentist stared up at the expanse of windows.

"Because of his wife, you mean?"

"Tommy Sandman lived there, too."

"I remember." I kept my voice neutral.

The dentist chuckled. "I wonder how he likes his new home?"

The chuckle held a distinct British pleasure at a rich man's downfall. My father, who had once been so brilliantly successful, was now in jail. "I imagine he'll survive," I said drily.

"More than his poor bloody son. Crippled for life, I hear."

I kept silent, pretending an interest in the ugly houseboat moored at my wharf. She had once been a working boat, perhaps a trawler, but her upperworks had been sliced off and a hut built there instead. There was no other word for it: a hut that was as ugly as a container on a barge. The hut had a sloping roof covered with tarpaper. A stainless steel chimney protruded amidships. At the stern there was a railing which enclosed an afterdeck on which two deckchairs drooped. Washing was pegged to the railings. "Who lives in that?" I asked the question with some distaste.

"Bannister's racing crew. Bloody apes, they are."

The presence of the houseboat on my wharf suggested that it had been Bannister himself who had removed *Sycorax*, but I did not want that to be true. Anthony Bannister's public image was that of a strong and considerate man; the kind of person any of us might turn to for advice or help, and I was reluctant to abandon that imaginary friend. Besides, he was a yachtsman who had lost his wife, which made me feel sympathetic towards him. Someone else, I was sure, must have moved *Sycorax*.

We were in line with the cut now and I could see a second Bannister craft in the boathouse: this boat was a low, crouching, twin-engined speedboat with a polished hull and a flashy radar arch. I could see her name, *Wildtrack II*, and I remembered that Bannister's yacht which had so nearly won the St Pierre had been called *Wildtrack*. There was a sign hanging in the roof arch above the powerboat: "Private. Keep Out".

"Are you sure we should be here?" The dentist throttled back, worried by other strident signs which had been posted along the river's bank: "Private", "No Mooring", "Private". The lettering was bright red on white; glaring prohibitions that jarred the landscape and seemed inappropriate from such a well-loved man as Bannister.

"The broker said it was OK." I jerked my head towards *Sycorax*. "He said anyone could view her."

"You're buying her?"

"I was thinking of it," I answered guardedly.

The explanation seemed to satisfy the dentist that I was not a burglar, and my accent was presumably reassuring, but he still looked dubious. "She'll take a bit of work."

"I need the therapy." I was staring at *Sycorax*, seeing how she had been dragged a full twenty feet above the high-water mark. There were stones in that slope which would have gouged and torn at her planking as she was scraped uphill. Her stern was towards me and her keel was pointing down the hill. I could see that her propellor had gone, and it seemed obvious that she'd been dragged into the trees and left to die. "Why didn't they just let her rot on the water?" I said angrily.

"Harbour Authority wouldn't allow that, would they?" The dentist span the dinghy expertly and let its stern nudge against the end of the wharf where a flight of stone steps climbed towards the woods. He held the dinghy fast as I clambered awkwardly ashore. "Wave if you want a lift back," he said.

I was forced to sit on the steps while the pain receded from my back. I watched the dentist take his dinghy to the upstream moorings. When his motor cut there were only the gentle noises of the river, but I was in no mood to enjoy the peace. My back hurt, my boat was wrecked, and I wondered why Jimmy Nicholls had allowed *Sycorax* to be moved. God damn it, that was why I had paid Jimmy a fee. The money had not been much, but to earn it Jimmy had merely to keep an eye on *Sycorax*. Instead, I'd returned to find her high and dry.

The climb was hard. The first few feet were the most difficult, for there were no trees to hold on to and the ground had been scraped smooth by *Sycorax*'s passage. I had to stop after a few feet and, bent double, catch the breath in my lungs. There were low branches and undergrowth that gave handholds for the last few feet, but by the time I reached *Sycorax* the pain was like white-hot steel burrowing into my spine. I held on to her rudder, closed my eyes, and forced myself to believe that the pain was bearable. It must have been all of two minutes before I could straighten up and examine my boat.

She lay on her side, dappled with the wintry sun. At least a third of the copper sheathing had been torn away. Floating ice had gouged, but not opened, her planking. The keel had been jemmied open and the lead ballast stolen. Both her masts and her bowsprit were gone. The masts had not been unstepped, but sawn off flush with the deck. The teak grating in the cockpit, the washboards, and both hatch covers were missing. The compasses had disappeared.

The brass scuttles had been ripped out. The fairleads and blocks were gone. Anything of value had been taken. The coachroof must have snagged on a tree-stump halfway up the slope for it had been laid open as if by a tin-opener. I leaned on the broken roof and peered into the cabin.

It took a moment for my eyes to adjust to the gloom. At first all I could see was the black gleam of still water lying deep in her canted hull, then I saw what I expected: nothing. The radios were gone, the stoves had been stolen and all the lamps were missing. The main cabin's panelling had been stripped. A mattress lay in the rain water. There would be rot in the boat by now. Seawater pickles wood, but fresh water destroys it. The engine, revealed because the cabin steps had been tossed aside, was a mass of rust.

I was feeling oddly calm. At least *Sycorax* was here. She had not disappeared, not sunk, and she could be rebuilt, and all it would take would be my time and the money of the bastard who had done this to her. The damage was heart-rending, but, rather than anger, I felt guilt. When I had been eight years old my dog, a fox terrier, had been hit by a milk lorry. I had found the bitch dying in the grass beside the lane. She'd wagged her tail to see me and I'd wept beside her and felt guilty that all her innocent trust in me had been betrayed. I felt that way now. I felt that I had let *Sycorax* down. At sea she looked after me, but back in the place where men lived I was her protector, and I heard myself talking to her just as I used to talk to her when we were at sea. I patted her ripped coachroof and said everything would be all right. It was just her turn to be mended, that was all.

I stumbled back down the hill. I planned to cross the river, then walk to the pub and give Jimmy Nicholls a few hard moments. Why the devil hadn't he done something? The freehold of the wharf was mine and there was no law on God's earth by which anyone could take it. The wharf had been built two hundred years before when lime was exported from the river, but now the sixty feet of old stone wall were mine. Even the Harbour Authority had no rights over the wharf, which I'd bought from my father because it would provide a haven for *Sycorax* and a place I could call home. It was my address, God damn it, my only address: the Lime Wharf, Tidesham, South Devon, and now Anthony Bannister had his ugly houseboat moored to it. I still found it hard to believe that a man as celebrated as Bannister had stolen the wharf by moving *Sycorax*, but someone had stranded my boat and I swore I would find them and sue them for every penny my broken ship needed.

I stepped over one of the springs which held the houseboat safe against my wharf. I was going to hail the dentist for a lift across the river, but glanced first into the boathouse.

And saw my dinghy there. She lay snugly moored against *Wildtrack II*'s starboard quarter. My ownership was proclaimed in flaking paint on her transom: 'Tender to *Sycorax*'. She was a clinker-built wooden dinghy, my dinghy, and she was tied alongside Bannister's flash speedboat.

I think perhaps it was the ugliness of that speedboat which convinced me of Bannister's guilt. Anyone who owned a boat so flash and sharp could not be as considerate as his decent image suggested. To me, suddenly, he became just another rich bastard who thought his money gave him privileges beyond the law.

So sod the bastard. He'd wrecked my boat, stolen my wharf, but I was damned if he would steal my dinghy. I decided I would take the tender back into my ownership, then row myself on the ebb tide to the village pub. "Hello!" I shouted aloud. No one answered. I thumped on the side of the houseboat, but no one was on board.

The boathouse could either be entered by water or by a single door which led from the garden. I had to use the garden door which was padlocked. I paused for a moment, balancing the legalities in my mind, but decided against the possibility that Bannister had rescued the dinghy and was keeping it against my return. The presence of his filthy houseboat on my wharf suggested otherwise, and so I decided to break in.

My back ripped with pain as I lifted a heavy stone and hammered at the brass lock. The sound of my attack echoed dully from the manicured grass slope beneath my father's old house. It took six sharp blows before the hasp came away from the wood and the door splintered open.

I stepped inside to find *Wildtrack II* rocking gently to the falling tide. She had a green tarpaulin cover which stretched from her forward windscreens back to the massive twin engines on her stern. Her bows, sharp as a jet fighter's nosecone, were slicked with chrome. She was a monster, spawned by greed on vulgarity, and my father would have loved every inch of her.

I walked round the boathouse's internal dock. My cotton sails, still in their bags, were heaped against one wall next to my fisherman's anchor. The name *Sycorax* was stencilled on the canvas sailbags. I stooped, hissing with the pain, and felt the treacherous dampness in the bags. God damn Bannister, I thought. God damn his greed.

I found two oars and tossed them into my dinghy, then climbed gingerly over *Wildtrack II*'s stainless steel guardrail. She shivered as I stepped on her deck. I saw that the two springs which held my dinghy close to the speedboat's flank were cleated somewhere beneath the tarpaulin, so I began by unlacing the stiff material and peeling it away from the windscreens. Once the cover was folded back, I stepped down on to the helmsman's black leather chair.

And found my brass scuttles.

And my radios. The VHF and the short-wave were both there, and both with their aerial and power connections snipped short.

The radios were among heaps of similar items that were piled in two tea-chests which had been hidden beneath the tarpaulin. Most of the items had come from other yachts. There were echo-sounders, electronic logs, VHF sets, compasses, and even Lewmar winches that must have been unbolted from the decks of moored boats. There's little profit in stealing boats in England, not when the registration is so good, but there has always been a profit in plundering them of valuables. I stared down into the chests, guessing that the value of their contents must be three or four thousand pounds at black-market prices. Why in God's name would a man as rich as Bannister meddle with bent chandlery?

"Don't move."

The voice came from the door which I'd broken open.

I turned.

"I said don't move, bastard!" The man shouted it, just as we used to shout when we went rifle-butt first into a backstreet house in Northern Ireland. The first command always made the people inside jump in alarm and we would then scream the second order to freeze them tight.

I froze tight.

The man was silhouetted in the doorway. The sun was bright on the pale lawn behind him while the boathouse was in deep shadow, so I couldn't see his face; only that he was a huge man, well over six feet tall, with muscle-humped shoulders and a cropped skull. It certainly wasn't Bannister who faced me. The man carried a double-barrelled shotgun that was pointed at my chest.

"What do you think you're doing?" He had a harsh and grating voice which clipped his words very short. The accent was born of that bastard offspring of the Dutch language, Afrikaans.

"I'm taking my property," I said.

"Breaking and entering," the South African said. "You're a fucking thief, man. Come here." He jerked the gun to reinforce his command.

"Why don't you piss off?" I shouldn't have been belligerent, not in my weakened state, but I was feeling mad as hell because of what had happened to *Sycorax*. I stooped to my tender's bowspring and jerked it off the stainless-steel cleat.

Wildtrack II rocked violently as the man jumped on to her bows. The movement made me stagger, and I had to clutch the radar arch for support just as he reached over the windscreen with his left hand. I caught his hand with my own, instinctively trying to unbalance him by hauling him towards me.

I'd forgotten how little strength there was in my legs. I pulled him so far, then my right knee gave way and I staggered back into the tea-chests. The South African laughed and I saw the gun, brass-butt towards me, coming forward.

I was off balance, I could not parry, and the butt thumped like a piledriver into my ribs. I jabbed fingers at his eyes, but my co-ordination was lost. The gun came again, throwing me back, then he contemptuously reached for my jacket to haul me out of the speedboat's cockpit.

I heard myself scream as he scraped my spine over the windscreen's top edge. I hit at him, and he must have found that amusing for he gave an oddly feminine, high-pitched chuckle before he threw me like offal on to the dock. I sprawled on my own sailbags which were not soft enough to prevent the pain forking down my legs like blazing phosphorus. The gun slammed down again into my ribs.

He stood over me and, confident that I had been battered into submission, discarded the gun. "Get up," he said curtly.

"Listen, you bastard . . ." I tried to push myself upright, but the pain in my spine struck like a bullet and I gasped and fell again. I had been going to insist, not necessarily politely, that the South African help me remove my property from the boathouse, but the pain was gagging me.

He must have been worried by my twitching and gasping body. "Get up!" he paused. "You're faking it, fairy." There was worry in his voice. "You're not hurt, man. I hardly touched you." He was trying to convince himself.

He must have leaned down to me, because I remember his hands under my shoulders, and I remember him yanking me upright. He let go of me and I tried to put my weight on to my right leg, but it buckled like jelly. I fell again, and this time my wounded back must have speared down on to the upturned fluke of the fisherman's anchor.

And I screamed myself into blessed unconsciousness.

When I woke up I could see a cream-coloured ceiling. There was no hairline crack, instead there were two brilliant fluorescent tubes which were switched on even though daylight seemed to be coming from a big window to my right. I could hear the pip of a cardiograph. To my left there was a chrome stand with a saline drip suspended from its hook. There was a tube in my left nostril that went thick and gagging down my windpipe. Two earnest faces were bent over the bed. One was framed in a nurse's white hat, the other belonged to a doctor who had a stethoscope at my chest.

"Jesus," I said.

"Don't talk." The doctor unhooked the stethoscope and began to feel my ribs.

"Christ!" I suddenly felt the pain. Not the old pain, but a new one in my chest.

"I said don't talk." The doctor had half-moon spectacles. "Can you move the fingers of your right hand?" I tried and must have succeeded for he nodded with satisfaction. "Now the left? That's good, that's good." His face did not reflect the optimism of his words. "If you speak," he warned, "do it very gently. Can you tell us your name?"

"My name?" I was confused.

"You were found without any identification. You're now in the South Devon General Hospital. Can you remember your name?"

"Sandman," I said. "Nick Sandman."

He showed no sign of recognizing the name. "That's good, Nick." He had been feeling my ribs as I spoke, but now he leaned forward to shine a light into my eyes. "Where do you live?"

"Here," I said, knowing it was not a helpful answer, but suddenly the new pain was melding with the old, washing through me, making me arch my back, and I saw the doctor's hand dart to the hanging drip and I knew what would happen, but I did not want to sleep yet. I wanted to know how badly I was hurt, and so I tried to protest, but no words came. I saw the nurse frowning at me and I wanted to reassure her that I'd been through worse than this, much worse, but I could not speak for I was once again falling down the soft, dark and familiar tunnel of chemical sleep.

Where I dreamed of *Sycorax*. At night, when the phosphorescence sparkles thick in the turned water of her wake, I like to peg her tiller and go forward. I go right forward, past the pulpit, until I'm standing on the bowsprit and holding on to the forestay. I turn there and stare back at her. That's what I dreamed I was doing, only in my dream I had two good legs. I dreamed I was standing on the bowsprit, as I had so often stood, and staring at the slim beauty of an empty hull driving through dark seas to leave an arrow's path of light beneath the stars.

Thus should *Sycorax* sail for eternity; breaking the glittering seas and, driven by the endless winds of night, free.

Sycorax had been built on my river as a rich man's toy, but built by men who only knew how to make a fisherman's workboat. She had the lines of a fishing smack, a Brixham mule, with a straight bow, a raked stern and a gaffed main. The design was old, and proven by generations of men who had worked the dangerous Western Approaches. She was an honest boat, sturdy and functional, but made pretty by her elegantly overhanging counter and by the workmanship of her fittings. Her first owner, uninterested in speed, had commissioned a safe cruising boat that would doggedly plunge through the worst of seas.

Sycorax had known five good years until the Depression had struck. Her rich owner sold her, and, until 1932, she was resold every season by a succession of owners who must have found her either too slow or too expensive to maintain. So summer by summer *Sycorax* had faded. Her brightwork had become tarnished, her sails had blown out, and her paint had peeled. Yet the copper sheathing had kept her hull-planks as sound and dry as the day they were laid.

By the mid-thirties she had become a working boat. Her cabin was stripped of luxuries and her coachroof ripped out to leave only a tiny cuddy aft of the mainmast. Her long raking stern was cut short and squared off, while her mizzen was thrown away, which must have made her an unbalanced brute at sea, but she took the mistreatment like the stubborn witch that she was. Her name was changed, which should have brought her bad luck, but as *The Girl Pauline* she did five safe seasons longlining and potting off the Devon headlands. The war ended that. She was abandoned; canted on her side in the sands of Dawlish Warren where the oxidised copper was ripped off her hull and the lead torn from her keel. Soldiers training for D-Day shot at her, her planks were sprung, and the rain seeped in to rot her oak frame.

My father found her on the Warren in the sixties. He was making his money then, pots of bloody money, more money than he knew what to do with. His leaseback deals on London's property market had brought him a Rolls, two Jaguars, three Maseratis, and two Nicholson racing cruisers that were moored in the river beside our house. That was the Devon house where I'd been born. There was also a London house, a Berkshire house, and a flat by the harbour in San Tropez. For some reason my father fancied an antique yacht to add to his fleet. He loved flash things like fast cars and painted women and a son at Eton. My elder brother wore a fancy waistcoat at Eton, but, to my relief, the College wouldn't even look at me. I was too dumb, too slow, and had to be sent to a dullards' boarding school where I rotted happily in ignorance.

I only cared about boats, and in that long summer holiday before I went to my dullards' school, I helped rebuild *Sycorax* in the yard where she'd been born. My father, like the first owner, ordered that no expense was to be spared. She was to be restored to her old and splendid beauty.

Her hull was repaired with a loving and almost forgotten skill. I helped caulk the planks and became used to the ancient sea sound of mallet blows echoing from harbour walls. We tarred and papered her, then laid new copper so that she gleamed like a boat of gold. We lengthened the truncated stern to accommodate the new mizzen mast's twin backstays. Teak decks were joggled home, and a new cabin was made where all the brass fittings my father had collected could be lovingly installed.

New masts were cut, carefully chosen from the north side of a spruce forest so that the trunk's heartwood would be central, and not drawn to one side by the sun on the southern forest flank. I helped the boatbuilders adze the spruce down, corner by corner, until two treetrunks had become smooth and shining masts. We soaked the new spars in linseed oil and paraffin, then put on coat after coat of varnish. I can still close my eyes and see that finished mainmast lying on its trestles; straight as a clothyard arrow and gleaming in the sunlight.

Sails were made, sheets were rove, oil-lamps polished, and a dead boat came to life on the slips of a Devon yard. Her old name was deeply incised into her new transom, then painted with gold: *Sycorax*. A diesel engine was put in her aft belly, and the day came when she was lifted by slings into the mucky water of the yard's dock. She still had to be rigged, but I watched that hull float in the tide's wrack, and swore that so long as I lived she would be my boat.

My father saw my devotion, and was amused by it. Once she was launched, though, he lost interest in *Sycorax*. She was as beautiful as he had imagined, but she was not the slow docile craft he had dreamed of. He wanted a boat for long sunsets with gin and melting girls, but *Sycorax* could be a hard-mouthed bitch when she set her mind to it. She was a stiff sailor in sea winds, and too long-keeled for easy river cruising. My father would have sold her, but he could never bear to part with pretty things, and *Sycorax* was dazzlingly pretty with her gleaming brass and shining varnish. He moored her below the house like a garden ornament. Once in a long while he would motor her upriver, but I was the only person who bothered to hoist her sails. Jimmy Nicholls and I would take her out to sea and set her bows to the vast waves that came in from the Atlantic. She could be stubborn, but Jimmy said she was as fine a seaboat as any that had sailed from Devon. "She only be stubborn when you wrestle her, boy," he would say to me in his deep Devon brogue. "Let her be and she'll look after you."

Six years after *Sycorax* was relaunched I joined the Army. I had rarely seen my father so angry. "For Christ's bloody sake!" he had shouted. "The Army?" There was a pause, then a warily hopeful note. "The Guards?"

Not the Guards.

"Why not the bloody Navy? You like sailing, don't you? It's about the only bloody thing you do like. That and skirt."

"I don't like sailing in big ships."

"You're throwing your bloody life away!"

I might not have been bright, but my father thought I could hack a living at banking or broking, or one of the other pin-striped forms of thievery at which he and my elder brother so excelled.

I joined the Army, but I would still go down to Devon and take the stiff cotton sails out of the boathouse loft so that *Sycorax* could go to sea. I married. Melissa and I would motor down to the Devon house for long weekends, but, as time passed, my father was rarely there to entertain us. Later I discovered why. He was borrowing money he could not repay on the strength of promises he could not keep. He was even ready to sell me both *Sycorax* and the wharf to raise some money. His battle became ever more desperate and flamboyant; and he lost it. He was sent down for seven years; a savage sentence, but the judge wanted to make it plain that just because a crime was committed in an office by a businessman it was no less a crime for that. But by then I was sailing to the South Atlantic and everything was changing.

Except for *Sycorax*. Because she was now all that I had and all that I wanted.

"You don't remember me, do you?" A tall, cadaverous man in a shabby grey suit appeared at my bedside. He was in his fifties and looked older. He had yellow teeth, bloodshot eyes, thin grey hair and a lugubrious face nicked with shaving cuts.

"Of course I remember you," I said. "Detective Sergeant Harry Abbott. As toothsome as ever was."

"Inspector Abbott now." He was pleased I'd remembered him. "How are you, Nick?"

"I'm bloody well." I found it hard to speak clearly because the pain in my chest made breathing difficult. "I might go for a bike ride if the rain holds off."

"It isn't raining," Abbott said gloomily. "It's actually quite spring-like, for a change. Mind if I smoke?" He lit up anyway. Abbott used to play golf with my father who loved to be friendly with the local law. My father had encouraged their gossip and relied on their help when he drank and drove. He gave wonderful parties, my father. You could hear them a mile upriver, but there were never any complaints, not while the local police were so fond of him. "Seen Wednesday's papers?" Abbott asked me now.

"No."

He held a tabloid over the bed. 'Falklands VC Hero Assaulted at TV Tony's Hideaway,' it read. Front page. There was a photograph of me in uniform, a big picture of Anthony Bannister, and a photograph of the house. "Bloody hell," I said.

"Mr Bannister was in London." Abbott folded the paper away. "So it wasn't him that beat the shit out of you."

"It was a South African."

"Figured it was." Abbott showed no surprise, nor much interest. He picked a grape from the bunch beside my bed and spat the pips on to the floor. "A big sod?"

"Built like a barge."

Abbott nodded. "Fanny Mulder. He's Mr Bannister's professional skipper." There was an infinite derision in the last two words.

"Fanny?"

"Francis, but always known as Fanny. He's pissed off, of course. Probably in France by now. Or Spain. Or gone back to the Fatherland. Whatever, he's waiting for things to quieten down before he comes back." Abbott stared at my face. "He certainly took care of you, didn't he?"

"He nicked my wallet. And my bag. And everything off my boat."

"He bloody tried to murder you, didn't he?" Abbott did not sound very concerned. "He dumped you on the foreshore and probably hoped the tide would wash you away. Some dentist found you. Mr Bannister says you broke into his boathouse?"

"He had my bloody dinghy in there!" I protested too forcibly, and the pain in my chest whipped at me like the recoil of a frayed wire cable. I coughed foully. There were tears in my eyes.

Abbott waited till I was silent. "Mr Bannister wants it all hushed up. He would, of course."

"He would?"

"Not good for the image, is it? He doesn't want the scum papers saying that a war hero was scuffed over by one of his pet gorillas. Image is very important to Mr Bannister. He's one of those blokes who straps himself into a fighting chair just to catch a bloody mackerel." Abbott laughed scornfully. "You know the kind, Nick, a bloody Londoner who comes down at weekends to show us dumb locals how it's all done."

"Isn't he meant to be a brilliant sailor?" I asked.

"His wife was. She insisted on buying the Devon house. She was here a lot, but then she was always bloody sailing." Abbott pulled open the drawer of the bedside cabinet and tapped a long drooping piece of ash into its emptiness. "I didn't like her so much. American." He added the last word as though it explained his distaste, then blew a plume of smoke towards my drip. "I miss your old man, Nick."

"Not surprising, is it, when you consider how generously he gave to the police orphan and champagne fund?"

Abbott sniffed disapproval. "Have you been to see your dad, Nick?"

"I haven't had time," I said, then, to change the subject, "When did Bannister buy the house?"

"Couple of years back. It took the courts that long to sort out your old man's mess."

"Did Bannister take my boat out of the water?"

"Lord knows." Abbott did not seem to care. "Could have been anyone. There was some mischief on the river this winter. Usual thing. Radios and depth-sounders nicked."

"That was Mulder," I said. "There were crates of stuff in the boathouse. Including my gear."

"Won't be there any longer, will it?" Abbott said carelessly. "He'll have shipped it all off to George Cullen. Remember George?"

"Of course I remember George."

"He's still as bent as a pig's tail. We reckon Mulder's been doing business with Georgie, but it's hard to prove."

"I thought we taxpayers paid you to prove hard things."

"Not my job, Nick, not my job." Abbott went to the window and frowned his disapproval at the cloudless sky. "I'm off crime now."

"What are you? Traffic? Giving parking tickets to the grockles?" Grockles were tourists.

Abbott ignored the gibe. "I'll tell CID about the stolen stuff, Nick, of course I will. But I doubt they'll do anything. I mean rich fellows whose shiny yachts get ripped off aren't exactly the highest priority on our list. Not while we've got orphans and widows being robbed. Orphans and widows tend not to have insurance, you see, unlike the floating rich."

"My boat wasn't insured. My ex-wife didn't forward the renewal notice."

"You are a bloody fool," Abbott said.

"It was hard for Melissa to remember everything when she was having fun. Besides," I shrugged, "Jimmy Nicholls was supposed to be looking after *Sycorax*."

"Jimmy's been in hospital since November," Abbott said, thus explaining why *Sycorax* had been abandoned. "Emphysema.

He smokes too much." He looked down at his cigarette, shrugged, and stole another grape. "Seen your kids, have you?"

"They visited me in the other hospital." I wondered why Abbott was so deliberately sheering away from more pressing matters. "Are you going to charge Mulder?" I demanded.

"I doubt it, Nick, I doubt it. Wouldn't do much bloody good, would it?"

"For Christ's sake! He stole all my stuff!"

"Difficult to prove. You can prefer a charge of assault against him, if you like." Abbott did not sound enthusiastic.

"Why don't you arrest him?"

"You're the one who got clocked," Abbott pointed out reasonably, "not me."

"Aren't you supposed to charge him?"

"I told you. I'm not crime. I just volunteered to come and have a chat with you. For old times' sake."

"Thank you, Harry," I said mockingly.

"But if I was you, I wouldn't bother pressing charges," Abbott said airily. "Bannister looks after Fanny, he does. He'll hire him a top lawyer who'll muddy the waters, and you'll end up with the court's sympathy because of the medal, but they'll still pin a bloody great bill for costs on to you." He shook his head. "Not worth it, Nick. Forget it."

"I don't want to forget it. I've got to sue someone if I'm going to find the money to repair *Sycorax*."

Abbott jerked his head towards the door. "There's a whole lot of bloody lowlife out there who'd gladly write you a cheque. The press, Nick. They've been trying to see you for days."

"Keep them out, Harry, for Christ's sake. And I want to press charges against Mulder."

Abbott sighed at my stubbornness. "If you insist, Nick. If you insist. I'll arrange for a bloody lawyer to come and see you." He went to the door, pausing there. "You know your old man was proud of you, Nick? Really proud." He waited, and when I made no response, he explained, "The VC."

"The other two earned it," I said. "I just disobeyed orders."

"It's still a Victoria Cross, Nick. It can change your life, earning a thing like that."

"I don't want it to change my life. I just want to get it back."

Abbott frowned. "Get what back?"

"The medal, Harry. Bloody Mulder stole it with everything else. It was in my bag."

Abbott flinched as if, at last, he recognized that I'd suffered a misfortune. "I am sorry, Nick."

"Now do you see why I need to sue the bugger?"

"If it's any consolation to you, he'll have the devil's own job to sell it. Any collector will know it's stolen, and I can't think Fanny knows the right fence. He usually only deals with George Cullen, and Georgie wouldn't touch your medal."

"Put the word out, will you, Harry?"

"I'll do that, Nick." Abbott nodded a farewell.

The next day I swore out a complaint against Francis Mulder, accusing him of assault and theft. The lawyer was sympathetic, but pessimistic. Mulder, he said, had disappeared and was unlikely to return to England so long as the writ threatened. He thought my chances of recovering the medal were slight, and my chances of successfully recouping the costs of repairing *Sycorax* even slighter.

"Suppose we sue Bannister for the boat damage?" I asked.

"We'd need to prove that Mulder was acting on his behalf." The lawyer shook his head to show how little hope he placed on that idea.

After the lawyer was gone I lay back and stared at the ceiling and wished it had a hairline crack. The pain was insidious. By holding my breath and lying very still I could trick myself into thinking that it was going away, but as soon as I breathed again it would surge back. I felt at rock bottom. An ambulance siren wailed and a trolley rattled in the hall outside. I wondered how long I would have to stay here. The doctor had said I might limp again, but he had not prophesied how long it would take.

I closed my eyes and thought of *Sycorax* broken and beached, lying dismasted on a hill, with her hull rotting. The damage would be blamed on Fanny Mulder, and he was gone. I'd lashed out at him with the law, but that was a puny weapon, and there was no certainty that he would ever be found or that, even if he was, he would have funds that could rebuild *Sycorax*. The repairs, I knew, would be up to me. I thought of my small bank account. I could patch the hull with salvaged iroko and slap marine ply on the coachroof. I could make new masts if someone would give me the trees. I could replace the stolen lead with pig iron, but it would all take time, so much time, and the sailing season would slip by and *Sycorax* would not be ready for the water till the winter gales were filling the channel.

And even then she would not be ready. I knew I could not afford the blocks and lamps and propellor and sails and sheets and wire and instruments. She would take a fortune and I knew I was trying to stretch a few hundred pounds to fill a bottomless pit. The crane fees to lift her on to legs would half break me. I couldn't even afford a new VHF radio, let alone the seasoned oak for her rotted frames. I'd have to sell her for scrap value and I'd be lucky if I saw five hundred pounds. Or else I could whore to the newspapers and sell my story. I wouldn't do that.

So if I wouldn't whore I would have to sell *Sycorax*. I knew it, and I tried to fight the knowledge. She was a rich man's toy, not a penniless man's dream. I could not afford her, so she would have to go.

The door creaked and I opened my eyes.

A tall man stood watching me. I did not recognize him immediately. I should have done, but his long jaw was slightly jowlier than it appeared in photographs, his blond hair less glossy, and his tanned skin more pitted. It took a second or two before I realized this really was the famous Anthony Bannister, but Anthony Bannister without either television make-up or the kindly, flattering attention of a photographer's airbrush. He looked older than I had expected, but then he smiled, and instantly the imperfections were overwhelmed by an obvious and beguiling charm. "Captain Sandman?" His familiar voice suggested dependability and kindliness.

"Who the hell are you?" I wanted to resist his charm and shatter his confident assumption that I would instantly recognize and trust him.

"My name's Bannister. Tony Bannister." There were nurses standing behind him with silly looks on their faces; they were excited because the great Tony Bannister was in their hospital.

It was like a royal visit, and the staff seemed struck mindless by the occasion. Bannister smiled on them in gentle apology, then closed the door, leaving the two of us alone. He looked fit and trim in his superbly tailored tweed jacket, but as he turned from the door I noticed how his shirt bulged over his waistband. "I think we have a mutual problem," he said.

I was surprised to detect a nervousness in him. I'd expected a man like Bannister to stalk through life with an insouciant and unconquerable confidence. "My only problem is a boat" – I could feel the insidious seduction of his fame and wealth, and I fought against it – "which your Boer wrecked."

He nodded in immediate acceptance of the responsibility. "My fault, but I was assured the boat was abandoned. I was wrong and I apologize. Now, I imagine, you want it restored to perfection?"

He'd stolen the wind clean from my sails. I stared up at the famous face and, despite my reluctance to join the world's uncritical admiration of the man, I found myself feeling sympathetic towards Bannister. He had shown honesty, which was the quality I admired above all things, but I also felt flattered that such a famous man was here in my room. My belligerence faded. "I can do the work on her myself," I said, "but I can't buy the materials. I'm a bit skint, you see."

"I, fortunately, am not skint." He smiled and held out his right hand. He wore a gold bracelet, a gold wristwatch and two heavy gold rings.

For some reason I thought of one of my father's favourite sayings: that principles are very fine things, but are soluble in cash. But for *Sycorax*'s sake, only for *Sycorax*, I shook the golden hand.

"You have to understand," Matthew Cooper said, "that it's a rough cut."

"A rough what?"

He gestured energetically with a right hand that was so stained with nicotine that it looked as if it had been dipped in ochre paint. "It's just scraps of film we've assembled." He frowned, seeking an image I might understand. "We've hammered it together instead of dovetailing it." Matthew, a nervous man in his mid-thirties, was a film director sent to visit me by Anthony Bannister. He had chain-smoked ever since he'd walked into the house.

"And the film isn't dubbed," Angela Westmacott said flatly.

"Dubbed?" I asked.

"The sound isn't polished," Matthew answered for her, "and there's only ten minutes. The final film will probably run at sixty."

"Or ninety," Angela Westmacott said, "but it's a risk." She did not look at me as she spoke, which gave me the chance to look at her. Bannister, when he had telephoned me from London to tell me that Matthew was coming, had not mentioned this girl. If he had I might have looked forward to the meeting with more enthusiasm. Angela was a tall, ethereal blonde, so slender and seemingly fragile that my protective instincts had been immediately roused when she had walked in. Her hair was gathered by combs and pins from which it escaped in cirrus wisps of lightest gold. Her jacket was a shapeless white and pink padded confection from which loops and belts and fasteners stuck like burrs, while her trousers were baggy white and stuffed into pink ankle-length boots. She was fashionably unkempt and devastatingly, even disturbingly, beautiful.

Two years in hospital had sharpened that particular appetite into a ravenous hunger. I could not resist watching her, thinking how vulnerable and delicate her face was in its cloud of gold untidiness. She wore, I noted, neither wedding nor engagement ring. Her clothes, so deliberately casual, were clearly expensive and I had decided, when she first came into the house, that she must have been a television presenter. I had said as much and she had shaken her head dismissively. I now wondered whether Anthony Bannister's television company had sent her as bait. She made good bait.

"It's a risk," she said again, "because without your agreement then the footage we've already shot is wasted."

"Already shot?" I was puzzled.

"The rough cut," Matthew explained. "Tony thought you would feel happier if you could see what we had in mind."

We were in the new front room of Bannister's house. The house had all changed, and how my father would have loved it. This new room must have been seventy-five feet long and every foot of it offered a splendid panoramic view of the river which curled about the garden beneath. Three carpeted steps climbed to the top half of the room where, rippling gently, there was now sixty feet of indoor swimming pool. Between the steps and the windows was a raised fireplace built as an island in the centre and topped with a massive copper hood. White leather sofas were scattered to either side of the fire while at the northern end of the room there was a space-age array of sound and vision equipment. There were radios, cassette players, CDs, record-players, speakers, video-disc players, VCRs and a massive television; the largest TV in a house filled with TVs.

On to which television screens Anthony Bannister now planned to put me. He wanted to make a film of my life, my injury and my recovery, and he had sent Matthew and Angela to seek my co-operation. Matthew Cooper took the video cassette from his briefcase. "Shall we watch it now?" he asked.

I had gone to stand at the window and was gazing at an aluminium-hulled yacht which was running under main and jib to the moorings in the upper pool. The only person on deck was a man in a black woollen hat and I admired the exquisite skill with which he picked up his mooring buoy. It looked easy from up here, but there was a deceptively gusting wind blowing against a flooding spring tide and I knew I had just witnessed a marvellous piece of seamanship. I watched the boat rather than betray my self-torturing interest in Angela Westmacott. It was unfair, I thought, to be tantalized by such careless beauty.

"Are you ready?" Matthew insisted.

"That's a French boat." I spoke as if I had not heard his question. "First I've seen this year. He's probably run over from Cherbourg. He's good, very good."

"The video tape?" Angela said. I assumed now that she was Matthew's assistant, and I wondered if she was also his lover. That thought made me jealous.

Matthew pushed the video tape into the slot. "It's a very rough cut indeed," he said apologetically.

"Fine." I spoke as if I was content, but in truth I was struggling not to show my annoyance. I'd spent months avoiding the press, and now Bannister was trying to make me the subject of a television film, and I could only blame myself. Bannister, coming to the hospital, had offered me everything I wanted. A refuge, security and the means to repair *Sycorax*. No legal tangles, no unpleasantness, just peace and forgiveness. I should have known what the price would be when, the next day, the papers trumpeted Bannister's generosity. 'TV Tony Rescues VC Hero'. There had been no mention of Fanny Mulder. One paper claimed I had been attacked by vandals who had been damaging my boat, while the others blandly reported that my attackers were unknown.

None of the papers had connected the attacker with Anthony Bannister. Bannister had come out of the stories like driven snow; odourless and white. Something nasty had happened in his boathouse while he was in London, and he was now putting it right. I'd left the hospital to come to Bannister's house where, in these last three weeks, I had mended fast. I was attended by Bannister's doctors, swam in Bannister's pool and was fed by Bannister's housekeeper. *Sycorax* had been lifted out of the trees and stood in cradles on Bannister's lawn. The materials for her repair were on order, and they were nothing but the best; mahogany, teak, mature oak, copper, spruce and Oregon pine. TV Tony had worked his magic, but now the price for all that kindness was being exacted.

"Here it is," Angela said sharply, chiding me for being insufficiently attentive to the television screen on which numbers counted down, then the picture changed to show a wild and bleak landscape darkened by dusk and edged by a pink-washed sky. Plangent music played as the title appeared: '*A Soldier's Story*, a film by Angela Westmacott'. I glanced at her with surprise. Clearly I had appraised my visitors wrongly, imagining Matthew to be in charge.

"It's only a working title." Matthew seemed to think my glance was critical.

"It's just to give you an idea." Angela was irritated by Matthew's interruption.

The titles went and the picture changed to a night skyline. Tracer bullets flicked left to right, arcing in their distinctive and deceptive slowness. There was an explosion in the far distance and I recognized the sudden flare of white phosphorus. Our 105s, I remembered, firing from Mount Vernet. Or was it a cocktail round? High explosive and phosphorus lobbed through a mortar. They were nasty bloody things. I looked away.

"The Falklands" – Anthony Bannister's distinctive and warm voice was redolent with a grave sincerity – "fourteenth of June, 1982. British troops were closing on Stanley, the battles of Goose Green and the mountains were behind them, and there was a sense of imminent victory in the cold South Atlantic air. Captain Nick Sandman was one of the men who – "

I stood up. "Do you mind if I don't watch this?"

There was not much they could say. I limped to the window and stared down at the cradled *Sycorax*. She'd been drained of water, cleaned out, and the patches of rot had been cut out of her hull. The old copper sheathing, oxidised to the thickness of rice-paper, had been stripped off and the nail holes plugged with pine. The stumps of her masts had been lifted out like rotten teeth and her coachroof stripped off. Now she lay swathed in a tarpaulin and waiting for the new timber that would be patched and scarfed into her old hull.

I looked upstream to the French yacht just in time to see the skipper take off his hat. He was a she, shaking out her black hair. She went to the foredeck to bag the jib and I envied her the simple task. I remembered the sweet luxury of arriving on a mooring and knowing that once the small chores were done there would be time for a drink as the tide ebbed. Behind me Bannister's famous and sonorous voice was telling my story. I tried to block it out, but failed. I turned despite myself, to see my own photograph on the screen. It was a photograph taken five years before and had once stood on my wife's dressing-table. I wondered how the television people had come by a copy. It did not look like me, at least I did not think so. My rat-tail mouse-coloured hair was unnaturally tidy, suggesting that a cheap wig was perched on my ugly, long-jawed face. "We'll replace the caption with film, of course." Angela saw I had turned from the window.

"Caption?"

"The photograph. We'll have film of you instead."

My face was replaced by Sergeant Terry Farebrother who looked nasty, brutish and short in his combat smock. He had been filmed at one of the Surrey exercise grounds where thunderflashes smoked in the far distance to lend the screen a suitably warlike background. Farebrother had cleaned up his accent and language for the camera and the result was a bland and predictable tribute to a wounded officer. It was as unreal as reading one's own obituary. I remembered that Terry still had my kit in his house. Some day I should go and fetch it. He described the moment I was wounded; the same moment that had led to the medal. I did not recognize the description. I had not felt heroic, only bloody foolish, and instead of expecting a medal I thought I would be reprimanded for breaking orders.

Doctor Maitland's pink and plump face filled the screen. "Frankly we were surprised he hadn't died. The body can only stand so much shock, and Nick had been very badly mauled. But that's our specialization here, you see. We make the lame to walk."

The picture changed to one of the physiotherapy rooms.

"We'll cover these pictures with wildtrack," Angela said, "describing how they treated you."

"Wildtrack," Matthew helpfully explained, "is an unseen voice."

"Like God?"

"Exactly."

Doctor Plant appeared and said I had an unnaturally high quotient of bellicosity that was more usual in a criminal than in a soldier. Most army officers, she said, were conformists, but it was undoubtedly my pugnacious traits that had forced me to prove the hospital wrong by making myself walk. Somehow it did not sound like a compliment. She added that my bellicosity was tempered with very old-fashioned conceptions of honour and truth, which did not sound like a compliment either. I saw how Matthew and Angela were intent on the film, staring at it like acolytes before an altar. This was their work; a rough-cut film which told how I had been written off as a hopeless casualty of a bitter little war in a lost corner of the Atlantic. A West Indian nurse described how galling it had been to watch me trying to walk. "Nice to have the ethnic input," Matthew murmured to Angela, who nodded.

"He'd be bent over," the nurse said. "I know he was hurting himself, but he wouldn't give up."

"Nick Sandman wouldn't give up," Tony Bannister's voice broke in, "because he had a dream." The picture cut to *Sycorax* as she had been when I first saw her lying abandoned in the trees. "He had a boat, the *Sycorax*, and he dreamed of taking her back to the Falklands. He would sail in peace where once he had marched in anger."

"Oh, come on!" I protested. "Who makes up this garbage?"

"We can change anything," Angela said dismissively. "We're just trying to give you an idea of what the final film could look like."

The film described how the *Sycorax* had chafed her warps and been driven on to a mudbank in the river. "That's a bloody lie!" I was angry. "Bannister wanted my berth! He had his bloody Boer move my boat."

"But we can't say that." Angela pressed the pause button and her voice intimated that I was being unreasonably tiresome. "What happened was a regrettable accident, for which Tony is making amends." She released the button and the film showed the caterpillar-tracked crane which had lifted *Sycorax* out of the trees and on to the front lawn. "Boat and man," Bannister's wildtrack intoned, "would be restored together, and this film follows their progress." The screen went blank. They had been ten bad minutes, and now they wanted my co-operation to make the rest of the film.

"There," Angela switched the set off. "That wasn't too painful, was it?" She used the same patronising inflection that had so grated on me in hospital.

"What's painful" – my anger made me forget just how attractive I found her – "is getting a bullet in the back. That's not painful." I waved at the set. "That's rubbish. Bannister took my boat and my wharf. Now, because he doesn't want the bad publicity, he'll foist that gibberish on the public!"

"Tony rented Lime Wharf from your wife in good faith," Angela said primly.

"My ex-wife," I corrected her, "whose power of attorney expired when she walked out on me to marry that soggy MP."

"Tony didn't know that. And you have to admit he's trying to put matters right, and very generously, I would say."

"At least your bloody film didn't mention my father," I said.

"We wanted to talk to you about that." Matthew, clearly made nervous by the animosity between Angela and myself, lit a new cigarette from the stub of his old.

"Bloody hell." I turned to stare out of the window, but the French girl had gone down to her cabin. I limped to the far end of the room where Bannister had hung a whole slew of pictures of his dead wife, Nadeznha. The photographs showed Nadeznha at sea, Nadeznha in Rome, Nadeznha and her brother at Cape Cod, Nadeznha and Bannister in Sydney, Nadeznha in oilskins, Nadeznha at a fancy-dress ball. Nadeznha had been a very beautiful girl, with dark eyes and a happy smile which made me presume that no one had ever tried to coerce her into being an unwilling TV star. I turned back to Matthew and Angela. "Just out of interest," I said, "who exactly is paying to repair *Sycorax*?"

Angela was pouring herself some Perrier water. For a second I thought she was going to answer, then she gave me a very cold look. "We are, naturally."

My ribs hurt beneath the bandages. "We?"

"It's a television production, Mr Sandman. If the programme wants to film the boat's restoration then the programme budget will have to find the funds."

So Bannister wasn't even paying for *Sycorax*? He'd towed her ashore, then allowed his Boer brute to strip her of valuables, and the TV company would now pay to put it back together? It was astonishing. It was a venality that even my father would have admired, but not me. "No," I said. "No way."

"No?" Angela enquired delicately.

"Bannister wrecked my boat. Bannister can put it back

together. Why the hell should I make a spectacle of myself for something he did?"

"You drink whisky, don't you, Nick?" Angela asked.

I ignored her attempt at conciliation. "I've spent the last two years running away from publicity. Can you understand that? I don't want to spend the rest of my life being a man who won a medal. I've got other things to do and I want to be left alone. I am not a hero, I'm just a damn fool who got shot. I don't want to be made into something I'm not, I don't want to make money out of something that I didn't deserve, and I'm not doing your film. So take the wretched thing back to London and tell Bannister to send me a big cheque."

There was silence for a few seconds, then Angela stood and walked to the window. "Look at it this way, love." Her voice dropped nastily on the last word. "You accepted Tony's hospitality. Your boat's on his lawn. The first ten minutes of the film are already shot. Do you think any law court in the land will think you didn't agree to all of that? Or to all of this?" She waved at the lavish room with its sunken pool and electronic gadgets and raised fireplace. "Of course you can fight the case, Mr Sandman. You can claim that you always planned to sue Tony, but that you first decided to rip off his hospitality." She mocked me with a smile. "Do you think you'll win?"

"He wrecked my boat!"

"Don't be tedious! He was assured that it was abandoned!" I was beginning to see that this slender and beautiful creature had the sting of a scorpion. She looked at me with derision. "Your wife assured Tony it was abandoned. She assured him personally. Very personally."

Sod you too, I thought, but didn't say it. I wondered how Melissa and Bannister had met, then supposed it must have been when Bannister wanted to rent the wharf. And how Melissa would have loved to add a celebrity like Bannister to her conquests.

"Well?" Angela asked coldly.

"Well what?"

"What's your answer, Nick?" She used my first name, not in friendliness, but with condescension. When I didn't answer she went back to the table and took a cigarette from Matthew's packet. He lit it for her, and she blew smoke towards me. "We want to make a film, Nick. It will be a very truthful and very meaningful film. It will tell the story of a man who achieved something quite remarkable. It will also tell of triumph over pain, of ambition over despair. It will give new hope to other people who are suffering." Her voice was now sweet reason itself. "At the same time it will give you a peaceful convalescence and a beautifully rebuilt boat. I assume you do want *Sycorax* rebuilt?"

"You know damn well I do."

"Then you should understand that none of the necessary materials for the repair will be delivered until you sign the contract." She stared at me in cool challenge.

"And we'll pay you an appearance fee," Matthew said encouragingly.

"Shut up, Matthew." Angela kept her eyes on me.

I turned and looked at *Sycorax*. I hated to see her out of the water. "Let me get this straight," I said. "Bannister took my boat out of the water because he thought it was abandoned?"

"He was told it was abandoned, yes," Angela said.

"And Melissa rented him the wharf, even though it wasn't hers to rent?"

"So you say." Angela was guarded.

"And it was Bannister's thug who beat the crap out of me."

"That was not on Tony's orders. Fanny believed you were stealing the powerboat, but we agree that he over-reacted."

"I'd call two fractured ribs an over-reaction, too." My irony was lost on her. "And where is Mulder, anyway?"

"We really don't know," Angela said. Bannister had promised me he would try and find Mulder, then persuade the South African to return the medal, but there had been no news. Bannister had also tried to persuade me to drop my charges against Mulder, arguing that Fanny would be more likely to reappear if no legal threat loomed, but I had refused. Mulder had wounded *Sycorax* and myself, and I wanted him nailed.

But nailing Mulder was a separate business from restoring *Sycorax* and it seemed, whether I liked it or not, that the only way to achieve that was to co-operate with Angela's bloody film. I said as much, which irritated Angela. "I wouldn't describe it as a bloody film," she said tartly. "It will be a very truthful and very moving human story."

"What control do I have?"

She frowned. "Control?"

"Over untruths. I can't have you saying that I want to go back to the Falklands. It's not that I'm frightened of going, it just doesn't happen to be one of my ambitions. I want to sail to New Zealand."

"You mean editorial control?" Angela said calmly. "Let me explain. You were clearly a very good soldier, Nick, but you're hardly a trained television producer. You'll have to understand that our skill lies in the shaping and transmission of information. We're very good at it, and we don't surrender the control of those skills to anyone. If we did, then we'd be forced to bend to the whim of any politician or public-relations man who wanted to conceal the truth. And that's what we tell, the truth. So you get no editorial control. You tell us your truth, and we tell it to the world."

There did not seem to be much to say to that. "I see."

Angela stubbed out her half-smoked cigarette. "So perhaps you'll sign the contracts?" She opened her bag and took out a thick wad of documents. "Head contract." She separated and dropped three copies of each document on to the table as she spoke. "The sub-contract with Bannister Productions Ltd, who will actually make the film. An insurance indemnity form. Your undertaking not to talk with any other television company or newspaper while the film's being made. And a medical form." She dropped the last pieces of paper, then held a pen towards me. "Sign wherever I've pencilled a cross, then please initial every separate page of the two contracts."

I took the pen and sat. I tried to follow the good advice to read whatever I was signing, but the contracts were dense with sub-paragraphs about syndication rights and credits.

"They're standard contracts." Angela seemed frustrated by my hesitation. "And I'll leave you copies."

"Of course," I said. The truth is that I've always found it

embarrassing to keep people waiting while I read the small print. It seems so untrusting, and I never understand the legal language anyway. I signed in triplicate, then scribbled my initials on all the separate pages. "Now do I get the timber for *Sycorax*'s hull?"

"It will come next week." Angela pushed the documents to Matthew, who witnessed them. "Your first call," she said to me, "is next Tuesday, mid-day. The location will be the town marina. Do you know it?"

"I grew up in it."

"And you do understand what you've signed, Captain Sandman?"

"To make your film," I said.

"To make yourself available and co-operative for the successful completion of the film." She separated my copies of the documents and handed them to me. "That means I'd appreciate it if you were to always let me know where you are."

"I'll be in London tomorrow," I said, "to see my children. Is that permitted, ma'am?"

She ignored my clumsy sarcasm. "I'll see you on Tuesday," she said instead, "when we'll be going to sea. Do you need us to provide waterproofs?"

"I have my own."

"I hope our co-operation will be very constructive," she said coldly, "and might I recommend that you watch Tony's show tonight? Matthew and I will see ourselves out. Till Tuesday, Captain Sandman."

"It's Mister," I said. "I left the Army."

She paused. Her blue eyes appraised me for a second and did not seem to like what they saw. "Till Tuesday, Nick. Are you ready, Matthew?"

They left, and I began to understand how General Menendez must have felt in Port Stanley; slashed to bloody ribbons and with nowhere to turn.

And it was all my own fault.

I watched *The Tony Bannister Show* that night. I was hurting. For some reason the pain in my back had decided to tighten and flare, while my right leg, which I kept telling myself was almost healed, felt numb and flaccid. Alone in the lavish house, I felt the temptation of despair; of accepting that I would never walk properly. I swallowed four aspirins that I helped down with two large glasses of Irish whiskey, none of which helped, then I diverted my self-pity by switching on Bannister's programme.

It was a nightly programme, shown from autumn until spring, and transmitted after the late news. I'd watched more than a few of the programmes since I'd been a guest in Bannister's house, and I hadn't much enjoyed them.

That night's show was the final programme in the present series. It kept to Bannister's usual formula: a handful of celebrity guests, a rock group and an excited audience. I watched the programme in Bannister's big living-room where I lay on a sofa trying to persuade myself that the weakness of my right leg was only imaginary. I'd left the windows open to air the room of the lingering smell of cigarettes.

Bannister's first guest was an American actress, then there was a British politician who seemed wittier than most practitioners of the evil trade. I turned the sound down while a rock group caterwauled, then turned it up again for a comedian who rattled off jokes at the speed of a light machine-gun.

It was a standard kind of television chat show, even an average show, yet there was one very special ingredient – Tony Bannister himself. I didn't need to be an addict of the television to understand that he was very good indeed at his job. He had a natural and immediate charm, a quicksilver wit, and a very reassuring presence that made him an ideal intermediary between the audience and the gilt-edged celebrities that were his guests. He seemed so very trustworthy, which made Angela Westmacott's prickly-sour attitude so puzzling. I warmed to Bannister as I watched him, and was proud that I'd met him. Damn it, I liked him. I noticed how much younger he looked on television. When I'd met him in hospital I'd thought him in his mid-forties, while tonight he looked no older than thirty.

At the show's end Bannister talked about the films he would be making during the coming summer months. I'd been told he always made films in the warm months, and nearly all the films contributed to his tough-but-tender image. They showed Bannister climbing mountains, or diving to wrecks, or training with the Foreign Legion. This year's films, all of the same ilk, would be dominated by an account of his assault on the St Pierre. He spoke with real dignity of his dead wife, recalling her loss, but promising that this year he would sail *Wildtrack* to victory in her memory. The screen showed a film of *Wildtrack* as he spoke. She was a Farley 64, a British-made racing cruiser that appealed to wealthy customers about the world. I'd often sailed by the Farley yard and seen their sleek products being sea-tested. The 64-footer, Farley's largest production model, was a typical modern boat; wedge-shaped, flat-arsed, and with a stabbing fin keel. They were undoubtedly quick, but I wouldn't want to be in one when a real Atlantic storm struck. Give me a deep, heavy boat like *Sycorax* any day. *Sycorax* might not be fast, but she was built for the bad seas.

The picture cut back to Bannister in the studio. "And I'll be making another, and very special, film this summer," he was saying, "a film about bravery and recovery. A film about a man who has modestly refused to make any profit from his hard-won fame." I knew now why Angela had told me to watch this show, and I cringed back in the sofa. "Indeed," Bannister continued, "a man who has so far shunned the limelight, but who has finally agreed to tell his story as an encouragement to anyone else who finds themselves in adversity." The screen showed a photograph of me. I was in uniform, sitting in a wheelchair, and it must have been taken on the day I received the medal. "In the autumn we'll be bringing you the true story of Britain's most reluctant Falklands hero, Captain Nicholas Sandman, VC." The audience applauded.

Pain scoured my back as I wrenched myself off the sofa to turn the television off. I gasped from the vivid agony, then sat back in sullen silence. God damn it, but why had I agreed to their damned film? Only for *Sycorax*, of course, but I felt a fool; a damned, damned fool. I could hear the halliards slapping at the masts on the river, and the sound made me fretful and lonely. God damn it, God damn it. I unscrewed the cap of the whiskey bottle.

The telephone rang suddenly, forcing me to abandon the whiskey to pick up the handset.

"So that's why you did it?" It was Inspector Harry Abbott chuckling at me.

I closed my eyes against the sullen and insistent throb of pain in my spine. "Why I did what, Harry?"

"I told you Bannister looked after his friends, and I suppose you're a friend of the great man's now. Going to be a telly star, are you? But remember what they say about supping with the devil, Nick."

"What have I done, Harry?"

He paused, evidently to gauge the innocence of my question. "You've withdrawn your charges against Fanny Mulder, Nick, that's what you've done."

"I have not!"

"Then how come that a television company's lawyer has been on the telephone to our office?"

"Saying what?"

"Saying you've withdrawn your charges, of course. He's sending the paperwork down to us. He claims he's got your signature, but are you telling me you don't know anything about it?"

"Bloody hell," I said softly, remembering all the pages I'd signed and initialled, but hadn't read. "I know about it."

"Long spoon, lad, long spoon." Harry sighed. "Still got your gong, has he?"

"Yes."

"If it's any interest to you, Nick, the bugger's staying at Bannister's London house. We think he's been there ever since he raked you over."

"If you knew that," I said irritably, "why hasn't someone gone to arrest the bastard?"

Abbott paused. "I told you, Nick, I'm not crime any more."

"What are you, Harry?"

"Good-night, Nick."

I put the phone down, then found my copies of the contract documents and, sure enough, there was a clause which said that I unreservedly relinquished any legal claims, actions, or proceedings that might be pending against any member of the production company. I turned yet more pages to find that Francis Mulder was named as boatmaster for the production; responsible for the supply and safe handling of all vessels needed for the filming.

And all the time Bannister had sworn he did not know where Mulder was. All the time.

I limped to the window, lurching my weight on to my right leg in an attempt to convince myself that it would not buckle and that I was strong enough to sail alone into emptiness. Once at the window I stared into the night and reflected on the art of committing a reluctant enemy to battle. You sucker them in, offering an easy victory, then you clobber them with all the nasties that you've kept well hidden.

And I'd just been clobbered.

It was easy to find Bannister's London address by going through the papers in his study. I thought of phoning him, but an enemy warned was an enemy prepared.

Next morning I caught the first London train, but still did not reach Richmond Green until nearly eleven o'clock. I was supposed to collect my children from the tradesmen's entrance of Melissa's Kensington house at mid-day, so I was in a hurry. My back was hurting, but not so badly as on the previous night.

Perhaps it was the weather that made me feel better, for it was a lovely spring morning, warm and fragrant with blossom. A cherry tree shed petals in the front garden of Bannister's house, which was expensive, and flamboyantly marked as such by the burglar alarm fitted high on its imposing façade. The downstairs windows were all barred and shuttered.

I climbed his steps and rang the bell. The milk and newspapers were still on the top step. I rang the bell again, this time holding my finger on the button so that the bell rang insistently.

I took my finger off when I heard the rattle of bolts and chains. A thin, balding man in black trousers and waistcoat opened the door. He was evidently offended by my behaviour, but I gave him no time to protest. "Is Mr Bannister at home?" I demanded.

He looked me up and down before answering. I did not look very impressive; I was dressed in old jeans, torn deck-shoes and a frayed shooting jacket. "Mr Bannister is not yet up, sir." He spoke with the haughty reserve of a trained servant and, though he called me 'sir', I saw his hand go towards the alarm system's hidden panic button that would alert the police station that an intruder had bluffed his way past the front door.

"My name is Captain Nicholas Sandman, VC." I used the full rigmarole and my crispest accent to reassure him, and it must have worked for he took his finger away from the button. "I really came to see Fanny Mulder."

"Mr Mulder has a private entrance by the garage, sir."

"I've arrived by this one now," I said, "so send him up to me. Is there somewhere I can wait?"

"Indeed, sir." He showed me into a lovely high-ceilinged room where he drew back the curtains and unfolded the shutters to let the morning sun stream on to an expensive pale carpet. "I believe Mr Mulder is also still sleeping, sir. Would you like some coffee while you wait?"

"A large pot of it, please. Milk, no sugar."

"I shall inform Mr Mulder that you're here, sir." He gave a hint of a bow, and left.

I waited. The room was beautifully furnished, with a fine Impressionist painting over the mantelpiece and a profusion of watercolour landscapes on the opposite wall. A lovely photograph of Nadeznha Bannister stood on a side table. Behind it, and echoing the array in Bannister's Devon house, was a bank of electronic equipment. In front of the fireplace was an expensive glass-topped coffee table at least twelve feet square. Its smoked glass had prettily bevelled edges. The previous day's paper lay there and I idly read it while I waited for the coffee. The miners' strike was a month old and police and pitmen were fighting pitched battles outside coke depots and coalmines.

"Coffee, sir." The manservant put a large silver Thermos jug on to the table. "I've informed Mr Mulder of your arrival, sir, and he will join you as soon as he can. Would you like today's paper, sir?"

"No. Is there a back gate to the house?"

He hesitated, then shook his head. Which meant that if Mulder wanted to escape me then he would have to leave by the front gate and I would see him run for it. If he did, I planned to phone the police.

But Mulder did not run for it. He kept me waiting ten minutes, but finally appeared in jeans and a sweatshirt that carried the name *Wildtrack* in big letters. He stood sullen and huge. He had winch-grinder's hands, a face battered by sun and sea, and the confidence of his giant size. "What is it?" he asked curtly.

"You heard that I withdrew my charges against you, Fanny?"

"I heard." He was suspicious.

"But you still owe me an apology, Fanny."

A look of hurt pride flicked over the big face, then he shrugged. "I didn't know you were a crip, man."

I suppose that passed for a Boer apology, meaning that if he'd known I was crippled he'd have only broken one rib. I smiled. "And you've got something that I want, Fanny."

He said nothing, but just glowered in the doorway.

"I said you've got something I want, Fanny. Or did you find a buyer for the medal?"

He tried to brazen it out. "What medal?"

I crossed to the glass table, picked up the silver Thermos jug, and smashed it hard down. The smoked glass was toughened, and all I managed to do was crack it. I lifted the dented jug higher, slammed it down again, and this time the precious glass splintered into crazed fragments. Magazines, dried flowers and ashtrays collapsed among the broken glass. I smiled pleasantly at Fanny again. "You've got two minutes to find my medal, you bastard, or I break up this house."

Fanny was staring aghast at the table's wreckage. "You're mad!"

"One minute and fifty seconds."

"Jesus bloody wept!" For a second I thought he was going to attack me, but he stayed rigid at the door.

I unscrewed the jug's lid and upturned it. A mixture of hot coffee and broken vacuum lining spilt on to the fine carpet. "One minute forty seconds, Fanny. The picture over the mantel will be next."

"I'll get it, man! I'll get it!" He held his hands wardingly towards me. "Don't do any more! I'll get it!"

The medal arrived within one minute. Just seconds after Fanny had thrust the slim case towards me, Bannister himself appeared in the doorway. He was wearing a bathrobe of flamboyant silk. He stared appalled at the horrid mess where his table had stood, then looked at me in newly-woken astonishment. "Captain Sandman?"

"Good morning," I said politely. "I came here to retrieve my medal. Mr Mulder was reluctant to admit that he still possessed it." I opened the lid of the case and looked down at the dull cross of bronze with its claret ribbon. "I'm sorry I had to use unfair methods to persuade him, but clearly you were making no effort at all."

"Ah." Bannister appeared to be naked under his silk robe. He also seemed incapable of collecting his wits.

"You told me you didn't know where Fanny was," I accused him.

"I . . ." He stopped, trapped by his lie, helpless to know what to say.

"But, as you can see, I found him." I put the medal into my pocket.

"I can explain everything, Nick." Bannister had found his charm now, and deployed it hurriedly. "Fanny only arrived last night. I was going to talk to you about him, of course – "

"I'm in a hurry," I cut him off. "But I also want to tell you that I've no intention of making your film, none. I'll ask my lawyer to send you a bill for *Sycorax*'s restoration. Unless you'd prefer to write me a cheque now?"

"Nick!" Bannister's hurt tone suggested he had been grievously wronged. "It's going to be a very good film, very good!"

"I'd rather have a cheque," I said.

"You've signed a contract." Angela Westmacott stepped into the room. Until now I'd been in charge of the confrontation, but her sudden appearance flabbergasted and silenced me. "You've signed a contract," she said again, "and I expect you to fulfil it." Like Bannister she was in a silk robe and, like him, she seemed to be naked under the bright garment. Her hair was loose, cascading in a golden flood down her back. She had no make-up, yet she looked very beautiful. I understood now why she always behaved with such imperiousness; she had Anthony Bannister as a lover, and she had assumed his power along with his bed. She looked with disgust at the mess I'd made. "Are you telling us that you plan to withdraw from your contract, Mister Sandman?"

"I shall talk to my lawyer about it on Monday."

"Do that. And once you've wasted his time and your money I shall still expect to see you at mid-day on Tuesday." Her scorn was biting and her voice like a whip. "Get out, Fanny," she snapped at Mulder, who fled.

"I need Fanny, Nick," Bannister offered the feeble explanation. "If I'm going to win the St Pierre, I shall need him."

"Do you plan to vandalize anything else in the room?" Angela did not believe in explanation, only attack. "Or did I understand you to say that you were in a hurry, Mister Sandman?"

She made me feel clumsy and boorish. "I'm in a hurry."

"Then don't let us detain you." She stepped back from the door to let me pass. "If you're not at the marina on Tuesday, I shall consider you in breach of contract. Your lawyer will doubtless inform you of our remedy. Good day, Mr Sandman."

I went down the front steps into the sunlight, and I was suddenly jealous of Anthony Bannister. Angela might be a bitch incarnate, she was probably a liar, she was certainly a cheat, but I was the one who was jealous. Damn the glands, I thought, but I was jealous.

I delivered the children safely back to their Swedish nanny at teatime. Melissa, hearing our voices in the kitchen, graciously accorded me an audience. She let me pour her a martini and myself a whiskey, then she grimaced at my clothes. "I do hope the children don't resent being seen with you. Don't passers-by think they've been kidnapped?" Melissa has a voice like a diamond gouging slate. I never liked that voice, but it hadn't stopped me marrying her.

"I don't want to spend money on clothes," I said. "Not that I've got any money for clothes."

"I do hope you're not going to be frightfully boring and tell me you have money problems?"

"My money problems are no longer your concern."

"They are very much my concern, darling," she said. "School fees. Or had you forgotten?"

"School fees." I imitated her perfect enunciation.

"You can't expect Mands and Pip to slum it in a state school. Be reasonable, Nick." I flinched from Melissa's nicknames for our children. Amanda was the eldest, six now, while Piers was four. I'd been in Belfast when Amanda was born and in Germany when Piers arrived; two postings that explained why I had been given no say in the choice of names. Melissa picked up an emery stick and lightly buffed the tip of a fingernail. "Or do you want them to become communist perverts, Nick? That's all they teach children in London schools these days."

"I'm already paying their school fees," I said. "There's a standing order at the bank."

"But in a few years, Nick, Mands will want to be at a decent boarding school and Piers will go to the Dragon. Then Eton, of course, and you can't expect Hon-John to pay. They're not his children."

"But the Honourable John's filthy rich," I said as though it was a most reasonable objection.

Melissa sighed. "And Mumsy and Dadsy won't pay." Melissa's parents were always called that, Mumsy and Dadsy. I imagined how very relieved Mumsy and Dadsy were that Melissa had rid herself of the jailbird's son and married the Honourable John instead. Melissa was a most beautiful rat who had abandoned the sinking ship with immaculate timing. She was also, though it pleased her to disguise it, a most clever rat. Cleverer than I was. "Or Dadsy won't pay unless you're dead," she said now.

I put two fingers to my head. "Bang."

"So if you're spending all your money on that silly boat, Nick, you won't have the funds for the school fees, will you? And then I shall have to sue you again, which will be awfully boring."

"Jesus wept." I walked to the window. "You've got my bloody Army pension that I've hocked for their bloody school fees. You've got the God-damned tin handshake which paid for their bedrooms in this palace. What more would you like? A pint of my blood? Or would you like to fry one of my kidneys for their breakfast?"

"I see that being out of hospital hasn't helped your temper." Melissa frowned at her fingernail, then decided it came close enough to perfection. She smiled at me, evidently satisfied with victory in the opening skirmish and now prepared to offer a truce. "I saw you on the moving wallpaper device last night. I think it'll be jolly nice to see a proper film about you. Do you think they'll want to interview me?"

"Why don't you ask your friend Tony. Your very close friend, Tony."

Melissa looked at me dangerously. She is a most beautiful woman, and I, with the foolishness of lust, had married her only for those looks. She married me for my father's wealth, and once that had gone Melissa went straight to the divorce courts. By that time I was on a hospital ship. "Do I hear jealousy?" She asked me sweetly.

"Yes."

She smiled, liking that answer. "I know Tony quite well." Her voice swooped judiciously on the word "quite", investing it with special meaning. "He's a bit rough trade, don't you think? But of course he married frightfully well."

"Rough trade? He seems bloody smooth to me."

"I mean that he's not top drawer, Nick. But then, nor are you. And of course he's another sailor, isn't he? Do you think I have a weakness for sailors?"

"All I know," I said bitterly, "is that your friend Tony has a weakness for a bloody Boer brute."

"That's hardly surprising, is it? If you had that ghastly man threatening you, you'd have a Boer bodyguard too."

I stared in astonishment at her. I'd spoken in resentment of the trick Angela had played with the contracts, but my words had achieved the effect of tossing a grenade into an apparently empty foxhole and being rewarded with a body. The foxhole, in this case, was Melissa's prodigious memory for gossip. "Who's threatening him?" I asked.

The long lashes went up and the big blue eyes looked suspiciously at me. Gossip, for Melissa, was a precious coin that should not be squandered. Her first remark about someone threatening Bannister had been made on the casual assumption that I shared the knowledge, but now, upon discovering my ignorance, she was wondering what advantage there might be in revealing more.

"Who?" I insisted.

She put the emery board down and evidently decided there was no advantage in revealing her knowledge. "Did you have a lovely time with the children?"

"We went to Holland Park."

"How very thrilling for you all, but I hope you didn't fill them up with grease-burgers, Nick?"

"I gave them fish and chips. Piers had three helpings."

"I think that's very irresponsible of you."

"What am I supposed to do? Feed them avocado mousse? Fish and chips is all I can afford." I scowled out of the window at the mirror image of Melissa's house across the street. The London home of the Honourable John and Mrs Makyns is one of those tall and beautiful stucco houses. The Honourable John complained that Kensington was far too far from the House of Commons, but I sensed how much Melissa loved this expensive home. Now, in spring, her road was thick with cherry blossom, in summer the stucco would reflect brightly white, while in winter the windows would reveal the soft gleam of wealth inside high-corniced living-rooms. "And talking of money," I said, "when are you going to pay me the rent you've been taking for my wharf?"

The faintest note of alarm entered Melissa's voice. "Don't be ridiculous, Nick."

I turned on her. "You rented my bloody wharf when you had no right to do it, no justification for doing it, and no need to do it."

"I might have known that if I invited you up for a chat you'd become tiresome." Melissa opened her hands like a cat stretching its claws. She inspected her nails critically. "Actually, Nick, I had to rent the wharf."

"Why? Did the Hon-John misplace one of his millions?" The Honourable John had oiled himself on to the board of a merchant bank and had somehow persuaded the selection committee of a safe Shire seat to make him their candidate. The Honourable John, in short, was sitting pretty, was already tipped as a future minister, and, so long as he wasn't caught dancing down Whitehall with a prostitute in either arm, he would inexorably rise to become Secretary of State for Pomposity, then a lord, and finally a Much-Respected Corpse. Whatever the Hon-John was, he wasn't rough trade.

"They're not Hon-John's children, Nick," Melissa said.

"Mands and Pip need ponies, and I really can't use Hon-John's private account for your children's necessities."

"Why didn't you just ask me for some cash?"

"You had some?" The interest was immediate.

"I could have pawned the gong." I protected my flank. I had a small amount of cash, but only enough to provision a repaired *Sycorax* and I did not want Melissa to fritter it away on a week's supply of lip-gloss.

"Do you have the medal?" she asked eagerly.

"As a matter of fact I do."

"May I see it, Nick. Please?"

I gave it to her. She turned the medal in her hands, then held it against her left breast as if judging its suitability as a brooch. "Is it worth a lot?" she asked.

"Only in scarcity value." I held out my hand.

She wouldn't give it back. "Pip should have it, Nick."

"When I'm dead, he can."

"If you're going to lead a ragamuffin life, then perhaps it will be safer here?"

"May I have it, please?"

She closed her hand over it. "Think about it, Nick. In all fairness it ought to go to your son, shouldn't it? I mean, you can always come back here and see it, but it will be much safer if I keep it for you."

I limped to a side table and lifted a porcelain statuette of a shepherd girl surrounded by three soppy-looking lambs. For all I knew the ornament might have been bought in a reject shop, but it looked valuable. This tactic had worked in Richmond this morning, and a tactic that works should never be abandoned. I hefted the porcelain, aiming its dainty delicacy at one of the big window panes.

"Nick!" Melissa contritely held the medal out to me and I tenderly restored the statuette to its side table. "I was only asking," she said in a hurt tone.

"And all I'm asking, Melissa dear" – I put the medal back into my pocket – "is why you rented Lime Wharf to Bannister."

"You were crippled, weren't you? That frightfully pudgy doctor said you'd never walk again, so it seemed hardly likely that you'd ever need the boat, let alone the smelly wharf. And your boat was nothing but scrap, Nick! It was a wreck! No one was looking after it."

"Jimmy Nicholls was. Except he was ill."

"He certainly wasn't doing a very good job," Melissa said tartly. "And frankly, Nick, I thought you could do with the extra money. For the children, of course, and I really think, Nick, that you should thank me. I was only doing what I thought right, and it took quite a lot of my time and a great deal of effort to arrange it."

The nerve of it was awe-inspiring. I reflected that if the boat's registration papers had not been safe in my lawyer's office Melissa would have sold *Sycorax* off to get herself a new hat for Royal Ascot. "How much rent is loverboy paying you for the wharf?"

"Don't be crude, Nicholas."

I met her gaze and wondered how many times she'd been unfaithful to me during our marriage. "How much?" I asked again.

The door opened, saving Melissa the need to answer, and the Honourable John came into the room. He looks every inch as expensive as his wife. The Honourable John is tall, thin, very pin-striped, with sleek black hair that lies close to a narrow and handsome head. He checked as he saw me. "Ah. Didn't know you were here, Nick. I hear you're going to be a telly personality?"

"They want me to encourage the nation to its duty."

"Splendid, splendid." He hovered. "And are you recovering well?"

"Fine most of the time," I said cheerfully, "but every now and then a fuse blows and I go berserk. I killed an investment broker last week. The doctors think the sight of a pin-striped suit makes me unstable."

"Jolly good, jolly good." The Honourable John was uncomfortable with me, and I don't much blame him. It's probably fitting that a man should be nervous around the ex-husband he cuckolded. "I just came in," he explained to Melissa, "for the Common Market report on broccoli."

"In the escritoire, darling, with your other thrillers. Nick was being tiresome about his wharf."

"And quite right, too. I said you didn't have any right to rent it out." The Honourable John shot up in my estimation.

Melissa glared at her husband. "It was for Mands and Pip," she said.

"Like auctioning my golf-clubs! I don't suppose there's a child born who's worth a good iron, what?" He dug about in the papers on the desk and found whatever he wanted. "I'm off to see someone. Will I see you for dinner, darling?"

"No," I said. They ignored me, kissed, and the Honourable John left.

"Don't take any notice of him," Melissa said. "He's really very fond of Mands and Pip."

"Does he know about you and Anthony Bannister?" I asked.

She twisted like a disturbed cat. "Do not be more tiresome than you absolutely need to be, Nicholas."

I stared into her face. A wedge-shaped face, narrowing from the broad clear brow to the delicate chin. It was, as my father had liked to say, a face where everything was wrong. Her nose was too long, her eyes too wide apart, her mouth was too small, yet altogether, with her pale, pale hair, it was a face that made men turn on the pavements as she went by. It was impossible, watching her now, to imagine that I had once been married to this pale and silky beauty.

"Who," I said, returning to the earlier question that Melissa had avoided answering, "is threatening Anthony Bannister?"

My previous question had been about Melissa's relations with Bannister and she smelt blackmail. "My marriage is very happy, Nick. Hon-John and I are both grown up." Melissa said it in a warning tone of voice.

"I hope it stays very happy," I said, thus becoming a blackmailer, and at the same time curious to hear what would be churned up from Melissa's remarkable memory.

"It's only a story." Melissa opened an onyx box, took out a cigarette and waited for me to hasten forward with a lighter.

I did not move so Melissa lit her own cigarette. "I mean, there are bound to be stories, Nick. There always are. About glamorous men like Tony." She paused to blow out a stream of smoke. Her overmantel was thick with embossed invitation cards. There was one, I saw, from my old mess. Good old loyalty. "You mustn't repeat this, Nick," she said dutifully.

"Of course not."

"It's all to do with Nadeznha, his late lamented. Awful name, isn't it? Sounds like one of those Russian ballet dancers who defect to the West as soon as they discover pantyhose and underarm deodorants. Anyway, you know she died last year?"

"I know."

"People were full of sympathy for Tony, of course, but there is just the teensiest whim of suspicion that he might have wanted her out of the way." Melissa watched me very carefully. "It's the perfect murder, isn't it? I mean, who's to know?"

"Overboard," I said.

"Exactly. One splash and you don't even have to buy a coffin, do you? Perhaps that's why I never went sailing with you?" She smiled to show she had not meant it. "Anyway, Nadeznha died at night and there was only one other person on deck."

"The Boer?"

"Score a bull's eye."

"But why would Bannister want her dead?"

Melissa rolled her eyes to the ceiling. "Because she was going to walk out on him, of course! That's what everyone thinks, anyway. And she'd have skinned him. Think of the alimony!" Melissa's voice took on an unaccustomed enthusiasm. "And I'm sure Tony's not exactly playing the taxman with a straight bat. He's got endless offshore companies and shady little bank accounts. Nadeznha would have revealed all, wouldn't she?"

"He must have good lawyers," I said. "And divorce must be as common as tealeaves among TV people."

"As common as cocaine, anyway," Melissa corrected me. "But Nadeznha would have had much better lawyers. She was frightfully wealthy. And anyway, Tony's pride couldn't have endured losing a catch like Nadeznha."

"Was she a catch?"

"Only Kassouli's daughter." Melissa's tone showed how

disgusted she was by my ignorance. "Oh, come on, Nick! Even you must have heard of Yassir Kassouli!"

I'd heard of him, of course. It was a name mentioned in the same breath as Getty, or Rockefeller, or Croesus. Yassir Kassouli owned ships, oil companies, finance houses and manufacturing industries around the globe. He had been born in the Levant, but had married an American wife and become an American citizen. He was rumoured to be richer than God.

"His money," Melissa said, "will go to his son, but Nadeznha can't have died poor, can she? She was the genuine American Princess."

"She was certainly pretty." I thought of the photographs in Bannister's Devon house.

"If you like bouncing tanned flesh and Girl Guide eyes, yes." Melissa shuddered. "Mind you, there was something quite eerie about all that mixed blood. She married Tony on the rebound, of course, and Kassouli never really approved. She was slumming in his eyes. And Yassir Kassouli has never forgiven Tony for her death. I mean, at worst it was murder, and at best carelessness. And you can imagine how sinister someone like Kassouli can be if he decides he doesn't like you. He's hardly likely to send you a solicitor's letter; much more likely to slip a cobra into your bed." She laughed.

"Do you think Bannister murdered Nadeznha?" I asked.

"I never said any such thing!"

"You think the Boer pushed her overboard?" I pressed her.

Melissa adopted a look of hurt innocence. "I am merely telling you the faintest, most malicious, trace of gossip, and I will utterly deny ever mentioning Tony's name to you." She tapped ash into a crystal bowl. "But the answer to your question, Nick, as to who might have threatened Tony, is Yassir Kassouli. The current whisper is that Yassir's sworn that Tony's not going to win the St Pierre."

"Which is why Bannister keeps that Boer brute around?"

"You're very slow, Nick, but you do eventually grasp the point. Exactly." Melissa stubbed out her cigarette to show that the subject was closed. "So what are you going to do now, Nick?"

"I'll see the kids in two weeks."

"I don't mean that, Nick. I mean with what passes for the rest of your life?"

"Ah! I'm going to repair *Sycorax*, then sail her to New Zealand. I'll fly back to see the kids when I can."

"You think money grows on trees?"

"My affair."

She picked up the emery board again. "Get a job, Nick. I mean, it's frightfully brave of you to think you can sail round the world, but you really can't. Hon-John will help you. He has oodles of friends who'd be jolly pleased to hire a VC. You can buy a grown-up suit and call yourself a public-relations man."

"I'm going to sail round the world."

She shrugged. "I shall need security from you, Nick. I mean, you can't just abandon your children in destitution while you gallivant in the South Seas, can you?"

"Why ever not?"

"I shall have to tell my lawyers that you're planning to run away, Nick. I hate to do it, you know that, but I really don't have any choice. None."

I smiled. "Dear Melissa. Money, money money."

"Who'll look after the children if I don't?"

"Their nanny?" I kissed her upturned cheeck. "I'll see you in two weeks?"

"Goodbye, Nicholas. The maid will see you out." She pulled the bellrope.

I left Melissa empty-handed, but in truth I had not expected to get any of Bannister's rent money.

But nor had I expected to hear the sibilant whisper of a rumoured crime. Was that what Inspector Abbott had meant when he spoke of using the long spoon? I limped through the drifts of fallen blossom and remembered Nadeznha Bannister's face from her photographs; she had been so pretty and happy, and now she lay thousands of feet deep with her body rotted by gas and drifting in the sluggish darkness.

And there was a whisper, nothing more than a catspaw of wind rippling a perfect ocean calm, that she had been murdered.

And Bannister was clearly protecting the Boer.

And, I told myself, it was none of my damned business. None.

It was none of my business, but I couldn't shake it out of my head.

When I got back to Devon I searched amongst the yachting magazines in Bannister's study for an account of the accident that had killed Nadeznha. I found something even better; in a brown folder on his desk there was a transcript of the inquest into Nadeznha's death.

It told a simple story. *Wildtrack* had been on the return leg of the St Pierre, some five hundred miles off the Canadian coast, and sailing hard in a night watch. The seas were heavy, and the following wind was force six to seven, but gusting to eight. At two in the morning Nadeznha Bannister had been the watch captain. The only other person on deck was Fanny Mulder, described in the inquest papers as the boat's navigator. That seemed odd. I'd been told Fanny was the professional skipper; and anyway, why would a navigator be standing a night watch as crew?

Mulder's evidence stated that the wind had risen after midnight, but that Nadeznha Bannister had decided against reducing sail. In the old days a yacht always shortened sail to ride out gales, but in today's races they went hell for leather to win. The boat, Mulder testified, had been going fast. At about two in the morning Nadeznha noticed that the boom was riding high and she had asked Fanny to go forward and check that the kicking strap hadn't loosened. He went forward. He wore a safety harness. He testified that Nadeznha, who was at the wheel in the aft cockpit, was similarly harnessed. He remembered, as he went through the centre cockpit, thinking that the seas were becoming higher and more dangerous. He found the kicking strap's anchor had snapped. Just as he was re-rigging the strap to a D-ring at the mainmast's base, *Wildtrack* was pooped. A great sea, larger than any other in that dark night, broke on to the yacht's stern. She shuddered, half-swamped, and Fanny told how he had been thrust forward by the rush of the cold water. His harness held, but by the time he had recovered himself, and by the time that *Wildtrack* had juddered free of the heavy seas, he found that Nadeznha was gone. The yacht's jackstaff, danbuoys, guardrails and lifebelts had been swept from the stern by the violence of the breaking wave.

Bannister, who was named as skipper of *Wildtrack*, was the first man on deck. The rest of the crew quickly followed. They dropped sail, started the engine and used white flares to search the sea. At daybreak they were still searching, though by then there could have been no hope, for Nadeznha Bannister had not been wearing a lifejacket, trusting instead to her safety harness. An American search plane had scoured the area at dawn, but by mid-day any hopes of a miracle had long been abandoned. Nadeznha Bannister's body had never been found.

The coroner remarked that *Wildtrack* had not shortened sail, and he criticized the attitude of yachtsmen who believed that risks should be taken for the ephemeral rewards of victory. That was the only criticism. He noted that the decision not to shorten sail had been taken by the deceased, whose skill at sailing and whose bravery at sea were not in question. It was a tragic accident, and the sympathy of the court was extended to Mr Anthony Bannister and to Nadeznha's father, Mr Yassir Kassouli, who had flown from America to attend the inquest.

The verdict was accidental death, and the matter was closed.

"Force six or seven?" Jimmy Nicholls said. "I wouldn't shorten sail either."

"You think it was an accident?" I asked.

"I weren't there, boy. Nor were you. But it just shows you, don't it? Always unlucky if you take a maid to sea. Maids should stay ashore, they should."

It was Tuesday. My lawyer had advised me that, if I wanted *Sycorax* restored, I should make the film, and so Jimmy was taking me to the marina in his thirty-foot fishing boat. It was a warm day, very warm, but Jimmy was dressed in his usual woollen vest, flannel shirt, serge waistcoat and shapeless tweed jacket that hung over thick tar-stained trousers which were tucked into fleece-lined sea-boots. Ne'er cast a clout till May be out, they say in England, but Jimmy did not intend discarding any clothing until he was stripped for his coffin.

He had almost found the coffin this last winter. "Buggers put me in hospital, Nick." He had told me this twenty times already, but Jimmy never liked to let a point drop until he was convinced it had been well understood. "T'weren't my fault, nor was it. Bloody social workers! Told me I were living in a slum, they did. Told me it were the Government's doing. I told 'em it were my home." He coughed vilely and spat towards the houseboat that was still moored on my wharf. Mulder was supposed to live in the ugly floating hut, but I had not seen the South African since my visit to Bannister's house in Richmond.

"You should give up smoking, Jimmy," I said.

"Buggers would like that, wouldn't they? There was a time when an Englishman were free, Nick, but we ain't free now. They'll be stopping our ale next. They'll have us all on milk and lettuce next, like the Chinese." The Chinese diet was one of the many matters on which Jimmy was seriously misinformed. The one subject of which he was a complete master was seamanship.

He was seventy-three now. In his twenties he had sailed in a J-class racing yacht; one of the twenty hired hands who lived in the scuttleless fo'c'sle of a rich man's racer with a single bucket for all their waste. Jimmy's job had been mastheadman, spending his days a hundred feet high on the crosstrees to ensure that the big sails did not tangle with the standing rigging. He had been paid three pounds and five shillings a week, with two shillings added for food and an extra pound for every race won. During the war he'd served in destroyers and been torpedoed twice. In 1947 he had become a deckhand on a small coaster that shuttled china clay and fertilizers about the Channel. Later he'd worked in trawlers, while now, notionally retired, he owned this clinker-built boat that hunted bass, crab and lobsters off the jagged headlands. Jimmy was a Devon seaman, tough as the granite cliffs that tried to suck his boat into their grinding undertow. I suspected that when his time came Jimmy would arrange his own death in those dark waters rather than surrender to the hospital's oxygen tent.

Now, as we chugged downstream, I again probed Jimmy's opinions of Nadeznha Bannister's death. "I don't reckon she'd have taken a risk," Jimmy said. "She could sail a boat right enough, I'll say that for the maid."

That was like Socrates admitting that someone was a reasonably clear thinker. "Right enough to fall overboard?" I asked.

"Ah!" It was half cough and half spit. "You're all the same, you youngsters. You think you know what you're doing out there! I've seen men who knew the sea like a hound knows its master, and they still went oversides. There isn't a law, Nick, not about the water. How long you been sailing, now?"

"Since I was twelve."

"How long's that?"

I had to think. "Twenty-two years."

Jimmy nodded happily. "And in another twenty-two, boy, you just might have learned a thing or two."

I kept trawling for gossip. "Did you ever hear anything about Mrs Bannister?"

He shook his head. "Not that would surprise you, no."

"I heard she might have been having an affair."

"T'weren't with me!" He roared with laughter, and the laugh turned into a hacking cough.

I waited for the coughing to finish. "I've heard rumours, Jimmy, that it wasn't an accident."

"Rumours." He spat over the side. "There are always rumours. They say she was pushed, don't they? I heard that. And they say as how it wasn't that Mulder fellow on deck with her, but Mr Bannister."

"That's new to me."

"Just pub talk, Nick, just pub talk. The maid be dead, and nothing'll bring her back to harbour now."

I tried another tack. "Why does Bannister keep Mulder with him?"

"Buggered if I know. He don't talk to me, Mr Bannister don't. I ain't high and mighty enough. But I don't like that other bloke. Keeps bad company, he do. Drinks with Georgie Cullen. Remember George?"

"Of course I remember George."

Jimmy lit one of his stubby pipes. We were turning into the wide sea-reach that was edged by the town and he stared across the river to where two Dutch pair trawlers were being scraped and painted by the old battleship buoys. The Dutch government subsidized their fishermen who could therefore afford a new trawler every other year. Their rejects were sold to us. Just short of the trawlers a motor-cruiser was trying to pick up a mooring buoy. The skipper was bellowing at his crew, a woman, who reached vainly with a boathook, but the skipper had misjudged the tide which made the woman's task hopeless. "You useless bloody cow!" the man shouted.

Jimmy chuckled. "Most of 'em couldn't float an eggbox round a bloody bathtub. Call themselves sailors! It would be easier to train a bloody chimp."

A French aluminium-hulled boat was motoring in from the sea. I recognized the same yacht that had been moored in the pool beneath Bannister's house the previous week. The same black-haired girl was at the tiller and I nodded towards her. "She's a good sailor."

"Boat comes from Cherbourg. Called *Mystique*." There was very little Jimmy did not know about the river. Tourists, seeing his filthy clothes and smelling his ancient pipe, might avoid him, but his old rheumy eyes saw everything and he picked up news in the river's small pubs with the merciless efficiency of a monofilament net. "The maid ain't a Froggy, though," he added.

"She isn't?"

"American. Her father were here in the War, see. She be seeing his old haunts." The Americans who had landed in Normandy had trained on the Devon beaches. "And she be writing a book, she do say."

"A book?" I tried to hide my interest in the girl.

Jimmy cackled. "Reckoned you'd be hungry when you came out."

"Thanks, Jimmy."

"She say she be writing a pilot book. I thought there were plenty enough pilot books for the channel, but she do say there ain't one for Americans. 'Spose that means we'll be swamped by Yankee boats next." He span his wheel to turn his boat towards the entrance of the town boatyard. It no longer made boats, but instead was a marina for the wealthy who wanted protected berthing for their yachts. I could see *Wildtrack* waiting for me at one of the floating pontoons. She was long, very sleek, with a wide blue flash decorating her gleaming white hull.

"Have you heard anything about someone wanting to stop Bannister from winning the St Pierre?" I asked Jimmy.

"The Froggies, of course. They'd do anything to keep him from winning it, wouldn't they?" Jimmy had a true Devon man's distrust of the French. He admired them as seamen, probably preferred them to any other nation, but was dubiously aware that they were not English.

Jimmy brought the heavy fishing boat alongside the pontoon with a delicacy that was as astonishing as it was unthinking. He looked over at *Wildtrack* and grimaced at the small crowd that waited for me. Mulder was in *Wildtrack*'s cockpit. Matthew Cooper was on the pontoon with his film crew, and Anthony Bannister waited to one side with Angela beside him. Angela was wearing shorts and Jimmy growled in appreciation of her long legs. "That be nice, Nick."

"She'd bite your head off as soon as look at you."

"I like a maid with a bit of spirit in her." He held out a hand to check me as I went to step on to the pontoon. "You never did have any sense, Nick Sandman, so you listen to me. You takes their damned money and you mends your boat. You let them make their daft film, and then you go off to sea. You hear me? And you don't mess about with the dead, boy. It won't get you nowhere."

"I hear you, Jimmy."

"But you never were one to listen, were you? Go on with you, boy. I'll see you in the pub tonight." He glanced at the waiting film crew. "Do you have to wear lipstick, Nick?"

"Piss off, Jimmy."

He laughed, and I went to make a film.

I can't say that we went to sea as a happy ship. Mulder did not speak to me, his crew were surly, while Matthew and his camera team stayed out of everybody's way. Angela retired to the after cockpit.

Tony Bannister grasped the nettle, though. "I'm glad you've come, Nick."

"Somewhat under protest," I said stiffly.

"I'm sure." We were motoring across the bar, between the rocky headlands where the breakers smashed white. To starboard I could see the waves breaking on the Calfstone Shoal. "I think," Bannister said awkwardly, "that we'd better let bygones be bygones. We behaved badly, but I would have told you about Fanny, and you would have got your medal back."

"I just don't like dishonesty."

"I think you've made that very plain. Let's just agree that we'll try harder?"

For the sake of peace, and because we seemed stuck with each other's company, I agreed.

We had bucked our way across the bar and Mulder now ordered the sails hoisted. He killed the engine, folded the propellor blades, and instantly *Wildtrack* became a creature in her element. She was no longer defying the sea with her diesel fuel and churning blades, now she was caught in the balance of wind and water. The sails were vast and white, swooping her gracefully southwards into the face of a brisk south-westerly wind.

Bannister and I sat in the central cockpit. Mulder must have known I was watching him and he must have guessed how I wanted to despise his seamanship.

But he was good.

I wanted him to be a butcher of a helmsman. I wanted him to be as crude as his physical appearance suggested. But instead he displayed a confident and rare skill. I'd expected him to be that most hateful of creatures, the loud and strident skipper, but his orders were given without fuss. His crew of seven men, identically dressed in blue and white kit, were drilled to a quiet efficiency, but the star of the boat was Fanny Mulder. He had an instinctive, almost gentle, touch and I knew, right from the beginning, that he was a natural. He was good.

And I was suddenly, unexpectedly happy. Not because I'd made a precarious peace with Bannister, but because I was at sea. I was watching my dark Devon coast slip away. Already the small beaches were indistinct, hidden by the heave of grey waves. I could look back into the river's mouth and I saw what I had forgotten; how the inland hills were so green and soft, while the sea-facing slopes were so wind battered and dark that it almost seemed as if the river was a wound cut into a crust of matter to reveal the softer flesh within.

I looked seaward. A Westerly was beating under full sail towards Dartmouth. A grey misshapen mass on the horizon betrayed a fleet auxiliary heading for Plymouth. A lobsterman coming from Start Point thudded past us in a stained boat heaped with pots and buoys and I thought I detected a derisive expression on the skipper's face as he glanced at Bannister's fancy boat. I would not have chosen a boat like *Wildtrack* to take me back to the ocean, but suddenly that did not matter. I was back where the hospital had said I would never be, and I could smell the sea and I could feel its lash in the spray and I could have cried for happiness when I saw the first fulmar come arrowing down to flick its careless flight along a wave's shifting face.

"You look happy." Bannister had taken the wheel from Mulder.

"It's good to be back." There was an awkward moment when neither of us had anything to say. Mulder had disappeared, sent down to the main cabin while Bannister conned the boat. I suspected, and later confirmed by observation, that Mulder was not to be included in the film. The audience would have to understand that it was the beloved Tony Bannister who was rescuing me. He looked impressive as he stood at the big wheel. His legs were braced, his face tanned, and his hair wind-stirred. On film he would look marvellous, like a Viking in a designer floatcoat.

"What do you think of the boat?" he asked me.

"Impressive." The truth was that I preferred my yachts to be old-fashioned. I'd never cared overmuch for speed, but *Wildtrack* cared so much that her digital log was accurate to one hundredth of a knot.

Yet, in her way, I suppose *Wildtrack* was an impressive boat. She was certainly expensive. The main cockpit was in the boat's centre, but there was a rear cockpit, aft of the owner's cabin, which would serve as a sundeck when the boat was in warmer seas. She was a boat built for the world's rich, complete with digital logs offering a ludicrous accuracy and motor-driven winches and weather faxes and satellite receivers and running hot water and air-conditioning and ice-making machinery and power-steering. The old seamen who had sailed from Devon, Raleigh and Drake, Howe and Nelson, would have understood *Sycorax* immediately, but they would have been flummoxed by the silicon-chip efficiency of this sleek creature.

They would have been flummoxed, too, by the extraordinary equipment which the film crew had deployed on the coachroof. Bannister saw my nervousness and tried to reassure me. "The idea is to film a background interview today. How you learned to sail, where, who taught you, why. We'll chop it all to ribbons, of course, and cut it in with some old home movies of you as a kid. Does that sound good to you?"

"It sounds bloody foul."

"Let's give it a whirl when we're ready."

The cameraman was filming general views of the boat, but was inexorably working his way aft to where Bannister and I waited in the central cockpit. I noticed how Bannister fidgeted with the boat. He constantly checked the wind-direction indicator on the dashboard, then twitched the helm to keep the small liquid-crystal boatshape constant on the tactical screen. Mulder had not needed the electronic aids to sail *Wildtrack* at her highest speed, but Mulder was a natural helmsman and Bannister was not. He suddenly seemed uncomfortably aware of my gaze. "Would you like to take her, Nick?"

"Sure."

"We're steering 195," Bannister said as he stepped aside.

"195." I glanced down at the compass. So long as the wind did not change, and this wind seemed set for eternity, I only had to keep one finger on the big stainless-steel and power-assisted wheel to compensate for *Wildtrack*'s touch of weatherhelm. The sea was not big enough to jolt the big yacht off her course. A few waves shuddered the hull, but I noted with relief how my balance seemed unaffected by them. I sensed a gust, luffed into it for speed, and then paid off with the extra half knot staying on the fancy speedometer. I did it without thinking and knew in that moment that nothing had changed.

It isn't hard to sail a boat. The hard bit is the sea's moods and the wind's fretting. The hard bit is surviving shoals and squalls and tidal rips. The hard bit is navigating in a filthy night, or reefing down in a shrieking storm when your body is already so wet and cold and tired that all you want to do is die. But putting a boat into a wind's grip and holding her there is as easy as falling off a cliff. Anyone can do it.

However, sailing a boat well takes practice that turns into instinct. I had found, at that moment when I added the small pulse of speed to the long hull, that the instincts had not been abraded by the years of hospitals and pain. Nothing had changed, and I was back where I wanted to be.

The cameraman had appeared close in front of me. The clapperboard snapped, and I gritted my teeth and tried to forget the lens's intrusive presence.

"Tell me when you first sailed, Nick?" Bannister asked.

"Long time ago." I was watching the wind-kicked spray shredding from the rocks off Start Point. We were overtaking a big Moody that was idling along while its crew lunched in the cockpit. They waved.

"Tell me how you started?" Bannister insisted. The sound-recordist crouched at my feet and thrust a long grey phallus of a microphone up towards my face.

Bannister had to coax me, but suddenly I found it easy to talk. I spoke of Jimmy teaching me in a dipping-lug dinghy, and I talked of stealing my father's boats to explore the Channel coast, and I described a bad night, much later on, when *Sycorax* had clawed me off the Roches Douvres, and I still swear that it was *Sycorax* who saved my life in that carnage of rock and rain. I should never have been under the lash of that northerly gale, but I'd promised to pick up a fellow lieutenant in St Malo and somehow *Sycorax* had kept the promise for me. I must have talked enthusiastically, for Bannister seemed pleased with what he heard.

"When you were wounded," he asked, "did you ever think you'd be back in a boat?"

"I thought of nothing else."

"But at the very first, in battle, didn't you give up hope?"

"I wasn't too aware of anything at that moment." Now that he was talking about the Falklands I heard my answers becoming sullen and short.

"What actually happened," he asked, "when you were wounded?"

"I got shot."

He smiled as though to put me at my ease. "What actually happened, Nick, when you won the VC?"

"Do you want to cross the Skerries?" I nodded ahead to where the shallow bank off Start Point was making the tide turbulent.

"The VC, Nick?" he prompted me.

"You want to go inshore of the Skerries?" I asked. "We'll get the help of the tidal current there."

Bannister, realizing that he was not going to draw me on the medal, smiled. "How does it feel," he asked instead, "to be in a boat again?"

I hesitated, searching for the right words. I wanted to say I'd let him know just as soon as I was in a proper boat, and not in some hyper-electronic Tupperware speed-machine, but that was unfair to the pleasure I was having, and the thought of that pleasure made me smile.

"Cut!" Matthew Cooper called to his cameraman.

"I didn't answer!" I protested.

"The smile said everything, Nick." Cooper looked back towards Angela in the aft cockpit and I saw him nod. The performing dog, it seemed, had done well.

Bannister, off camera now, crouched to light a cigarette with a gold-plated storm lighter. "You're going to have to answer those unwelcome questions, Nick."

"I am?" I let *Wildtrack*'s bows fall off the wind to take us east of the broken water.

"You can't be coy about the medal, you know. The reason we're making the film is because you're a hero."

"I thought we were making it because it was your thug who damaged my boat?"

He smiled. "*Touché.* But you will have to tell us. Not today, maybe, but one day."

I shrugged. It seemed that this day's filming was over because the camera crew began to pack up their equipment as Mulder took the wheel from me. To escape from the South African's sullen company I explored *Wildtrack*. I'd been worried before I came aboard that my injuries might have made my balance treacherous, but I found no difficulty in keeping my footing as I went to the foredeck. There was pain in my back, though I fancied that the regular morning swimming in Bannister's pool had done wonders to strengthen the muscles and dull the discomfort. I was more worried about my right leg which still shook uncontrollably and threatened to spill me like a drunk. That weakness was at its worst when I was tired, which was hardly an encouragement for single-handed sailing across the world, but at least my mobility on *Wildtrack*'s deck gave me optimism. I used the handrails and shrouds for support, but I would have done that even if I had never been wounded.

I dropped down a hatch and saw how the forepeak had been stripped empty to make the bows light. The main cabin showed the same dedication for speed. I'd expected a lavish comfort pit, but luxury had been sacrificed for lightness. What money had been spent had gone on navigational equipment; there was Loran, Decca, Satnav, even an Omega to trap very low frequency radio waves transmitted around the globe. The only thing I could not see was a sextant.

The rear cabin, approached through a narrow tunnel that ran abaft the centre cockpit, was more lavishly furnished and it was clear that these were Bannister's quarters. There was an air-conditioner, a heater, even a television and a VCR built into the bulkhead at the foot of the bunk.

Above the double bunk, framed and screwed to the bulkhead, was a photograph of Nadeznha. There was a line of print on the photograph's vignette and I knelt on the bunk to read it: 'Nadeznha Bannister, 1956–1983, 49° 18' N, 41° 36' W'.

I stared into the dead girl's dark eyes that were now so familiar to me from all the other pictures I'd seen. She had been no attenuated blonde like Melissa or Angela, but a robust girl with dark skin and strong bones. It seemed a terrible waste that her bones were in the ocean's deep darkness.

The cabin's rear hatch slid forward and Bannister swung himself down. He seemed surprised to find me in his quarters, but made no protest. He nodded towards the photograph. "My wife."

"She was very beautiful," I said.

He pulled open the sliding door to the head and took something from a locker there. I saw it was a phial of sea-sickness capsules. He turned and stared at the photograph. "Greek, Arab, French, Persian and American blood. A wonderful mix. Mind you, it also gave her a fearful temper." He somehow made the temper sound like one of his wife's more endearing characteristics. "She could be very determined," he went on, "especially about sailing. She was so damned sure she could win the St Pierre, which is why she was pushing the boat so hard."

"Is that what killed her?" I asked brutally.

"We don't know, not really." He offered a theatrical pause as though speaking of his wife's death was painful. "It was a dirty night," he said at last, "a following sea, and *Wildtrack* was pooped. That's usually caused because you're travelling too fast, isn't it? And I think Nadeznha must have unclipped her safety harness for a few seconds."

He'd told me nothing that I had not read in the inquest's transcript. "She was alone?" I prompted him.

"She was alone at the aft wheel." He nodded towards the small rear cockpit. "The other person on watch had gone forward to tighten the vang." He'd used the American term for the kicking strap. "The rest of us were sleeping. But she was a marvellous sailor. Grew up in Massachusetts, you see, near the sea. She was sailing a boat when most of us are still learning to ride a tricycle. I used to tease her that she had Phoenician blood, and perhaps she did."

I looked back to the photograph.

"We searched, of course. Quartered the sea for the best part of a day." Bannister's voice was toneless now, as though the events had been numbed by repetition. "But in those waters?

She'd have been dead in minutes." He clutched at a handrail as the boat lurched from the starboard on to the port tack. Mulder was putting the crew through their racing paces and *Wildtrack*'s motion was becoming rough. Bannister plucked a blanket from the foot of the bunk. "Will you forgive me? Angela's not exactly a born sailor."

I followed him up the companionway to the aft cockpit where Angela, now with a heavy sweater over her shorts and shirt, lay sprawled in abject misery. She grimaced to see me, then heaved, twisted, and thrust her head through the guardrails. I looked at her tall body draped over the scuppers and I saw in her long bare legs part of the reason why Bannister kept company with this prickly and angry girl. She was truly beautiful. He saw me looking, and I felt his pride of possession like a small sting.

Angela came back inboard and curled herself into the crook of Bannister's arm. He wrapped her in the blanket, then fed her two of the pills which, I knew, would do no good now. "There's only one cure for seasickness," I said heartlessly.

"Which is?" Bannister asked.

"Stand under a tree."

"Very funny." He held her tight. "What do you think of Fanny now?" he asked me.

"I think he's a Boer brute."

Bannister offered me an assured and tolerant smile. "I mean, what do you think of him as a helmsman?"

"He's good." I tried to sound ungrudging. Mulder was gybing the boat now, swinging her stern across the wind so that the boom slammed across the hull. It could be a dangerous manoeuvre, but his control was so certain that there was never a single jarring thud. At the same time he had his foredeckmen changing jibs. As soon as one was made fast Mulder ordered it changed. "He's very good," I added truthfully.

"Nadeznha found him. He was running a charter service in the Seychelles. She nicknamed him Caliban. Don't you find that a good omen?"

Caliban was the monstrous son of the witch, Sycorax. "No." I looked at the prostrate Angela. "Is she your Ariel?"

Bannister did not want to pursue the fancy. "Fanny's good,"

he said, "and very few people know just how good he is. Think of him as my secret weapon to win the St Pierre. That's why I need him, Nick."

I grunted. The hour and a half I'd spent on *Wildtrack* was not enough to tell me whether this boat and crew could lift the St Pierre off the French, but I allowed it was possible. The boat was fast, Fanny was clearly brilliant, and Bannister had the ambition.

And he would need it, for the St Pierre is the greatest prize of racing-cruisers.

The French organize it. There's no big prize money, and it isn't really a race at all because an entrant can choose his or her own starting time. The only rules are that a boat must be a production monohull and not some skinny one-off built for the event, that it must begin at Cherbourg, sail round the islands of St Pierre and Miquelon off the coast of Newfoundland, then, without touching land, run home to Cherbourg again. The course is around four and a half thousand nautical miles: a windward flog all the way out against currents and gales; a lottery with fog and ice at the turn; and a fast run back in heavy seas. At the end of the season, whoever has made the fastest voyage holds the prize.

Odd rules, but there's wily method in the Gallic madness. For a start, there's a political method. European rule of North America ended long ago, except in two tiny and forgotten islands, St Pierre and Miquelon. They're French possessions, ruled from Paris, unconsidered island trifles that were never swept up by the British and were overlooked by the Canadians. The race is thus a constant reminder to the French that the Tricolour still flies on North American soil.

Then there's a more hard-headed purpose to the rules. French boats are good. The Jeanneaus, Centurions and Beneteaus have dominated the St Pierre and each successive win has been an advertising triumph to sell more French boats around the globe. To win the St Pierre a boat has to be good, hardy and fast. Each year a score of factory-prepared boats from Britain, America, Holland, Germany and Finland try to crack the race, and each autumn, when the fog and ice sweep southwards to finally close the St Pierre season, the French are still the holders and a thousand more orders go to keep French boatyards busy. As a marketing tool, the St Pierre is a miracle, and if a foreigner could take the prize, even for a year, it would be seen in France as a disaster.

"I'm planning a late run," Bannister said now, "and the far north route. With any luck I'll come home just when the autumn programme schedule begins. That'll start next season's shows with a triumph."

"Is that why you're doing it?"

"I'm doing it to prove that a British boat can do it. And for Nadeznha's memory. And because the television company are paying me to do it, and because my audience want me to win." He rattled the reasons off as if by rote, then paused before adding the final justification, "And to prove that a TV star isn't just a powder-puff in an overlit studio."

He had given the final reason lightly, but I suspected it was the most important spur to his ambition. "Is that what people think?"

"Don't you?" he challenged me.

"I wouldn't choose the life," I said, "but I suppose someone has to do it."

He smiled. "Most of them are just powder-puffs in overlit studios, Nick. They think they're so damned clever merely because they're on the idiot box, while the truth is that the job demands a great deal less intelligence than people think. So if I want to make my mark properly then I have to achieve something rigorous, don't I? Something like the St Pierre. It may not be the VC, but it will do."

It was a remarkable admission, even beguiling in its candour, and it explained why Bannister surrounded himself by strong men like Mulder and his loutish crew. Acceptance by such brutes made Bannister feel strong. He laughed suddenly, perhaps embarrassed because he had betrayed something personal.

Angela's miserable eyes watched me over the edge of her blanket. I put a hand on the small wheel that was linked to the larger helm in the central cockpit and I felt the rudder's tremors vibrating the stainless-steel spokes. I was thinking of the night of Nadeznha's death. If *Wildtrack* had been running before a heavy sea then why, in the name of God, would an experienced sailor con the ship from the aft cockpit? The centre cockpit would be far more comfortable, but perhaps Nadeznha Bannister had chosen this smaller cockpit as a vantage point to watch for the great waves looming from the darkness behind. I shivered as I imagined the tons of freezing water collapsing on to *Wildtrack*'s stern. It would be just like being hit by a truckload of cement dropped from two floors up.

Angela twisted round to throw up the seasickness pills and I politely looked away, past the danbuoys, to watch *Wildtrack*'s seething and curling wake. A cormorant flew low and fast across our stern. "Do you think *Wildtrack* can win it?" Bannister asked abruptly.

"With luck, yes."

"Would you like to be a part of it, Nick? As navigator?"

"Me?" I was astonished by the offer. "You don't need a navigator, Bannister! You've got more bloody electronics on this thing than an Apollo mooncraft!"

"The race rules say we must carry a specialist navigator."

"I thought Fanny was your navigator?"

"He was, but he'll take Nadeznha's place as a watch captain this year." Bannister turned as his crew spilt the spinnaker from its chute. The gaudily coloured sail blossomed as he turned back to me. "It's really Angela's thought, not mine, but I like the idea very much. Why don't we end your film by showing you leaving Cherbourg in *Wildtrack*? The film will be transmitted while we're at sea, and it'll help whip up some public enthusiasm for the film about the race itself."

I didn't think he'd asked me because of any affection for me, but it was still somewhat demeaning to realize that he only wanted my film to be a taster for his own greater triumph. "I thought the end of my film was *Sycorax* sailing into the sunset?"

"Maybe we'll use that over the opening titles. But think of it, Nick! Winning the St Pierre!" Bannister spoke with a sudden enthusiasm. "Licking the Frogs at their own game!"

Angela watched me like a sick hawk. I shook my head. "I've never been a speed-merchant. I like going slow."

"But do think about it," he urged me. "In a couple of months I'll be giving a big party to formally announce my bid for the trophy. I'd like to say you'll be a part of the effort, Nick. Will you think about it?"

"You need a specialist navigator," I said. "Some guy who's a race tactician as well. I'm really not going to be of any use to you."

"Not in the race, maybe" – Angela forced the words out – "but you'll help the ratings."

"Ratings?" I somehow took the word to refer to the members of Mulder's crew; as if they were naval ratings.

"The viewing figures," Angela said with an acidity which implied that my misunderstanding betrayed an astonishing stupidity. "The VC makes you interesting, Mr Sandman, interesting enough to guarantee us more than twenty million viewers. Anticipating that kind of audience rating will mean we can increase the price of the advertising slots, and that's how you'll be useful to us."

At least she had been honest, though that did not soften the offence I felt. So my Victoria Cross was to become an advertiser's weapon? A means of selling more dogfood and baked beans? I was framing an outright and offended refusal when a violent lurch of *Wildtrack*'s hull ended the conversation. Angela jerked upright, vomiting, and I saw the mainsail's shadow whip over us. There was a noise like a bass-string thumping the sky, and the boat was suddenly gybing, broaching and falling on her beam. I grabbed the small wheel for support. The tall mast was bending, breaking, then falling to leeward. Broken water boiled up the scuppers and spilt cold into the self-draining cockpits. A shroud whipped skywards, flicking a broken spreader with it. The unleashed spinnaker billowed ahead as the mast fell. The slick hull rolled, recovered and slowed. The seas were low, no more than two or three feet, but even so *Wildtrack*'s bows were buried and the boat staggered as if she'd sailed into a sandbank. Rigging was tangling and the mainsail was shredding with a noise like the fire of an automatic weapon.

Bannister stood, half fell, and shouted incoherently. A crew-member was overboard, tangled in the fallen shrouds. Angela was curled on the thwart, sobbing. Mulder's voice bellowed above the din and chaos, inflicting order on the panic.

A port shroud had parted. The stainless-steel wire, made to carry all the weight of great winds on a towering mast, must have snapped. The mast and sails had ripped overboard. It had taken no more than two or three seconds, and now *Wildtrack* lay wallowing and draining in the gentle seas. No one was hurt. The boat had pulled up short and it was a simple matter to pull the crewman who had gone overboard back to safety. The film crew, who had been staying out of the way in the main cabin, poured in panic up to the centre cockpit and were curtly told to get the hell out of the way.

"Fuck." Bannister was staring helplessly at the shambles.

"Wire-cutters!" Mulder shouted.

I stayed out of the way. The crew knew what to do. The broken and fallen rigging was secured, then the remaining stays and shrouds were cut so that the wreckage could be dragged inboard. The engine was started. All in all it had been a mild accident, impressive to watch, but harmless except to Bannister's purse.

And to his anger. He took me forward and showed me the turnbuckle that had taken up the tension of the broken shroud. It had not been the wire which snapped, but rather the turnbuckle that had simply let the shroud go. It was threaded inside, and someone had taken a circular file to the threads and worn them almost smooth. The sabotage was clumsily obvious; there were even shards of filed metal still sticking to the grease which had been put on to the abraded threads. Just enough purchase had been left to grip the shroud but as soon as Mulder put the spinnaker's extra weight on the mast the threads had given way. Once that shroud had gone, the others on the port side had snapped like cheesewire under strain.

"Fanny!" Bannister was livid with anger. "From now on you live in the boatyard. All of you!"

"Does that mean I get my wharf back?" I asked tactlessly.

For a second I thought Bannister was going to hit me, but

then he nodded. "You get your damned wharf back." His anger was showing as petulance, like a child losing a treat. He pushed past me, going back to the stern where his girlfriend was still slumped in the stomach-churning misery of the sea. For the moment Bannister appeared to have forgotten his offer that I should sail to St Pierre triumph as part of this boat's crew.

But I hadn't forgotten.

And I wouldn't do it. There are lucky boats and unlucky boats. That isn't a fancy, nor a superstition, but a fact. *Sycorax* was a lucky boat, but I smelt the stench of disaster about *Wildtrack*. She had already killed Bannister's first wife, and now someone had dismasted her. She was crewed by a surly pack and skippered by a kleptomaniac. I did not care what fame or fortune might come to the crew of this boat if she won the St Pierre, but I would not share it, for I would not sail in a boat that so reeked of ill-luck.

Bannister could sail the Atlantic without me. I knew he'd repeat the offer again, but so far I'd given him too much for too little. This time the answer would be no. When I sailed my next ocean it would be in *Sycorax* and in no other boat, just *Sycorax*.

Mulder scowled at me, pushed the throttle hard open, and we motored ignominiously home.

PART TWO

Inspector Abbott came to the village pub three weeks after *Wildtrack* had been dismasted. He was wearing trousers made of a wide blue and pink check that looked like dismantled curtains.

"You're looking better," he said to me in a rather grudging voice.

"I'm fine, Harry." I said it confidently, but it was not really true. I was swimming two miles every morning in Bannister's indoor pool and the exercise was laying new muscle beneath the scar tissue, but my leg could still betray me with a sudden and numbing weakness. Only the day before, while walking down from the village post-office, I'd sprawled helplessly on the pavement. One minute my right leg had been doggedly reliable, the next, and for no apparent reason, it had just gone limp. But I would not admit to the weakness, lest I persuaded myself that I was not fit enough to sail across the world. "I assume from the fancy dress that you're not on duty?"

Abbott plucked at the trousers. "Don't you like them, Nick?"

"They're bloody horrible."

"They're American golfer's trousers," he said with hurt dignity. "They're meant to improve the swing. Plenty of room in the crotch, you see? You want a lemonade, Nick? A bottle of cherry pop, perhaps?"

"A pint of best, Harry."

He carefully carried the two full pints of beer to my table. It was early evening and the pub was still empty, though in a few weeks the crush of tourists would make the riverside bar uninhabitable. Abbott sipped the top off his beer and sighed with pleasure. "Got your medal back, did you?"

"I did, and thank you."

He acknowledged the thanks with a gracious wave of his cigarette lighter. "What do you think of the Boer now?"

"He's a good sailor," I said neutrally.

"So was Bluebeard." Abbott lit a cigarette. "I haven't seen Mr Bannister lately."

"He's on Capri with his girlfriend. They're on holiday."

"I wonder why he's stopped going to America for his holidays," Abbott said with an air of puzzled innocence, then shook his head. "Me? I get a week with the wife's sister in bloody Frinton. Who's the girlfriend?"

"Girl called Angela Westmacott. She's a producer on Bannister's programme."

Abbott frowned, then clicked his fingers. "Skinny bint, blonde hair?"

"Right."

"Looks a bit like your ex-wife; starved. How is Melissa?"

"She struggles on."

"I've never understood why men go for those skinny ones." Abbott paused to drain his pint. "I nicked a bloke once who'd murdered a complete stranger. The victim's wife asked him to do it, you see, so he bashed the bloke's head in with a poker. Very messy. She'd promised him a bit of nooky, which is why he did it, and the woman was as scrawny as a plucked chicken. You know what he told me when he confessed?"

"No."

"He said that it was probably the only chance he would ever get to go to bed with a pretty woman. Pretty? She was about as pretty as a toothpick. And to cap it all she didn't even give it to him! Told him to sod off when he trotted round with his pecker sharpened." Abbott stared ruefully across the river. "It was almost the perfect murder, wasn't it? Having your best-beloved turned off by a stranger."

The slight stress on 'perfect murder' was the second hint that Abbott was not here entirely because he was thirsty. His first hint had been the gentle query why Bannister no longer visited America. "Perfect murder?" I prompted him.

"My beer glass is empty, Nick, and it's your round."

I dutifully fetched two pints. "Perfect murder?" I asked again.

"The thing about a perfect murder, Nick, is that we'll never even know it's happened. So officially there's no such thing as a perfect murder. So if you hear about one, Nick, don't believe in it."

The comments were too pointed to ignore. "Does that mean," I asked, "that it was an accident?"

"That what was an accident?" Abbott pretended innocence.

"Nadeznha Bannister?"

"I wasn't there, Nick, I wasn't there." Abbott was obscurely pleased with himself. I'd been given a message, though I wasn't at all sure what or why. Abbott fixed me with his hangdog look. "Have you heard these rumours that someone's trying to scupper Bannister's chances of winning the St Pierre?"

"I've heard them."

"And you know what happened two nights ago in the marina?"

"I heard." *Wildtrack*'s warps had been cut in the dead of the night. There was a spring tide at the full and, if it had not been for a visiting French yachtsman, Bannister's boat might have been carried out to sea. Mulder and his crew had been sleeping alongside in the houseboat that had been moved from my wharf and the Frenchman's shout of warning had woken them just in time. It had all ended safely, and it might all have been dismissed as a trivial incident but for the fact that the warps had been cut. That made it into another attempt at sabotage.

"But clumsy," Abbott now said. "Very clumsy. I mean, if you wanted to stop a bugger from winning the St Pierre, would you knock his mast off now? Or cut him adrift now? Why not wait till he's in the race?"

"Does somebody want to stop Bannister winning the St Pierre?" I asked.

Abbott blithely ignored my question. "Kids could have climbed the marina fence and cut the mooring ropes, I suppose."

"The mast wasn't wrecked by kids," I said. "I saw the turnbuckle, and it was sabotage."

"Whatever a turnbuckle might be," Abbott said gloomily. "It was probably buggered up by a crew member who just wanted a week off."

That was a possible answer, I supposed. Certainly, if Melissa was right and Yassir Kassouli did want to end Bannister's chances of winning the trophy, then the two incidents were very trivial, especially for a man of Kassouli's reputed wealth. "Are you making enquiries?" I asked Abbott.

"Christ, no! I don't want to get involved. Besides, as I told you, I'm not crime any more."

"What are you, Harry?"

"Odds and sods, Nick. General dogsbody." He sounded bored.

And I was confused. Abbott was sailing very close to the rumours I'd heard, but always sheering off before anything definite was said. If a message was being given to me, then it was being delivered so elliptically that I was utterly at a loss. I also knew it would be no good demanding elucidation, for Abbott would simply say he was just having an idle chat. "Seen your old man lately?" he asked me now.

"I've been busy."

"You and Jimmy Nicholls, I hear," Abbott said. Jimmy was helping me to repair *Sycorax*. "How is he?"

"Coughing."

"Not long for this world, poor old sod. He shouldn't smoke so much, should he?" Abbott contemplated putting out his own cigarette, then decided to suck at it instead. He blew smoke at me. "When's the big party, Nick?"

He was referring to the party that was to be held at Bannister's riverside house in the early summer. The party was not just a social affair, but also the occasion on which Bannister would formally announce his entry into the St Pierre. It did not matter that he had already broadcast his intention on nationwide television, he would do it again so that his bid would receive further attention in the newspapers and yachting magazines.

"I hear," Abbott said, "that Bannister's introducing his crew at the party?"

"I wouldn't know, Harry."

"I just wanted to say to you, Nick, that I do hope you won't be one of them?"

He was not being elliptical now, far from it. "I won't be," I said.

"Because I did hear that Bannister asked you."

I wondered how Abbott had heard, but decided it was simply riverside gossip. I'd told Jimmy, which was the equivalent of printing the news on the front page of the local newspaper. "He did ask," I said. "I said no, and I haven't heard anything since."

"Will he ask again?"

I shrugged. "Probably."

"Then go on saying no."

I finished my pint and leaned back. "Why, Harry?"

"Why? Because in an unperverted sort of way, Nick, I'm reasonably fond of you. For your father's sake, you understand, and because you were stupid enough to win that bloody gong. I wouldn't want to see you turned into sharkbait. And that boat of Bannister's does seem to be," he paused, "unlucky?"

"Unlucky," I agreed, then wondered if the vague stress Abbott had laid on the word was yet another hint. I tried to force him into a straight answer. "Are you telling me that someone is trying to stop him?"

"Buggered if I know, Nick. Perhaps Bannister's paranoid. I mean being on the fucking telly must make a man paranoid." He drained his pint. "I know you'd like to buy me another one, Nick, but the wife has cooked some tripe and pig's trotters as a special treat, so I'll be on my way. Remember what I said."

"I'll remember."

I heard his car start and labour up the hill. Out on the river a kid doggedly tacked a Mirror dinghy upstream. Behind it, motoring into the wind, came *Mystique*. The American girl stood at her tiller and I hoped she might swing across to the pub's ramshackle pier for a drink, but she stayed on the far bank's channel instead.

A heron flew past her aluminium-hulled boat and climbed to its nest. Three swans floated beneath the trees. It was a spring evening, full of innocence and charm.

"What did Harry want?" the landlord asked me.

"He was just having a chat."

"He never does that. He's a clever bugger, is Harry. Mind

you, his golf swing's lousy. But that's the only thing Harry wastes time on, believe me."

I did believe him, and it worried me.

As the days lengthened and warmed, I forgot my worries. I forgot Bannister and Mulder, I forgot the rumours about Nadeznha Bannister's death and the whispers about sabotage, I even forgot the unpleasantness that had marked my introduction to the television business, because *Sycorax* mended.

Jimmy Nicholls and I mended her. They were weeks of hard work, and therefore of pleasure. We scarfed new timbers into *Sycorax*'s hull and caulked them home. We shaped new deck planks and joggled them into place. We raised the cockpit's sole and put gutters out to the transom so that, for the first time, *Sycorax* had a self-draining cockpit.

Jimmy selected trunks of Norway spruce from the timber yard and fetched them upriver on his boat. He made me listen at one end of the trunks while he tapped the other with a wrench and I heard how the note came clear and sharp to prove the timber's worth. We put the spruce on the wharf and adzed the trunks down; first we turned them into square sections, then we peeled away each corner, and each new corner, until they were rounded and we had our masts, gaff and booms. We used a hefty piece of pitch-pine for the bowsprit. Each evening, when the work was done and before I went to the pub, I would treadle a grindstone to put an edge back on tools blunted by good wood.

They were good days. Sometimes a spring rain thundered on the tarpaulin that we'd rigged overhead, but mostly the sun shone in promise of summer. We made a new coachroof, but strengthened it with oak beams so that the cabin could resist a knock-down in heavy seas. A smith from the town put lead into *Sycorax*'s keel and forged me new hounds to take the rigging on her mast. As spring turned into summer Jimmy and I began to lay bright new copper sheets over the finished hull, bedding them on layers of tar and paper and fixing them with flat-headed nails of bronze. The copper was expensive, but superior to any anti-fouling paint, and I wanted its protection before I sailed my wooden boat to where the tropical worms could turn iron-hard mahogany into a porous sponge. Jimmy and I did a good, old-fashioned job. On our rare days off we went to boat auctions on the river and bought good second-hand gear – an outboard for the dinghy, warps, blocks, cleats, flares and smoke floats, fire-extinguishers – and all the receipts were sent to the television company who repaid the money without demur. They were even paying Jimmy a cash wage that the taxman would never hear about. Life in those days was good.

Wildtrack had moved to the Hamble where a larger marina offered uniformed guards and large dogs as security. There were no more incidents of sabotage. Anthony Bannister, when he returned from his holiday, stayed in Richmond and sailed out of the new marina, so I did not see him. Angela sometimes came to the house to oversee her film, but rarely. When she did come she was businesslike and brusque. She pretended no great interest in *Sycorax*'s progress, except to insist that the boat was moved off Bannister's lawn before the party. I assured Angela the boat would be ready in time.

She frowned at the cradled hull that was still only half-coppered. "How can it be ready? You haven't finished the masts yet!"

I ignored her sharp critical tone. "We don't step the masts till she's in the water. So all I have to do before we launch is finish the coppering and put in the engine."

She snatched at a chance to hurry the process. "Can't the engine wait till she's afloat?"

"Not unless you want the river coming in where the propellor ought to be."

"You know best, I suppose." She sounded very grudging. I waited for her to mention Bannister's invitation that I should sail on the St Pierre, but she said nothing and I assumed the invitation was forgotten. I was relieved when she stalked away; a cold girl with a clipboard. She went to the terrace of the house where she chivvied Matthew Cooper into making faster progress.

It seemed to me that it was Matthew who did the real work for the television company. He and his camera crew came down every other week to film *Sycorax*'s rebuilding. When Angela was absent they were relaxed, except about their expense sheets on which they spent hours of devoted work. Their union rules insisted that they travelled in a monstrous herd, which meant that most of them had no work to do, but one of the drivers and the assistant cameraman proved to be enthusiastic carpenters and happily helped with whatever work was on hand. Yet the film crew's presence inevitably meant frustration and delay. A piece of work that Jimmy and I might have finished in an hour could take a whole day with Matthew fussing about camera angles and eyelines. Sometimes he'd arrive to find a job finished and would insist that we dismantle the careful joinery and recreate it for the camera. Then he would shoot it from every conceivable angle. "Nick? Your right arm's in the camera's way. Can you drop your elbow?"

"I can't tighten a bolt if I'm screwed up like Quasimodo."

"It won't show on film." He waited patiently till I'd finished my grotesque impression of the hunchback of Notre-Dame. "Thank you, Nick. Dropping the elbow will be enough. That's better."

Then the sound-recordist would stop everything because a light aircraft was ruining his tape, and when the plane's sound faded a cloud would arrive and the cameraman would insist on remeasuring the light. I perceived that film-making was very like soldiering in that it consisted of hours of idle waiting punctuated by moments of half-understood panic.

I was frustrated by the delays, but in turn inflicted frustration on Matthew. Often, while the camera rolled, he would spring questions on me. In the finished film, he told me, his own voice would be replaced by Bannister's so that the viewers would think that the great man had been constantly present during the filming. The frustration occurred every time Matthew asked the one question that lay behind the film's purpose. "Can you tell us how you won the medal, Nick?"

"Not right now. Anyone seen the tenon saw?"

"Nick?" Chidingly.

"I can't remember what happened, Matthew, sorry."

"Don't call me Matthew. Remember I'm supposed to be

Tony. So what happened, Nick?" Long pause. "Nick, please?"

Another long pause. "What was the question, Matthew?"

"Nick!"

"Nothing to say, Matthew, sorry, Tony."

"Oh, fuck it. Cut!"

Jimmy would chuckle, the film crew would grin, and Matthew would glare at me. I liked him, though. He had a shaggy black moustache, unruly hair, and a face which looked tough but which on closer inspection proved rather sad and dogged. He was hag-ridden with self-doubt and smoked more than a fouled engine, but, like his cameraman, Matthew cared desperately about the quality of his work. He did what Angela ordered him to do, but he invested those orders with a concern for the very best pictures. He would spend hours waiting for the light to touch the river in just the right way before he started shooting. He was an artist, but he was also the conduit for Angela Westmacott's instructions and worries; the chief of which still remained that *Sycorax* would not disfigure Anthony Bannister's lawn on the day of his big party.

Angela need not have worried, for Jimmy and I finished the hull ten days ahead of our schedule. The engine was still in pieces, the boat was unrigged, and the sails were still being repaired, but it was a great day when we could walk round the gleaming hull and see all the hard work come to a satisfying wholeness. I phoned Matthew and told him we could launch in a week's time, just as soon as the engine was back in the boat's belly, and he promised to bring the crew down for the event. Thus we would be in the water the day before the party.

I spent the next two days repairing the diesel and replacing the propellor. The new strength that the swimming had put into my back helped during the tedious hours of installing the engine. I rigged a jury crane with chains and blocks and spent frustrating hours settling the shims under the engine-block so that the propellor shaft ran true. It was probably the most difficult job of the whole repair, but eventually it was done. The self-starter would not work, but there was a handle and a flywheel, so I threw the damn thing away.

Melissa went to Paris for a fashion show and sent the children down to Devon for the next three days to get them off her hands, and I borrowed a Drascombe Dabber to potter about off the river's mouth where we caught mackerel on hand lines. Their nanny came to fetch the children back to London in Melissa's new Mercedes. "Mrs Makyns says the children are in need of the summer clothes, Mr Sandman." The nanny was a lolloping great Swede with a metronome voice.

"Tell Mrs Makyns that there are shops which sell the children's clothes."

"You are yoking, I think. She says you are to give me the money."

"Tell her I will send her a cheque."

"I will tell her. She will see you next week at Mr Bannister's party, I think." It sounded like a threat.

That same afternoon a crane arrived ready to lift *Sycorax* into the water. The launch was scheduled for the next morning and I had a bottle of champagne ready to break over the fairlead at her bows. Preparations for Bannister's party were also well advanced; caterers were setting up tables on the terrace, florists were delivering blooms, and gardeners were tidying up the lawns. Matthew arrived that evening and found me still working. The newly-laid copper reflected the dying sun so that *Sycorax* looked as if she had been cast in red-gold.

"She looks good, Nick," Matthew said.

"She is." I was dressed in swimming trunks and felt happily filthy with tar, paint and varnish stains. I was on *Sycorax*'s deck, varnishing the boom-gallows. "One month for rigging, then she's finished."

Matthew lit a cigarette and helped himself to a beer from the crate I kept by the sheerlegs. "I've got bad news for you."

I peglegged down the ladder and took a beer. "Tell me."

"Medusa wants you out of the house by tomorrow night." We had nicknamed Angela 'Medusa' – the snake-haired female with the basilisk gaze that turned her enemies to stone.

"That's fine," I said.

"She says it's only till next Tuesday. Because they've got weekend guests staying, you see. I'm sorry, Nick." Matthew sounded miserably embarrassed at having to make the request.

"I really don't mind, Matthew." I was getting too used to the luxury of Bannister's house and would happily move into a relaunched *Sycorax*. She had no berths yet, no galley and no lavatory, but I had a sleeping bag, a primus stove and the river.

"And Medusa also asked me to tell you not to use the swimming pool till all the guests are gone."

I laughed. "She doesn't want a cripple to spoil the decor?"

"Something like that," Matthew said unhappily. "But, of course," he went on, "you're invited to the party."

"That's nice."

"Because Bannister wants to announce that you'll navigate *Wildtrack* for him."

For a second I did not respond. I was watching the shining-hulled *Mystique* that had suddenly appeared at Sansom's Point. The boat had been absent for the last two months and I presumed the American girl had been exploring the harbours she would describe in her pilot book.

"Did you hear me?" Matthew asked.

"I heard."

"And?"

"I'm not bloody doing it, Matthew."

"Medusa wants you to do it," Matthew said warningly.

"Sod her." I was watching the American girl who was motoring *Mystique* against the tide with just a jib to stiffen her. She had chosen the eastern channel which was both narrower and shallower than the main channel, and which would bring her close to where Matthew and I stood.

"Medusa's set her mind on it," Matthew said.

"She never mentions it to me."

"She will, though."

"I'll say no again."

"Then she'll probably refuse to pay for *Sycorax*'s rigging."

"Sod her!" I said again. "I'll buy the rigging wire out of the fee you're paying me."

"What fee?" Matthew said. "Medusa says you've been living in Bannister's house, so he ought to get some rent out of you."

"He wrecks my boat, now I'm paying him to mend it? You're joking!"

The misery on Matthew's face told me that he was not joking. He tried to soften the blow by saying that perhaps it was just a rumour, but he was not convincing. "It's Medusa's fault," he said at last. "She was nothing till she started screwing Bannister. Now she virtually runs the bloody programme." He sounded envious that such a route of advancement was denied to him. "Bannister insisted she was made a full producer before he signed his last contract. Never let it be said, Nick, that you can't get to the top of British television by lying flat on your back. It is still the one certain, well-tried and infallible method of success."

I felt somewhat uncomfortable with the criticism, even if it was true. "She seems good at her job?" I offered mildly.

"Of course she's good at her job," Matthew said irritably. "It doesn't take much intelligence to be a good television producer. It's not nearly so demanding a job as teaching. All that being a producer takes is a capacity for expense account lunches and the ability to pick the right director." He shrugged. "What the hell. Perhaps she'll marry Bannister and leave us all in peace?"

"Do you think that's likely?" I asked.

"With all his money? She'd love to marry him." He drew on his cigarette. "She'd like to get her hands on his production company." Bannister's company, as well as making his own summer films, also made rock videos and television adverts. It was, I gathered, a most lucrative business.

"Hi!" The voice startled both of us and we turned to see that it was the black-haired American girl who had hailed us from *Mystique's* cockpit. She was standing by the tiller. She was only a stone's throw away now, but the setting sun's sheen on the rippling water made her face into an indistinct shadow. "Can I stay in this channel for the pool?"

"What do you draw?" I asked.

"Four foot three." Her voice was businesslike and quick. As she glanced forward I had an impression of bright eyes and a tanned, lively face.

"When you get alongside the perch," I pointed, "steer 310."

"Thanks!"

"Been far?"

"Far enough." She tossed the answer back. I stared at her

silhouette and I suddenly very much wanted to be in love with a girl like her. It was a ridiculous wish; I hadn't seen her face properly, I didn't know her name, but she was a consummate sailor and she had nothing whatever to do with the writhing jealousies and greed of television.

I crouched for a bottle, noting how the pain in my back was almost bearable. "You want a welcome-home beer?"

Her black hair lifted as her head turned. "No, thanks. 'Preciate the help, though. Thanks again." She stooped to push the throttle forward and *Mystique*'s exhaust blurred blue at the transom.

Matthew chuckled. "Not your day, Nick."

"Take me to the pub," I said. "We'll get drunk."

So we did.

We got drunk the next day, too. We put *Sycorax* in the water at the tide's height and we broke champagne across her bows, then we raided Bannister's cellar for more champagne. The cameraman was ceremoniously thrown into the river, then Matthew, then me. The American girl watched from her cockpit, but, when Matthew shouted at her to join us, she just shook her head. An hour later she hoisted sails and went downstream on the tide.

Sycorax looked much smaller now she was in the water. She floated high so that a wide belt of her new copper shone above the river. Jimmy had tears in his eyes. "She's a beauty, Nick."

"We'll go somewhere in her together, Jimmy."

"Maybe." I think he knew he was dying, and that he would never sail out of sight of land again.

Angela did not come for the launching, which was why we enjoyed it. After the ceremonial throwings-in we all went swimming, then finished the champagne as we dried in the late-afternoon sun. We stole strawberries and clotted cream from Bannister's fridge, then more champagne, and that night I sat on the river bank and stared at my boat in the water. I admired her lines and I dreamed the old dreams of far-off seas that were now so much closer. *Sycorax* still had no masts, rigging or sails, but she was afloat and I was happy. I could afford to forget

Angela's insistence that I sailed in *Wildtrack*'s crew; I had my own boat in the water again, and that was enough.

I slept aboard *Sycorax* that night. I'd cleared my room in Bannister's house and carried my few belongings down to the wharf. I made a space on the cabin sole where I could spread the sleeping bag. I cooked soup on the primus and ate it in my own cockpit. It did not matter that *Sycorax* was a mess, that her decks were a snake's honeymoon of tangled ropes, or that her scuppers were cluttered with tools, timber and chain; she was floating.

I woke the next morning to the good sound of water slapping my hull. I went topsides to see *Wildtrack*'s gleaming white hull with its broad and slanting blue streak moored in the channel. She must have come upriver on the pre-dawn tide, and Mulder and his crew were stringing flags up the forestay, doubtless ready for the night's party. *Mystique* was still off her mooring.

Later that morning Bannister and Angela arrived with the first of their house-guests. Angela ignored me, but Bannister strolled down to look at *Sycorax*. He brought two of the guests with him, which was perhaps why neither of us mentioned the St Pierre, nor my eviction from his house. This was the first time I'd seen Bannister since his holiday, and he looked very fit, suggesting that freedom from the studio programme had been good for him. He treated me with a jocular familiarity, though I noted that he took pains to mention my VC to his two friends and the medal went some way towards redeeming my reputation that had been spoilt by my raggedly stained appearance. Bannister stared up at *Sycorax*'s mainmast which I'd stood against the boathouse wall so that the linseed and paraffin in which I'd soaked it could drain down to the heel. "You wouldn't feel happier with a metal mast, Nick?"

"No." I said.

"Nick's a traditionalist," he explained to his friends; a London couple. The woman told me she was an interior designer and thought my boat was 'cute'. The husband, a stockbroker, opined that *Sycorax* was a splendid sort of boat for knocking about the Channel. "Just the ticket for a jaunt to Jersey, what?"

I explained that I'd crossed the Atlantic twice in *Sycorax*, which somewhat damped down the hearty atmosphere of bonhomie that Bannister had tried so hard to create. He looked at his watch as though he had urgent business elsewhere. "We'll see you at the party tonight, of course?"

"Am I invited?" I asked disingenuously.

"And do bring a friend, won't you? Drinks at six, end time unknown, and tomorrow will be celebrated as Hangover Sunday."

I promised to be there and, once they'd gone, I spent a happy day fixing the bowsprit against its oak bitts, then bracing it with a bobstay made of galvanized chain. It was hard work, and therefore satisfying. At around four o'clock, when I was tightening the gammon iron's last bolt, *Mystique* returned.

I finished the job, washed off the worst of the dirt, then rowed myself out to the anchorage. The American girl had gone down into her cabin so, as I approached, I hailed her. "*Mystique! Mystique!*"

"Wait a minute." The voice was sharp. "Who is it?"

"A neighbour."

"OK. Wait."

I was quite ridiculously apprehensive. I wanted to like her, and for her to like me. She must have been washing for when she appeared she had a big towel wrapped round her body and a smaller towel twisted about her hair. She seemed very suspicious of me. "Hi."

"Hello." I was holding on to *Mystique*'s starboard guardrail and the setting sun, reflecting from the polished aluminium hull, was blinding. I was stripped to the waist. "My name's Nick Sandman."

"Jill-Beth Kirov. Kirov like the ballet." Close up I saw that Jill-Beth Kirov had a tanned face, dark eyes, and the strong American jawline that my father always claimed came from chewing too much gum. My father always had a theory for everything and I remembered him explaining the gum theory as we sat having tea in New York's Plaza Hotel. He'd liked to take his children on his travels, and I thought how much the old goat would have liked this girl. I looked to see if she had a wedding ring. She did not. "Do you mind if I don't shake hands?" she asked.

If she had offered a hand then the towel round her body could have fallen. I solemnly excused her the politeness, and said there was a party at the house tonight and I wondered if she'd like to come as my guest.

"Tonight?" She seemed somewhat taken aback by the immediacy of the invitation, but I noted she did not immediately refuse. Instead she looked up at Bannister's lavish house. "He's a celeb, right?"

"A celeb?"

"Famous," she explained. "A celebrity."

"Oh! Right."

"Are you his boatman?"

"No."

"OK." She was clearly unimpressed with me, despite my denial of servant status. "What time's this party?"

"Drinks at six. I gather it goes on most of the night."

"Formal?"

"I don't think so."

"Remind me what the guy's name is?"

"Anthony Bannister."

She clicked her tongue in sudden recognition. "The television guy, right? He was married to Kassouli's daughter?"

"That's the fellow."

"That was kind of messy." She stared up at the house again as if expecting to see blood trickling down the neatly striped lawn. I watched her. It would be foolish to say I fell in love, but I wanted to. "It might be fun," she said dubiously.

"I hear you're writing a book?" I asked in an effort to prolong the encounter.

"Maybe we'll have a chance to talk about it." She did not sound as if she was looking forward to the opportunity. "Thanks for the invitation. Can I leave it open? I'm kind of busy."

"Of course."

"Thanks again." She stayed on deck to make sure that I pushed my dinghy away from her boat. "Hey! Nick?"

"Yes." I had to turn round on the dinghy's thwart to see her face again.

She was grimacing. "What did you do to your back?"

"Car accident. Front tyre blew out. No seatbelt."

"Tough." She nodded to show that as far as she was concerned the encounter was over.

I rowed back to my wharf, disappointed. I asked myself what I had expected. An invitation to board *Mystique*? An adolescent sigh and a melting of two hearts into one? I told myself that I was not in love, that all I had done was focus my frustrations on a girl who was a symbol of freedom and release, yet, even as I tried to persuade myself of that good sense, I failed. I tried to turn her wary words into an acceptance of my invitation, and I failed at that too.

"Gone fishing, Sandman?" It was Fanny Mulder who lounged in *Wildtrack*'s centre cockpit and who must have been watching me talk to the American girl. "Catch anything?" he asked mockingly.

"Lost any masts recently, Fanny? Gone drifting in the night again, have you?"

"Not since we left you, Sandman."

I rowed past him, watched all the way by his knowing and cunning gaze. But I was thinking of other things, of a girl with a strong face and a name just like the ballet. My boat was in the water, and I was ready for love.

Over two hundred people arrived for the party. Cars blocked the driveway and two helicopters drooped their rotors on the upper lawn. It stayed blessedly fine so drinks were served on the wide terrace that looked down on the river. A rock band played loudly enough to inflict a physical punch on the belly with their sound waves. Chefs carved at joints of beef and ham, the bar was frantic, and the party an evident success from its very beginning. A lot of the faces were famous: actresses, actors, television people, politicians – all enjoying being recognised. Behind the band was a giant chart of the North Atlantic on which a notional route for *Wildtrack*'s assault on the St Pierre was marked. Matthew's film crew had lit the podium ready for Bannister's announcement. *Wildtrack* herself was dressed overall with flags and coloured lights, and guests were invited to cross a rickety gangplank to inspect the boat.

Melissa, in a dress of silk that swirled and floated like gossamer, glimpsed me across the terrace. She greeted me with an affectionate kiss. "Tony wants me to look at his ghastly boat, but I told him I suffered quite enough of boats when I was married to you. How are you?" She did not wait for an answer. "We're staying in some frightfully twee hotel up on the moor. A hundred and fifty pounds a night, and with spiders in the bath. Can you believe it? Did you know I was coming?"

"Yes. It's nice to see you. Are you with the Honourable John?"

"Of course I am. He's found a socialist MP so they're agreeing on just how ghastly the miners are. Is that your boat?" She peered down at *Sycorax*, which huddled a hundred yards away against my wharf. "It looks very dinky. Where are its thingummybobs?"

"Masts?"

"Don't tell me, I'd only be bored." She stepped back and looked me up and down. "Haven't you got anything better to wear?"

I was dressed in flannel trousers, a washed but un-ironed white shirt, and was using an Old Etonian tie as a belt. I was wearing my only pair of proper shoes, valuable brogues, and thought I looked fine. "I think I look fine."

"A trifle louche, darling."

"I don't have any money for clothes. I'm paying it all in child support."

"You'd better go on paying it, Nicholas. I told my lawyer you were planning to sail round the world and he says we might have to nail a writ to your mast. Are you going to do a scarper?"

"Not immediately."

"You'd better get the mast ready, anyway. And that reminds me, your cheque hasn't arrived for the children's summer outfits."

"I can't think why. It was sent by native runner."

"It had better arrive soon. Oh, look! Isn't that the bishop who wants us all to be bigamists? It's going to be such a lovely party. Just like old times. Doesn't it seem odd to be back in the house? I keep expecting your father to pinch my bum. Would you be a treasure and get me some more champagne?"

I was dutifully a treasure. There was no sign of Jill-Beth Kirov coming, and every time I glanced down at the anchorage I saw her dinghy still moored to *Mystique*'s transom. I saw the Honourable John deep in conversation with a bearded MP who seemed to be nodding fervent agreement. Anthony Bannister was having an animated conversation with a young and pretty actress whom I recognized but could not name. As Melissa had said, it was just like one of my father's old parties; nothing had changed, and I felt just as out of place as ever. I knew very few of the guests and liked even less of them. Matthew was present, but was tied up with his preparations for filming Bannister's announcement.

Dusk came. The last guest had evidently inspected *Wildtrack*, and the gangplank, which had precariously rested on two inflatable dinghies, was dismantled. A pretty girl accosted me, but when she discovered I was not in television she abandoned me for a more hopeful prey. The bishop was introduced to me, but we had nothing in common and he too drifted away. Jill-Beth Kirov had still not arrived. I saw Melissa teasing Bannister.

Angela Westmacott, seeing the familiarity with which Melissa treated her man, waylaid me. "Do you mind your ex-wife being here?"

"I've been pleasurably feeding her champagne. Of course I don't mind."

Angela edged towards the balustrade and, out of courtesy, I followed. "I'm sorry we had to ask you to move out of the house," she said abruptly.

"It was time I moved out." I wondered why Angela had suddenly become so solicitous of my comfort. Her long hair was twisted into a pretty coil at the back of her narrow skull and she was wearing a simple white dress that made her look very young and vulnerable. I supposed that such a simple white dress probably cost more than *Sycorax*'s mainsail.

She looked at her diamond-studded watch. "Tony's going to make his announcement in forty-five minutes."

"I hope it goes well," I said politely.

Angela looked at me coldly. "I should have spoken to you before, Nick, but things have been very busy. Tony will make the announcement, then introduce Fanny. I'd like you to be next. You won't have to say anything."

"Me?" I glanced towards the dark shape of *Mystique* and saw that Jill-Beth's dinghy was no longer there, which meant she must have left her yacht, but I could see no sign of her on the terrace.

"Tony will introduce you after Fanny," Angela explained pedantically.

I looked back to her. "Why?"

She sighed. "Please don't be difficult, Nick. I just want to have on film the moment when you're named as *Wildtrack*'s navigator." She saw I was about to protest, and hurried on. "I know we should have talked earlier. I know! That was my fault. But please, tonight, just do as I ask."

"But I'm not going to navigate."

She kept her patience. Perhaps, as she claimed, she had overlooked the small matter of my agreement, but I suspected she had preferred to try and bounce me into Bannister's crew. By catching me in company and presenting me with a *fait accompli* she gambled on my spontaneous acceptance. She clearly feared my refusal, for she fed me a passionate argument about the advantages of ending the film in the way she wanted;

how it would knit the two programmes together, and how it would offer me a double appearance fee as well as the fame of being on a winning team. She then painted an heroic picture of Nick Sandman, victorious navigator, encouraging the handicapped by his achievement.

I shook my head. "But I'd be about as much use to Bannister as a pregnant pole-vaulter."

That checked her. She frowned. "I don't understand?"

"I told you before; I'm not a tactician navigator, and that's what you need. You need someone who'll hunt down every breath of wind and trace of current. You need a ruthless taskmaster. I hate that sort of sailing. My idea of sailing is to bung the boat in front of a convenient wind and open a beer."

"But you're a brilliant navigator," she said in protest. "Everyone says so."

"I can generally find the right continent," I agreed, "but I'm not a racing tactician. That's what Bannister needs. For me to be in his crew just wouldn't be honest, or fair."

"Honest?" She bridled at that word.

"I really hate making yachts go fast for no other reason than to win races. So it would be excessively dishonest of me to pretend that I cared about the St Pierre. I don't. And I fear I don't really care about your audience ratings, either."

The last comment touched her to the quick, perhaps because it attacked the holy grail of television producers. "You're so goddamned righteous!" There was anger, almost hysteria, in her voice that had been loud enough to attract embarrassed looks from the nearer guests.

"I just like to be truthful," I said gently, thereby hoping to deflect the threatening storm.

But Angela's patience snapped like a rotted hawser. "Do you really want my film to be truthful? Because the honest truth, Nick Sandman, is that you're nothing but a privileged public-schoolboy who chose the mindless trade of soldiering because you didn't care to exert yourself in the real world. You were wounded in an utterly pointless war, fighting for a quite ridiculous cause, and you probably went down there like an excited puppy with a wet nose and a wagging tail because you thought it would be fun. But we won't say that in our film. We won't say that you were a vacuous upper-class layabout with a gun, and that if it hadn't been for a stupid medal you'd be nothing now, nothing! And we won't say that you're too proud or too stubborn or too idiotic to make a proper living now. Instead we'll applaud your sense of adventure! Nick Sandman, eccentric rebel, refusing to recognize life's misfortunes. We'll say you were a war hero! Doing your bit for Britain!" Her passion was extraordinary, unleashed in a corrosive flood of emotion that lacerated the evening and appalled the terrace into an awed silence. Even the musicians ceased playing. "And the real truth, Nick Sandman, is that you can't even be an eccentric rebel without our help, because you haven't got a boat. And when you do get it, if you ever get it, you'll be finished inside six months because you'll run out of money and you'll be too lazy to earn any more! Is that the truth you want my film to tell?"

A very embarrassed Bannister appeared at her side. "Angela?"

She shook him off. There were tears in her eyes; tears of pure rage. "I'm trying to help you!" She hissed the words at me.

"Good-night," I said to Bannister.

"Nick, please." He was every bit as excruciated as his guests.

"Good-night," I said again, then backed off from the two of them. The guests were turning away in the clumsy pretence that nothing had happened. I saw that Jill-Beth Kirov had arrived, but she too turned abruptly away from me. Everyone was awkward, looking away from me. The evening, which had been such a success, was suddenly foully soured, and I was the focus of the embarrassment.

Then Melissa knifed through the crowd. "Nick, darling! I thought you were going to dance with me?"

"I'm leaving." I said it quietly.

"Don't be such a bloody fool." She said it just as quietly, then turned imperiously towards the rock group. "You're paid to make a noise, not gawp at your betters. So strum something!"

A semblance of normality returned to the terrace. Melissa and I danced, or rather she danced and I rhythmically disguised my limp. I was furious. Angela had disappeared, leaving Bannister with his actress. A whispered rumour that Angela was suffering from overwork circled the terrace. I forced myself to dance, but was saved from the indignity by the sudden collapse of my right leg that spilt me sideways to clutch desperately at the flagpole.

"Are you drunk?" Melissa asked with amusement.

"My leg's still buggered up."

"We'll sit." She took my arm and steered me to the terrace's edge where she lit a cigarette. "I must say that loathsome girl was quite right. You did go off to the Falklands with a wet nose and a wagging tail. You were frightfully bloodthirsty."

"I got paid for being bloodthirsty, remember?" I was massaging my right knee, trying to force sensation back into it.

Melissa watched me. "Poor Nick. Was it an awful little war?"

"Not awful, just unfair. Like playing soccer against a school for the blind."

"It was awful, I can tell. Poor Nick. And I was beastly to you. I thought your leg was cured?"

"It is, most of the time." But not now. My back felt as if it was being harrowed by fire, while my leg seemed nerveless. I felt the old panic that I would never be functional. I knew I'd never be fully fit again; I'd never run uphill with a heavy pack or step down a wicket to drive a ball sweetly through the covers, but I did want to be functional. I wanted a leg that would hold me on a pitching foredeck while I changed a staysail. It didn't seem much to ask, and for days it seemed possible until, quite suddenly, like now, the damned knee would disappear beneath me and the pain would start tears to my eyes.

Melissa blew out a stream of smoke. "Do you know what your problem is, Nick?"

"An Argentinian bullet."

"That's just self-pity, which isn't like you. No, Nick, your problem is that you fall in love with all the wrong women."

I was so astonished that I forgot my knee. "I don't!" I protested.

"Of course you do. You were quite soppy about me once, and you're just the same about that sordid little television tart who's just clawed you."

"That's ridiculous."

Melissa laughed at my shocked expression. "I saw you fancying her before she exploded in your face. You always fall helplessly in love with pale blondes, which is extremely silly of you because they're never as vulnerable as you think they are."

"Angela isn't vulnerable."

"But she looks it, which triggers you. I know you, Nick. You should settle for some sturdy girl with whacking great thighs. You'd be much happier."

"Like that one?" I said, rather ungallantly, for Jill-Beth hardly fitted Melissa's prescription. The American girl was dancing with Fanny Mulder and, to my chagrin, seemed intensely happy to be in his arms.

Melissa watched till Jill-Beth and Mulder were swallowed up by the other dancers. "She'd do," she finally said, "except you prefer your women to look like wounded birds." She sighed. "Lust is so frightfully inconvenient, isn't it? Do you remember when we first met? You were positively festooned with weapons and smothered in camouflage cream. You looked endlessly glamorous; not at all like the sort of man who'd ever worry about a mortgage." We'd met at the Bath and West Show where my regiment had staged a display. Melissa's father, a retired brigadier, had insisted on giving the officers a drink in his hospitality tent where I'd been dazzled by Melissa. Who now shrugged. "I don't understand lust at all. That bishop probably does." She waved her cigarette towards the bishop who, in clerical purple, was dancing with a girl who seemed to be wearing nothing but a sequinned fishing net. "Do you know he groped me?"

"The bishop did?"

"It was a positive and ecclesiastical fumble. Do you want to dance again?"

"I don't think I can. My back still hurts."

"So long as it isn't your pride. You should have slapped her silly face."

"I'm not into hitting women."

"Good old chauvinist Nick." She kissed me. "Do you mind if I slither off?"

Melissa had generously salved my pride after Angela's mauling, and I was grateful for it, yet I still felt foully awkward. Jill-Beth, dressed in a simple shirt and white trousers, was ignoring me, preferring Mulder's company, while the other guests treated me as though I had smallpox or the plague. It was clearly not to be my evening. I saw Matthew's cameraman setting up his gear ready for the announcement, and, wishing no more part of it, I gingerly stood and limped down the garden steps. I kept my leg stiff so the knee could not buckle.

As I peglegged down the last few steps Mulder and Jill-Beth came arm-in-arm to the terrace's balustrade. They leaned there, heads close together, and the American girl's laughter struck me like a jealous dart. I limped down the long lawn to where the reflected lights shimmered on the black water. I flinched with pain as I stepped down on to *Sycorax*'s deck, and again as I huddled down in the cockpit among the heaped stores that would soon go into the rebuilt cabin lockers. I could smell the linseed from the spars which lay on trestles on the bank, and the tar varnish which I'd smeared into the bilges.

I sat for a long time as the pain ebbed away from my spine. The moonlit sky seemed almost luminous above the black trees which edged the river. The Romans had seen this river thus, and they must have stared into the dark deep woods and wondered what strange misshapen creatures moved like wraiths among the leaves. It must have seemed a weird, hostile place, and I wondered if some Roman officer had been wounded here and then gone back to Rome where he fell in love with a dark-haired girl who rejected him for a hairy Phoenician sea-captain. Damn Jill-Beth, and damn Mulder, and damn the fact that I could not slip my moorings on this high tide and take *Sycorax* to sea. I straightened my right leg and pressed my foot against the bridge deck hard enough to stab a lance of pain up my thigh. I went on pressing, welcoming the pain as evidence that the leg would mend. I pressed till there were tears cold on my cheeks.

Applause sounded from Bannister's house and I knew he must be announcing his entry for this year's St Pierre. I opened a beer and drank it slowly. Bannister could sail without me. From this day on I wanted sailing to be a whim, dictated only by wind and sea. I wanted to wander and drift through a busy world, freed of tax and bills and the loud voices of politicians and pompous men. Perhaps Medusa was right, and perhaps I was a layabout, and perhaps I was too stupid to make a proper living, but, God damn it, I was not a piece of television slime.

I drank another beer. Silver-edged clouds were heaping above Dartmoor to make aery and fantastic battlements that climbed higher and ever higher as the ocean winds were lifted by the slopes above the Tamar. I decided I would rig the boat with my last savings and I would sail south, penniless, just to escape Bannister and Angela. I would strap my right knee, lay in a stock of painkillers, and disappear.

Jill-Beth Kirov's voice stirred me from my morose thoughts. I raised my head over the cockpit's coaming and saw her walking down the lawn on Fanny Mulder's arm. "I won't see anything!" I heard her say.

"You'll see fine, girl."

She stopped at the river wall and stared at *Wildtrack*. "It's so beautiful!"

Mulder pulled a dinghy to the garden steps. Jill-Beth laughed as she stepped down into the small boat and I felt the sting of jealousy. She'd preferred Mulder to me, or to any other man at the party for that matter, and my pride was offended. A daft thing, pride. It had once driven me up a hill on an Atlantic island to meet a bullet.

I heard Jill-Beth's soft laughter again as Mulder rowed the dinghy the few strokes to *Wildtrack*. He helped Jill-Beth on to its long rakish deck, then gave her the full guided tour of the topsides. He turned on the deck lights that were mounted beneath the lower spreaders and their brilliant light showed me Jill-Beth's dark hair and strong jaw and bright excited eyes. I stayed still, a shadow within a shadow, watching.

They stood in the aft cockpit and I could hear every word they said because water carries sound as cleanly as glass carries light. And suddenly, very suddenly, I forgot my misery because Jill-Beth was encouraging Mulder to tell the story of Nadeznha Bannister's death. "I'd gone forward, see?" Mulder pointed to the mast. "The kicking-strap had worked loose."

"And Mrs Bannister stayed here?" Jill-Beth asked.

"She liked being aft in a big sea, and that sea was a bastard. But nothing we hadn't seen before. Then one broke and pooped us. She just disappeared."

Jill-Beth turned and looked at the array of lifebuoys and Danbuoys that decorated *Wildtrack*'s stern. "She wasn't wearing a harness?"

"She could have taken it off for a moment, you know how you do? Maybe she wanted to go forward? Or maybe it bent. I've seen snaphooks bent straight in a gale. And it was a crazy night," Mulder said. "I didn't see she'd gone at first, you know, what with being busy with the kicking-strap and the water everywhere and the boat bucking like a jack-hammer gone ape. Must have taken me five minutes to get back to the wheel."

Jill-Beth stared up at the masthead where the string of lights was bright above the floodlights. "Poor girl."

"*Ja*." Mulder pulled open the aft cabin hatch. "A drink?"

Did I sense a hesitation in Jill-Beth? I prayed for her to say no. I didn't want to watch her go into that aft cabin with its wide double bunk. She said no. "I've got an early start in the morning, Fanny, but thanks."

"I thought you were interested." He sounded hurt. "I mean I've still got that night's log down here if you want to see it."

She hesitated, but then her curiosity about Nadeznha Bannister's death swayed the issue. "Sure."

It was like that moment when, during a calm, the water shadows itself beneath the first stirrings of a killing wind. For these last weeks, as I had lost myself in the restoration of *Sycorax*, I had forgotten the stories of Nadeznha Bannister's death. But other people had not forgotten. Harry Abbott had warned me off the stories, but here was an American girl stirring up the dangerous rumours. And the dead girl's father was American too. It was a cold wind that was disturbing my calm. I shivered.

Wildtrack's deck lights were doused and the cabin lights glowed through the narrow scuttles until curtains were snatched across the glass.

I thought of what I'd heard. It matched the evidence given to the inquest, and made sense. A safety harness would have saved Nadeznha Bannister's life, but safety harnesses are not infallible. A harness is a webbing strap that encases the torso and from which a strong line hangs. At the end of the line is a steel snaphook that can be attached to a jackstay or D-ring. I'd known a snaphook open simply because it was wrenched at an odd angle. I'd known them bend open, too. Snaphooks were made of thick, forged steel, but water is stronger than steel, especially when the water comes in the form of a breaking ocean wave. I imagined a heavy following swell, lifting *Wildtrack*, surging her forward, then dropping her like a runaway lift into the deep trough. The next wave would steal the wind from the sails, there'd be a moment of unnatural quiet, then Nadeznha Bannister would have heard the awesome melding roar as the great tongue of breaking death curved over the stern. She might have looked up to see her death shredding high and white in the night above her. If she had unsnapped her harness for a moment she would have screamed then, but too late, because the cold tons of white water would be collapsing on to the boat to turn the cockpit into a maelstrom of foam and berserk force.

Wildtrack would have staggered, her bow rising as her stern was pile-driven downwards, but a good boat would survive a pooping and *Wildtrack* would have juddered upwards, shedding the flooding water. But Nadeznha Bannister would already have been a hundred yards astern, helpless in the mad blackness. The wind would have been shrieking in the rigging, the decks would have been seething, and her cries would have been lost in the welter of foam and wind and banging sails.

Or else she was pushed. But the cries in the darkness would have been just as forlorn.

Then, from *Wildtrack*'s aft cabin, Jill-Beth screamed.

The scream was more of a yelp, and swiftly cut off as though a hand had been slapped over her mouth. I detected panic in the quick sound, but the music on the terrace was far too loud for anyone but me to have heard the truncated scream.

I picked up a full beer bottle and hurled it. *Wildtrack* lay no further than good grenade distance away and the bottle crashed with a satisfying noise on her main coachroof. The second ricocheted off a guardrail and shattered a cabin window, the third missed, but the fourth bottle broke against the metal mainmast and showered fragments of glass and foaming beer on to the boat.

The aft cabin door opened, and Jill-Beth came out like a dog sprung from a trap. She did not hesitate, but scrambled over the guardrail and dived into the river. Mulder, bellowing in frustrated anger, followed from the cabin as I hurled the fifth full bottle. By pure chance it hit him clean on the forehead, throwing him back and out of sight. He shouted in anger or pain. I'd thrown the bottle hard enough to fracture his skull, but he seemed quite unhurt as, seconds later, he reappeared with his shotgun in his hands. He aimed it at *Sycorax*'s cockpit.

I dropped.

He fired. Both barrels.

The noise slammed across the water and I saw the glare of the barrel flames sheet the sky above me. The pellets went high, spattering into the bushes above the wharf. I listened for the sound of Jill-Beth swimming, but could only hear the sharp click as Mulder broke the gun for reloading.

I scrabbled through the tangled mess of stores that clogged the cockpit. Jimmy Nicholls' and my hauls from the boat auctions lay in an unseamanlike confusion. I cursed, then found the net bag I wanted. I heard the cartridges slap home in Mulder's gun and the click as the breech was closed.

When in doubt, an old commanding officer of mine liked to say, hit the buggers with smoke. I had bought some old emergency smoke floats and I prayed that they still worked as I pulled the first ring. I counted as though it were a grenade, then lobbed it out of my shelter.

There was a pause as the water entered the floating can, then I smelt the acrid scent and I raised my head to see a smear of orange smoke boiling up from the river. The lurid smudge spread to hide *Wildtrack*'s hull. The ebb had just begun and the can was floating downstream, but the sea breeze was conveniently carrying the smoke back towards Mulder. I thickened it with a second can, then leaned over *Sycorax*'s side to search for Jill-Beth. I could hear people calling from the terrace. I tossed yet another float to keep Mulder blinded, and the can landed just feet away from a sleek black head that suddenly surfaced in the river. "Miss Kirov?" I called politely.

"Nick?"

I held out my hand for her, and as I did so Mulder unleashed his next weapon. Perhaps he had realized that one volley of gunfire was enough, and that more might land him in trouble with the law, so now he fired a distress flare in *Sycorax*'s direction. The flare was rocket-propelled, designed to sear high into the air where it would deploy a brilliant red light which dangled from a parachute. I heard the missile fizz close overhead. It struck the coping of the wharf and bounced up into the night trailing smoke and sparks. A second rocket followed from the mass of orange smoke. Either could have killed if they had hit my head, but both went high.

Jill-Beth's hand took hold of mine and I pulled her dripping from the water. I was given haste and strength by a third rocket which went wide. The first flare had exploded in the trees above the boathouse and the brilliant dazzle of the red light made it seem as if the wood had caught fire. I hurled my last smoke float towards *Wildtrack* and searched among the mess in the cockpit to find my own flares. Jill-Beth was panting. Her expensive silk shirt and white trousers were soaked and dirty. "Climb the wall," I said, "and run like hell for the house." There were people streaming down the lawn, shouting, and I hoped their presence would deter Mulder's madness. I found a flare that I pointed towards the bigger boat.

"No!" Jill-Beth said the word with panicked force. "I can't stay here! For God's sake get me out! Have you got a dinghy?"

"Yes."

"Come on, Nick! Let's go!"

I abandoned the flare and we scrambled over the stern into my tender. I had the presence of mind to toss a duffelbag of spare clothes in first, then I slashed the painter. Jill-Beth pushed us away and we drifted on the tide towards the overhanging trees beyond the boathouse cut. Jill-Beth poled us with an oar and we reached the shelter of the thick branches just as the first guests reached the river bank to stare in awe at the rolling orange smoke that was meant to mark an emergency at sea for searching helicopters. The cloud had shrouded *Wildtrack* right up to her gaudy string of lights and was made even more spectacular by the brilliant light of the burning flares.

"The smoke was smart of you," Jill-Beth said. "Sorry, Nick."

"Sorry?"

"Never mind. Sh!" She touched a warning finger to her lips, then pointed behind me as if to say that we could be overheard by the people who now crowded the river bank. I was rigging the dinghy's outboard, an ancient and small British Seagull that I'd bought for a knockdown price at auction.

"Fanny!" It was Bannister's angry voice. "What the hell do you think you're doing?"

"Fireworks, sir!" Fanny must have realized that he had over-reacted and now he proved sharp enough to find an explanation that fitted the night's mood. "Just using up old flares, sir!"

"I heard a gunshot." The Honourable John's voice.

"Lifeboat maroon." Mulder's voice came out of the thick smoke.

"How awfully exciting." Melissa's voice. "Have you got an Exocet?"

"Nothing to be excited about." That was Bannister again, thinking ahead to the possibility of headlines. He knew it was illegal to set off distress flares unnecessarily. "Are you drunk, Fanny?"

"A bit, sir!"

"I'll paddle!" That was Jill-Beth, in a whisper. She pushed the dinghy along the bank, keeping under the trees' cover. "That bastard wanted to kill me!" she whispered.

"I thought he was raping you."

"That was just for starters. Does that engine work?"

"I was cheated of ten quid if it doesn't." Seagulls might not be flash, but by God they work. I pulled, the old engine coughed and caught, and the noise brought the stab of a torch beam that swept round towards us from Bannister's garden, but we were now well under the cover of the overhanging trees. The branches whipped at us as I opened the throttle, and I heard Jill-Beth giggle, apparently in reaction to the panicked escapade. "There are dry clothes in the bag," I said.

"You're a genius, Nick."

I waited till we had rounded Sansom's Point before I broke out from under the trees' shelter. We were hidden from Bannister's house by now and I curved the dinghy towards the main channel and opened the throttle as high as it would go. Seagulls might work, but they're not fast and we were going at no more than a hearse's crawl as we left the black shadows under the trees and emerged into the moonlight where I found myself sharing the dinghy with one very wet, very tanned and entirely naked girl who was rubbing herself dry and warm with one of my spare sweaters. She seemed quite unabashed, and I had time to notice that she was tanned all over and how nice the all over was before I politely looked away. "Enjoying the view?" she asked.

"Very much."

She pulled on the sweater and a pair of my dirty jeans that she rolled up around her calves. She pushed at her soaking hair, then looked upriver. "Where are we going?"

"Jimmy Nicholls' cottage. You know Jimmy?"

"I've met him." The village lights were bright on the starboard bank while two miles further south the town lights quivered on the water. Beyond that was the sea. Jimmy's cottage was just short of the town.

Jill-Beth was searching through the duffelbag. "Got any sneakers here?"

"No shoes, sorry."

She looked up at me and smiled. "Thank you for the rescue."

"That's what we white knights are for," I said.

At which point the dragon growled, or rather I heard a percussive bang and then the throaty roar of big engines, and I knew it was too late to reach Jimmy's house. I pulled the outboard's lever towards me and prayed that the puttering little two-stroke could outrun the gleaming monster engines on *Wildtrack II*'s stern. I'd forgotten the threat of the big powerboat crouched in Bannister's boathouse.

Jill-Beth turned as the engine noise splintered in the night. She knew immediately what the sound meant. "That bastard doesn't give up, does he?"

"A Boer trait." I was running for the darker western bank where more overhanging trees might hide us. I glanced behind to where the dying flares still silhouetted Sansom's Point. They also lit the shredding remnants of my smokescreen through which, as yet, there was no sign of the big powerboat.

Jill-Beth was suddenly scared. "He knew why I'm here," she said in astonishment.

I suspected that I knew why she was here too, but it was no time for explanations because a brilliant stab of white light suddenly slashed across the river. Mulder, if it was Mulder in *Wildtrack II*, had turned on the boat's searchlight. He was still beyond Sansom's Point and the light was far away from us, but I knew it would only be seconds before the powerboat came snarling into our reach of water.

"Come on, you bastard!" I enjoined the engine.

"Jesus!" Jill-Beth cowered as the sharp prow of *Wildtrack II* burst into view. There was a speed limit of six knots on the river and he must have been doing twenty already and was still accelerating. That was his mistake, for the acceleration was throwing up his bows so he could not see straight in front. The wake was like twin curls of moonlit gossamer that spread behind him.

"Head down!" I called out. Jill-Beth ducked and the dinghy scraped under branches. I killed the engine as the dinghy's bows jarred on some obstruction. The searchlight whipped past us as the powerboat slewed round into the main channel. She must have been doing thirty knots now and her engines could have woken the dead in village graveyards a mile away. I scrambled past Jill-Beth and tied the dinghy's painter to a low bough. "Give me your wet trousers," I said.

She frowned with puzzlement, but obeyed. I hung the white trousers over the dinghy's side, looping one leg over the gunwale and hanging the other straight down into the water. "Breaking our shape," I explained. "He's looking for a wooden dinghy, not a brown and white pattern." The drooping tree branches would help confuse our shape, but I knew Mulder's searchlight was powerful enough to probe through the leaves and I hoped the white cloth would disguise us.

"He's stopping." Jill-Beth was down in the dinghy's bilge and her voice was scarce above a whisper.

The power-boat was slowing and I heard its engines fade to a mutter as its bow dropped and its shining aerofoil hull settled into the current. Mulder had accelerated to where he thought we might be; now he would search. "Head down!" I crouched with Jill-Beth in the boat's bottom.

The light skidded past us, paused, came back, then went on again. I breathed a sigh of relief. *Wildtrack II* was burbling along the river now, searching. Mulder had missed us on his first pass. But he would be back.

Jill-Beth tweaked the trousers I'd hung over the gunwale. "A soldier's trick?"

"Is it?" I said.

"Because you weren't injured in a car crash, were you?"

"You shouldn't listen to gossip at parties."

"Gossip?" She laughed softly, and her face was so close to mine that I could feel her breath on my cheek. "You're Captain Nicholas Thomas Sandman, VC. Your last annual report before the Falklands was kind of non-committal. Captain Sandman's a fine officer, it said, and did well in Northern Ireland, but seems frustrated by the more commonplace duties of soldiering. In brief, he's not very ambitious. He spends too much time on his boat. The men liked you, but that wasn't sufficient reason for the regiment to recommend you for staff college. They really wanted you to leave the regiment to make room for some younger gung-ho type, right? You lacked the motivation to excel, they said, then someone gave you a real live enemy and you proved them all wrong."

I said nothing for a moment. The water gurgled past our fragile hull. I had pulled away from Jill-Beth, the better to see her face in the shadows. "Who are you?"

"Jill-Beth Kirov, like the ballet." She grinned, and her teeth showed very white against her dark skin. I raised my head high enough to see *Wildtrack II* searching the far bank and I made out Mulder's distinctive silhouette against the glare caused by his searchlight on the thick leaves.

"Who are you?" I asked again.

"I work for a guy called Yassir Kassouli. Heard of him?"

"Bannister's father-in-law."

"Ex-father-in-law," she corrected me, then stiffened suddenly as the searchlight whipped round and seemed to shine straight at the two of us. I saw the willow leaves above our heads turn a mixture of bright silver-green and jet black as the light slashed into the branches. "Jesus!" Jill-Beth hissed.

"It's all right." I put an arm over her shoulder to keep her head low. The light swept on, probing another shadow, but I kept my arm where it was. She did not move.

"What do you do for Kassouli?" I whispered the question almost as if I feared Mulder might hear us over the growl of his idling engines.

"Investigator."

"A private detective?" I asked in some astonishment. I thought private detectives only existed on television, but how else could she have discovered the details of my confidential army file?

"Insurance investigator," she corrected me. "I work for the marine division of an insurance company that's a subsidiary of Kassouli Enterprises."

"What do you investigate?"

"Hell," she shrugged, "whatever? I mean, if some guy says a million bucks' worth of custom-built motor yacht just turned itself into a submarine off the Florida Keys, and now he wants us to fork out for a new one, we kind of become curious, right?"

I tried to imagine her dealing with crooks, and couldn't. "You don't look like an investigator."

"You expect the Pink Panther? Shit, Nick, of course I don't look like a cop! Hell, if they see some chick in a bikini they don't start reaching for their lawyer, do they? They offer me a drink, then they tell me all the things they wouldn't tell some guy with a tape-recorder." She peered upriver, but Mulder was now far off the scent.

"And just what are you investigating here?" I asked.

"Nadeznha Bannister's life was insured with her father's company for a million bucks. Guess who the beneficiary is?"

"Anthony Bannister?"

"You got it in one, soldier." She grinned. "But if Nadeznha was murdered, then we don't have to pay."

There was something chilling about the calm and amused confidence with which she had spoken of murder; so chilling that I took my arm from her shoulder. "Was she murdered?"

"That's what I'm trying to prove." She spoke grimly, intimating that she was not having any great success.

"What else are you doing?" I asked.

She must have heard the suspicion in my voice, for her reply was very guarded. "Nothing else."

"Dismasting *Wildtrack*?" I guessed. "Cutting its warps?"

"Jesus." She sounded disgusted with me. "You think I'm into that kind of stupidity? Just what kind of a jerk do you think I am?"

Then if not her, who? Yet I believed her strenuous denial, because I wanted this girl to be straight and true. "I'm sorry I suggested it," I said.

"Hell, Nick, I'd love to know who's bugging Bannister, but it sure as hell isn't me. Ssh!" She put a finger to my lips because *Wildtrack II* had swung round, accelerated, and now the searchlight slid towards us again. Mulder cut the throttles once more and I cautiously raised my head to see the big powerboat coming slowly down this western bank. I could sense Mulder's confusion from the erratic movements of the light, but there was still a chance that he would find us.

Jill-Beth wriggled herself into a semblance of comfort. "How long will that bastard keep looking?"

"God knows."

"I need to get back to *Mystique*. I left all my papers in the cabin."

"We'll just have to wait." I paused. "Is that why you were with Mulder tonight? Hoping he'd say something incriminating?"

"Sort of." She grinned at me. "You must have thought I was a real creep, but the chance to talk to him was just too good. But the bastard set me up. He knew just why I was here."

"How did he know?"

"Beats me." She raised her head to watch the light, then subsided again. "Why was that girl chewing you up?"

"Bannister wants me to be his navigator in the St Pierre. I've refused. She got upset."

She stared at me in silence, perhaps puzzled that I should refuse such an offer. Then she shrugged. "I'm sorry to involve you, Nick."

"Don't be sorry. I wanted to be involved."

Her big eyes reflected dark in the night. She said nothing, nor was there anything that I cared to say, so instead I leaned forward and kissed her on the mouth.

She returned the kiss, then placed her head on my shoulder. We stayed still. I did not know just what tangle she was drawing me into, I only knew that I wanted to be a part of it. I sensed a tension flow out of her.

We talked then. Mulder searched for us, but we crouched in the dinghy and talked. She told me she came from Rhode Island, but now lived on Cape Cod. Her father was in the US Navy. I told her that my father was in jail, and that Bannister's house had been my childhood home.

She told me *Mystique* was a cow to sail, but she had not wanted to bring her own boat over from Massachusetts because the crossing would have wasted valuable time. I asked her if hers was a big boat and she said yes, then wrinkled her nose prettily and told me she was kind of affluent. I told her I was kind of poor.

She said *Sycorax* was a great-looking boat. I agreed. I also decided that fate had been kind in sending this girl to my river. She was swift to laugh and quick to listen. We talked of sailing and she told me of a bad night when she'd been single-handed on the western side of Bermuda. I knew those reefs, and sympathised. She'd been a watch-captain on one of the boats caught in the '79 Fastnet storm and I listened jealously to her descriptions.

We talked, almost oblivious of Mulder's fumbling search, but then his light suddenly went out and the sound of his twin engines died away to leave an ominous silence. We both twisted to stare at the river, but nothing moved on the water except the dying disturbance of the powerboat's wake.

"He's given up," Jill-Beth breathed.

"No," I said.

"He's gone!" she insisted.

"He wants us to think he's gone." I climbed over the dinghy's thwart, wound the starting lanyard on to the Seagull, then yanked it. The motor belched into life and its distinctive sound echoed across the river. I let it run for five seconds, then cut the fuel just as the searchlight split the darkness in an attempt at ambush. Mulder had been hiding in the shadows, but his guess of where the outboard's sound had come from was hopelessly wrong. I chuckled at having successfully tricked him.

Jill-Beth was less pleased. "He's a stubborn bastard."

"He'll wait all night," I said.

"Jesus! Shee-it!" She was suddenly vehement in her frustration. "I need to get those damned papers! Hell!" She stared across the river to where *Wildtrack II* was searching the far bank. The searchlight flickered quick and futile across the empty leaves. "Suppose I swim back?" Jill-Beth asked suddenly.

"What if he finds you?" I asked in warning.

"I can't just do nothing!"

In the end she helped me to hide the dinghy by filling it with stones and sinking it at the river's edge. We concealed the Seagull under a pile of grass and leaves, then worked our way northwards. It was too dangerous to stay close to the river while Mulder searched so we looped up to Ferry Lane through the hill pastures. I made Jill-Beth wear my brogues to save her bare feet from the nettles and thorns. It was an awkward journey through hedgerows and across rough fields, but I noticed how my leg did not buckle once and how the pain in my back seemed to relent in the face of our urgency.

The urgency was to rescue Jill-Beth's papers which, she said, must not fall into Bannister's hands. We planned to go as far as the ferry slip from which we would swim to *Mystique*. If Mulder had abandoned his search by then, and restored *Wildtrack II* to the boathouse, Jill-Beth would slip her moorings and sail out to sea. If there was still danger, then we would just remove the papers and swim ashore again.

But our planning was all in vain for, as we reached the shadows at the head of the ferry slip, we saw that Bannister had anticipated our fears. A dinghy was moored beside *Mystique* and two men, perhaps from Mulder's crew, were searching her. Their torchlight flickered on the small boat's deck. There was still a hint of orange smoke skeining the moorings, though the fires in the woodland had died to a dull glow.

Jill-Beth swore again.

"How important were the papers?" I asked.

"There's nothing in them he doesn't already know," she said, "but they'll tell him just how much I know. Shit!"

"Shall we call the police?" I asked. "I mean, they don't have any right to search your boat."

"Come on, Nick!" she chided me. "How long will it take for us to reach a phone? And how long before the goddamn police arrive? Bannister will have his answers by then." She stared at the flickering shapes on *Mystique*, then shrugged in resignation. "You can't put the toothpaste back in the tube, so there's no point in trying."

She shivered, and I put an arm around her. She resisted for a second, then subsided against me. "Hell," she said, "but you're a very inconvenient man, Nick Sandman."

"I thought I was rather convenient for you tonight."

"I don't mean that." She went silent because *Wildtrack II* had appeared at Sansom's Point. I thought Mulder was going to bring the big powerboat up to the moorings, but instead, in a swirl of moonlit foam, he accelerated in a semicircle to speed downriver again.

"What I meant," Jill-Beth said softly, "is that it's very inconvenient to get emotionally entangled during a case."

"Are you emotionally entangled?"

She did not answer the question, and I did not press her. Instead we crouched together in the deep shadows at the slip's head and stared at the bright lights on Bannister's terrace from whence came the tumbling sounds of music and laughter. The night's alarums were over for the party guests, but there was still a grim game of cat and mouse happening on the darkened river. Jill-Beth could not escape to sea so long as Mulder blocked the river, and the South African had shown no signs of giving up the chase.

"I'm finished here," Jill-Beth finally said. "I guess I screwed up, right?"

"I don't see how you could have ever got your evidence," I said in an attempt to make her feel better. "I mean, if Bannister did push his wife overboard, how could you ever prove it?"

"That's my job," she said bitterly, then pulled herself gently away from my embrace. "But what's important now is to get you safely back. I can't show my face here again, but you're still kosher. Tell them that, as far as you know, you just rescued me from that God-damned rapist, OK? We haven't talked about Kassouli, and you think I'm just a girl writing a pilot book."

"It doesn't matter about me," I said, "except that I don't want to leave you."

She smiled at my protestation, then kissed me. "If you disappear now, Nick, Bannister will think you've been working with me. How long do you think your boat will be safe then? Jesus! You saw how ready that South African is to pull a trigger! He'll stop at nothing, Nick."

The thought of *Sycorax* at risk made me silent.

"Stay here," Jill-Beth urged me, "and I'll get in touch with you. I'll leave a message with Jimmy Nicholls and it'll be real soon, Nick."

"I want it to be soon."

"Real soon." She said the words softly, in promise, and I felt a shiver of excitement. Jill-Beth gently pulled away and stood up. "Can I keep the shoes for tonight?"

"Where are you going?"

"I've got to reach a telephone. I'll call one of Kassouli's British executives and tell him to send a car for me. I need to go to London, I guess, in case Kassouli wants me to fly home." She shrugged. "He's not real keen on people who screw up."

"You did your best," I said loyally.

"Yassir Kassouli's not interested in my best, only success."

I shivered. The parting was awkward, and made more so by

the unasked questions and unsaid words. I smiled. "Don't leave England without meeting me."

"I've got to return your shoes, right?" She laughed, then tied the laces as tightly as she could. "Take care, Nick."

"You take care, too."

She impulsively leaned towards me and kissed me warmly. "Thank you for everything." She said it softly, then pulled away from me and bundled up the wet clothes she'd fetched from the dinghy.

"What about *Mystique*?" I asked.

"The charterers will fetch her back. I'll call them from London." We kissed again, then she started uphill. I watched her shadow moving in the lane and listened to the scuff of the heavy shoes.

The sounds faded and I was alone. The men who'd searched *Mystique* rowed towards the far bank. Mulder was still downriver and I felt suddenly forlorn. I tried to conjure back the sensations of Jill-Beth's skin and voice. Till that moment I had not thought of myself as lonely, but suddenly it seemed to me that the American girl would fit so easily into *Sycorax*'s life.

I sat for a long time, thinking. I should have been thinking about murder and proof and justice, but I had been entranced by a girl's smile and a girl's voice and by my own hunger. The music sounded across the water. I consoled myself that Jill-Beth had promised to call me soon, and somehow that promise seemed to imply a whole new hope for a whole new life.

I waited a good hour, but Mulder was as stubborn as I feared and did not return. In the end I stripped naked, bundled my clothes at the small of my back, and went quickly down the ferry slip and into the river. I breaststroked through the quicksilver shimmer of moonlight to my wharf where I pulled myself over *Sycorax*'s counter. I dried off, went below, and tried to imagine the finished cabin as a home for two people. Then, dreaming the dreams of love's foolish hopes, I locked the washboards and hatch, then waited for dawn.

No one stirred in the dawn. The litter of the night's party was strewn down the garden where a vague and sifting mist curled from the river. *Wildtrack II* was back in its dock. I'd heard the powerboat come in during the night and I had waited with a hammer in case Mulder should try to enter *Sycorax*'s cabin, but he had ignored me. I'd slept then.

Now, waking early, I took one of Bannister's inflatables and went downstream to where I'd left my dinghy. I emptied it of water, then dragged tender and outboard over the mud and towed them home. If Mulder saw me from *Wildtrack*, he did nothing.

I washed my hands in the river, took some money from its hiding place in *Sycorax*'s bilge, then walked up to the house. Some of the guests slept in the big lounge, others must have been upstairs, but no one was stirring yet. I made myself coffee in Bannister's kitchen, then took the keys to one of his spare cars. There was a Land-Rover that Bannister kept deliberately unwashed so that tourists would think he had a working farm, and a Peugeot. I took the Peugeot for my long overdue errand.

I hadn't driven in over two years, and at first my right leg was awkward on the pedals. I missed the brake once and almost rammed the heavy car into a ditch, but somehow I found the hang of it. I drove north and east for three hours, arriving at the housing estate at breakfast time. Concrete roads curved between dull brick houses. I parked in a bus-stop and waited for an hour, not wanting to wake the household.

Sally Farebrother was still in her brushed nylon dressing-gown when she opened the door to me. She had a small child clutching at her right leg and a baby in her arms. She looked surprised rather than pleased to see me; indeed, she must have wondered if I was in trouble, for I looked like a derelict in my filthy jersey, torn jeans, and old sea-boots. Sally did not look much better herself; she had become a drab and shapeless girl burdened with small children and large resentments. Her dyed hair was lumpy with plastic rollers and her face was pasty. "Captain?"

"Hello, Sally. Is Terry in?"

She shook her head. "They're on exercise."

"I didn't know. I'm sorry." I was embarrassed to find her so obviously joyless. I'd been a guest at Sergeant Farebrother's wedding, and I remembered even then fearing that the pretty bride of whom Terry was so proud had the sulky look of a girl who would resent the man who took her from the discos and street-corners. Terry had proved no better than I at choosing a wife. "It's just that I've got some kit here," I explained lamely. "Terry said he'd keep it for me."

"It's in Tracey's room." Tracey was one of the children, but I couldn't remember which. Sally opened the front door wide, inviting me in.

"Are you sure?" I knew how swiftly malicious rumours went round Army housing estates.

Sally did not care. "Upstairs," she said, "on the left." She cleared a path for me by kicking aside some broken plastic toys. "I'll be glad to have the space in the cupboard back."

"I'm sorry if it's been a bother."

"No bother." She watched me limp upstairs. "Are you all right now?"

"Only when I laugh." The house had the ammonia stench of babies' nappies. "How's Terry?"

"They want him to be a Weapons' Instructor." It was said unhappily, for Sally was always nagging Terry to resign the service and go home to Leeds.

"He'd be good at that." I tried to be encouraging as I reached the landing. "This room?"

"In the cupboard." A child began crying downstairs and Sally shouted at it to be quiet and eat its bloody breakfast. The house was thin-walled and cheap; married quarters.

I found my bergen under a broken tricycle in the child's cupboard. I dragged the heavy rucksack out and hauled it downstairs. "Give Terry my best, won't you?"

"He'll be sorry to have missed you."

"I'll be in touch with him. Thanks for keeping this."

"Sure." She closed the door on me. I saw the curtains twitch in other houses.

I drove back to Devon, reaching Bannister's house at

lunchtime. I'd filled the Peugeot's tank with petrol as amends for borrowing it, but no one seemed to have missed the old car which Bannister kept solely for local errands. I could hear voices in the house, so I took the path through the woods down to the wharf where *Sycorax* lay.

I emptied the bergen on the cabin floor. There were sweaters still smeared with dark peaty Falklands soil. There was a shaving kit, canteen, monocular, two shirts, and a camera which still had a roll of undeveloped film in it. There was a situation map, a cigarette lighter, a letter from my bank manager which I'd never opened, and a deck plan of the *Canberra*. This was the kit we'd left behind as we marched to the start line for the last attack. There was a letter from Melissa's lawyer demanding that I surrender pension rights, bank accounts, all joint savings, everything. Like a fool, I'd given in on every demand. At the time it had seemed a most irrelevant letter and I had simply wanted the matter out of the way before the grimmer reality of taking the heights above Port Stanley began. There was a letter from my father that I had not answered, and two photographs of my children. There were three pairs of underpants that needed washing, a towel, a pair of gloves, and a tin of camouflage cream. There was, God alone knew why, a map of the London Underground. There was my beret, which gave me a pang of old and still bright pride. There were no bad dreams.

And underneath it all was the reason why I had driven so far. It was a souvenir wrapped in a dirty towel. I'd taken it from a dead Argentinian officer who'd been lying in the burnt gorse on Darwin Hill. I unwrapped the towel to find a leather belt from which hung a pouch and a holster. In the holster was a .45 calibre automatic pistol, made in the USA; a Colt. It was ugly, black, and heavy. I turned it in my hand, then ejected the full magazine. I emptied the magazine of rounds and noted that the spring was still in good condition, despite being compressed for so many months. I cocked the empty gun and pulled the trigger. The sound seemed immense inside the *Sycorax*'s hull. The words *Ejercito Argentina* were incised on the barrel's flank.

I opened the pouch and took out the spare magazines and rounds. I did not want to use this weapon, indeed I had hoped never to fire a gun like this again, but Jill-Beth's warning, and the memory of how easily Fanny Mulder had resorted to his shotgun, had persuaded me to retrieve this trophy of a faraway war. Now, staring at the gun's obscene and functional outline, I was suddenly ashamed of myself. I wasn't a prisoner, there was no need to stay. Holding the heavy gun I was suddenly disgusted that my affairs with Bannister had come to this. I would get out now, I would resign. I would leave Bannister. There was no sense in staying in a place where I had been driven to arm myself with a weapon.

My disgust tempted me to hurl the gun far into the river, but there are still seaways where such a thing is needful, and so I oiled and greased the pistol, loaded it, then sealed it in two waterproof bags. I hid the gun deep in *Sycorax*, deep down where the sun would never shine, deep beneath the waterline in a dark place where such a thing is best kept.

A hand rapped on the outside of the hull and I jumped like a guilty thing.

"Mr Sandman?" It was one of Mulder's crew. "Mr Bannister wants to see you. Now."

It wasn't a request, but an order. But I wanted to see Bannister too, so I obeyed.

Bannister was waiting for me in his study. He had taken care to provide himself with reinforcements. Fanny Mulder stood to one side of a table littered with charts and weather maps, while Angela slumped in a deep chair in the corner of the room. They all three looked tired.

"Ah, Nick!" Bannister seemed almost surprised that I'd come. I sensed that there had been an argument before I arrived. Angela was sullen, Mulder silent, and Bannister was nervous. He crossed to his desk and shook a cigarette out of a packet. "Thank you for coming," he said.

"I wanted to see you anyway."

He clicked a lighter, puffed smoke. "Angela tells me you borrowed a car this morning?"

"I filled it with petrol," I said. "I should have asked you before I borrowed it. I'm sorry."

"That's all right." His denial was too hasty. Bannister, it was clear, did not have the guts to go for a confrontation. Clearly Angela and Mulder were expecting a fight, and I guessed that was what the argument must have been about. They wanted to attack me, while Bannister wanted to keep things gentle. For all his tough-guy image, he crumbled at the first touch.

"Is that all you wanted?" I asked. "Because I've also got something to say to you."

"Where did you go in the car?" Mulder asked in his flat voice.

I ignored him. "I've come to tell you that you can count me out," I said to Bannister. "Not just out of the St Pierre, but out of everything. I don't want any more of your film, any more of your company. I'm through."

"Where did you go?" Mulder insisted.

"Answer him," Angela said.

"I've got nothing to say to you! Nothing!" I turned on her furiously, stunning the room with my sudden anger. "I'm sorry," I said to Bannister. "I don't want to get angry. I just want out. After last night" – I glanced at Angela, then looked back to Bannister – "I don't see how I can decently stay. And as I understand things, you promised to restore my boat, so give me a cheque for a thousand pounds and I'll finish *Sycorax* myself and leave you alone."

Bannister hated the confrontation. "I think we should talk things over, don't you?"

"Just give me a cheque."

Mulder seemed to despise Bannister's pusillanimity. He moved close and looked down at me. "Where did you go in the car, man?"

"Get out of my way."

"Where did – "

"Get out of my bloody way or I'll break your fucking neck!" I astonished myself by my own savagery. Mulder, even though he could surely not have feared me, stepped back. Angela gasped, while Bannister stayed motionless.

I made my voice calm again. "A cheque, please."

Bannister found some courage for the moment. "Did you go to see Miss Kirov, Nick?"

"No. A cheque, please."

"But you did invite her to the party?" Bannister insisted.

"Yes, but I didn't know Fanny was going to try and rape her. Are you going to give me a cheque?"

"I didn't – " Fanny began.

"Shut up!" I snapped. I'd harried them all into submission. They'd summoned me to this room to dress me down as if I was a small schoolboy, but they were all now silent. Mulder stepped away from me, while Angela fumbled in her bag for a cigarette. I could hear the murmur of voices from the terrace beneath where the guests gathered for brunch. "I want a cheque," I said to Bannister.

I thought I'd won, for Bannister walked to his desk and pulled open a drawer. I expected him to bring out his chequebook, but instead he produced a stack of cardboard folders. "Please look at those, Nick."

I didn't move, so he lifted the top one, opened it, and handed it to me.

My own photograph was in the file and curiosity made me take it from Bannister. "Read it," he said quietly.

There were only two sheets of paper in the folder, both topped with a printed letterhead: 'Kassouli Insurance Fund, Inc. (Marine)'. My photograph was pasted on to one of the sheets with my career, such as it had been, carefully typed out beneath. The citation for the Victoria Cross was reproduced in full. The other sheet was handwritten in what, I supposed, was Jill-Beth's writing. "Captain Sandman's presence in AB's house is unexpected, but could be fortunate for us. Captain Sandman, like many soldiers, is a romantic. In many ways he lives in La-la land, by which I mean he's a preppy drop-out who wants to do a Joshua Slocum, but undoubtedly his sense of honour and duty would predispose him to our side." I was wondering where La-la land was, and whether Jill-Beth would like to live there.

"That," Bannister said quietly, "is your Miss Kirov's pilot book. We found these files on her boat." He handed me another opened file which had a photograph of Fanny Mulder doing his morning exercises on *Wildtrack*'s bow. The sparse career details said that Francis Mulder had been born in Witsand, Cape Province, on 3 August 1949. His schooling had been scanty. He'd served in the South African Defence Forces. He had a police file in South Africa, being suspected of armed robbery, but nothing had ever been proved. The next entry recorded his purchase of a cutter in the Seychelles where he had run his charter business until Nadeznha Bannister had spotted his undoubted talent.

Again there was a handwritten comment. "Despite being a protegé of your daughter's, there can be no doubt of Mulder's loyalty to AB. AB has promoted him, pays him well, and constantly demonstrates his trust in Mulder." The rest of the page had been raggedly torn off, making me wonder if Bannister had destroyed comments that discussed Mulder's presumed involvement in Nadeznha Bannister's murder.

I was tempted to ask by what right Bannister had searched *Mystique*, but, faced with the evidence in the files, it would have been a somewhat redundant question. Bannister took the two files from me. "Do you understand now why we're somewhat concerned that you might be a close friend of Miss Kirov's?" He turned to stare at a large portrait of his dead wife that stood framed on the study bookshelves. "Do you know who owns the Kassouli Insurance Fund?"

"I assume your ex-wife's father?"

"Yes." He said it bleakly, almost hopelessly, then sat in a big leather chair behind the desk and rubbed his face with both hands. "Tell him, Angela."

Angela spoke tonelessly. "Yassir Kassouli is convinced that Tony could have prevented Nadeznha's death. He's never forgiven Tony for that. He also believes, irrationally and wrongly, that by making another attempt on the race this year Tony is demonstrating a callous attitude towards Nadeznha's death. Yassir Kassouli will do anything to stop Tony winning. Last night Miss Kirov tried to persuade Fanny to sabotage our St Pierre attempt. Fanny refused. In turn he accused Miss Kirov of dismasting *Wildtrack*. They had an argument. That's when she pretended to be attacked, and when you played the gallant rescuer." Angela could not resist unsheathing a claw. "That's the truth, Mr Sandman, of which you're such a staunch guardian."

I said nothing. There had been a ring of truth in her words, however much they contradicted what I'd seen and what Jill-Beth had said, and I felt the confusion of a man assailed by conflicting certainties. Jill-Beth had spoken of murder, and of a million-dollar insurance claim, while Angela now spoke convincingly of a rich man's obsession with preserving his daughter's memory. I supposed that the real truth of the matter was that there was no real truth. Nor, I told myself, was it any of my business. I had come here to resign, nothing more.

Bannister swivelled his chair so he could stare at the portrait. If he'd murdered her, I thought, then he was putting on an award-winning performance. "I can't explain grief, Nick," he said. "Yassir Kassouli's never forgiven me for Nadeznha's death. God knows what I was supposed to do. Keep her ashore? All I do know is that so long as Kassouli lives he'll hate me because of his daughter's death. He isn't rational on the subject, he's obsessed, and I have to protect myself from his obsession." He shrugged, as if to suggest that his explanation was inadequate, but the best, and most honest, that he could provide. He tapped the folders. "You can see that Miss Kirov believes that you'll help sabotage my St Pierre run this year."

"I'm not in a position to help," I said to Bannister, "because I've resigned from your life. No film, no St Pierre, I just want your cheque. A thousand pounds will suffice, and I promise to account for every penny of it."

"And how will you account for the money already spent?" Angela snapped into her most Medusa-like mood, echoing her vituperation of the previous night. "Do you know how much money we've invested in this film? A film that you undertook to make? Or had you forgotten that you signed contracts?"

I still refused to look at her or speak to her. I kept my eyes on Bannister. "I want a cheque."

"You just want to do what's most comfortable!" Angela had worked herself into another fine anger. "But I want a film that will help people, and if you back out on it, Nick Sandman, then you're reneging on a contract. It's a contract we trusted, and we've spent thousands of pounds on realizing it, and if you tear it up now then I promise you that I'll try and recoup that wasted money. The only property of yours that the courts will consider worth confiscating is *Sycorax*, but I'll settle for that!" Her voice was implacably confident, suggesting she had already taken legal advice. "So if you don't fulfil your contractual obligations. Nick Sandman, you will lose your boat."

I still ignored her. "A thousand pounds," I said to Bannister.

"You're not going to walk out on this!" Angela shouted.

"A thousand pounds," I said to Bannister again.

Bannister was caught between the two of us. I suspected he would gladly have surrendered to me at that moment, but Angela wanted her pound of Nick Sandman's flesh and Bannister, I assumed, was afraid of losing her flesh. He prevaricated. "I think we're all too overwrought to make a decision now."

"I'm not," I insisted.

"But I am!" He betrayed a flash of anger. "We'll talk next week. I need to look at the budget, and at the film we've already shot." He was making excuses, trying to slide out from making a decision. "I'll phone you from London, Nick."

"I won't be here," I said.

"You'd better be here," Angela snapped, "if you want to keep your boat."

So far, except for the first time she'd spoken to me, I'd succeeded in ignoring her. Now I told her to go to hell, then I turned and walked from the room. The guests on the terrace fell silent as I limped past them. I didn't know whether I'd resigned, been fired from the film, or was about to be baked in a lawyer's pie. Nor did I much care.

I stumped down the lawn, skirted the boathouse, and saw that Jimmy Nicholls had come upriver and tied his filthy boat alongside *Sycorax*. He was lifting two sacks into *Sycorax*'s scuppers. "Chain plates and bolts," he told me. "Ready for the morning."

"Bugger the morning. Can you tow *Sycorax* away today?"

"Bloody hell." He straightened up from the sacks. "Where to?"

"Any bloody where. Away from bloody television people. Bloody stuck-up, arrogant powder-puffs." I climbed down to *Sycorax*'s deck.

Jimmy chuckled. "Fallen out with your fancy friends, boy?"

I looked up at the house and saw Angela watching me from the study window. "Up yours, too." I didn't say it loud enough to carry. "The bastards are threatening to get the bailiffs on to *Sycorax*. Where can I hide her?"

He frowned. "Nowhere on this river, Nick. How about the Hamoaze?"

"Georgie Cullen's yard?"

"He liked your dad."

"Every thief likes my dad." I scooped up a coiled warp and bent it on to a cleat ready for the tow. I wanted Angela and Bannister to see me leave. I wanted them to know that I didn't give a monkeys for their film or their threats. "Have you got enough diesel to get me there today, Jimmy?"

"You don't want to go anywhere right now," Jimmy said sternly. "I've got a letter for you. Boy on a motorbike brought it from London! Said I was to get it to you, but no one was to notice, like, so that's why I hid it with the bolts, see?" He pointed to one of the sacks. "From London, Nick!" Jimmy was just as astonished as I that someone should hire a messenger to ride all the way from London to Devon. "The boy said as how an American maid gave it he. You want to read it before you bugger off?"

I wanted to read it. A moment ago I had been full of certainty as to what I should do, but the sudden and overwhelming memory of a naked girl in my dinghy, of her smile, of her competence, made me carry the heavy sack down into *Sycorax*'s cabin. The creamy white envelope was marked 'Urgent'.

I tore it open. Two things fell out.

One was a first-class ticket for British Airways, London to Boston and back again. The ticket was in my name, and the outbound flight left Heathrow the very next morning. The return had been left open.

The second thing was a letter written in a handwriting that I'd just read in Bannister's study. 'If you haven't got a visa then get one from the Embassy and come Tuesday. I'll meet you at Logan Airport.' The signature was a child's drawing of a smiling face, a sketched heart, and the initials JB.

I did not consider the choices. Not for one heartbeat did I sit and think it through. It never occurred to me that I was being asked to take sides, nor did I think it odd that a girl would send me an expensive air ticket. At that moment, after years in which I had known nothing except fighting, pain, and hospital, I was being offered a great gift. The gift seemed to imply all the things that a soldier dreams of when he's neck-deep in wet mud with nasty bastards trying to bury him there forever.

In short, with visa and passport ready, I would go.

There would be no time to hide *Sycorax*, but a stratagem would have to protect her while I was away. I also asked Jimmy to keep an eye on her. "If they tow her off, Jimmy, follow them."

"I'll do what I can, boy." He eyed the air ticket. "Going far, are you?"

"Out of the frying-pan, Jimmy, and straight into bed." I laughed. It seemed like a madcap thing to do, an irresponsible thing to do, but a wonderfully spontaneous and exciting thing to do, and there had been precious little spontaneous and enjoyable excitement in my life since the bullet caught me. So I locked the cabin hatch, rode Jimmy's boat downriver to the town, and caught a bus. For Boston.

The stratagem to protect *Sycorax* involved telephoning my mother in Dallas.

"Do you know what time it is, Nick?" She sounded horrified. "Are you dying?"

"No, you are." I fed another fifty-pence piece into the coinbox.

"It's half-past four in the morning! What do you mean, I'm dying?"

"I apologize about that, Mother, but if anyone calls from England and asks after me, then say you're not well. Say you asked me to visit your deathbed. It'll only be for a few days."

There was a pause. "It bloody well is half-past four!"

"I'm sorry, Mother."

"Where are you, for God's sake?"

"Heathrow."

"You're not really coming to see me, are you?" She sounded appalled at the prospect.

"No, Mother."

"Your sister came a month ago and I'm still exhausted. Why am I dying?"

"Because I've told some people that I'm visiting you. I'm actually going somewhere else and I don't want them to know."

Another pause. "I really don't understand a word you're saying, Nick."

"Yes, you do, Mother. If anyone telephones you and wants to know if I'm there, then the answer is that I am there, but I can't reach the telephone straight away, and you're dying. Will you tell your maid that?"

There was another long pause. "This is uncommonly tedious, even for you. Are you drunk?"

"No, Mother. Now will you help me?"

"Of course I will, I just think it's terrifying to be telephoned at half-past four in the morning. I thought the Russians must have invaded. Did you transfer the charges?"

"No, Mother."

"Thank God for that." She yawned down the telephone. "Are you well?"

"Yes. I'm walking again."

"How's your father?"

"I haven't seen him."

"You ought to. You were his favourite. How are Piers and Amanda?"

"They're very well."

"So crass of you to have lost Melissa. Do you mind if I go back to sleep now?"

"Thank you, Mother."

"You're very welcome."

I pressed the receiver rest, put in more coins, and dialled Devon. No one answered in Bannister's house, or rather the relentlessly cheerful answering machine responded. "This is Sandman," I said, "and I'm phoning to say that my mother's been taken ill in Dallas and her doctors think I should be with her. I'll discuss our other problems when I get back."

I was taking precautions. I feared that Angela might interpret my disappearance as a desertion of her wretched film, and that she would then carry out her legal threats. I had no idea how long it took to get a court order, or whether the court could really order *Sycorax*'s sequestration, but I reckoned the fiction of a dying mother would confuse the lawyers for long enough. Then, just as soon as I returned to England, I planned to take the boat away. I'd had enough of Bannister, more than enough of Medusa, and I would take *Sycorax* to another river and there rig and equip her. But first, America.

They looked at me very oddly at the check-in desk. I was wearing a pair of my oldest deck-shoes, duck trousers which were stained with varnish and linseed oil, and a tatty blue jumper over one of the unwashed Army shirts I'd found in the bergen. It was my cleanest shirt. "Any luggage?" the girl asked me.

"None."

But my ticket was valid, and my visa unexpired, so they had to let me on.

I went with excitement. I forgot Bannister and I forgot his

threats because a girl with bright eyes and black hair had summoned me to Boston.

It was raining at Boston's Logan Airport. There was no Jill-Beth. Instead a chauffeur with a limousine the size of a Scorpion tank waited for me. The chauffeur apologized that Miss Kirov was unable to be personally present. He was civilized enough to overlook my lack of luggage and the state of my clothes. The US Immigration officers had been less courteous, though a phone call to the Military Attaché at the British Embassy in Washington had finally convinced them that I had not come to corrupt the morals of the Republic. I rather hoped that I had.

In which hope I was driven south through a thunderstorm.

We drove to Cape Cod. I remembered, as we crossed the canal, how I had sailed *Sycorax* down this waterway to the East Boat Basin six years before. I'd had a crew from my regiment on board and we'd all been awed by the glossy boats amongst which *Sycorax* had seemed like a poor and shabby relation.

Now, taken deep into the Cape, I was wafted to a hotel of unimaginable luxury where I was expected and, despite my appearance, treated as a most honoured guest. I was shown to a door that carried a brass plate inscribed "Admiral's Quarters", but few admirals could ever have lived in such sybaritic splendour. It was a suite of rooms which overlooked a harbour. I had a jacuzzi, a bath, a bedroom, a living-room and a private balcony.

I went to the window. My father had always loved America; he loved its freedom, its excesses and its shameless wealth. I found the Republic more frightening, perhaps because I had not inherited my father's talent for manipulating cash. I stared now at the busy harbour where boats that cost more than an Army officer could earn in a lifetime jostled on their moorings. The rain was clearing, promising a bright and warm evening. A motor-yacht with a flying bridge, raked aerials, fighting chair and a harpoon walkway accelerated towards the sea, while behind me the air-conditioning hissed in the Admiral's Quarters. It all suddenly seemed very, very unreal; like a splendid dream that will end at any moment and return the sleeper to a commonplace reality. I turned on the television to find that the Red Sox were four runs ahead at the bottom of the eighth with three men on base. A printed card planted on the television set assured me that Room Service could bring me the Bountiful Harvest of the Sea or Land at any hour of the Day or Night. I felt as though I was drowning in casual affluence. There was a shaving kit laid out for me in the bathroom, a towelling robe waiting on the bed, while in one of the walk-in cupboards I found my old brogues which had been re-heeled, then polished to a deep shine. The sight of them, and the memory of the last time I had worn them, made me smile. There were also four pairs of new shoes sitting alongside the brogues.

Above the shoes, and hanging in protective paper covers, were clothes. There were two dinner-jackets; one white, one black. There were slacks, shirts, unnecessary sweaters, even a rain-slicker. Some ties hung on a door-rack and I noticed, with astonishment, that my old regiment's striped tie was among them. A label was pinned on to the regimental tie: "With the Compliments of Miss Kirov." At the bottom of the paper slip was the legend, 'Kassouli Hotels, Inc., a Division of Kassouli Leisure Interests, Inc.'.

I suppose I'd really known right from the moment when I'd opened that thick creamy envelope in *Sycorax*'s cabin. I'd known who had paid for the ticket, and who wanted me in the States, but I'd deceived myself into thinking that it was love; as bright and shiny and new as a fresh-minted coin. Of course it was not. It was Kassouli. The compliments slip only confirmed it, but still I thought I could pluck my fresh coin out of the mess.

The telephone startled me.

"Captain Sandman? This is the front desk, sir. Miss Kirov has requested us to inform you that she'll come by at seven o'clock with transportation. She suggests formal dress, sir."

"Right. Thank you."

He enjoined me to have a nice day. On the television the batter hit a grand slam home run, the ball rising so that the picture was shattered by the starburst of stadium lights. I turned the set off and drew a bath. It was madness, but I had volunteered to come here because of a girl. I felt my right leg trembling and I feared that the knee would buckle, so I lowered myself into the bath and told myself that there was no need for apprehension, that it was an adventure, and that I was glad to be here.

My sense of unreality, that I was a sleepwalking participant in a sleek dream, only increased when Jill-Beth arrived. She came in a white BMW convertible, and was wearing an evening dress of black and white speckled silk. She had a triple strand of pearls beneath a lace shawl. Her hair seemed glossier and her skin more glowing than I remembered. "Hi, Nick."

"Hello." I was shy.

She laughed. "I knew you'd choose the black tux."

"I'm sorry to be so conventional."

"Hell, no. I like a black tux on a man. You don't want to look like a waiter, do you?" She leaned over and gave me a quick kiss. "How's the jet lag?"

"As bad as yours, I imagine?"

"I feel great. You'd better, too, because we're partying." She accelerated the BMW from under the hotel's awning. It was a hot sticky evening, but, though the BMW's hood was down, she had the air-conditioning on full blast so that my legs froze while my chest became sticky with sweat.

"I didn't bring much money," I said warningly.

"A thousand bucks should see you through the night." She saw the expression on my face, and laughed. "Hell, Nick! You're Kassouli's guest, OK?"

"OK," I said, as though I'd known all along that it was Kassouli who'd plucked me across an ocean and not love.

Jill-Beth swung into a marina entrance where an armed guard recognized her and opened the gate. We drove past a row of moored motor-cruisers, each the size of a minesweeper and each with an aerial array that would have done service to a frigate.

"La-la land," I said, echoing the comment Jill-Beth had written about me in the file that Bannister had shown me.

Jill-Beth instantly understood the allusion, and laughed. "Did you see the files?"

"Only those that Bannister wanted me to see."

"That figures. Were you offended by what I wrote?"

"Should I have been?"

"Hell, no." She waved to a man on board one of the moored cruisers, then offered me a deprecating smile. "I guess I'm not exactly flavour of the month with Tony Bannister?"

"Not exactly. Nor am I."

"Tough." She swung the BMW into a parking slot opposite a berth where a white cutter was moored. She put the gear into neutral and kept the motor running as she nodded at the yacht. "Like it?"

I knew that make of boat, and liked it very much. She was called *Ballet Dancer* and had been built on America's West Coast; a 42-foot cutter with a canoe stern, bowsprit, and the solid, graceful lines of a sturdy sea boat. She was made of fibreglass, but had expensive teak decks and rubbing-strakes. "Yours?" I guessed.

"Mine. I always wanted to be a ballet dancer, you see, but it doesn't help if you're built like a steer."

"You should have qualified then."

She smiled at the compliment. "I grew too tall. Anyway, I prefer sailing now."

"She's a lovely boat," I said warmly. *Ballet Dancer* had the good look of a well-used boat. You can always tell when a boat is sailed hard; it loses its showroom gloss and accretes the small extra features that experience has demanded. *Ballet Dancer*'s cleats and fairleads were worn, there were extra warps neatly coiled in her scuppers, and there was a ragged collection of oars, poles and boathooks bundled beside the lashed-down liferaft. The teak decks and trim had faded to a bone white. In a month or two *Sycorax* would have this same efficient and weathered look. "She looks beautiful," I said.

"And all mine," Jill-Beth said happily. "Paid off the final instalment last month." She switched off the BMW's engine and opened her door. "Coming?"

I followed her on to the floating pontoon and watched as she disconnected the shoreside electricity and unlooped the springs. "We're going out?" I said with surprise.

"Sure. Why not?"

It seemed very odd to be crewing a boat while dressed in evening clothes, but that was evidently Jill-Beth's plan. She started the engine. "You want to take her out, Nick?"

The boat's long keel made it hard to turn in the marina's restricted water, but I backed and filled until the bow was facing the channel. Once there Jill-Beth unrolled the genoa from the forestay, then hoisted the main. I'd never seen a girl in evening dress rig a yacht before. "The trick to it," she said happily, "is a damned good anti-perspirant." She came and sat next to me in the cockpit where she opened a locker. "Champagne?"

"I thought you'd never ask."

The evening had been sparked with a spontaneity that matched the irresponsibility of flying the Atlantic. I felt happy, even light-headed. It was cooler out on the water where the small wind spilt down on us from the mainsail's curve. "How does she compare to *Sycorax*?" Jill-Beth asked.

"*Sycorax* carries more windage aloft. The gaff, all those blocks and halliards, the topsail yard. So she has to have a lot of metal underwater. That makes her stubborn."

"Like you?"

"Like me. And like me she's not too hot to windward, but I don't plan to fight my way round the world." A motor-cruiser surged past us. There was a party in evening dress on its covered quarterdeck and they raised their glasses in friendly greeting. I could see the first stars pricking the sky's pale wash where an airliner etched a white trail. "Thank you for the air ticket," I said.

"*Nada*." Jill-Beth grinned. "Isn't that why white knights rescue damsels in distress? For a reward?"

"Is this my reward?" I asked.

"What else?" She touched my glass with hers. The wake of the cruiser jarred *Ballet Dancer*'s double-ended hull and made Jill-Beth's champagne spill on to my black trousers. She wiped the excess off. "I like you in a tux. It makes you look elegantly ugly."

I laughed. "I think it's the first time I've worn a tie since they gave me the medal." We passed a moored boat which had a smoking barbecue slung from its dinghy davits. The skipper waved a fork at us and we raised our champagne flutes in reply. I thought how the pleasure of this evening compared to the bitter paranoia of Bannister's life; the jealousies and ambitions, the sheer squalidness of his suspicions. No wonder, I thought, that his American wife had tired of it. Had she wanted to come back to this elegant coast with its sprawl of luxuries?

I pushed the mainsheet traveller across as the wind backed a point or two. We were going softly eastwards, past shoals, but keeping within the buoys that marked the offshore channel. Two more motor-cruisers passed us, and both carried yet more people in evening dress. "Where's the party?" I asked.

"There." Jill-Beth pointed directly ahead towards a massive white house that occupied its own sand-edged promontory. The house was shielded on its landward side by trees while wide terraced lawns dropped to the private beaches and to the private docks that this night were strung with lanterns and crowded with boats. A string of headlamps showed where other guests drove along the spit of sand that led to the promontory. "The house belongs to Kassouli's wife," Jill-Beth said. "She's not there, but Kassouli is. He wants to thank you."

"Thank me for what?"

"For rescuing me."

I suddenly felt nervous. There's something about the very rich that always makes me nervous. Principles, I remembered, are soluble in cash, and I had already surrendered my privacy to Bannister's cash and feared that something more might be asked of me this night. I pushed the helm away from me. "Why don't we just bugger off to Nantucket? I haven't been there for years."

Jill-Beth laughed and pulled the helm back again. "Yassir wants to see you, Nick. You'll like him!"

I doubted it, but obediently steered for the dock where servants waited to berth our yacht. I could hear the thump of the music coming from the wide, lantern-hung gardens. I chose a windward berth, spilt air from the sails, and two men jumped aboard to take our warps.

We entered the garden of Kassouli's delights. A pit had been dug on one of the beaches and a proper clambake of driftwood and seaweed sifted smoke into the evening and tantalized us with the smells of lobster, clams and sweetcorn. Higher up, on one of the terraces, steaks dripped on barbecues. There was champagne, music and seemingly hundreds of guests. It was clearly an important social occasion, for there were photographers hunting through the shoals of beautiful people. One flashed a picture of Jill-Beth and myself, but when he asked my name I told him I was no one important. "A Brit?" He sounded disappointed, then cheered up. "Are you a Lord?"

I told him my name was John Brown. He wrote it down, but it was plain I was not destined to be the evening's social lion.

"Why didn't you say who you were?" Jill-Beth protested.

"I'm no one important."

"Nonsense. You want to dance?"

I said my back hurt too much and so we sat at a table where we were joined by a noisy group. One of the men, after the introductions, told me how I could refinance my boat on a twelve-year amortization schedule. I made polite noises. I gathered that a good few of the guests worked for Kassouli, either in his finance houses, shipping line or oil companies. I looked for Kassouli himself, but the man who wanted to lend me money said that the boss probably wouldn't show himself. "Yassir's not a great partygoer. He likes to give 'em, though." The man peered round the garden. "That's his son, Charlie."

I recognized the son from the pictures I'd seen in Bannister's house, but there was one thing I was not prepared for. Charles Kassouli was now in a wheelchair. He was only in his early twenties, but had withered legs slewed sideways on the chair.

"What happened?" I asked my new acquaintance.

"Motorbike." The reply was laconic. "Too many bucks and not enough sense. What do you expect of rich kids?"

Jill-Beth introduced me to the son a few moments later.

Charles Kassouli's face was startlingly handsome, but his character was distant and churlish. I thought he might be doped into lethargy with painkillers, though he proved snappish enough when Jill-Beth told him I was a sailor.

"Sailing sucks." The resentful face turned to see whether I

would take offence. I took none. If anything I felt a chill pity, for here was a boy born to the pleasures of the richest society on earth, and who had thrown them away with one twist of a motorcycle's grip. At the same time I felt some scorn. I'd known scores of people in hospital who, denied the chance to walk, faced their lives with a courage that made me feel inadequate. Charles Kassouli, though, was clearly not cut from the same cloth.

"You've never sailed?" I asked him.

"I told you. Sailing sucks."

"Charles owns a motor-cruiser," Jill-Beth said in an attempt to chivvy him into cheefulness.

"Are you dancing, JB?" He threw away his cigarette and swivelled his chair away from me.

"Sure, Charlie." She walked beside his electric wheelchair on to the dance floor and I watched how unself-consciously she gyrated in front of him. She grinned at me, but I turned away because a voice had spoken in my ear. "Captain Sandman?"

The speaker was a tall and fair-haired man who had broad shoulders beneath his white and braided uniform coat. He offered me a slight bow of his head. "Captain Sandman?" he asked again. He had a Scandinavian accent.

"Yes."

"If you're ready, sir?" He gestured towards the big house.

I looked for Jill-Beth, but she had disappeared with Kassouli's son, and so I followed the uniformed manservant into the great house that was more like a palace. We entered through a garden room hung with cool watercolour landscapes. A door led to a long air-conditioned hallway lined with the most superb ship models of the eighteenth century. Naval museums would have yearned for just one such model, but Kassouli owned a score of them. The walls were hung with pictures of ancient naval battles. An open door revealed a conservatory where a long indoor swimming pool rippled under palms.

At the hallway's end the Scandinavian opened both leaves of a gilded door and bowed me into a library where he left me alone.

It was a lovely room; windowless, but perfectly proportioned.

It was lined with expensive leather-bound editions in English, French, Greek and Arabic. On rosewood tables in front of the library stacks were more ship models, but these were of Kassouli's modern fleet. There were supertankers and bulk carriers, all painted with the Kassouli Line's emblem of a striking kestrel. Each ship's name began and ended with a K. *Kalik*, *Kerak*, *Kanik*, *Komek*. In the trade it was called the Kayak Line; a slighting nickname for one of the world's great merchant fleets.

And a fleet run, I thought, by a modern merchant prince; a Levantine who had drawn me across the globe. I was suddenly very nervous. I stared up at the paintings which hung above the bookshelves. They were not pictures calculated to reassure a nervous Briton; they showed the battles of Bunker Hill, Saratoga, Yorktown, and, from a later war, New Orleans. The canvases were dark with varnish; the patina of ancient wealth giving gloss to a new American's fortune.

On a table in the room's centre there was a handsomely mounted family photograph. Yassir Kassouli, his plump face proud, sat next to his wife. She was a fair-haired, good-looking woman with amused eyes. Behind them stood Nadeznha and Charles; proud children, wholesome children, the finest products of the world's richest melting pot. I saw how their father's Mediterranean blood had dominated in their faces, but on Nadeznha I could see an echo of her mother's humorous eyes.

"A photograph taken before the tragedies." The voice startled me.

I turned to see a tall, thick-set and balding man standing in a doorway. It was Yassir Kassouli. His skin was very pale, as though he had seen little sunlight in the last few months. What was left of his hair was white. In the family photograph he had appeared as a man in his prime, but now he had the look of old age. Only his eyes, dark and suspicious, showed the immense and animal force of this immigrant who had made one of America's great fortunes. He was in evening dress and bowed a courteous greeting. "I have to thank you, Captain Sandman, for coming all this way to see me."

I muttered some inanity about it being my pleasure.

He crossed to the table and lifted the photograph. "Before the tragedies. You met my son?"

"Indeed, sir." The 'sir' came quite naturally.

"I raised my children according to Western tenets, Captain Sandman. To my daughter I gave freedom, and to my son pleasure. I do not think, on the whole, that I did well." He said the last words drily, then crossed to a liquor cabinet. "You drink Irish whisky, I believe."

"Yes, sir."

"Jameson or Bushmills?" He had a New England accent. If it had not been for his name, and for the very dark eyes, I'd have taken him for a Wasp broker or banker.

"Either."

He poured my whiskey, then helped himself to Scotch. As he finished pouring, the door opened and his son, escorted by Jill-Beth, wheeled himself into the room. Kassouli acknowledged their arrival by a gesture suggesting they helped themselves to liquor. "You don't mind, Captain, if my son joins us?"

"Of course not, sir."

He brought me my whisky that had been served without ice in a thick crystal glass. "Allow me to congratulate you on your Victoria Cross, Captain. I believe it is a very rare award these days?"

"Thank you." I felt clumsy in the face of his suave courtesy.

"Do you smoke, Captain Sandman?"

"No, sir."

"I'm glad. It's a filthy habit. Shall we sit?" He gestured at the sofas in front of the fireplace.

We sat. Jill-Beth and Charles Kassouli positioned themselves at the back of the room, as if they knew they were present only to observe. The son's earlier and surly defiance had been muted to a respectful silence and I suspected that Charles Kassouli lived in some fear of his formidable father. He certainly did not light a cigarette in his father's presence.

Yassir Kassouli thanked me for rescuing Jill-Beth. He thanked me again for coming to America. He spoke for a few minutes of his own history, of how he had purchased two tank-landing craft at the end of the Second World War and used them to found his present fortunes. "Most of that fortune," he said in self-deprecation, "was based on smuggling. A man could become very rich carrying cigarettes from Tangiers to Spain in the late forties. Naturally, when I became an American citizen, I gave up such a piratical existence."

He asked after my father and expressed his regrets at what had happened. "I knew Tommy," he said, "not well, but I liked him. You will pass on my best wishes?" I promised I would. Kassouli then enquired what my future was, and smiled when I said that it depended on ocean currents and winds. "I've often wished I could be such an ocean gypsy myself," Kassouli said, "but alas."

"Alas." I echoed him.

The word served to make him look at his family portrait. I watched his profile, seeing the lineaments of the thin, savage face that had become fleshy with middle age. "In my possession," he said suddenly, "I have the weather charts and satellite photographs of the North Atlantic for the week in which my daughter was killed."

"Ah." The suddenness with which he had introduced the subject of his daughter's death rather wrong-footed me.

"Perhaps you would like to see them?" He clicked his fingers and Jill-Beth dutifully opened a bureau drawer and brought me a thick file of papers.

I spilt the photographs and grey weatherfax charts on to my lap. Each one was marked with a red-ink cross to show where Nadeznha Bannister had died. I leafed through them as Kassouli watched me.

"You've sailed a great deal, Captain Sandman?" he asked me.

"Yes, sir."

"Would you, from your wide experience, say that the conditions revealed in those photographs were such that a large boat like *Wildtrack* might have been pooped?" Kassouli still spoke in his measured, grave voice, as though, instead of talking about his daughter's death, he spoke of politics or the Stock Market's vagaries.

I insisted on looking through all the papers before I answered.

The sequence of charts and photographs showed that *Wildtrack* had been pursued, then overtaken, by a small depression that had raced up from New England, crossed the Grand Banks, then clawed its way out into the open ocean. The cell of low pressure would have brought rain, a half gale, and fast sailing, but the isobars were not so closely packed as to suggest real storm conditions. I said as much, but added that heavy seas were not always revealed by air pressure.

"Indeed not," Kassouli acknowledged, "but two other boats were within a hundred miles, and neither reported exceptional seas."

I shuffled the photographs with their telltale whirl of dirty cloud. "Sometimes," I said lamely, "a rogue wave is caused by a ship's wake. A supertanker?"

"Miss Kirov's researches have discovered no big ships in the vicinity that night." Kassouli had the disconcerting trick of keeping his eyes quite steadily on mine.

"Even so," I insisted, "rogue waves do happen."

Kassouli sighed, as though I was being deliberately perverse. "The best estimate of wave height, at that time and in that place, is fifteen feet. You wish to see the report I commissioned?" He clicked his fingers again, and Jill-Beth dutifully brought me a file that was stamped with the badge of one of America's most respected oceanographic institutes. I turned the typed pages with their charts of wave patterns, statistics and random sample analyses. I found what I wanted at the report's end: an appendix which insisted that rogue waves, perhaps two or three times the height of the surrounding seas, were not unknown.

"You're insisting that such seas are frequent?" Kassouli challenged me.

"Happily very infrequent." I closed the report and laid it on the sofa.

"I do not believe," he spoke as though he summarized our discussion, "that *Wildtrack* was pooped."

There was a pause. I was expected to comment, but I could only offer the bleak truth, instead of the agreement he wanted. "But you can't prove that she wasn't pooped?"

His face flickered, as though I'd struck him, but his courteous tone did not falter. "The damage to *Wildtrack*'s stern hardly supports Bannister's story of a pooping."

I tried to remember the evidence given at the inquest. *Wildtrack* had lost her stern guardrails, and with them the ensign staff, danbuoys and lifebelts. That added up to superficial damage, but it would still have needed a great force to rip the stanchions loose. I shrugged. "Are you saying the damage was faked?"

He did not answer. Instead he leaned back in his sofa and steepled his fingers. "Allow me to offer you some further thoughts, Captain. My daughter was a most excellent and highly experienced sailor. Do you think it likely that she would have been in even a medium sea without a safety harness?"

I saw that Kassouli's son was leaning forward in his wheelchair, intent on catching every word. "Not unless she was re-anchoring the harness," I said, "no."

"You are asking me to believe" – Kassouli's deep voice was scornful – "that a rogue wave just happened to hit *Wildtrack* in the two or three seconds that it took Nadeznha to unclip and move her harness?"

It sounded lame, but sea accidents always sound unlikely when they are calmly recounted in a comfortable room. I shrugged.

Kassouli still watched closely for my every reaction. "Have you seen the transcript of the inquest?" he asked.

"Yes, sir."

"It says that the South African, what was his name?" He clicked his fingers irritably, and Jill-Beth, speaking for the first time since she had come into the room, supplied the answer. "Mulder," Kassouli repeated the name. "The report says Mulder was on deck when my daughter died. Do you believe that?"

"I don't know." I hesitated, and Kassouli let the silence stretch uncomfortably. "There's a rumour," I said weakly, "that Mulder lied to the inquest, but it's only pub gossip."

"Which also says that Bannister was the man on deck." Kassouli, who had clearly known about the rumour all along, pounced hard on me as though he was nailing the truth at last. "Why, in the name of God, would they lie about that?"

I was beginning to regret that I had come to America. It had seemed like a blithe adventure when Jimmy had delivered the ticket to *Sycorax*, but now the trip had turned into a very uncomfortable inquisition. "We don't know that it was a lie," I said.

"You would let sleeping dogs dream," Kassouli said scathingly, "because you fear their bite."

I feared Kassouli's bite more. He was not a sleeping dog, but a very wideawake wolf. "There is something else." Kassouli closed his eyes for a few seconds, as if his next statement was painful. "My daughter, I believe, was in love with another man."

"Ah." It was an inadequate response, but my Army training was not up to any other reaction. I could discuss the sea with a fair equanimity, but I was discomforted by this new, embarrassing and personal strain in the conversation.

Kassouli, oblivious to my embarrassment, turned to his son. "Tell him, Charles."

Charles Kassouli shrugged. "She told me."

"Told you what?" I asked.

"There was another fellow." He was laconic, and his voice was very slightly slurred.

"But she did not say who he was?" his father asked.

"No. But she was kind of excited, you know?"

I did know, but I kept from looking at Jill-Beth. "Isn't it odd," I said instead, "that she sailed with her husband if she was in love with someone else?"

"Nadeznha was not a girl to lightly dismiss a marriage," Kassouli said. "She would have found divorce very painful. And, indeed, she shared her husband's ambition to win the St Pierre. It was a mistake, Captain. She sailed to her murder."

He waited once more for me to chime in with an agreement that her death had been murder. I'd even been fetched clean across the Atlantic to provide that agreement, but I did not oblige.

Kassouli gave the smallest shrug. "May I tell you about Nadeznha, Captain?"

"Please." I was excruciatingly embarrassed.

He stood and paced the rug. Sometimes, as he spoke, he would glance at the family photograph. "She was a most beautiful girl, Captain. You would expect a father to say that of his daughter, yet I can put my hand on my heart and tell you that she was, in all honesty, a most outstanding young lady. She was clever, modest, kind and accomplished. She had a great trust in the innate decency of all people. You might think that naivety, but to Nadeznha it was a sacred creed. She did not believe that evil truly existed." He stopped pacing and stared at me. "She was named after my mother" – he added the apparent irrelevance – "and you would have liked her."

"I'm sure," I said lamely.

"Nadeznha was a good person," Kassouli said very firmly as if I needed to understand that encomium before he proceeded. "I believe that I spoilt her as a child, yet she possessed a natural balance, Captain; a feel for what was right and true. She made but one mistake."

"Bannister." I helped the conversation along.

"Exactly. Anthony Bannister." The name came off Kassouli's tongue with an almost vicious intensity; astonishing from a man whose tones had been so measured until this moment. "She met him shortly after she had been disappointed in love, and she married him on what, I believe, is called the rebound. She was dazzled by him. He was a European, he was famous in his own country, and he was glamorous."

"Indeed."

"I warned her against a precipitate marriage, but the young can be very headstrong." Kassouli paused, and I noted this first betrayal of a crack in the perfect image he had presented of his daughter. He looked hard at me. "What do you think of Bannister?"

"I really don't know him well."

"He is a weak man, a despicable man, Captain. I take no pleasure in thus describing one of your countrymen, but it is true. He was unfaithful to my daughter, he made her unhappy, and yet she persisted in offering him the love and loyalty which one would have expected from a girl of her sweet disposition."

There was confusion here. A sweet girl? But headstrong and wilful too? There was no time to pursue the confusion, even if I had wanted to, for Kassouli turned on me with a direct challenge. "Do you believe my daughter was murdered, Captain Sandman?"

I sensed Jill-Beth and the crippled son waiting expectantly for my answer. I knew what answer they wanted, but I was wedded to the truth and the truth was all I would offer. "I don't know how Nadeznha died."

The truth was not enough. I saw Yassir Kassouli's right hand clenching in spasms and I wondered if I had angered him. The son made a hissing noise and Jill-Beth stiffened. I was among believers, and I had dared to express disbelief.

Yet if Kassouli was angry, his voice did not betray it. "I only have two children, Captain Sandman. My son you see, my daughter you will never see."

The grief was suddenly palpable. I hurt for this man, but I could not offer hi.n what he wanted – agreement that his beloved daughter had been murdered. Perhaps she had been, but there was no proof. I was prepared to admit that it was unlikely that Nadeznha Bannister had been unharnessed in a stiff sea, I could even say that it was possible she had been pushed overboard, but such lukewarm support was of no use to Yassir Kassouli. I was in the presence of an enormous grief; the grief of a man who could buy half the world, but could not control the death of a child he had loved.

"It was murder," Kassouli said to me now, "but it was the perfect murder. That means it cannot be proved."

I opened my mouth to speak, found I had nothing to say, so closed it again.

"But just because a murder is perfect," Kassouli said, "does not mean that it should go unavenged."

I needed to move, for the sofa's rich comfort and the man's heavy gaze were becoming oppressive. I stood and limped to the room's far end where I pretended to stare at a model of a supertanker. She was called the *Kerak*. It struck me, as I stared at the striking kestrel on her single smokestack, that despite Kassouli's Mediterranean birth he had one very American trait;

he believed in perfection. The *Mayflower* had brought that belief in her baggage, and the dream had never been lost. To Americans Utopia is always possible; it will only take a little more effort and a little more goodwill. But a large part of Yassir Kassouli's dream had died in the North Atlantic, in nearly two thousand fathoms of cold water. I turned. "You need proof," I said firmly.

He shook his head. "I need your help, Captain. Why else do you think I brought you here?"

"I – "

He cut me off. "Bannister has asked you to navigate for him?"

"I've refused him."

Kassouli ignored the words. "I will pay you two hundred and fifty thousand dollars, Captain Sandman, if, on the return leg of the St Pierre, you navigate the *Wildtrack* on a course that I will provide you."

Two hundred and fifty thousand dollars. The sum hung in the air like a monstrous temptation. It spelt freedom from everything; it would give *Sycorax* and me the chance to sail till the seas ran dry.

Kassouli mistook my hesitation. "I do assure you, Captain, that your life, and the lives of the *Wildtrack*'s crew, will be entirely safe."

I did not doubt it, but I noted how one man's name was excepted from that promise of mercy; Bannister's. I'd known Kassouli was Bannister's enemy, now I saw that the American would not be content until his enemy was utterly and totally destroyed. Something primeval, almost tribal, was at work here. A tooth for a tooth, an eye for an eye, and now a life for a life.

I still had not answered. Kassouli picked up the framed photograph and turned it so I could stare into the dead girl's face. "Can you imagine the pure terror of her last moments, Captain?" He paused, though no answer was needed, then he sighed. "Now Nadeznha is among the *caballi*."

He had said the word very softly. I waited for an explanation, but none came. "The *caballi*?" I prompted him.

"The souls of the young dead, the untimely dead." Kassouli's voice was very matter of fact, almost casual. "They roam the world, Captain, seeking the consolation of justice. Who, but their families, can provide such solace?"

I said nothing. My father had often told me that the very rich, having conquered this world, set out to conquer the next, which was why spiritualist frauds so often found patrons among practical men and women whose dour talents had made vast fortunes. Kassouli, having failed to convince me with the science of meteorology and oceanography, had retreated to the claptrap of the ghost world.

But neither ghosts, nor weather charts, nor even two hundred and fifty thousand dollars could make me accept. I needed the money, God knows how *Sycorax* and I needed the money, but there was an old-fashioned dream, as old as the dream that was carried in the *Mayflower*, and it was called honour. There was no proof that Bannister had done murder, and till that proof was found there could be no punishment. I shook my head. "I'm not your man, sir. I've already told Bannister I'm not sailing with him."

"But that decision could be reversed?"

I shrugged. "It won't be."

He half smiled, as though he had expected the refusal, then carefully replaced the silver-framed family portrait. "You are a patriot, Captain?"

The question surprised me. "Yes, sir."

"Then you should know that I have given myself one year to avenge my daughter's death. So far, Captain, I have tried to achieve that satisfaction through conventional means. I pleaded with your government to re-open the inquest, I went on my knees to them! They have refused. Very well. What your government will not do, I will do. But I need the help of one Englishman, and that is you. Miss Kirov assures me you are a brave and resourceful young man."

I looked at Jill-Beth, but she gave no sign of recognition. "But you have no proof," I protested to the father.

Kassouli was long past that argument. "If no Englishman will help me, Captain, then I will wash my hands of your country. I don't flatter myself that I can bring Great Britain to its knees, as

I went on my knees to Great Britain, but I will withdraw all my investments out of your country and I will use my influence, which is not negligible, to deter others from investing in your economy. Do you understand me?"

I understood him. It was blackmail on an enormous scale; so enormous that it defied belief. My face must have reflected that incredulity, for Kassouli raised his voice. "Every cent of every investment I have in Britain will be withdrawn. I will become an enemy of your country, Captain Sandman. Whenever it will be in my power to do it harm, that harm will be done. And when I die, I will charge my son to continue the enmity."

Charles Kassouli, under the thrall of his father's powerful voice, nodded.

Kassouli smiled. "But this is a nonsense, Captain Sandman! Fate has sent you to me. Fate has put you into Anthony Bannister's confidence, and I do not believe that fate is so very capricious." He held up a hand to check my protest. "I understand, Captain, that I am asking you to take on trust that my daughter was murdered. You must reflect that not every course of action in this world is underpinned by cause and proof, by validation and reason, or by the natural justice of good sense and right feeling. Sometimes, Captain, we have to trust our God-given instincts and act!" The last word was stressed by a punch of his right fist into his left. "Did you?" he asked, "consider the sense and rationality of your actions when you assaulted the Argentinian positions on the night you won your medal?"

"No," I said.

"Then do not become a weak man now, Captain."

"It isn't weakness . . ."

"My daughter is dead!"

I closed my eyes. "And you cannot prove it was not an accident." I opened my eyes to see that, surprisingly, Kassouli was smiling.

"You have not disappointed me, Captain. I would have been shocked had you offered instant agreement. I like strong people. They are the only ones on whom I can rely. So, I wish you to do one thing for me." He held out a hand to indicate that I should accompany him to the door. As we walked he made one last effort to sway me. "I want you to consider everything I have said. I want you to consider the meteorological conditions, the sea conditions, and the experience of my daughter. I want you to weigh in the balance the value of her immortal soul against that of Anthony Bannister. I want you to search your conscience. I want you to consider the damage I can cause to your country. And when you have done all of those things, then I want you to inform me whether or not you will help me. Will you do that, Captain?"

I glanced towards Jill-Beth, but she just smiled and lifted a hand in farewell.

"Will you do that, Captain?" Kassouli insisted.

"Yes, sir," I said lamely.

He pressed a button beside the doorframe and the tall Scandinavian servant appeared instantly. Kassouli gripped my hand. "Goodnight, Captain. I will send for your answer in due time."

The door closed on me. The Scandinavian asked whether I wanted to rejoin the party, but I shook my head. Instead I was shown to a limousine that took me back to my lavish hotel. I waited there half expecting a knock on the door or a telephone call, but none came.

So I slept uneasily. And alone.

In the morning I walked about the harbour and tried to persuade myself that Kassouli's threats had been nonsensical. I could not convince myself. I walked back to the hotel where I was informed that a car would be taking me to the airport that afternoon, and that Miss Kirov was waiting for me in the Lobsterman's Saloon.

The saloon was decorated with old-fashioned lobster pots, nets and plastic crustaceans. I found Jill-Beth sitting alone at the polished bar. She smiled happily. "Hi, Nick! Irish whiskey?" Her ebullience was like a mockery of the evening before. "How did you sleep?" she asked.

"Alone."

"Me too." She shrugged, and I knew I had been brought to

this town only to meet Kassouli. Jill-Beth had been nothing but the bait and, like a greedy mackerel snapping at a gaudy feather, I'd bitten. "So what did you make of Yassir?" she asked me.

"Mad."

She shook her head. "He's a grieving father, Nick. He lost a daughter and he wants to sleep better. It isn't madness. You want to eat lobster?"

I took the menu out of her hands and laid it down. "He isn't talking about sabotaging Bannister's attempt at the St Pierre, Jill-Beth, he's talking about killing Bannister!"

Her eyes widened in mock horror. "I didn't hear him say that!"

"Not in so many words."

She shook her head disapprovingly. "Then you're talking out of turn, Nick. Maybe Yassir just wants to talk to Bannister? Maybe he wants a signed confession so the courts can take it over? Hell, he probably wants to save his insurance company paying out a million bucks! Maybe he just wants to put Bannister over his knee and tan his hide? I don't know what he wants, Nick."

"He's mad! He can't declare economic war on a whole country!"

"Sure he can! Hotels, chemical works, computers, investments, oil, shipping. I guess his companies employ thirty thousand people in Britain? I know that's not many, but there are subcontractors too. Still, why should you care about unemployment?"

"For God's sake!" Her insouciance angered me.

"Nick." She touched my hand. "He's a very, very angry man."

"He hasn't got a shred of proof!"

"There can't be proof of a perfect murder."

I sipped the whiskey that was drowning in crushed ice. "Who was Nadeznha Bannister in love with?"

"Goodness knows." Jill-Beth shrugged. "Charlie doesn't know, or won't say."

"But that's part of Kassouli's evidence," I protested. "A love affair that no one even knows existed, a weather map that doesn't describe the sea conditions, and the probability that she'd have been wearing a safety harness. That's it, Jill-Beth! On that thin basis he's predicating murder!"

"You got it, Nick."

"You can't believe it," I challenged her.

She stirred her drink with a lobster-shaped swizzle stick. "I work for Kassouli, so I guess I'm predisposed to believing what he wants me to believe. But if I weigh the evidence?" She stared up at the net-hung ceiling. "Yeah, I guess it was murder. I mean, who's to know? Bannister doesn't want a divorce, he's kicking around with that new blonde of his, he knows Nadeznha will give him grief with the taxman, so he pushes her over the edge five hundred miles out on the return leg? I'd call that the perfect murder."

"It isn't me who lives in La-la land," I said bitterly. "Kassouli goes on about unquiet souls? About ghosts?"

Jill-Beth smiled. "La-la land, my dear Nick, is where everything is simple, where the virtuous always triumph, and where honour rules. This isn't La-la land. You're dealing with a guy who's very angry, very frustrated, and who wants justice. He only has two children; one's crippled, one's dead, and he can't have any more."

"Why can't he have any more?" I asked.

Jill-Beth ordered herself another drink. "Dorothy's got cancer. Dying very slowly."

"Jesus." I flinched.

"Yassir loves her very much. He's given sixteen million to cancer research. Is that mad?"

"No."

"He built a whole research wing around her in Utah. He read somewhere that Utah has the lowest rate of cancer in America." She shrugged, as if to show that nothing Kassouli could do would save his wife. "Yassir isn't mad, Nick, but he's very, very determined. Hell, all he's got left now is his son, and you've seen him."

"Surly," I commented.

"Sky-high, you mean."

It took me a second or two to realize what she implied. "Drugs?" I sounded astonished.

"Drugs, though he hides it from his father." She stirred her drink. "People envy Kassouli. He's rich. But he's been dealt a bad hand with his family, and he wants to hit back."

I looked at her, and I thought how very American Jill-Beth was; bright-eyed, firm-faced, shining hair, and it struck me how like Nadeznha she must be. Yet this lovely girl was condoning murder. She would deny it, but I was convinced that Kassouli planned murder. "Suppose I went to the police?" I said. "Suppose I tell them that you're trying to make me an accessory to piracy on the high seas? Or murder?"

"Try it," she said cheerfully.

"They'd have to believe me," I said, without too much conviction. "How many peasants like me get invited to Kassouli's house?"

"Lots of people."

"I can prove you flew me over here!"

"Your ticket was paid for in cash. If necessary we'll say that you met me in Devon and followed me here because you were besotted by my beauty. You wouldn't be the first guy to bug me like that." She grinned. "I'm empowered to increase the offer to four hundred thousand dollars. One hundred thousand in cash when you agree, and the rest after completion. Payable in any tax haven and in any currency you like."

"I'm not helping you. When I get back to England I'm moving *Sycorax* to a hiding place. Somewhere a long way from Bannister and a long way from you."

She ignored me. "I'll be over in England soon, Nick. I'll get in touch, OK?"

"You won't find me."

She touched my forearm. "Don't be a pain, Nick. Chivalry died with Nadeznha. Stay with Bannister, say you'll navigate his boat, and buy yourself a calculator that goes up to four hundred big ones." She picked up the menu again. "You want to eat?"

I shook my head.

"OK." She slid off the stool, her new drink untouched. "I'll see you soon, Nick, and I'll have one hundred thousand dollars cash with me. If you're not there, then kiss a lot of British jobs goodbye. Safe home."

I turned as she reached the door. "Why me, Jill-Beth?"

She paused. "Because you're there, Nick. Because you're there." She smiled, blew me a kiss, and went.

I felt like a frog that had sought out the princess, been kissed, but stayed a frog all the same. In short, I felt damned foolish. And up to my neck in trouble.

The Honourable John Makyns, MP, pretended that he was not embarrassed by lunching with his wife's cast-off husband, but I noted how he had chosen one of the West End's less prestigious clubs for our meeting. "I thought you were a member of Whites?" I teased him.

"The food can be better here," he lied smoothly, then waved his fish knife towards the *trompe l'oeil* ceiling. "And it's an amusing place, don't you think?"

"Side-splitting. Is Melissa well?"

"Very well, thank you." He paused. "I probably won't mention to her that we've lunched."

"Don't worry, I won't either."

He gave me a quick smile of thanks. "Not that she dislikes you, Nick. You mustn't think that."

"But she might think we were swopping dirty secrets?"

"Something like that, I suppose." He seemed rather sombre, but perhaps that was understandable. It isn't every day that you're telephoned from Heathrow to be told that a major foreign industrialist is declaring economic war against your country. The Honourable John broke off a piece of an over-baked bread roll that he thickly smeared with butter. "How was America?"

"Hot, shining, busy."

"Quite. It is like that, isn't it?" He fussed over the choice of wine and recommended the lamb to me. I ordered it, then listened as he told me a long and disjointed story about his mother's kitchen garden and the problems of finding craftsmen who could repair Tudor brickwork. He was avoiding the subject, which was Yassir Kassouli. He'd tried to ignore the subject on the telephone, but as soon as I threatened to call the Fleet Street newspapers he had hastened to suggest this luncheon. He was still evasive, though, asking about Devon, the weather in America, my health and my opinion of the lamb.

"I've tasted better out of cat-food tins."

"They're rather proud of their lamb here." He was hurt.

"Tell me about Kassouli." I decided to cut through to the reason for our meeting.

"Ah." The Honourable John speared a piece of meat with his fork and energetically sawed at the gristle with his knife. "Kassouli did approach HMG. Not officially, of course. As a private citizen of a foreign state, Kassouli has no diplomatic standing, you understand?"

"But he's rich, so Her Majesty's Government listened?"

He frowned at my crudity, but nodded. "We like to be accommodating to influential foreigners. Why shouldn't we be?"

"Indeed."

He was still frowning. "But we really could not help him."

"What did he want?"

The Honourable John shrugged. "I think he wanted us to put Bannister on trial, but there really was no cause, nor justification, nor reason."

"A dead girl?" I suggested.

He shook his head. "An incident happened on the high seas, beyond the limits of our or anyone else's sovereignty. Agreed that the boat is British registered, which is why there was a British inquest, but the coroner's findings were quite clear. It was an accident."

"Couldn't you have given Kassouli another inquest? Just to satisfy him?"

"There was no legal reason for doing so. There would have had to be fresh evidence, and there was none."

"There was a rumour," I said, "that lies were told at the inquest. I hear Bannister was on deck when Nadeznha died, not Mulder."

"As you say," John said delicately, "a rumour. Insufficient, alas, to initiate new proceedings."

"But it was explored?" I persisted.

"I really couldn't say."

Which meant that the Government had toyed with the idea of re-opening the inquest, but had sheered away for lack of real evidence. "So Kassouli's been threatening you?" I accused John.

He gave a tiny and frosty smile. "One does not threaten HMG."

"He told me he'd pull all his jobs out of Britain, then follow it with his investments, and then persuade all his rich pals to do the same thing. That won't look good on the unemployment figures."

The Honourable John concentrated on chewing, but finally decided he would have to reveal something from his side of the table. "You aren't the first person to bring us this message, Nick. A Kassouli embargo on Britain?" He frowned as he drew from his meat a length of string which he fussily placed at the side of his plate. "I do trust, Nick, that you won't be telling any of this to the newspapers? HMG wouldn't like that."

I ignored that. "Could Kassouli hurt us?"

The Honourable John leaned back and stared at the painted ceiling for a few seconds, then jerked his head forward. "Not as much as he thinks. But he could embarrass us, yes. And he could damage confidence at a time when we're working hard to attract foreign investment."

"How bad would the damage be?"

"We'd survive." He said it without much fervour. "The longer-term damage would be to unemployment. If all Kassouli's jobs went to Germany or Ireland or Spain, we'd never see them again. And most of them are in just the kind of sunrise industry we need to encourage."

"So he could hurt us?" I insisted.

"Embarrass," he insisted.

"So what do I do?"

The Honourable John grimaced with a politician's dislike of a direct question which needed a straight answer. "I really can't say," he said primly. "I'm merely a humble back-bencher, am I not?"

"For Christ's sake, John. You've been briefed on this! Just as soon as I telephoned you trotted round to the Department of Industry or whatever honey-pot has got the problem and told them what I told you!"

"I might have mentioned it to the Permanent Secretary," he allowed cautiously. The real truth was that HMG had moved with the speed of a scalded cat; partly because they were terrified of Kassouli, and even more terrified that I'd spill the whole rotting can of worms into Fleet Street's lap.

"So what do I do?" I insisted.

He swirled the white wine around in his glass, trying to look judicious. "What do you feel is best, Nick?"

"I'd hardly be coming to ask for your help if I knew what to do, would I? I've got some madman threatening economic warfare against Britain unless I help turn Anthony Bannister into fish food. Wouldn't you say that was a matter for government, rather than me?"

"Fish food?" The Honourable John could be wonderfully obtuse when he wanted to be.

"They want me to turn out his lights, John. Switch him off. Banjo him. Kill the fucker."

He looked immensely pained. "Did Kassouli say as much?"

"Not exactly, but I can't think what the hell else he wanted. I'm supposed to steer the good ship *Lollipop* straight to point X on the chart. What do you think is going to be waiting for us? Mermaids?"

"I shall really have to insist that I've heard no implications of murder. So far as I know, all Kassouli wishes to do is deny Bannister the chance of winning the St Pierre."

"Don't be pompous, John. The bastard's up to no good. You want me to go and squeal this tale down Fleet Street? Someone will listen to me. I've got a fragment of bronze that will insure that."

"They'll listen only too avidly, I fear. Nothing excites the press so much as a chance to damage our relationship with the United States." He stared at me helplessly.

"Then for Christ's sake, reassure me! Tell me the Government's on top of this problem. Don't you have friends in Washington who can tell Kassouli to rewire his brain?"

"Not with the amounts of money he contributes to members of Congress, no." He shrugged. "And you forget that Kassouli has never made these threats openly. They have been – how shall we say? – hinted at. Usually by intermediaries like yourself. Kassouli naturally denies making such threats, nevertheless HMG is forced to take them seriously,"

"Then give him his God-damned enquiry! Why ever not?"

"Because counter to the squallings of the left-wing press,

Nick, HMG do not actually control the judiciary. A new inquest can only be instituted if there are fresh revelations of fact. There are not. So we must look to you – "

"Hold it!" I said. "Here's a revelation of fact. I'm not going to help Kassouli, because I don't fancy joining my father in jail. What I'm going to do is go back to Devon and, if Bannister's bloody mistress hasn't stolen my boat, I'm going to tow it off to a nice safe place where I shall rig it. Meanwhile you'll be losing lots of jobs, but don't blame me, I've done my bit for the country and I've got a fucked-up spine to prove it. And you can tell Melissa not to try and find me before I sail, because I'll have disappeared. The kids' school fees are in the bank, and there isn't any more money, so it isn't worth her looking. Will you tell her that, John? Tell her I'm up a bloody creek and bankrupt."

"Nick, Nick, Nick!" The Honourable John held up a pained hand. "Of course we're not asking you to adopt responsibility for this situation."

"You're not?"

He waved away a waiter. "I repeat that I am not a member of Her Majesty's Government . . ."

". . . yet."

"But I think I can fairly reflect what the Government is thinking. Frankly, Nick, we'd rather Mr Kassouli did not press his threats against us. I think that's a fair stance, and a sensible one. But, as I said, the threats have not been made openly and we need to know a great deal more about their nature. Your information is valuable, but we'd like more. Is it a real threat, for example? Do I make myself clear?"

"The answer to your first question is yes; to the second, no."

He wouldn't look at me. "What I think I'm saying is that HMG would be most grateful, most grateful indeed, if you were to keep us informed of Mr Kassouli's intentions. Nothing more, Nick. Just information."

"How grateful would HMG be?" I mimicked his pronunciation.

He gave a small laugh. "I don't think we're talking about fiscal remuneration, Nick. Shall we just agree that we would silently note and privately approve your patriotism?"

"Jesus bloody wept." I waited till he looked at me. "You want me to go along with Kassouli, don't you?"

"We want you to keep us informed. Through me, though naturally I shall deny this request was ever formally made. It's entirely unofficial."

"But the only way I can keep an eye on Kassouli is by going along with his plans, isn't it? So I do help him, and HMG will be very grateful in the most nebulous and undeniable manner. Is that it?"

The Honourable John thought about his answer for some time, but finally nodded. "Yes, I think that is it. And you do want your boat back, don't you? This would seem to effect that desideratum."

It was all so very delicate. Kassouli justified revenge as righteous anger. The Honourable John was making it a case of expediency. And I was to be the instrument. "Why don't I just go to the police?" I asked.

He gave me a very small, very tight smile. "Because you would discover that the matter was beyond their competence."

"Meaning HMG put it there?"

"Indeed."

I thought of Harry Abbott; always so close to me, nudging me away from trouble like an escort ship taking a merchantman past a minefield. Except Abbott's job, I suddenly realized, was to steer Bannister into the mines. "God, but you're a slimy lot." I stared at him. "Do you think Bannister murdered his wife?"

"I think it would be unscrupulous to make any conjecture."

"If you want him dead," I said brutally, "why don't you use your thugs to do it? Or are you telling me that those chaps who used to disappear from my regiment went into monasteries?"

"Our thugs," he said in a pained voice, "don't have boats on Bannister's lawn, nor the honour of Bannister's acquaintance."

"You could introduce them," I said helpfully. "I thought Bannister was a friend of yours?"

"Rather more of Melissa's, I think." He did not look up at me as he spoke.

Poor sod, I thought. "Really? I never got that impression."

He tried to hide his relief, but couldn't. "Not that they're especially close, I think, but she has more time for a social life than I do."

More time to slide in and out of bed, he meant. Both the Hon-John and I wore Melissa's horns. "So HMG," I said instead, "would be jolly grateful if I helped knock off Melissa's friend Tony, and you're telling me, in the slimiest and most roundabout manner possible, that the police will turn a blind eye."

"You may put whatever construction you choose upon my words, Nick, and once again I entirely deny any imputation of a conspiracy to murder. All I am prepared to say, and that unofficially, is that we would like you to be helpful to a most important industrialist who could bring a great deal more investment and many more jobs to Britain."

"Is that what Kassouli promised you if you turned a blind eye? Jobs?"

That made him twitch. "Don't be ridiculous, Nick."

"The man's as mad as a hatter, John. He talks about unquiet souls. He's probably chatting to his daughter on a planchette board, or through some half-mad fucking spiritualist!"

"Was madness an occupational risk of hatters? I don't know." He looked at his watch. "Good Lord. Is that the time? And Nick?"

"John?"

"Not a word to the press, there's a very good chap."

He paid and left me. I had gone to the Government for help, and I'd been abandoned. So I did the one thing they did not want me to do. I phoned Fleet Street.

The pub was dingy, smelly and, compared to the Devon pubs, expensive, but it was close to the newspaper offices which was why Micky Harding had suggested it. Harding had been one of the reporters who had marched every step of the Falklands with my battalion which, inevitably, had nicknamed him 'Mouse'.

Mouse now brought four pints of ale to the table. Two for each of us. "You look bloody horrible, Nick."

"Thank you."

"Never thought I'd see you again."

"You could have visited me in hospital."

"Don't be so fucking daft. I spent bloody hours outside your door, didn't I? But you were being coy. What's the matter? Do we wear the wrong perfume for you? Cheers." He downed the best part of his first pint. "Saw your ugly face in the papers. Who beat you up?"

"Friend of Anthony Bannister's. South African."

"Well, well, well." He looked at me with interest, sensing a story.

"But you can't say that," I said hastily, "because if you do I lose my boat."

He closed his eyes, clicked his fingers irritably, then gave me a look of triumph. "*Sycorax*, right?"

"Right."

"Three bloody years and I haven't forgotten." I remembered how Micky prided himself on his memory. "God," he went on, "but you were boring about that bloody boat. Still afloat, is it?"

"Only just."

"How come you lose her if I say that you were beaten up by a mate of Bannister's?"

"Because I need Bannister's money to repair it."

Micky gave me a long and disbelieving look. "If I recall correctly, which I bloody well do, us taxpayers gave a hundred thousand quid to everyone who got badly wounded in the Falklands. Didn't you qualify?"

"I got stitched up by a divorce lawyer."

"Bloody hellfire. A hundred grand?"

"Damn nearly."

"Jesus, mate. You need a bloody nanny, not a newspaper reporter. So tell me all."

I told him about *Sycorax*. I also told him about Bannister, Jill-Beth, Kassouli and the Honourable John. I told him everything. I told him how I had let myself be suckered into Kassouli's house and how, as a result, I now had a problem. I wanted to head Kassouli off, not because I was on Bannister's side, but because it was impossible to do nothing when so many jobs were threatened. It had become a matter of patriotism. Micky grimaced when I used the word. "So why don't you just play shtum?" he asked. "Clearly the fucking Government's happy for Bannister to get knocked over, the jobs get saved, and you keep your boat. What do you need me for?"

"Because there's no proof that Bannister did kill his wife."

"Oh. You want to be honourable as well, do you?" He said it in friendly mockery, then lit a cigarette and stared at the smoke-stained ceiling. He was a big man with a coarse tongue and a battered face and a mind like a suspicious weasel. He gave me an overwhelming impression of world-weariness; that he had seen everything, heard everything, and believed very little of any of it. Now he looked dubious. "It's the word of a convict's son versus the British Government and one of the world's richest men?"

"That's about it."

"The VC will help, of course – " he thought about it some more – "but Kassouli will deny talking to you?"

"Utterly."

"And the Government will say they never heard of you?"

"I'm sure."

"Dodgy." He went silent again for a few puffs of his cigarette. "Do you think there's a chance Bannister did it?"

"I haven't the first idea, Mouse. That's the whole point about a perfect murder. It's so perfect you don't even know if it was murder."

"But if we say it was murder, Nick, or if we even bloody hint at it, Bannister will slap a bloody libel writ on us, won't he?"

"Would he?"

"Of course he would. Worth hundreds of thousands, that libel. Tax-free, too." He shook his head. "It just can't be proved that he murdered his wife, can it?"

"No."

"It would be the perfect bloody murder." He said it admiringly. "And a damn sight cheaper than divorce." He lit another cigarette. "I want it. It's a lovely little tale. A stinking rich Yank with a wog name, a murdering Brit bastard, a pusillanimous government, a copper-bottomed war hero, and a corpse with big tits. Just right for a scummy lowlife rag like mine. Cheers, Nick."

"So can you help?" I felt the relief of a weight being lifted, the relief that I was no longer alone between the rock and a hard place. If the British Government would not take on Kassouli's obsession, then the press certainly would. Kassouli's threats would disappear in the face of publicity, for he would surely not dare acknowledge that he was trying to blackmail a government or plan revenge on the high seas. I would let the newspapers stir up the sludge and make a huge stench. The stench might even give Kassouli what he wanted; another enquiry into Nadeznha's death. The stench would also release me from the whole mess. I had wanted help, and now I had it from the very people I'd been avoiding for over two years.

"I'll help," Micky said grimly, "but I need proof." He wrinkled his face as he thought. "This Jill-Beth Kirov-like-the-fucking-ballet. She's coming back to talk to you?"

"She said so. But I'm planning to move my boat tomorrow. I'm not going to be around to be talked to."

"You have to move the boat?"

"Bloody hell, yes. Bannister's threatening to repossess it, and I've had enough."

"No." Micky shook his head. "No, no, no. Won't do, Nick. You'll have to stay there." He saw my unwilling expression, and sighed. "Look, mate. If you're not there, then the American girl won't talk to you. If she doesn't talk to you, then we haven't got any proof. And if I haven't got proof then we don't have a story. Not a bloody dicky-bird."

"But how does her talking to me provide proof?"

"Because I'll wire you, you dumb hero. A radio mike under your shirt, an aerial down your underpants, and your Uncle Micky listening in with a tape-recorder."

"Can you do that?"

"Sure I can do it. I have to get the boss's permission, but we do it all the time. How do you think we find all those bent coppers and kinky clergymen? But what you have to do, Nick, is go along with it all, understand? Tell Bannister you'd love to navigate his bloody boat. Tell Kassouli you're itching to help him trap Bannister. String them along!"

"But I don't want to stay at Bannister's," I said unhappily.

"In fact I've already told them I'm through with their damned film."

"Then bloody un-tell them. Eat crow. Say you were wrong." He was insistent and persuasive; all his world-weariness sloughing away in his eagerness for the story. "You're doing it for Queen and Country, Nick. You're saving jobs. You're staving off some Yankee nastiness. It won't be for ever, anyway. How long before this American bint turns up with the hundred thousand?"

"I don't know."

"Within a month, I'll wager. So, are you game?"

Bannister had not been able to persuade me to stay on to be filmed, nor had Kassouli, nor even the Honourable John, but Micky had done it easily. I said I'd stay. But only till the story broke, and after that I would rid myself of all the rich men into whose squabble I had been unwillingly drawn. "Of course we'll pay you for the story," Micky said.

"I don't want money for it."

He shook his head. "You are a berk, Nick, you are a real berk."

But I was no longer alone.

I took the train to Devon next morning. It was raining. *Wildtrack* had left the river, either gone back to the Hamble marina or else to her training runs. *Mystique* had also disappeared; probably reclaimed by an angry French charter firm.

But *Sycorax* was still at my wharf. I had half expected to find her missing, but she was safe and I felt an immense relief.

I limped down to her and climbed into her cockpit. I saw that Jimmy had bolted the portside chainplates into position, ready for the main and mizzen shrouds. I unlocked the cabin padlock and swung myself over the washboards. I lifted the companionway and found the gun still in its hiding place under the engine. If Mulder had been willing to search *Mystique*, I wondered, why not *Sycorax*?

I went topsides, but there was no sign of Jimmy. Nothing moved on the river except the small pits of rain. I had the tiredness of time zones, of being dragged by jets through the hours of sleep. I slapped *Sycorax*'s coachroof and told her we'd be off soon, that there was not much longer to stay on this river, only so long as it took to trap a coterie of the world's wealthy people.

There was no beer on board *Sycorax*, nor anything to eat, so I trudged up to the house only to find that the housekeeper was out. I knew where she kept a spare house key, so I let myself in and helped myself to beer, bread and cheese from the kitchen. I ate the meal in the big lounge from where I stared out at the rain falling on the river. A grockle barge chugged upstream and I saw the tourists' faces pressed against the glass as they stared up at Bannister's big house. Their guide would be telling them that this was where the famous Tony Bannister lived, but in a few weeks, I thought, the newspaper's scandalous stories would bring yet more people to gape at the lavish house. I supposed the grockle barges must have done good business during my father's trial.

The sound of the front door slamming echoed through the house. I turned, expecting to hear the housekeeper go towards the kitchen, but instead it was Angela Westmacott who came into the lounge. She stopped, apparently surprised at seeing me.

"Good afternoon," I said politely.

"I thought you'd resigned," she said acidly.

"I thought we might talk about it," I said.

"Meaning you need the money?" She was carrying armfuls of shopping which she dropped on to a sofa before stripping off her wet raincoat. "So are you making the film or not?" she demanded.

"I thought we might as well finish it," I said meekly. I'd planned to go this very afternoon, but, true to the promise I'd made to Micky Harding, I would stay.

"And how is your mother?" Angela asked tartly.

"She's a tough old bird," I said vaguely, and feeling somewhat ashamed at being taxed with the lie I'd recorded on the answering machine.

"Your mother sounded quite well when I spoke to her. She was rather surprised at first, but she did eventually say you were in Dallas, though not actually in the house right at that moment." Angela's voice was scathing. "I said I'd phone back, but she said I shouldn't bother."

"Mother's like that. Especially when she's dying."

"You are a bastard, Nick Sandman. You are a bastard."

I felt immune to her insults because I was no longer in her power. I had Micky's newspaper behind me. I turned to watch rainwater trickling down the window. The clouds were almost touching the opposite hillside, which meant the moors would be fogged in. I prayed that Jill-Beth would come to England soon so that I could get the charade of entrapment done, and free myself of all these spoilt, obsessed and selfish people.

A sob startled me. I turned and, to my astonishment, I saw that Angela was crying. She stood at the far end of the long window and the tears were pouring down her face and her thin shoulders were shuddering. I stared, appalled and embarrassed, and she saw me looking at her and twisted angrily away. "All I want to do," she said in between sobs, "is make a decent film. A good film."

"You use funny methods to do it," I said bitterly.

"But it's like swimming in treacle!" She ignored my words. "Everything I do, you hate. Everything I try, you oppose. Matthew hates me, the film crew hate me, you hate me!"

"That's not true."

She turned like a striking snake. "Medusa?" She waited for a response, but there was nothing I could say. She sniffed, then wiped her eyes on the sleeve of her jacket. "Can't you see what a good film it could be, Nick? Can't you, for one moment, just think of that?"

"Good enough to blackmail me? No supplies till I do what you want? If I won't do everything you want, just as you want it, you threaten to steal my boat!"

"For God's sake! If I don't force you, you'd do nothing!" She wailed it at me. She was still crying; her face twisted out of its beauty by her sobs. "You're like a mule! The bloody film crew spend more time reading the Union regulations than they do filming, Matthew's frightened of them, you're so bloody casual, but I'm committed, Nick! I've taken the company's money, their time, their crew, and I don't even know whether I'm going to be able to finish the film! I don't know where you are half the time! And if I do find you, and want to talk to you, you look at me as if I'm dirt!" It was as if a great chain had snapped inside her. She hated to be seen thus, and she tried to shake the demeaning misery away, but she could not stop her sobs. She found her handbag, took out a packet of cigarettes, but only succeeded in fumbling them across the carpet. She cursed, picked one up, and lit it. "I swore I'd give up bloody cigarettes," she said, "but how can I with bastards like you around? And Tony."

"What's wrong with Bannister?"

"He's frightened of you! That's what's wrong with him. He won't tell you what's expected of you, so I have to do it. Always me! He's so God-damned bloody lazy and you're so God-damned bloody obstructive, and I'm so bloody tired!" She shook with great racking sobs. "I'm so bloody tired."

I limped towards her. "Is it such a good film?"

"Yes." She wailed the word. "God damn you, you bloody man, but it is! It's even an honest film, though you're so full of shit that you won't see it!"

"God damn me." I trod on her spilt cigarettes. "But I didn't know." I put my hands on her shoulders, turned her, and held her against me. She did not resist. I took the burning cigarette from her fingers and flicked it into the swimming pool. "I'm sorry," I said.

"I'm sorry, too." She sobbed the words into my dirty sweater. "Hell," she said, "I didn't want this to happen." But she did not pull away from me.

"I did," I said. From the very first I'd wanted it to happen, and now, on a rainy afternoon, and to confuse everything, it did.

It rained all afternoon, all evening. For all I knew or noticed, all night too.

We talked.

Angela told me about her childhood in the Midlands, about her Baptist minister father and oh-so-respectable mother, and about the redbrick university where she had marched to abolish nuclear weapons and save the whales and legalise marijuana. "It was all very normal," she said wistfully.

"Did your father think so?"

"He was all for saving the whales." She smiled. "Poor Daddy."

"Poor?"

"He'd have liked me to have been a Sunday School teacher. Married by now, of course, with two children."

Instead she had met a glib and older man who claimed to run a summer radio station for English tourists in the Mediterranean. She'd abandoned university in her last year, and flown south, only to find that the radio station had gone bankrupt. "He didn't want me for that, anyway."

"What did he want you for?"

She rolled her head to look at me. "What do you think?"

"Your retiring and gentle nature?"

She blew smoke at the ceiling. "He always said it was my legs."

"They're excellent legs."

She lifted one off the bed and examined it critically. "They're not bad."

"They'll do," I said.

So then she had used the letterheaded stationery of the defunct radio station to land herself a job with a real radio station in Australia. "It was cheeky, really," she said, "because I didn't know the first thing about radio. I got away with it, though."

"Legs again?"

She nodded. "Legs again. God knows what would have happened if I'd been ugly." She thought about that for a time, then frowned. "I've always resented the looks, in a way. I mean, you're never sure whether they want you for your looks or abilities. Do you know what I mean?"

"It's a problem I have all the time," I said, and she laughed, but I was thinking that her passionate drive to make a good film must have been part of her answer to that question. She desperately wanted to prove that her abilities could match those of a clever and ugly person.

Not that Angela had ever been coy about using her good looks. She'd moved from the radio station to its parent TV company, and it was there that she had met Anthony Bannister who had been filming in Australia. He had promised her a job on his programme if she should ever return to England. "So I came back."

"Just for him?"

She shrugged. "I wanted to work in English television. I wanted to come home."

"And Bannister was the price?"

She looked at me. "I like him, Nick. Truly."

"Why?"

"I don't know." She stubbed out the cigarette then rolled on to my left arm. I held her against me and she crooked her left leg over mine. "He's like me, in some ways."

"He's got good legs?" I asked in astonishment.

"He's so vulnerable. He's very good at his job, but he doesn't have any confidence outside of it. Have you noticed that? So he wears his success like a mask."

"He's weak," I said.

"It's easy for you to say that. You're strong."

"You should see me in telephone boxes. There's nothing but a blur, then I reappear with my underpants outside my trousers."

She laughed softly. "Tony doesn't think anyone likes him. That's why he tries to be nice to everyone. People think he's so successful and confident, but all the time he's frightened and he'll always agree with what any opinionated person says because he thinks that will make them like him. That's what makes him good on the telly, I think. He draws people out, you see. And he's very good-looking." She added the last in a rather defensive voice.

"He's spreading round the waist," I said idly.

"He won't exercise. He's always buying the equipment, but he never uses it."

"Was he married when you met?"

She nodded, but said nothing more.

We lay quietly for a while, listening to the rain. I pulled a strand of her long hair across my chest. "Will you marry him?" I asked.

"If he wants me to, yes."

"Will he?"

"I think so." She fingered the scar on my shoulder. She had very long thin fingers. "He'd prefer someone like Melissa, someone with social acceptance, but he may settle for me. I'm efficient, you see, which is good for his career. I think he's frightened he might lose me to a rival programme."

"Do you love him?"

She appeared to think about it, then shook her head.

"Then why marry him?"

"Because . . ." She fell silent again.

"Why?" I insisted.

"Because he can be good company." She spoke very slowly, like a child rehearsing a difficult lesson. "Because he's very successful. Because I can give him confidence when he meets people who he thinks despise him. He thinks you despise him."

"Maybe that's because he's despicable?"

She pulled a hair out of my chest in punishment. "He's not despicable. He's insecure and he's only confident when the television cameras are pointing at him."

"You'll have a wonderful marriage," I said sourly, "with the bloody cameras following you around."

"And perhaps I can change him," she said. "He'd like to be more like you."

"Poor?"

"He envies you. He wishes he'd been a soldier."

"Good God." I lay in great contentment, my left hand stroking her naked back.

"That's why he likes Fanny, I think," Angela said. "Fanny's tough."

"That's true."

"And if tough people respect him, Tony feels tough himself." She shrugged. "Perhaps, in time, and if enough people offer him acceptance, he will become strong?"

It seemed a rum recipe to me. "You're strong," I said.

"I don't cry very often," she said, "and I don't like it when I do." She lay silent for a few moments. Gulls were calling harshly on the river. "There's something else about Tony," she went on. "He doesn't have close friends. He'd like to have one really close friend. Not me, not any woman, just some man he could be totally honest with."

"Friends are harder to find than lovers," I said.

"Do you have friends, Nick?"

"Yes." I thought about it for a second. "Lots."

"He doesn't. Nor do I, really. So, yes, I'll marry him because it will make me feel safe."

"Safe?"

Angela raised her face and kissed my cheek. "Safe."

"I don't understand."

"I'm tired of being chased by men. Now, because people know that I belong to Tony, they don't try."

"Belong?"

"He's very possessive." She said it in a slightly apologetic tone, then lay staring at the ceiling for a moment. "He wants me to give up my job if we marry."

"Would you?"

"It wouldn't be fair to other people if I didn't, would it? I mean, they'd say I got all the best jobs because I was Tony's wife." I reflected that people must already be thinking that, wedding ring or no. She shrugged. "And I'd never have any more money worries, would I? And I'd get this house, and I could see you whenever you sailed *Sycorax* back to the wharf. That wouldn't be bad, would it?"

It was a long way, I thought, from a semi-detached Baptist minister's house in the Midlands to a mansion above a Devon river. "It might not be bad," I said, "but would it be good?"

"That's a romantic's question."

"I'm a romantic. I'm in love with love."

"More fool you." She wriggled herself into comfort against me as the wind slapped rain at the window. It was a north wind and I imagined the small yachts beating hard towards shelter through the bucking waves at the river's bar. Angela was still thinking of love and its dishonest shifts. "Tony isn't faithful to me, but I'm not to him any longer, am I?"

"Would he be angry about this?"

She nodded. "He'd be horribly angry. And hurt. He's unfaithful to me all the time, but he never thinks that it might hurt me." She shrugged. "He has a terrible pride. Terrible. That's why I think he might ask me to marry him."

"Because he thinks you'll stay faithful to him?"

"And because I'm decorative." She twisted her head to see if I thought her immodest.

I kissed her forehead. "You're very decorative. The very first moment that I saw you, I thought how decorative you were. It was lust at first sight."

"Was it?" She surprised me by sounding surprised.

"Yes," I said gently. "It was."

She smiled. "You were very gaunt and frightening. I remember being very defensive. I didn't think I was going to like you, and I was sure you were going to hate me."

"I was just fancying you," I said, "but I was nervous of you. I thought television people would be much too clever and glamorous."

"We are," she said with a smile, then went back to thinking about Bannister. "It's very important to Tony to have a beautiful wife. It's like his car or house, you see; something to impress other people with. And it helps in the business, too."

"What happens if he wants to trade the wife in for a younger model?"

"Alimony," she said too swiftly, "is a girl's best friend."

We lay in silence for a long while. I heard an outboard on the river as someone made a dash through the rain towards the pub. Angela fell lightly asleep. Her mouth was just open and her breath stirred a wisp of her pale hair. I thought she looked very young and innocent as she lay in my arms. All the tense anger had leached out of her face in this afternoon; as if by coming to bed we had stopped fighting some foul gale and just let ourselves run before the wind. I kissed her warm skin, and the kiss woke her. She blinked at me, recognition came to her eyes, and a smile followed. She returned my kiss. "Tell me about you," she said.

"I thought you were making a film about me. Don't you know everything already?"

"I don't know whether you're in love with Jill-Beth Kirov."

The suddenness of the question surprised me. In this new happiness I'd clean forgotten that I'd only just returned from America. "I'm not in love with her."

"Truly?"

"Truly."

Angela propped herself up on an elbow. "Did you fall out of love with her in these last few days?"

"I didn't . . ." I stopped. I had been about to say I had not met Jill-Beth, but I did not want to lie to Angela. Not now. Lies twist life out of true, and this afternoon I'd found something that I wanted to be very true.

Angela was pleased with herself. "You'd be amazed how co-operative people are to television companies. Airlines aren't supposed to reveal who's on their passenger lists, but when you say you're from the telly and that it's terribly important to find Mr Sandman who's flown to the States without his script, they do help. And Dallas, Nick, is a very, very long way from Boston. Or it was the last time I was in America. Has it moved?"

I smiled. "I thought I was being very clever."

"Fooling you, Nick Sandman, is like taking candy off a very dumb baby." She rolled away from me, lit another cigarette, and came back to my side of the bed. She lay on her belly, propped herself on her elbows, and blew smoke at my face. "So?"

I nodded. "I fell out of love with her in these last few days."

"Did you go to bed with her?"

"No."

She looked pensive. "You would say that, wouldn't you? Being a gentleman."

"Yes, I would. But I didn't."

"I'm glad." She ducked her head and kissed me. "Will you be in love with me now?"

"Probably."

"Only probably?"

I raised my head and kissed her. "Undoubtedly."

"Silly Nick." She laid her head on my chest, and I felt the heat of the cigarette as she drew on it. "Did you fly to America to go to bed with her?"

"No. Yes. She wanted to see me, but I wanted to go to bed with her."

"Did you pay the air fare?"

"No."

Angela laughed. "It would have been an expensive non-fuck if you had. Did she want to see you about the St Pierre?"

"Yes." I suddenly wondered if this was a clever Bannister trick to make me confess all. Angela must have instinctively felt my fear, for she lifted her face and looked into my eyes.

"I didn't tell anyone where you were, Nick."

"Why not?"

"Because I want to finish the film." She drew on the cigarette. "Are they going to sabotage *Wildtrack*?" I didn't answer and she pulled away from me. "Did you meet Yassir Kassouli?"

"Yes."

"What did you think of him?"

"Very impressive, very powerful, horribly rich, very obsessed, and quite possibly a touch mad."

She smiled, then rolled over and sat up with her ankles crossed in front of her. She put an ashtray on the sheet and tapped her cigarette into it. Her naked body looked uncannily like Melissa's, very thin and pale and supple. If love was a thing of lust, then I was already lost. "Kassouli's always hated Tony," she said. "He hated him for taking his daughter away. He thought Nadeznha had married beneath herself. She married him on the rebound, I think. That's what Tony says, anyway."

"Were they happy?"

Angela shook her head. "Not especially. But not especially unhappy either. But Kassouli didn't help. He used to visit them all the time. Nothing was too good for his darling Nadeznha. He made them buy this house and insisted they put the pool in for him. He was always here, nagging her to go home."

"Why didn't she?"

"Nadeznha always did just what Nadeznha wanted." I heard

the dislike in Angela's voice. "She quite liked queening it in England. Here she was the heiress married to the show star, while in America she'd just have been another little rich girl."

"I heard she was rather a sweet girl," I said as innocently as I could.

"Sweet?" Angela almost spat the word. "She was unbelievably selfish. She was a monster! I always thought Tony was terrified of her, though he denies it."

I thought how Bannister clearly fell for very strong women. "She was a very good sailor," I defended the dead.

"That's not necessarily a recommendation, is it?"

I smiled, rolled off the bed, and walked to the window. I had been embarrassed at first because of the scars on my back, but Angela had laughed at the embarrassment. Now I stood and stared down at the river. The tide was rising, swirling to cover the mudflats and lift the moored tenders on the far bank. "Was Nadeznha going to leave him?" I asked.

"I don't know." Angela frowned. "Tony hasn't said much, but he wouldn't. I mean, it would have been a terrible blow to his pride if she'd walked out. Marrying her was a great coup, after all. But he's sort of hinted at it. He thinks she was having an affair, but I don't know who with. He gets angry if I talk about it now."

"Does he often get angry?"

"Only with people he thinks he can bully. He's a very insecure man."

I leaned my backside on the sill and watched her angular body on the rumpled sheet. Her unbound hair hung to the base of her spine. The bedclothes, all but for the bottom sheet, had fallen in a heap on the carpet. It was time, I thought, to delve into yet another layer of truth on this wet afternoon. "Do you know what people say about Nadeznha's death?"

She looked up at me. "I know, Nick."

"And?"

She shrugged. "No."

"No, impossible? No, he didn't do it? No, you're not saying anything?"

She stared down at the sheet for a long time. "I don't think he's got the guts to kill someone. Killing someone must be horrible. Unless you're so angry that you don't know what you're doing. Or in self-defence, perhaps?" She shrugged. "You must know, Nick. Aren't you the expert?"

"Good God, no."

"The Falklands, I mean."

"It wasn't the same. It wasn't easy, either." I thought about it. "Afterwards is the worst, when you're clearing up. I mean, it's one thing to pull a trigger when you know the bastard is pulling his, but it's quite different when you see his body a few hours later. I remember there was one who looked just like a fellow I used to play rugby with."

"Was it really bad?" she asked, and I heard a trace of her television producer's interest in the question. She was wondering whether I would talk like this on her film.

"Just mucky," I said.

She heard the evasion and made a face at me. "But could you murder someone in cold blood? Someone you'd loved? Could you murder Melissa?"

"Good Lord, no!"

"What makes you think Tony could, then?"

"I don't know what I think." I paused. "Could Mulder?"

"For God's sake, Nick!" So far she had patiently indulged my interest in the subject, but now, in a flash of the old Angela, she became annoyed. "You think Tony would keep Mulder around if he'd murdered Nadeznha? Tony keeps Mulder as a bodyguard. He knows Kassouli has threatened to stop him winning the St Pierre. Why do you think we won't take any strangers into the crew?"

"But you asked me."

She ground the cigarette into the ashtray. "We know what kennel you crawled from, Nick. You're not one of Kassouli's people. He's trying to make you into one, though, isn't he?" The question was a challenge.

"Yes," I said honestly, "but he didn't succeed. And I'm sorry I asked you all these horrid questions about Bannister."

"Tony isn't a murderer," she said flatly.

"I'm sorry," I said again.

"Don't even speculate about it," she said firmly, and with another trace of impatience. "The last thing I want is for the gutter press to start on Tony's last marriage. Can you imagine the mud they'd sling if they thought he might have murdered Nadeznha?"

I could imagine it, and I'd already triggered the process by talking to Micky Harding. Now, however truthful I wanted to be with Angela, I did not think I had better mention Harding to her.

She lit another cigarette.

"You smoke too much," I said.

"Piss off, Nick." It was said gently enough; nothing more than irritation at being criticized.

"And can I give you some more advice?" I said.

"Try me."

"Don't let Bannister go on the St Pierre. Keep him ashore. I don't know what Kassouli plans, but it's more than just preventing him from winning the St Pierre."

She looked at me for a long time. "He wants revenge for his daughter's death?"

"I think so, yes." I wondered why I was being so solicitous of a man who was now my rival for this girl. Good old chivalry.

"Male pride. Old bull, young bull." Angela swung herself off the bed and walked to the window beside me. The thick clouds were bringing on an early dusk. "Tony's very proud, Nick, and he won't back down. He's told the whole world that he's going to win the St Pierre this year. He wants to become a hero for Britain on television; he wants to be the man who tweaked the noses of the French. Bloody hell, Nick, he wants a knighthood! Other telly people have got it, so Tony wants one, and he thinks that winning the St Pierre will help."

"So you'll be Lady Bannister?"

She smiled, but didn't answer, and I thought how she would love the title.

"Don't let him go," I said. "Does he know how determined Kassouli is?"

"Would you give up a dream just because you were threatened?"

"It would depend on who was doing the threatening," I said fervently. "I'm much more likely to repent for a Soviet armoured division than for the Salvation Army."

"He won't give it up, Nick." She took my arm and leaned against me. "That's why I want you to go with him. Because you'll be another bodyguard."

"Not for the ratings?" I asked.

"That, too, you fool." She laughed, then threw her cigarette out of the window.

I fell over.

It had not happened for days, but suddenly my right leg had switched itself off and I lurched sideways, grabbed the windowsill, then sprawled heavily on the thick carpet. Panic coursed through me. I felt stupid, frightened, and suddenly very helpless. The pain was in my back again; not the usual dull pain that I had learned to live with, but a sudden streak of hard and frightening agony.

"Nick? Nick!" There was genuine alarm in Angela's voice.

"It's OK." I had to force my voice to sound calm. I tried to stand, and couldn't. I heard myself hiss with the pain, then I managed to roll over, which helped, and I pulled myself across the floor towards the bed.

"What is it, Nick?" Angela tried to lift me.

"Every now and then the leg crumples. It'll be all right in a minute." I was hiding my fear. I'd thought that because the leg had stood up to my American trip then perhaps the sudden weakness had mended itself, but suddenly, and foolishly, I was a helpless cripple again. I managed to haul myself on to the rucked bed where I lay with eyes closed as I tried to subdue the pain.

"You never mentioned it before," Angela accused me.

"I told you, it'll be all right in a minute." I forced myself to turn over, then began to pound my knee in an attempt to force pain and feeling back into the joint.

"Have you seen a doctor?" Angela asked.

"I've seen millions of doctors."

"You God-damned bloody fool." She strode naked across the room and seized the telephone.

"What are you doing?" I asked in alarm.

She fended off my clumsy grab for the phone. "You're going to see a doctor."

"I'm bloody not." I lunged for the phone again.

She lifted the phone out of my reach. "Do you want to go to bed with me again, Nick Sandman?"

"For ever."

"Then you bloody well see a doctor." She paused. "Do you agree?"

"I told you," I insisted, "it'll cure itself."

"I'm not discussing it, Nick Sandman. Are you going to see a doctor or are you not?"

I agreed. I'd found Angela now and I was not going to lose her and I'd even see a quack for her. I lay back on the bed and willed my leg to move, and I thought, as I listened to her quick, competent voice arranging my appointment, how very nice it was to be cared for by a woman again. I was Nick in love, Nick in La-la land, Nick happy.

PART THREE

The doctor turned out to be a woman of my own age, but who seemed older because of her brusque and confident manner. She was a neurologist whom Angela had met during the filming of a medical documentary. Doctor Mary Clarke had a hint of humour in her green eyes, but none in her voice as she briskly put me through her various tests. At the end of the performance she led me back to her private office overlooking a rose garden, where Angela had waited for us. Doctor Clarke asked me to describe the exact nature of my wound. She grimaced as she took notes, while Angela, who had not heard the full story before, flinched from the gory details.

"I wish," Mary Clarke said when I'd finished, "that I'd had you as my patient, Mr Sandman."

"I rather wish that, too," I said gallantly.

"Because" – she pointedly ignored my clumsy compliment – "I'd have kept you strapped down in bed so you couldn't have done any more damage to yourself."

Silence. Except that a nearby lawnmower buzzed annoyingly.

"What do you mean?" I asked eventually.

"What I mean, Mr Sandman, is that your do-it-yourself physiotherapy has undoubtedly aggravated a fairly routine and minor oedematose condition. There's no medical reason why you shouldn't be walking normally, except that you forced the pace unreasonably."

"Bollocks," I said angrily, with all gallantry forgotten. "The bastards said I'd never walk again!"

"The bastards usually do." Mary Clarke half smiled. "Because a spinal oedema routinely presents itself as a complete severance. Naturally, if your spinal cord was cut, you'd be paralysed for life. It's only when some degree of mobility returns that an oedema can be diagnosed."

"Oedema?" Angela asked.

"A bloody swelling," I answered too caustically, and immediately regretted the tone. I might have lived too long with the doctors and their vocabulary, but Angela was new to it.

"Very literally a bloody swelling," Mary Clarke said to Angela, "which presses on the spinal cord to induce a temporary paralysis, but which can usually be expected to subside within a matter of weeks."

"Mine didn't," I said stubbornly, as though I was proving her wrong.

"Because you'd been severely traumatized. There was extensive burning as well as the bullet damage. In essence, Mr Sandman, you have a permanent oedema now." She paused, then gave a grin that was almost mischievous. "The truth is that you're a very remarkably scrambled mess. When you die they'll probably put your backbone in a specimen jar. Congratulations."

"But what's to be done?" Angela insisted, and I was touched by the look of real anguish on her face until I realized that she was probably just terrified for the future of her film.

"Nothing, of course," Mary Clarke said happily.

"Nothing?" Angela sounded shocked.

Mary attempted a nautical metaphor; explaining that my body had somehow lashed together some kind of nervous jury-rig that gave me control of my right leg. The problem was that the jury-rig sometimes blinked out and, though further surgery might help, the risks were too frightening. "Are you determined to sail round the world?" Mary asked me at the end of the bleak explanation.

"At least to New Zealand, yes."

"You shouldn't do it, of course. If you had any sense, Mister Sandman, you'd apply for a disabled person's grant, find a bungalow with a nice ramp for your wheelchair, then write your memoirs." She smiled. "Of course, if you do that, then you'll become a completely helpless cripple, so perhaps you should go to New Zealand instead."

"But . . ." Angela began.

"There's nothing I can do!" Mary said sturdily. "Either the leg will function, or it won't. All any doctor can do now is experiment on him, which I rather suspect won't meet with Mister Sandman's approval?"

"Too bloody right," I said.

"But supposing he's alone in the middle of the Atlantic when the leg fails!" Angela protested.

"I imagine he'll cope," Mary said drily, "and so far there's always been a recovery of function. The muscle tone is good" – she looked at me – "but if you detect that the numbness is lasting longer each time, or if you see a withering in the limb, then you'd better seek medical advice. Of course they won't be able to do anything, except slice you up again, but some people find the attentions of a doctor reassuring." She stood up. "My fee will be a bottle of Côte de Beaune '78, chateau-bottled."

That was a good year for Burgundy, and Mary Clarke was a good doctor who knew that sometimes, maybe most times, the best thing to do is nothing. With which treatment Angela had to be content, and I had to live, and so we went back to Devon.

The good times began then. Anthony Bannister was commuting between his London house and the Mediterranean where *Wildtrack* had been entered for a series of offshore races. Fanny Mulder was with the boat, so I had Devon to myself. I also had the non-sailing Angela.

Matthew and the film crew must have realized what had happened between Angela and me, but they said nothing, and they were happy for me that *Sycorax* could make such progress. Her rigging wire arrived and, for the price of a dozen pints of beer, we borrowed a buoy barge so that its onboard derrick could lower the varnished masts into their places. Before stepping the mainmast I carefully placed an antique penny in the keel chock where the mast's heel hid and crushed the silver coin. It was a traditional specific to bring good luck to the ship, but love brought better fortune as Angela freed all the materials for *Sycorax*. Suddenly there were no more conditions, only co-operation. I even gave the camera a limping description of what had happened on the night I won the medal. I heard nothing from Jill-Beth, and I let myself think that Kassouli's threat was a chimera. Micky Harding phoned me a few times, but I had nothing to report and so the phone calls stopped.

Day by day the rigging took shape. Wire, rope, timber and

buckets of Stockholm tar were hoisted aloft and turned into the seemingly fragile concoction that could withstand the vast powers of ocean winds. It was slow work, for if any part of the rigging was to fail then I would rather it failed on the berth than in an Atlantic force eight. I cut the belaying pins out of *lignum vitae* and rammed them home in oaken fife rails that were bolted to the mast beneath cheek pieces. The film crew gave up trying to understand what was going on; they said I was becoming nautical, which just meant that the vocabulary had become technical as Jimmy and I worried about deadeyes and gantlines, robands and leader cringles, worming and parcelling. The cameraman retaliated by presenting me with a dictionary, while Angela made *Sycorax* a gift of some antique brass scuttles. She called them portholes.

"Scuttles," I insisted. They were beautifully made, with thick greenish glass and heavy brass frames. They had hinged shutters that could be bolted down in bad weather.

I screwed and caulked the scuttles home. Beneath them I was rebuilding the cabin. I made two bunks, a big chart table and a galley. I turned the forepeak into a workshop and sail locker. I built a space for a chemical loo and Angela wanted to know why I didn't put in a proper flushing loo like the ones on *Wildtrack* and I said I didn't want any unnecessary holes bored in *Sycorax*'s hull. Why bother with a loo at all, she asked tartly, why not just buy an extra bucket? I said that the girls I planned to live with liked to have something more than a zinc bucket. She hit me.

The sails were repaired in a Dartmouth loft and came back to the boat on a day when the film crew was absent. Jimmy and I could not resist bending mizzen and main on to their new spars. The sails had to be fully hoisted if they were to be properly stowed on the booms and I felt the repaired hull shiver beneath me as the wind stirred the eight-ounce cotton. "We could take her out?" Jimmy suggested slyly.

I wound the gaff halliard off its belaying pin and lowered the big sail. "We'll wait, Jimmy."

"Put on staysails, boy. Let's see how her runs, eh?"

I was tempted. It was a lovely day with a south-westerly wind gusting to force five and *Sycorax* would have revelled in the sea, but I'd promised Angela I'd wait so that the film crew could record my first outing in the rebuilt boat. I lifted the boom and gaff so Jimmy could unclip the topping lift and thread the sail cover into place.

He hesitated. "Are you sure, boy?"

"I'm sure, Jimmy."

He pushed the cover on to the stowed sail. "It's that maid, isn't it? Got you right under her thumb, she do."

"I promised her I'd wait, Jimmy."

"You keep your brains in your trousers, you do, Nick. When I was a boy, a proper man wouldn't let a maid near his boat. It means bad luck, letting a woman run a boat."

I straightened up from the belaying pin. "So what about Josie Woodward? Who put her in the club three miles off Start Point?"

He laughed wickedly and dropped the subject. I promised him it would only be a day or two, no more, before we could film the sequence I had dreamed of for so long; the moment when *Sycorax* sailed again. Two months before, I reflected, I would have taken Jimmy's hint and we would have taken the old boat out to sea and debated whether ever to come back again, but now I was as committed to the film as Angela herself. I had even begun to see it through her eyes, though I still refused to contemplate sailing on the St Pierre, and Angela had agreed that we'd devise a different ending for the film; one with *Sycorax* beating out to sea.

I telephoned Angela at her London office that afternoon. "She's all ready," I said. "Sails bent on, ma'am, ready to go."

"Completely ready?"

"No radio, no navigation lights, no stove, no barometer, no chronometer, no compass, no bilge pumps, no anchors, no radar reflector, no . . ." I was listing all the things Fanny Mulder had stolen.

"They're ordered, Nick," Angela said impatiently.

"But she can sail," I said warmly. "*Sycorax* is ready for sea. She awaits your bottle of champagne and your film crew."

"That's wonderful." Angela did not sound very pleased,

perhaps because I was finishing a boat that would take me away from her, which made my own enthusiasm tactless. There was a pause. "Nick?"

"There's a train that leaves Totnes at twenty-six minutes past five this afternoon," I said, "and it reaches London at – "

"Twenty-five minutes to nine," she chimed in, and did sound pleased.

"I suppose I could just make it." I made my voice dubious.

"You'd bloody well better make it," she said, "or there'll be no radio, no navigation lights and no stove."

"Bilge pumps?"

She pretended to think about it. "Definitely no bilge pumps. Ever."

I made it.

Angela's flat was a gloomy basement in Kensington. She only used it when Bannister was away, but the very fact that she had retained the flat spoke for her independence. At least I thought so. The flat had a somewhat abandoned feel. It was sparsely furnished, the plants had all long died of thirst, and dust was thick on shelves and mantelpiece. Papers and books lay in piles everywhere. It was the flat of a busy young woman who spent most of her time elsewhere.

"Next Tuesday," she told me.

"What about it?"

"That's when we'll film *Sycorax* going to sea."

"Not till then?"

She must have heard my disappointment. "Not till then." She was sitting at her dressing-table wiping off her make-up. "We can't do it till Tuesday because Monday's the travelling day for the crew."

"Why can't they travel on Sunday?"

"You want to pay them triple time? Just be patient till Tuesday, OK?"

"High tide's at ten forty-eight in the morning," I said from memory, "and it's a big one."

"Does that matter?"

"That's good. We'll go out on a fast ebb."

She leaned towards the mirror to do something particularly intricate to an eyelid. "There's another reason it has to be Tuesday," she said, and I heard the edge of strain in her voice.

"Go on."

"Tony wants to be there." She did not look at me as she spoke. "It's important that he's there. I mean, the film is partly about how he helped you, isn't it? And he wants to see *Sycorax* go to sea."

"Does he want to be on board?"

"Probably."

I lay in her bed, saying nothing, but feeling jealousy's tug like a foul current threatening a day's perfection. It was stupid to feel it, but natural. I knew that Angela's prime loyalty was to Bannister, yet I resented it. I had lived these past weeks in a mist of happiness, revelling in the joys of a new love's innocence, and now the real world was snapping shut on me. This present happiness was an illusion, and Bannister's return was a reminder that Angela and I shared nothing but a bed and friendship.

She turned in her chair. She knew what I was thinking. "I'm sorry, Nick."

"Don't be."

"It's just that . . ." she shrugged, unable to finish.

"He has prior claim?"

"I suppose so."

"And you have no choice?" I asked, and wished that I had not asked because I was betraying my jealousy.

"I've got choice." Her voice was defiant.

"Then why don't we sail *Sycorax* out on Sunday." On Sunday Bannister would still be in France, even though *Wildtrack* had sailed for home three weeks before. "You come with me," I said. "We'll be in the Azores in a few days. After that we can make up our minds. You want to see Australia again? You fancy exploring the Caribbean?"

She twisted her long hair into a hank that she laid up on her skull. "I get sea-sick."

"You'll get over it in three days."

"I never get over it." She was staring into the mirror as she pinned up her hair. "I'm not a sailor, Nick."

"People do get over it," I said. "It takes time, but I promise it doesn't last."

"Nick!" I was pressing her too hard.

"I'm sorry."

She stared at herself in the mirror. "Do you think I haven't been tempted to get away from it all? No more of Tony's insecurity, no more jealousy at work, no more sodding around with schedules and film stocks and worrying where the next good idea for a programme will come from? But I can't do that, Nick, I can't! If I was twenty years old I might do it. Isn't that the age when people think the world will lap them in love and all they need do is show a little faith in it? But I'm too old now."

"Twenty-six is not old."

"It's too old to become a hippy."

"I'm not a hippy."

"What the hell else are you?" She shook a cigarette from its packet and lit it. "You think you're going to drift around the world like a gypsy. Who's going to pay you? What will you do when your leg collapses? What about your old age? It's all right for you, Nick, you don't seem to care. You think that it really will be all right, but I'm not like you."

"You want to be safe."

"Is that so bad?" she said belligerently.

"No. It's just that I'm in love with you, and I don't want to lose you."

She stared at me. "Get a job, live in Devon. Can't you parlay that medal into a job?"

"Maybe."

She grimaced and stubbed out the cigarette she'd only just lit. She stood, walked round the bed, and dropped her bathrobe on to the floor. She stood naked, looking down on me. "Let's make the film first, Nick, then worry about life?"

I threw back the bedclothes for her. "OK, boss."

She climbed in beside me. "You'll stay tomorrow?"

Tomorrow was Friday. "How about the whole weekend?"

"You know I can't." Bannister wanted her to go to France for the weekend. After *Wildtrack*'s successful series of races he had moved to the Riviera where he had been a judge at a television festival. That work was now completed and he wanted Angela to fly down for the festival's closing celebrations. The plan was that she would fly to Nice on Friday evening, then return with Bannister on Monday morning and drive down to Devon that same afternoon. We thus both sensed that this might be our last night of stolen freedom, for the old constraints would come back with Bannister's return.

Angela left early next morning, going to the studios where she was rough-cutting the film that had been shot so far. I made myself coffee in her tiny kitchen, bathed in her tiny bathroom, then sat and made a list of the charts I wanted to buy. The list was very long, but the money was typically short so I cut the list down to the Azores and the Caribbean. Every fare to London denied *Sycorax* another clutch of charts, but I didn't think *Sycorax* would deny me these visits. I looked at Angela's few belongings; the untidy papers left over from the research of past programmes, a pretty watercolour on her wall, the old and decrepit teddy-bear that was the one thing she had brought from her childhood home.

The phone rang. I did not move. The telephone was connected to an answering machine and, when I was in the flat, I left the machine's speaker turned up. If it was Angela calling me then I would hear her voice and know to pick up the telephone and switch off the machine. I hated the process, which struck me as a typical shift of adultery, but it was necessary. Sometimes Bannister called and I would listen to his peremptory voice delivering a curt message and the jealousy would spark in me.

This time I heard the usual tape of Angela's voice apologizing that she could not answer the phone in person. Please speak after the tone, she said, and the tone dutifully blipped. There was a pause, and I thought the caller must have hung up, but then another familiar voice sounded. "Hi. You don't know me. My name's Jill-Beth Kirov. We met at Anthony Bannister's house, remember? I'm kind of looking for Nick Sandman and I gathered you were filming him, and I wonder if you'd pass on a message to him? My number is – "

She broke off because I had switched off the answering machine and lifted the telephone. "Jill-Beth?"

"Nick! Hi!"

I was angry. "How the hell did you know I was here?"

"What's the drama, Nick?" She sounded pained. "I was just trying to reach you. I didn't know where you were. I was just going to leave messages everywhere. I need to talk with you, OK?"

For a second I forgot my careful arrangements with Micky Harding. "I don't think we've got anything to say to each other."

She paused. "You want to play hardball or softball, Nick?"

"I'm sorry?" I said, not understanding.

She sighed. "I once had to investigate a guy who had a boat pretty much like yours, Nick. His was a yawl, but it was really cute. He even had a figurehead, a mermaid with his wife's face. He was real proud of that boat. It burned. It was a real tragedy. I mean the guy had put his life into that yawl, and one careless cigarette end and suddenly it's the Fourth of July fireworks show."

"Are you threatening me?"

"Nick!" She sounded very hurt. "I just want to talk with you, OK? What's the harm in that?"

I remembered Micky Harding and his promise that the newspaper could ease me off Kassouli's hook. "All right." I spoke guardedly.

She suggested this very lunchtime and named a pub in Soho, but I didn't know if I could find Micky that quickly. I didn't even know if I could find him at all during the weekend. "I can't meet till Monday," I said, "and that's the earliest, and I'll be back in Devon by then."

She paused, then sounded warily accepting. "OK, Nick." She named a pub that I knew and a time.

I put the phone down. It seemed that Yassir Kassouli had not given up his pursuit of Bannister. The hounds of revenge were slipped and running, and I now had to head them into the light where they would be dazzled and confused by publicity. I telephoned Micky's paper and tracked him down to the newsroom. I told him where and when I was supposed to meet Jill-Beth. "Can you make it?" I asked.

"I'll make it." I heard anticipation in his voice. He was already relishing the headlines: "Tycoon Plots Piracy!", "Yank Billionaire Threatens UK Jobs," or, more likely from Micky's newspaper, "Piss Off Kassouli!"

Angela came home irritated because a film editor had taken off sick and she had needed him to cut a particular sequence and the replacement film editor was, she said, a butcher. She played the message tape on the phone. I'd rewound the spool after Jill-Beth's call and the American girl's voice had been overlaid with an invitation for lunch, a message about flights to Nice, and a call from an old acquaintance of Angela's who just wanted to say hello.

"What she wants is a job," Angela said scathingly. "What kind of a day did you have?"

"I bought two charts," I said, "and discovered a million things I can't afford."

"Poor Nick." She reached out a long thin hand and touched my cheek. "A friend has said I could borrow a cottage in Norfolk this weekend. There's no phone there, and he's got a dinghy in the creek. A Heron dinghy? Does that makes sense?"

"A Heron makes much sense." My joy at having Angela to myself all the weekend must have shown, but I still wanted to make certain of it. "And Nice?"

"Bugger Nice. I'll tell Tony I'm too busy."

So we buggered Nice, and I did not tell Angela about Jill-Beth's call. I wanted to, but I didn't know how to explain why I was meeting the American, nor did I care to say that I was only doing it because Micky would be there. Angela would have bridled at the thought of the bad publicity that would be flung at Bannister, and anyway I told myself I was only meeting Jill-Beth to end Kassouli's interference. I thought I was taking care of the matter and I did not need Angela's help, so I felt rather noble about it, and not in the least guilty, because, all things considered, and come Monday evening, Yassir Kassouli, just like Nice, would be buggered.

Micky Harding and I drove down to Devon on the Monday afternoon. I was nervous. "We're taking on one of the richest men in the world, Micky. They threatened my bloody boat!"

"Ah." Micky made the soothing noise sarcastically. "What we're going to do, Nick, is screw the bastard." He glanced at me as I twisted awkwardly to look through the back window. "You think we're being followed?"

"No." Instead I had been looking for Angela's Porsche. She had gone to meet Bannister at Heathrow and, if they left directly for Devon, they could well overtake us on the road. I did not want to see them together. I was jealous. I'd just spent a weekend of gentle happiness with a small sailing boat and with Angela to myself. She had not even been sea-sick. But now, with the horrid crunch of a boat going aground, the real world was impinging on me.

Micky lit a cigarette. "You are bleeding nervous, mate, that's what you are. I could do a story on that. VC revealed as a wimp."

"I'm not used to this sort of thing."

"Which is why you called in the reinforcements?"

"Exactly."

The 'reinforcements' were waiting for us at a service area where the cafeteria offered an all-day breakfast and where Terry Farebrother was mopping up the remains of fried egg and brown sauce with a piece of white bread. I've never known a man eat so much as Sergeant Terry Farebrother; he wasn't so much a human being as a cholesterol processor. Morning, noon and night he ate, and he never seemed to put an inch of fat on his stocky, hard body. The one thing he'd hated about the Falklands was the uncertainty of meal times and I'd once watched him pick his way into an Argentinian minefield to salvage an enemy pack on the off chance that it might have contained a tin of corned beef. His moustached face was impassive as the two of us approached his table. "Bloody hell," he greeted Micky Harding. "It's the Mouse."

The Mouse, who had known the Yorkshire sergeant in the

Falklands, shook Terry's hand. "You don't improve with time, do you?"

"I'm just waiting till the Army takes over this country, Mouse, then I'm going to Fleet Street to beat up all the fucking fairies."

"Not a chance," Micky said. "We've got dolly-bird secretaries who'd crucify you pansies."

Insults thus dutifully exchanged, Terry nodded a greeting to me and wondered aloud whether there was time to eat another plate of fried grease, but I said we should be moving on. "Shall I buy you a cheese sandwich?" I asked.

"Cheese gives me the wind something rotten. I'll have a couple of bacon ones instead." He half crushed my fingers with his handshake. "You're looking better, boss. Sally said you looked like something the cat threw up."

"How is Sally?"

"Same as ever, boss, same as ever. Bloody horrible." Terry was in his civvies; a threadbare blue suit that was buttoned tight round his chest. He'd probably bought the suit the year before he entered the Army as a junior soldier and had never replaced it. He did not really need to, for Terry was one of those men who only look at home in camouflage or battledress. He was a bullock of a man; short, stubborn and utterly dependable. It was good to see him again. "No trouble," he said when I asked if he'd had difficulties in getting away from the battalion. "They owed me leave after the bleeding exercise."

"How was the exercise?"

"Same as ever, boss; a bloody cock-up. Got fucking soaked in a turnip field and then half sodding drowned in a river. And, of course, none of the bleeding officers knew where we were or what we were bloody doing. I tell you, mate" – this was to Micky – "if the Russkies ever do come, they'll fuck through us like a red hot poker going up a pullet's arse."

"It's not surprising, is it?" Micky asked, "when most of our soldiers are as delicate and fastidious as your good self?"

"There is that," Terry laughed. "So what are we doing?"

"Nick's nervous," Micky said dismissively as we walked to the car.

I told Terry that I was indeed nervous, that I was meeting this American girl, and it was just possible, but extremely unlikely, that she might threaten my boat if I didn't agree to do whatever she wanted, and so I would appreciate it if Terry sat on *Sycorax* until Micky and I got back to the river.

"Nothing's going to happen." Micky accelerated back on to the motorway. "You just get to sit on a bloody boat while it gets dark outside."

Terry, eating the first of his cold bacon sandwiches, ignored Micky. "So what will these buggers do? If they do anything?"

"Fire," I said. Jill-Beth had hinted at arson, and it frightened me. A hank of rags, soaked in petrol and tossed into the cockpit, would reduce *Sycorax* to floating ash in minutes. If I turned Jill-Beth's proposal down, which I planned to do, *Sycorax* would be vulnerable, and never more so than in the hour it would take me to get back from our rendezvous to the river. That fear presupposed that Jill-Beth had already stationed men near the river; men whom she could alert by telephone. The whole scheme seemed very elaborate and fanciful now, but the fear had seemed very real as I had brooded on it during the weekend. Yassir Kassouli was a determined man, and a bitter one, and the fate of one small boat on a Devon river would be nothing to such a man. The fear had prompted me to phone the Sergeants' Mess from the public phone in the Norfolk village. I'd left a message and Terry had phoned back an hour later. I'd told Angela I'd been talking to Jimmy Nicholls about anchor chains and, though I had hated telling her lies, they seemed preferable to explaining the complicated truth. Now, with Terry's comforting solidity on my side, I wondered if I had over-reacted. "I don't think anything will happen, Terry," I confessed, "but I'm a bit nervous."

"End of problem, boss. I'm here." Terry slumped in the back seat and unwrapped another sandwich.

We reached the river two hours later and, as Micky waited on the road above Bannister's house, I took Terry down through the woods and behind the boathouse to *Sycorax*. I saw two of Mulder's crewmen preparing *Wildtrack II* in the boathouse, ready for tomorrow's outing when she would be the camera platform for *Sycorax*'s maiden trip. I assumed, from their presence, that Mulder must have returned from his victorious Mediterranean foray, but I did not ask. I looked up at the house, but could see no one moving in the windows. I thought of Bannister sleeping with Angela tonight and an excruciating bite of jealousy gnawed at me.

The tide was low. Terry and I climbed down to *Sycorax*'s deck and I unlocked the cabin. I did not tell him about the hidden Colt, for I didn't want his career ruined by an unlicensed firearm's charge.

"Any food, boss?" he asked hopefully.

"There's some digestive biscuits in the drawer by the sink, apples in the upper locker and beer under the port bunk."

"Bloody hell." He looked disgusted at the choice of food.

"And you might need these." I dropped the two fire-extinguishers on the newly built chart table. *Sycorax* might lack a radio, pump, anchors, log, chronometer, compass, loo and a barometer, but I'd taken good care to buy fire-extinguishers. She was a wooden boat and her greatest enemy was not the sea but fire. "And if anyone asks you what you're doing here, Terry, tell them you're a mate of mine."

"I'll tell them to fuck off, boss."

"I should be back by nine," I said, "and we'll go over the river for a pint."

"And a baby's head?" he asked hopefully.

"They do a very good steak and kidney pudding," I confirmed. If there was one certainty about this evening now, it was that *Sycorax* was safe. Kassouli would need an Exocet to take out Terry Farebrother, and even then I wasn't sure the Exocet would win.

I limped back up through the woods and got into Micky's car. We went north, threading the maze of deep lanes that led to Dartmoor. I was silent, wondering just what we had got ourselves into, while Micky was ebullient, scenting a story that would splash itself across the headlines of two nations.

We climbed up to the moor. Low dark cloud was threatening from the west and I knew there would be lashing rain before the evening was done. We left the hedgerows behind, emerging on to the bare bleak upland where the wind sighed about the granite tors. We were over an hour early reaching the village pub in the moor's centre where Jill-Beth had said she would meet me. Micky took me into the pub's toilet where he fitted me with the radio-microphone. It was a small enough gadget. A plastic-coated wire aerial hung down one trouser leg, a small box the size of a pocket calculator was taped to the small of my back, and the tiny microphone was pinned under my shirt. "I'm going back to the bar," Micky said, "so they don't think we're a couple of fruits, and you're going to speak to me." He had the receiver, together with a tape-recorder, in a big bag. To hear what was being recorded he wore a thin wire which led to a hearing-aid.

The device worked. After the test we sat at a table and Micky gave me instructions. The transmitter was feeble and if I went more than fifty yards away from him he'd likely lose the signal. He said the microphone was undirectional and would pick up every sound nearby so I should try and lean as close to Jill-Beth as I could. "You won't mind that, will you?" Micky said. "You fancy her, right?"

"I used to."

"Fancy her again. Get in close, Nick. And keep an eye on me. If I can't hear what she's saying I'll scratch my nose."

"Is this how we trap one of the world's richest men?" I asked. "With nose-scratching and toy radios?"

"Remember Watergate. It all spilt out because some CIA-trained prick couldn't tape up a door latch. You are suffering from the delusion that the world is run by efficient men. It isn't, Nick. It's run by constipated morons who couldn't remember their own names if it wasn't printed on their credit cards. Now, what are you going to say to her?"

"I'm going to tell her to get lost."

"Nick! Nick! Nick!" he groaned. "If you tell the birdie to fuck off, she will. She'll do a bunk and what will we have? Sweet FA, that's what we'll have. You have to chat her up! You have to go along with her, right? You've got to say all the things she wants you to say, so that she says all the things we want her to say. Especially, my son, you have to ask her just what Kassouli plans to do out there. Is he trying to knock Bannister off? Or is he just trying to scare the bastard? Got it?"

"Got it," I said. "What about the money?"

Micky closed his eyes in mock despair. "God, you're a berk, Nick. You take the ruddy money! It's proof!" He drained his whisky. "Are you ready for battle, my son?"

"I'm ready."

"To war, then. And stop worrying. Nothing can go wrong." He finished my whisky then took himself across the bar. I waited nervously. The pub slowly filled, mostly with hikers who shook water from their bright capes as they came through the door. It had begun to rain, though not heavily.

I switched from whisky to beer. I did not want to fuddle my wits, not with so much at stake. If I was successful this evening I would stop an obsessed millionaire from pulling thousands of jobs out of Britain. I would start a scandal in the newspapers. I would also drive Angela away from me, because I knew she would never forgive me for bringing Bannister's name into the story. I had so often, and often unjustly, accused her of dishonesty, now she would say that I had been dishonest. She would say that I should have told her everything, and perhaps she was right.

But I was going to sea anyway, and that always meant an abandonment of loves left behind. I would render Kassouli's threats impotent, then I would leave Bannister to make his attempt on the St Pierre and Angela to her ambitions. After tonight I would be free, and *Sycorax* and I would go to where the wind willed us.

I waited.

"Hi!" After Angela's slender paleness, Jill-Beth looked tanned and healthy; a glowing tribute to vitamin tablets, exercise and native enthusiasm. I wondered why Americans were so often enthusiastic while we were so often drab. She was wearing a blue shirt, tight jeans and cowboy boots, as if she had expected a rodeo. She carried a raincoat and a handbag over her arm. She stooped to offer me a kiss, then sensed from my reaction that such a gesture was inappropriate. Instead she sat next to me. "How are you?" she asked. Her back was towards Micky who offered me a surreptitious thumbs-up to indicate that he could hear her through the concealed microphone.

"You'd like a beer?" I asked.

She shook her head. "How about going for a walk?"

"In this?" I gestured at the rain that was now blurring the window panes.

"I thought you were a soldier! Are you frightened of rain?"

I was frightened of getting out of range of Micky's radio, but Jill-Beth would not take a refusal, so I followed her on to the road where she pulled on the raincoat and tied a scarf over her hair. "Yassir says hi."

"Great."

She seemed not to notice my lack of enthusiasm; instead she opened the handbag and showed its contents to me. "One hundred thousand dollars, Nick. Tax-free."

I stared at the tightly wadded notes, each wad bound in cellophane. I'd never seen so much money in my life, but it didn't seem real. I tried to look impressed, but in truth I found the situation ludicrous. Did Jill-Beth really believe I could be bought?

"It's all yours." She closed the bag. The rain was getting harder, but she seemed not to notice it as we crossed the bridge and headed towards Bellever Forest. I dared not look behind in case Jill-Beth also turned and saw Micky Harding's ungainly figure following us. My jacket was getting soaked and I hoped the microphone was not affected by damp. "Do we really have to walk in this muck?" I asked.

"We really do." She said it very casually, then frowned with a sudden and genuine concern. "Are you hurting? Is that it?"

"A wee bit."

She shrugged and took my arm, as though to help me walk. "I'm sorry, but I just couldn't abide all that cigarette smoke in the pub." She glanced up at the sky which was threatening an even heavier downpour. "Perhaps we'd better get into cover?" She led me into the pines of Bellever. The rain was too new to have dripped through the thick cover of needles and we walked in comparative dryness. I once heard a footfall behind us and knew that Micky had kept up. He'd be silently cursing me for dragging him out of the pub, but his sacrifice was small in comparison to the rewards that this evening would give him.

Jill-Beth let go of my arm and leaned against a tree trunk. For a moment neither of us spoke. I was awkward, and her self-assurance seemed strained. She offered me a quick smile. "It's nice to see you again, Nick."

"Is it?"

"You're being hostile."

She pronounced the word as 'hostel', and sounded so hurt that I could not resist smiling. "I'm not being hostile, it's just that my back's hurting."

"You should see a doctor."

"I did. She couldn't help."

"Then see an American doctor."

"I can't afford that."

"They are expensive bastards," she admitted.

We were both being wary, and I supposed that if I really was being 'hostel' then I was risking all the hard work that Micky had put into this meeting. I was here to convince this girl that I would help her, however reluctantly, and so I forced another smile. "Are you here to get me wet, or rich?"

She smiled back. "Does that mean you're going to help us, Nick?"

I was hopeless at telling lies, and did not think that an outright statement of compliance would be convincing. I shrugged, then began pacing beneath the trees as I spoke. "I don't know, Jill-Beth. I just don't share your conviction that Bannister's guilty. That worries me. I don't like him, but I'm not sure that's sufficient grounds for ruining his chances of the St Pierre." I was making noises to cover my nervousness, then I realized that by pacing up and down I was constantly turning the microphone away from Jill-Beth. Not that she was saying much, except the odd acknowledgement, but I stopped and faced her.

She sighed, as though exasperated by my havering. "All you have to do, Nick, is sail on Bannister's boat. You agree to do that, and you get one hundred thousand dollars now, and another three hundred thousand when it's over."

"I've already told him I won't sail," I said, as though it was an insuperable barrier to her ambitions.

She shrugged. "Would he believe you if you changed your mind?" It was very silent under the trees; the wind was muffled and the dead needles acted as insulation. It made our voices seem unnaturally loud.

"He'd believe me," I said reluctantly.

"So tell him."

"And if I don't do it – " I was trying not to make my voice stilted, even though I was stating the obvious " – Kassouli will pull all his jobs out of Britain?"

She smiled. "You've got it. But not just his jobs, Nick. He'll pull out his investments, and he'll move his operations to the Continent. And a slew of British firms can kiss their hopes of new contracts on American projects goodbye. It'll be tough, Nick, but you've met him. He's a determined guy. Kassouli doesn't care if he goes down for a few millions, he can spare them."

I paused. It seemed to me that Micky must have struck his pure gold for, in a few sentences, Jill-Beth had described Kassouli's threat and, with any luck, all that damning evidence must be spooling silently on to the take-up reel of Micky's recorder. All I had to do now was cross the Ts and dot the Is. "And Kassouli won't do that if I sail on *Wildtrack*?"

"Right." She said it encouragingly, as though I was a slightly dumb pupil who needed to be chivvied into achievement. "Because we need your help, Nick! You're our one chance. Persuade Bannister to take you as *Wildtrack*'s navigator, and count your money!"

It seemed odd to me that Yassir Kassouli, with all his millions, could only rely on me, but perhaps Jill-Beth was right. My arrival at Bannister's house must have seemed fortuitous, so perhaps that explained her eagerness. I was a very convenient weapon to Bannister's enemies, if I chose to be so. "And exactly what do I have to do?" I wanted her to spell it out for the microphone.

She showed no impatience at the pedantic question. "You just navigate a course that we'll provide you."

"What course?"

"Jesus! How do we know? That'll depend on the weather, right? All you have to do is keep a radio watch at the times we tell you, and that's it. The easiest four hundred thousand you ever earned, right?"

I smiled. "Right." That word, with its inflection of compliance, had been hard to say, yet I seemed to be convincing Jill-Beth with my act. And it was an act, a very amateur piece of acting in which I was struggling to invest each utterance with naturalness so that, consequently, my words sounded heavy and contrived. Yet, it occurred to me as I tried to seek my next line, Jill-Beth herself was just as mannered and awkward. I should have noted that with more interest, but instead I asked her what would happen when I had navigated *Wildtrack* to wherever I was supposed to take her.

"Nothing happens to you. Nothing happens to the crew."

"But what happens to Bannister?"

"Whatever Yassir wants." She said it slowly, almost as a challenge, then watched for my reaction.

I was silent for a few seconds. Jill-Beth's words could be taken as an elliptical hint of murder, but I doubted whether she would be more explicit. I think she expected me to bridle at the hint, but instead I shrugged as though the machinations of Kassouli's revenge were beyond me. "And all this," I asked with what I thought was a convincing tone of reluctant agreement, "on the assumption that Bannister murdered his wife?"

"You got it, Nick. You want the hundred thousand now?"

I should have said yes. I should have accepted it, but I baulked at the gesture. It might have been a necessary deception, but the entrapment was distasteful.

"For Christ's sake, Nick! Are you going to help us or not?" Jill-Beth thrust the handbag towards me. "You want it? Or are you just wasting my time?"

I was about to accept, knowing the money was the final proof that Micky needed, when a strangled shout startled me. It was a man's cry, full of pain.

I turned, but instantly, and treacherously, my right leg numbed and collapsed. I fell and Jill-Beth ran past me. I cursed my leg, knelt up, and forced myself to stand. I used my hands to straighten my right leg, then, half limping and half hopping, staggered on from tree to tree. I wondered whether my leg would always collapse at moments of stress.

I found Jill-Beth twenty yards further on, stooping, and I already knew what it was she crouched beside.

It was Micky. There was fresh vivid blood on his scalp, on his wet shirt, and on his hands. He was alive, but unconscious and breathing very shallowly. He was badly hurt. The bag lay spilt beside him and I saw the radio receiver but no sign of the small tape-recorder. Whoever had hit Micky had also stolen the evidence.

"Did you bring him?" Jill-Beth looked at me accusingly.

"Get an ambulance." I snapped it like a military order.

"Did you bring – "

"Run! Dial 999. Hurry!" She would be twice as fast as I could be. "And bring blankets from the pub!"

She ran. I knelt beside Micky and draped my jacket over him. I tore a strip of cotton from my shirt-tail and padded it to staunch the blood that flowed from his scalp. Head wounds always bleed badly, but I feared this was more than a cut. He'd been hit with too much power, and I suspected a fractured skull. Blood had soaked into the dry brown needles that now looked black in the encroaching and damp twilight. I stroked his hand for, though he was unconscious, he would need the feel of human warmth and comfort.

I felt sick. I'd guarded *Sycorax* against Kassouli, but I had not thought to guard Micky. So who had done this? Kassouli? Had Jill-Beth brought reinforcements? Had she suspected that I might try to blow Kassouli's scheme wide open? Those questions made me wonder whether she would phone an ambulance and, leaving Micky for a few seconds, I struggled to the edge of the trees and stared towards the village. My right leg was shaking and there was a vicious pulsing pain in my spine. I wasn't sure I could limp all the way to the village, but if Jill-Beth let me down then I would have to try.

I cursed my leg, massaged it, then, as I straightened up, I saw headlights silhouetting running figures at the bridge. I limped back to Micky. He was still breathing, grunting slightly.

Footsteps trampled into the trees. Efficient men and women, trained to rescuing lost hikers from the moors, came to Micky's rescue. There was no need to wait for an ambulance for there was a Rescue Land-Rover nearby which could take him to hospital. He was carefully lifted on to a stretcher, wrapped in a space blanket, and given a saline drip.

I limped beside him to the Land-Rover and watched it pull away towards the road. Someone had phoned the police and now asked me if I'd wait for their arrival. I said I wanted to go to the hospital, then remembered that Micky still had the car keys.

"I'll drive you," Jill-Beth said.

I hesitated.

"For Christ's sake, Nick!" She was angry that I did not trust her. She held out her car keys. "Do you want to take my car?"

I let her drive me. "Who is he?" she asked.

"A newspaper reporter."

"You're a fool," she said scornfully.

"Not me!" I snapped. "You're the bloody fool! Just because Kassouli's rich doesn't mean that he's right!"

"His daughter was murdered!"

"And who did that to Micky?" I waved towards the Land-Rover which was a mile ahead of us on the road. "You brought your thugs along, didn't you?"

"No!" she protested.

"Then who, for Christ's sake?"

She thought about it for a few seconds. "Did you drive straight here from London?"

"No. I went . . ." I paused. I'd gone to Bannister's house and seen evidence that Fanny Mulder was there. I hadn't thought, not once, to check that anyone had followed Micky and I to the moor. "Oh, Jesus," I said hopelessly. "Mulder."

Jill-Beth shrugged, as if to say that I'd fetched this disaster on myself. We drove in silence until we reached the hospital where the Land-Rover was standing at the entrance to the casualty department. An empty police car, its blue light still flashing, was parked in front of it.

Jill-Beth killed her engine. "I guess this means you're not going to help us, Nick?"

"I won't be the hangman for a kangaroo trial."

"You don't want the money?" she asked.

"No."

Jill-Beth shrugged. "It wasn't meant to be this way, Nick."

"What wasn't?"

"Americans against the Brits. Truly it wasn't. Kassouli believes his daughter was murdered. If you shared that belief you'd be helping us."

I opened the car door. "It isn't America against us," I said; "it's just a conflict of old-fashioned honesty, that's all. You don't have proof. You don't have anything but suspicion. You're playing games to make a rich man happy, and if he was a poor man you wouldn't be doing it at all."

She watched me get out of the car. "Goodbye, Nick."

I didn't reply. She started the motor, put it in gear and drove away.

The hospital smelt of disinfectant. It brought back memories I didn't want. I waited beneath posters which told me to have my baby vaccinated and that VD was a contagious disease. I waited for news that, at last, was brought to me by a very young detective constable. Mr Harding had a fractured skull and three broken ribs. He was unconscious. Why had I come to the hospital and asked after him? Because he was a friend of mine.

Had I seen the accident? No.

Was I aware that Mr Harding was a newspaper reporter? Yes.

Was I a newspaper reporter? No.

Had we gone to the moor together? Yes.

Why had I not seen the incident? Because I'd gone into the trees for a piss.

Did I know who had assaulted Mr Harding? No. Privately I was certain it was Mulder, but I could not prove it, so I repeated my denial.

How had I reached the hospital? In a friend's car.

Who was the friend? No one who mattered.

Would I go to the police station and give a statement? No, I would not.

I refused because it would be so utterly hopeless to explain. I was to accuse one of the world's richest men of threatening economic blackmail against Britain? I felt suddenly tired. And scared. Mulder, if he had the tape, would already be on his way back to Bannister. I needed to reach the river and stop Terry Farebrother murdering Mulder, because Mulder, as likely as not, would look for me on *Sycorax*. The last thing I needed to do now was sit in a police station and spin a tale that would most likely land me in the nearest mental hospital. "Mister Harding's just an old friend," I told the policeman. "We went to the moor for a walk, nothing more."

"In the rain?"

"In the rain."

The policeman, professionally suspicious, looked at me with distaste. "Very close friends, you and him?"

"Fuck off, sonny boy."

He closed his notebook. "I think you're coming to the station whether you want to or not."

"No," I said. "I'm going home. And what you're going to do is telephone Inspector Harry Abbott. You know him? Tell him I need a lift home bloody fast. Tell him the Boer War has broken out. So open your book and write down my name. Captain Nicholas Sandman. And remember the bit about the Boer War. Do it!" I snapped the last two words as if I was back in the battalion.

The policeman had read too many thrillers. "Is this special business, sir?" He stressed the word 'special'.

"It isn't your business. Phone him. Now."

I knew Abbott would give me hell when he got the chance, but he came through like a trooper on the night. I got my lift home. I told the copper to stop the car at the top of the hill and that I'd walk the rest of the way.

I was scared. Mulder was on the warpath, and didn't know just what an evil-minded bastard was minding the boat. Micky

Harding was unconscious. I wasn't sure how, but I'd screwed up.

Things had gone wrong.

I stopped halfway down the wooded slope. The tide was rising in the river. The rain was lessening now, but it was still driven by a brisk westerly wind that shook the branches above my head. I was soaked to the skin. There were lights in Bannister's house, but none down by the boathouse or near my wharf.

I went like a wraith down that slope. It was hard, for I was out of practice and my limp made me awkward, but I went as though I was on night patrol and a trigger-happy bastard with a full magazine waited for me. I stared for a long time at the shadows behind the boathouse. Nothing moved there, and nothing moved when I flicked a piece of earth into the rhododendrons to stir a hidden watcher's attention.

I crept down the last stretch of the hill and hid myself in the boathouse shadows. "Terry?"

"Been listening to you for the last ten minutes, boss. Bleeding noisy, aren't you?"

Relief flooded me. "Any trouble?"

"Not a bloody flicker. How did you get on?"

"Bloody disaster. Mouse got stitched up. We should have had you there, not here." I climbed down on to *Sycorax*'s deck. "Poor bugger's in hospital. Lost the bloody tape, too. Anything happened here?"

"One car arrived ten minutes after you'd gone. Another came an hour ago."

The first car would have been Bannister and Angela, the second Mulder. I suspected Mulder was in the house now with Micky's tape. He was telling Bannister and Angela that I'd met Jill-Beth Kirov on the moor. The implication was that I had been plotting against Bannister all along. The tape would bear that interpretation, too, but it was also possible that it would serve to warn Bannister of the real dangers of attempting the St Pierre. At this moment, though, I cared more about what Angela might be thinking of me. I stared up the slope to where a dark figure flitted across a lit window of the house. "I'm going up there," I said to Terry.

"Want me?"

"Yes, but keep out of sight."

I was going to the house because I could not let Angela think that I had betrayed her. I wanted her to know what had happened, and why I had met Jill-Beth. I would explain everything, not only to her, but to Bannister as well. Things had become muddled, but now was the time to let truth untangle the mess. That's the advantage of truth; it cuts through all the deception and muddle. I like truth.

Terry and I climbed the steep lawn and went on to the wide terrace. Terry whistled softly when he saw the luxury through the big windows. "Bleeding hell, boss. She's tasty."

The tasty one was Angela, who looked expensive and beautiful in black trousers and a lilac shirt. She was sitting, head bowed, apparently listening, and I could see the spools of a big tape-recorder revolving. The machine was part of the bank of electronic gadgets that decorated one end of the room. Bannister stood behind Angela's chair while Mulder and two of his crewmen stood respectfully to one side.

"Stay hidden, Terry," I said.

The sliding doors were not locked and everyone in the room jumped as I pulled one of the great glass panes aside. I heard my own voice coming from the tape-recorder, then Angela leaned forward and used the remote control to switch it off.

They all stared at me and I had the ridiculous notion that this was a scene out of a detective play when, at the end of the last act, everyone is gathered in the drawing-room to hear the culprit revealed. They seemed frozen by my appearance, as if caught in a flash photograph, then the tableau broke as Mulder moved towards me.

"Leave him!" Bannister's sudden command stopped Mulder, who contented himself with a threatening and derisive stare. Bannister shuddered as though he found it hard to even speak to me. "What the hell are you doing here?"

"I came here to explain." Rainwater dripped from my clothes on to the expensive carpet.

"You hardly need to explain." Bannister clicked his fingers at Angela. "Rewind it, then play it to Captain Sandman." He paused, then added with withering scorn, "VC."

"I know what's on the tape . . ." I began.

"Shut up!" Bannister shouted the command. Whatever courage he had lacked in the past was evident now; stung into the light by what he had heard on the tape.

But if Bannister was showing a new side to his character, Angela's demeanour was as it used to be before the rainy day when we had come together in this same room. Her face was a cold, pale mask of dislike. I caught her eyes once and there was not even a flicker of recognition in them. She leaned forward and I listened to the scribbling squall of a tape going backwards, there was a click, then Jill-Beth's eager, friendly, American voice filled the room. "Because we need your help, Nick! You're our one chance. Persuade Bannister to take you as *Wildtrack*'s navigator, and count your money!"

"And exactly what do I have to do?" My voice was much louder than Jill-Beth's, but the microphone had worked only too well and her words were quite distinct.

"You just navigate a course that we'll provide you."

"What course?"

"Jesus! How do we know? That'll depend on the weather, right? All you have to do is keep a radio watch at the times we tell you, and that's it. The easiest four hundred thousand you ever earned, right?"

"Right." There was a pause before my voice sounded again. "And what happens when we reach wherever it is that we're going?"

"Nothing happens to you. Nothing happens to the crew."

"But what happens to Bannister?"

"Whatever Yassir wants."

"And all this on the assumption that Bannister murdered his wife?"

"You got it, Nick. You want the hundred thousand now?" Jill-Beth's voice sounded eager; then there was nothing but the magnetic hiss of empty tape.

Angela leaned forward, turned off the tape-recorder, and

stood up. "You bastard!" She turned away from me and stalked out of the room.

"It isn't . . ." I had been going to say that the truth was not what they had heard on the tape, but Bannister, goaded to fury by hearing the damning evidence once more, shouted that I was to be quiet. Mulder took one threatening step forward and rubbed his hands in gleeful anticipation. His two crewmen looked nervous, but willing. Bannister flinched as the door slammed behind Angela, then repeated her insult. "You bastard."

"I turned the offer down," I said. "I only wanted to hear what they planned to do."

"You expect me to believe that?"

"Don't be such a bloody idiot!" I snapped back. "Ask the police about a poor bastard called Micky Harding who's unconscious in hospital right now! He's a newspaper reporter."

"He's lying," Mulder said laconically.

"And how the hell did you get that tape?" I demanded.

"I followed you," Mulder said coldly.

"Why?" I demanded. Mulder did not answer, and I pressed on in the belief that I had regained some of the initiative. "And why, for Christ's sake, would I be wired for sound? Why in hell's name would I risk doing that if I was on their side?"

"To make sure they wouldn't double-cross you, of course." Mulder's staccato voice was bleak.

"Micky Harding's a newspaper reporter," I said to Bannister, "and your thug beat him half dead." It was clear from Bannister's face that I was wasting my words. He was a media man, and for him a tape could not tell a lie. His world lay on tape and film, and my betrayal was proven by the magnetic ribbon. He stood between me and the tape-recorder as though he feared I might try and snatch the damning spool. "I'm through with you, Sandman."

"You know Harry Abbott," I said to him. "Phone him up! Ask him!"

Mulder moved so that he stood between Bannister and myself. "Why did you go to America?" Mulder challenged me.

I was surprised by the question and I hesitated. I'd told Angela the truth, but no one else.

My hesitation looked like guilt, and Mulder mocked it with a smile. "You said your mother was dying. So what about this, liar?" He reached into his jacket pocket and took out a folded glossy newspaper that he tossed on to the carpet by my feet. "Front page, liar."

It was an in-house news-sheet from Kassouli Enterprises, Inc. of New York, and on the front page, ringed in damning red ink, was the photograph of Jill-Beth and I which had been taken in Kassouli's Cape Cod garden. At the time I'd told the photographer I was nobody, just John Brown, but the caption said that Miss Jill-Beth Kirov, daughter of Rear-Admiral Oscar Kirov, USN, had been squired to a reception at Mr Yassir Kassouli's summer residence by Captain Nicholas Sandman, VC.

"Well?" Mulder's voice reeked of victory.

"Who the hell sent this to you?"

"What does that matter? They sent two." He took another copy of the news-sheet from his pocket and gave it to Bannister.

Bannister read it. I was at sea suddenly, my reasons swamped by this sudden twist. Mulder, in total control, stepped towards me. "You've done nothing but lie. You saved the American girl that night and you've been playing her game ever since. What else have you done, Sandman? Filed down a turnbuckle? Cut some warps? I think you just lost yourself a boat, Sandman. How else is Mister Bannister to recoup his losses?"

Bannister looked up from the paper. "What were you planning to do? Kill us all at sea?"

"I was trying to save your miserable life!" I shouted past Mulder's hulking figure.

"And where's the hundred thousand?" Mulder demanded.

"There isn't any money! I turned them down."

"You pathetic little bastard." Mulder was triumphant in his victory. "You scummy cripple. The money's on your boat, isn't it?"

"Get stuffed." It was a feeble response. I tried to think of an argument that might convince Bannister of my honesty, but the evidence against me was too overwhelming.

"You want me to get the money?" Mulder asked Bannister.

"There isn't any, you fool!" I backed towards the window.

"Stop him, Fanny!" Bannister said. "Then search his damned boat."

Fanny lunged towards me, and I twisted aside. "Now!" I snapped the word and Terry Farebrother appeared as if from nowhere. He made no sound. He must have been waiting just beside the window and he had been keyed up for this moment. If anyone in the room was astonished by his appearance they had no chance to display it before he crouched in front of Mulder who, dismissive of the much smaller man, went to push him aside.

Mulder stopped dead, then screamed. It was a horrid, almost feminine noise. Terry straightened up and I could not see what grip he was using, but I could see that Mulder was sinking to his knees.

The two crew members started forward and I snatched up a stone statuette that I swung like a short club. The threat checked them. I noted that Bannister made no move; he just gaped at the sudden violence which, with splintering speed, suddenly became more sickening as Terry swung his body, kicked with his right foot, and I heard a crunch as Mulder's nose was broken. The South African was finished, but our regiment never believed in half measures, and Terry felled the big man with a blow to his sternum. Mulder collapsed in breathless pain and Terry turned on the two crew men. "Come on, you fuckers." He was moving towards them, beckoning them to him, but they, seeing Mulder's agony, hung back. Bannister was white-faced and motionless.

"Come on!" That was me, shouting at Terry. I did not want to use his name, nor his rank, because by identifying him I could risk him having to face disciplinary proceedings. He had appeared like a small, very nasty force, and he had utterly cowed the room with his economical and swift violence. Now it was time to get him out before his face became memorable. "Come on!" I discarded my unused club. Mulder was writhing and gasping, his face bloodied, while Terry and I were doing the classic thing: shoot and scoot. Hit the bastards, then run like hell before they can muster reinforcements.

"Phone the police!" Bannister shouted.

Terry and I were already in the rainswept darkness. I was limping as fast as I could and Terry was staying with me, covering my retreat. "Did I do the right thing, boss?"

"God, yes." Why hadn't Bannister believed me? God damn it, but he was a fool! And Angela! The look she had given me before she stalked from the room had been one of pure reproach. More than that, a look of derisive hatred because she believed I had betrayed both her and Bannister.

I slipped on the grass, thought for a second that my damned leg was about to fold up on me, but it had only been a damp patch of lawn that had made me lurch. The sudden movement wrenched pain in my back, but the leg was still strong. I looked to see if anyone was following us, but Terry had plainly terrified them. Terry himself, high on the adrenalin of a successful fight, chuckled. "Orders, boss?"

"We get the fuck out of here. On *Sycorax*. You do the springs, then cast off the bow warp. Leave the stern till last."

Terry had sailed with me before and knew what he was doing. But did *Sycorax* know? She had been out of commission for over six months, she was untested, and I had to take her to sea in a fretting wind against a flood tide. I dragged the mainsail cover back, lifted the boom, and fumbled with the topping lift. I saw Angela appear on the balcony of Bannister's bedroom. She was staring down at me. "Micky Harding!" I shouted at her. "Phone Inspector Abbott!"

She turned away. "Springs and warp off!" Terry shouted at me. "Standing by!"

The tide was swinging *Sycorax*'s bows off the wall. She was moving in the water at last.

"Let's go!" The stern warp splashed off the wharf and *Sycorax* was unleashed. "Peak halliard, Terry!"

I did not trust the engine to start quickly, if at all. We were drifting on the tide and I needed a sail to give me some power. "Haul her up!"

I heard the rattle of the halliard and the flap of the big sail. It rose stiffly, stretching to the night wind, and there was a sudden creak as the starboard shrouds took the mast's weight and I felt a sudden surge of joy. It was not how I had imagined it, not in the least how I had dreamed of it, but *Sycorax* and I were going to sea.

"Did you kill that big guy?" I asked Terry.

"Christ, no!" He was scornful. "Just brought some tears to his fucking eyes. Have you got a light down here?"

"Only an oil-lamp."

He swore again. He had taken the companionway off to reveal the engine and was now trying to swing it into life. "Why can't you get a decent fucking motor?"

"Can't afford it." I pegged the tiller. "Throw up the yellow sail bag, Terry."

He struck a match, found the sail bag, and heaved it into the cockpit. I struggled forward with the heavy load. I hanked on the jib's head, ran its tack along the bowsprit with the traveller, then hoisted away. I tied the sheets on to the sail and threw them back towards the cockpit. I heard Terry swear at the motor again and I told him to abandon it and hoist the mizzen. I could see figures standing on Bannister's terrace. Would the police be waiting at the river's mouth? I dragged the staysail from its bag and fumbled with its shackle. Terry had to unpeg the tiller and adjust our course as I pulled the sail up. My back was hurting.

I rove the foresails' sheets through their fairleads, hauled the port sheets tight, and took over the tiller. We had no running lights, no compass, nothing but the boat, the sails and a pig of an engine that wouldn't start. Terry had gone below again, had lit the chart table's oil-lamp, and now swung the engine's handle. Nothing.

The wind was made tricky by the western hills. At moments it seemed to die completely, then it would back suddenly to gust in a wet squall. *Sycorax* was in confusion. She had not been ready for sea, but to sea she was going. I heard the blessed sound of water running by her hull. We were clearing Sansom's

Point which at last hid the lights of Bannister's house from us. "Topsail, Terry. Remember how to do it?"

"Yes, boss."

We now had jib, staysail, main, top and mizzen, and *Sycorax* was leaning to the wind, hissing the water, taking us fast down the river's buoyed channel. Fast, though, was a relative term. We were moving through the water, but the tide was moving against us. Our motion felt fast enough, but from the bank we would be creeping at less than walking pace. I was also uncomfortably aware that *Wildtrack II*'s sharp bows might appear at any moment.

Terry, the topsail hoisted, came back to the cockpit. "What happened, boss?"

"Two rich men are having a row. Both tried to involve me. Bannister thought I'd joined the other side. Now he wants *Sycorax*."

Terry took that lot on board, then squatted below the coaming to light a cigarette. "I thought Bannister was a decent bloke. He seems nice on the telly. Sally always watches his programme."

"He's a bloody wally," I said savagely, "and he wants to take *Sycorax*."

"Sod him, then." Terry complacently accepted my judgement.

"Exactly." But I was thinking of that look of mingled remorse and hatred which Angela had shot at me. She thought I was the enemy, that I had betrayed her. God damn it, I thought, but my emotions had become inextricably tangled with her. "Bloody women," I said.

"Bloody engine." Terry had gone back to the struggle, swung the handle again, and by some miracle the old engine banged into protesting life. "Give it some throttle, boss!"

I gave it some throttle, it threatened to die, then the cylinders settled into a proper, comforting rhythm and I slammed it into gear and *Sycorax* thrust forward against the tide.

"Where are we going?" Terry asked.

"I don't have a clue." I'd been trying to answer that myself. I needed to hide *Sycorax* from Bannister's bailiffs. The only refuge I could think of was George Cullen's boatyard on the

Hamoaze. "Plymouth," I suggested. "When do you have to be in barracks?"

"Fourteen hundred. Tomorrow."

"It'll be tight. You want me to drop you off at the town quay?"

He glanced behind. "Will those buggers chase you?"

"They might."

"I'll stay."

They followed us. The first I saw of our pursuers was a gleam of reflected lamplight from *Wildtrack II*'s polished bows. We were already abaft the town quay and the powerboat was a mile behind. It could close the gap in seconds if it wanted, but clearly Bannister, or whoever was at *Wildtrack II*'s helm, did not want to make an interception in full view of the quay. The powerboat hung back.

Our engine began to run rough. The diesel fuel was old, and I suspected there was water mixed in it. I hated bloody engines. There had been many times when I had been tempted to haul the damn thing out and sink it, but Terry coaxed it and we limped on. Someone shouted at us from the quay that we had no lights.

The headlands that marked the river mouth closed on us. I could feel the wind's uncertainty as it was confused by the masses of land. Rain was slapping on the sails. There was white water at the bar and it would be a rough passage. The engine was missing a beat now, thumping horribly in its bearings. "Kill it!" I shouted. I didn't want the shaft to shake the gland loose and let in sea water.

The engine died just as the bows juddered to the first sea. *Sycorax* was free at last, running to the ocean she was made for. Her sails were full and behind her the water whitened and spread. She took the steep, breaking seas like a thoroughbred and I whooped for the joy of the moment.

Terry grinned. "Happy, boss?"

"I should have done this bloody weeks ago!"

"And what about those bastards?" Terry nodded towards the river mouth where *Wildtrack II* had appeared.

"Screw them." I gave him the tiller and set about trimming

the sails. The topsail yard and jackyard were loose, the topping lift needed slackening and the foresail halliards tightening. We were heading westward, along the coast, and we were hard on the wind. We went perilously close to the Calfstone Shoal from which a breaking wave shredded foam across our bows. The rain was slackening, and there were gaps in the southern cloud that were edged by silver moonlight. *Sycorax* was slicing the wind and cutting into a head sea. The waves were big enough to dip her bows low and I saw the jib's foot come up dripping with water and there had been a time when I thought I'd never live to see that sight again. I was happy.

Except *Wildtrack II* still threatened us. "Bastards are closing!" Terry shouted.

I'd deliberately put *Sycorax* head to wind, and close to the Calfstone, in the hope that *Wildtrack II*, emerging at speed from the river mouth, might run aground on the shoal. It was a slender hope, and one that failed. I twisted in the cockpit to watch the slinking powerboat. I did not think they were likely to ram us. Most likely *Wildtrack II* had been sent to follow *Sycorax* and to betray our final position so the bailiffs could find us. Bannister, I thought, would be remorseless in his revenge on me, just as Kassouli was remorseless in his revenge on Bannister.

The night was not my helper. The sky was clearing. Soon we would be thrashing west under moonlight and would be in full sight of *Wildtrack II* without a hope of losing the powerboat. I needed time to think. I also needed to be comfortable. I was wet through and shivering. Terry was in the same discomfort and I told him to go below and find some warm clothes.

"Some proper bloody food would help, boss."

I fell off the wind slightly to put the floodtide on the starboard bow. I saw how gracefully the rebuilt *Sycorax* took the seas. It was a promise of what she would do with the bigger seas that waited in the years ahead. I trimmed her, belayed the sheets and pegged the tiller. She could sail herself now until we had cleared the transit of Start Point and could turn due west again. It would be a long hard thrash until the current ebbed, but we had all night.

I fetched my monocular and trained it on *Wildtrack II*. It was hard to hold her in sight, and harder still to see who was on board. I could see three men. No Angela. I thought I saw a man with a bandaged face, who had to be Mulder. "Could that fellow you clobbered be walking by now?" I asked Terry.

"Bloody hell, yes." Terry tossed me up a sweater and oilskin jacket. "I only tapped the fucker."

I wondered if Mulder had brought his shotgun, but surely they would not plan murder? Then the thought occurred that if Kassouli was right, these men had already committed one murder at sea. I stared at the powerboat. It was taking the seas badly, rearing its slick hull high on the wavecrests, then slamming down in discomfort. Would they try and end the discomfort by sinking *Sycorax*? I couldn't lose the thought of the shotgun. "Terry?"

"Boss?"

"If you feel under the engine you'll find a wooden box screwed to a frame on the starboard side. There's a package in it. Can you get it?"

He lifted off the companion steps and I heard him grunt as he groped in the bilge's darkness. "Jesus," he said as he felt the shape of the package. "Is that the bloody Colt I kept for you?"

"I don't want to use it, not unless I have to."

"No, boss." He sounded disappointed.

"But unwrap it. Then get some sleep."

Wildtrack II was still holding her distance. There were two fishing boats in sight, and I wondered if their presence was inhibiting Mulder. The beam of the Start Point light slid across the sky. I was sailing south now, aiming to go outside the tidal race at the Point. *Wildtrack II* was shadowing us. The powerboat was showing a white light at the top of its radar arch, another at its stern, and the proper red and green sidelights. My pursuers were letting me know where they were, and letting me know that I could not escape them.

They kept abreast of us for the three hours it took to claw past Start Point. There was a deeper swell offshore, and *Sycorax* seemed to revel in the longer, higher seas. She felt hard and good, well rigged and confident. But in the morning, I thought, just as soon as I put into shelter, Bannister's lawyers would descend on her with a writ. I had no idea how such a process was initiated, or how it was fought; only that I would be damned if Bannister took my boat from me. I had a talent, I reflected bitterly, for the making of wealthy enemies. First Kassouli, now Bannister. And all I had tried to be was truthful.

Terry slept for an hour, then came blinking up into the moonlight. "Still there?" he asked of *Wildtrack II*.

"Still there." We were on a port tack now and the powerboat was further out to sea. She was probably using her radar to follow us, but *Sycorax* made a small target, I had no reflector hoisted, and there were fishing boats about to give confusing echoes, and so *Wildtrack II* was staying well within easy visual range. A container ship, brilliant with deck lights, steamed eastwards beyond her. I was certain now that Bannister only wanted to discover my destination, but I was determined to lose him. "I think," I said slowly, "that it's time to scare the fuckers off. I'm going to tack."

Terry handled the foresails' sheets. *Sycorax*, never graceful in a tight turn, lurched round and settled on to the starboard tack. I let her off the wind, slackening the mainsheet into a broad reach so that we were running directly at our pursuers. "He's going to try and avoid us, Terry, but he won't really know what we're doing. So be ready for some smart manoeuvres. And get the gun. You'll need a couple of extra mags."

He gave me a surprised glance, but said nothing. He fetched the Colt, came back to the cockpit, and worked a round into the breech.

"What we're going to do," I said, "is scare the bugger witless. You're not going for the crew, but for the boat. Aim for the waterline or the engines. If you think there's the least danger of hitting any of the crew, don't fire. You understand?"

"Yes, sir." The "sir" was unconscious. He put the safety on, then thrust the pistol into a pocket of his oilskin jacket.

I used the monocular again, training it forward, and this time I clearly saw both Bannister and Mulder standing in the powerboat's cockpit. They were staring at *Sycorax*, doubtless wondering just what we intended, then they must have decided that we meant no good, for I saw Bannister bend down to the throttles and the boat dipped its stern as she accelerated away.

"Tacking!" I shouted. We tacked. Terry sheeted the headsails across, we tightened up, and were clawing almost head into the wind. The breeze seemed stronger, slicing over the coachroof and bringing a sting of spray from the bows. "Watch the bugger for me, Terry!"

"He's having a think, boss."

Wildtrack II, having gone ahead of us, had now slowed again.

I felt the tremble of water under *Sycorax*'s hull. We pitched once and the bows slammed down with a thump which banged back through the boat's skeleton. The waves were building. The wind was noisy in the rigging and was slatting the leading edges of the sails. I was pointing her up as much as I could, still aiming her bowsprit like a spear at *Wildtrack II*'s flank. "Where is he?"

"He's putting his foot down."

The powerboat, still puzzled by our behaviour, had accelerated again. She was going inshore of us now, perhaps planning to circle around to take position on our stern. I matched her move, spilling wind so that we were running north before the wind and banging into the cross seas. She was a hundred yards away, running across our bows, and I could see three faces staring from the cockpit.

"Turning to port," I warned Terry. "Get ready to fire!"

He brought out the gun and cradled it in two big and capable hands.

I turned back into the wind and hardened the sails. Now it looked as if we'd stopped playing games and resumed our westward progress. As I'd guessed and hoped, *Wildtrack II* also slowed. Her bows began to turn towards us. She was circling to follow us and, at its closest, her turn would bring her to within thirty paces. Long range for a Colt, but I wasn't after pinpoint accuracy.

I watched the powerboat. I was falling off the wind a touch, slowing and widening our own turn to close the range. *Wildtrack II* was also slowing. The sea was bucking *Sycorax*, thumping her hull and shaking her sails. "You're going to have ten seconds!" I shouted at Terry. "For Christ's sake don't hit anyone, but go for his hull! Aim as far for'rard as possible and as close to the waterline as you can."

"Got it, boss." He grinned, and I heard the snick of the safety going off, then the slam of the gun being cocked. He crouched on the starboard cockpit thwart, steadied by the coaming and the cabin bulkhead. The movement of our boat, and the heaving of the target, would make accuracy almost impossible and I prayed that Terry would not hit any of the three men. I almost told him to hold his fire, but then, when we were just thirty yards from the *Wildtrack II*, a wave heaved her up and I saw an expanse of her anti-fouling revealed in the moonlight. "Fire!"

Terry held the gun two-handed, braced himself, and opened fire at the speedboat's belly.

The noise was just like a sail flogging in a gale. The old sailors used to say the wind was blowing great guns when their canvas banged aloft and made a noise like cannons, and now the Colt filled the sea with the same murderous sound. The muzzle flash leaped two feet clear of the boat and I saw a streak of foam reflect red, then I looked at the powerboat and I saw the three faces disappear beneath the coaming. There was no way of knowing where Terry's bullets went, but water suddenly churned white at *Wildtrack II*'s stern and she shot away from us.

"Hold your fire! We're tacking!"

Terry changed magazines. I pulled the tiller gently towards me, wrenched in the mainsheet, and waited till *Sycorax*'s head was round before releasing the headsail sheets. The effort tore at my back, and I wondered if I ever could sail this heavy boat alone.

We were running now, stern to wind. *Wildtrack II*, like a startled deer, was circling at full speed. Her bows thumped the waves as she spewed a high wake sixty yards long. Once I saw her leap clear off a wavecrest before slamming down into a trough. Then she headed straight towards us and I suspected Mulder must have his gun and that he planned to have his revenge on *Sycorax*. "Get ready!"

The powerboat accelerated. I guessed they planned to swamp

us with their wash as well as loose a broadside at our sails. They would have to be dissuaded, and I decided against waiting to make our own broadside shot at them. "Into the bows, Terry. Fire!"

The powerboat's bows were high and its anti-fouled belly, pale against the night, reared vulnerably above the water. Terry stood, legs spread, and fired. He emptied a magazine at the approaching boat and I swore I saw a scrap of darkness appear in the hull where a heavy bullet ripped the fibreglass ragged.

Terry changed magazines. *Wildtrack II* was slowing, her bows dropping. Terry braced himself again, fired again and this time the powerboat's windscreen shattered in the night. The glass shards were snatched away like spindrift, and I saw the three heads twist away in panic. "Cease fire! Cease fire!" I was scared witless that the final shot might have hit one of the three men.

The powerboat veered off. I stared intently and thought I saw three figures still moving in the cockpit. That was a relief for me, but not for them, for they were in trouble. The powerboat would be taking water, needing to be pumped, and now their only safety lay in reaching harbour as soon as possible. They were forced to forget us, and Terry jeered as they fled. I sat down. "Make the gun safe, Terry."

"Already done it, boss."

We tacked again, sheeted home, and clawed into the south-west wind. The tide had long turned and the surging channel current was at last coming to our aid. I thanked Terry for his help.

"That's what the working class are for, boss. To get you useless rich sods out of deep shit."

"What the working class could usefully do now," I said, "is get some bloody beer."

I pegged the tiller. There was nothing to do now until we turned for Plymouth breakwater. We were a darkened ship sailing a black ocean. The wind was brisk, still chilled by the evening's rain. There was something mesmerizing about *Sycorax*'s motion; her plunging bow and rocking buoyancy.

Terry asked me about the filming and I told him how the television people kept asking me about the night I'd won the medal, and how I hadn't really told them anything at all. "I can't remember very much," I confessed.

"You were a bloody wally, boss," Terry said amicably.

"I remember going left round those rocks. The bastards were about ten yards behind, weren't they?"

"Ten! Bloody fifty."

"Truly?"

"I could hear you shouting," he said. "You were like a calf in the slaughterhouse. God knows how those buggers missed you at first. The Major had come up to tell us to keep our heads down and he was shouting at you to come back."

"I didn't hear him."

"He gave up in the end. He reckoned you were a dead 'un. He said it was your own bloody fault 'cos you'd taken us to the wrong place anyway. We should have been a bloody half-mile away, and instead you was doing a Lone Ranger on their headquarters company." He chuckled. "Then when you switched out their lights the Major told us to get the hell up after you."

"It worked," I said bleakly.

"We screwed 'em," Terry agreed. Somehow the conversation had made us both morose. I watched the loom of the Start light, then took a bearing on the entrance to Salcombe Harbour. We were making good time. I wondered how much water was in her bilges. There was bound to be some until the patched hull took up.

"Mind you," Terry went on, "I don't know what bloody good it did us. Life's still a bloody bastard."

"Is it, Terry?"

"Bloody women," he said.

I wished I had not heard the note of sad hopelessness in his voice. "As bad as that?" I asked.

"As bad as that, boss." He huddled in the cockpit's corner, sheltering from the wind. "You got out, didn't you?"

"Melissa left me. I didn't get out."

"Would you have bugged out on your own?"

I shook my head. "Probably not. I sometimes think women are more ruthless than us."

"I wish mine would be sodding ruthless. I wish she'd go back to her bloody mother. Then I could go back to barracks." He tipped a beer bottle to his lips. "I've got some good mates in the barracks."

"Is Sally still nagging you to get out of the Army?"

He nodded. "Never bleeding stops. She says there'll be jobs in the pits when the fucking strike's over, but what jobs? All this bloody Government wants to do is gut the miners."

"Would you want to work in the mines?"

"I've two uncles down the pits, so it's family, like." He paused. "And it might take Sally off my back, and I suppose it would be a better life for the nippers, but I don't know, boss. I like the Army, I do." His voice tailed away and we sat in companionable misery; he thinking of his Sally, I of Angela. I'd lost her, of course, but I, unlike Terry, was free.

"If you ever want to escape," I said to him, "there's always a berth in *Sycorax* for you. We're good together, you and I."

He toasted me with his beer bottle. "That's true, boss."

We fell silent. The cliffs to the north were touched with moonlight and the water broke on them in wisps of shredding white. Everything had gone awry, but at least *Sycorax* was back where she belonged. All I had to do now was to escape Bannister's lawyers, finish the boat, then go to where the lawyers couldn't follow; to sea.

George Cullen fidgeted with his pipe. He had reamed it, rammed it, now he tamped it with tobacco. "Times are hard, Nick."

"I'm sure."

"No one wants a proper boat any longer, do they? They just want plastic bowls with Jap engines." He lit the pipe and puffed a smokescreen towards his peeling ceiling. "Fibreglass," he said scathingly. "Where's the bloody craftsmanship in fibreglass?"

"Tricky stuff to lay properly, George."

"An epileptic bloody monkey could lay it properly. But not the bloody layabouts I get." He stood and went to the dusty window of his office. It was raining again. The office was a mess. George's big desk was heaped with old pieces of paper; some of them looked as if they were unpaid bills from at least twenty years before. The walls were thick with vast-breasted naked pin-ups who disconcertingly advertised valve springs, crankcases and gaskets. Among the display of lubricious and fading flesh were fly-spotted pictures of Cullen's Fishing Boats; sturdy little dayboats for long-lining or trawling. It had been years since the yard last built one; back, indeed, in the time of George's father. Now the yard survived on a dwindling supply of repair work and on making the despised fibreglass hulls for do-it-yourself enthusiasts who wanted to finish the boats for themselves. It also survived on crime. George was a fence for every boatstripper between the Fal and the Exe. "Seen your old man?" he asked me.

"No."

"I ran up there, when? Six months ago? Before Christmas, anyway. Said he was missing you."

"I was in hospital, George."

"Course you were, Nick, course you were." He began to fiddle with his pipe that had gone out. He was a vast-bellied man with a jowly red face, grey hair and small eyes. I'd never much liked him, but I understood George's attraction for my father. There wasn't a piece of knavery on the coast that George did not know about, and probably did not have a finger in, and he could spend hours regaling my father with the tales of rogues and fools that my father had so relished. From my earliest childhood I could remember George drinking our whisky and talking in his gravelly old voice. He'd seemed old then, but now I saw he was just in his seedy middle age. "Your old man's dead proud of you, Nick, proud of you," he said now. "The Vicky Cross, eh?"

"The other two earned it," I said. "I was just lucky."

"Rubbish, boy. They don't give that gong away with the cornflakes, do they? So what do you need?"

"VHF, short-wave, chronometer, barometer, anchors, lights, batteries, sea loo, compass, bilge-pumps . . ."

"Spare me, for Christ's sake." He sat down again, flinching from some inboard pain. George was for ever at death's threshold and for ever ingesting new kinds of patent medicines. He preferred whisky, though, and poured us each a glass now. It was only mid-day, but George had probably been on the sauce since seven o'clock. It was no wonder, I thought, that Cullen's Fishing Boats were no longer launched down his small slip.

Sycorax was tucked safe into a narrow dock beside George's office. He'd moored a wreck of a fishing craft outside to hide her. Terry Farebrother had been put on a train in nearby Plymouth. For the moment I'd found shelter. George's price had been to hear the story, or as much as I cared to tell him. "Mulder," he said now. "I know Fanny."

"Like him, do you?"

"Fanny's all right," George said guardedly. "Brings me in a bit of business from time to time. You know how it is, Nick."

"He nicks the business, George. He nicked a lot of bloody stuff off my boat. You've probably still got it, George."

"Wouldn't surprise me," George said equably. "I'll let you have a look later on, Nick, and if anything is yours I'll let you have it at cost."

"Thank you, George."

"Fair's fair, Nick," he said as though he was doing me a great favour. "And you are Tommy Sandman's boy. Anything for Tommy. And for a hero, of course." He knocked back the whisky and poured himself another. The glass was filthy, but so was the whisky that, despite its label, had never been anywhere near Scotland. "What sort of anchors do you want?"

"Two CQRs. One fisherman's."

He half closed his eyes. "We had a Dutchman run out of money here last year. Nice boat, too. You want his pair of 75-pound CQRs?"

"They'll do. Have you got any chain?" I knew it was hopeless to ask a price, because I would not be given one until George had worked out to a penny just what I could afford. Then he'd add something. He would welcome me at the yard so long as I could show him a profit, and the day he thought he'd squeezed me dry he'd turf me out.

"Fathoms of chain, Nick. Half-inch do you?"

There was a sudden commotion in the outer office where George's secretary, a shapely girl whose typing speed was reputed to be one stroke a minute, spent her days polishing her fingernails and reading magazines of true romance. "You can't go in there," I heard Rita squeal. "Mr Cullen is in conference."

"Mr Cullen can bloody well get out of conference, can't he?" The opaque glass door banged open and Inspector Abbott came inside. "Morning, George." He ignored me. I was sitting in an ancient leather armchair with broken springs, and I stayed there.

"Morning, Harry." George automatically reached for another filthy glass into which he splashed some of his rotgut whisky. "How's things?"

"Things are bloody. Very bloody." Abbott still ignored me. "Would you have seen young Nick Sandman anywhere, George?"

George flickered a glance towards me, then realized that Abbott must be playing some sort of game. "Haven't set eyes on him since he went to the Falklands, Harry."

Abbott took the whisky and tasted it gingerly. He shuddered, but drank more. "If you see him, George, knock his bloody head off."

Again George glanced my way, then jerked his gaze back to Abbott. "Of course I will, Harry, of course."

"And once you've clobbered him, George, tell him from me

to keep his bloody head down. He is not to show his ugly face in the street, in a pub, anywhere. He is to stay very still and very quiet and hope the world passes him by while his Uncle Harry sorts out the bloody mess he has made." Some of this was vehemently spat in my direction, but was mostly directed at George. I said nothing, nor did I move.

"I'll tell him, Harry," George said hastily.

"You can also tell him, if you should see him, that if he's got a shooter on his boat, he is to lose it before I search his boat with a bloody metal detector."

"I'll tell him, Harry."

"And if I don't find it with a detector, then I'll tear the heap of junk apart plank by bloody plank. Tell him that, George."

"I'll tell him, Harry."

Abbott finished the whisky and helped himself to some more. "You can also tell Master Sandman that it isn't the Boer War I'm worried about, but the War of 1812."

George had never heard of it. "1812, Harry?"

"Between us and America, George."

"I'll tell him, Harry."

Abbott walked to the window from where he stared down through the filth and rain at *Sycorax*. "I'll tell the powers-that-be that after an exhaustive search of this den of thieves there was no sign of Master Sandman, nor of his horrible boat."

"Right, Harry." The relief in George's voice that there was to be no trouble was palpable.

Abbott, who had still not looked directly at me, whirled on George and thrust a finger towards him. "And if you do see him, George, hang on to him. I don't want him running ape all over the bloody South-West."

"I'll tell him, Harry."

"And tell him that I'll let him know when he can leave."

"I'll tell him, Harry."

"And tell him he's bloody lucky that no one got killed. One of his bloody bullets went within three inches of Mr Bannister's pretty head. Mr Bannister is not pleased."

"I'll tell him, Harry."

"They always were rotten shots in that regiment," Abbott

said happily. "Unlike the Rifles of which I was a member. You don't need to tell him that bit, George."

"Right, Harry."

"And tell him his newspaper friend is out of danger, but will have a very nasty bloody headache for a while."

"I'll tell him, Harry."

Abbott sniffed the empty glass of whisky. "How much did you pay for this Scotch, George?"

"It was a business gift, Harry. From an associate."

"You were fucking robbed. I'm off. Have a nice day."

He left. George closed his eyes and blew out a long breath. "Did you hear all that, Nick?"

"I'm not deaf, Harry."

"So I don't need to tell you?"

"No, George."

"Bloody hell." He leaned back in his chair and his small, shrewd eyes appraised me. "A shooter, eh? How much do you want for it, Nick?"

"What shooter, George?"

"I can get you a tasty little profit on a shooter, Nick. Automatic, is it?"

"I don't know what you're talking about, George."

He looked disappointed. "I always thought you were straight, Nick."

So did I.

A hot spell hit Britain. The Azores high had shifted north and gave us long, warm days. It was not the weather for an attempt on the St Pierre. In the yachting magazines there were stories about boats waiting in Cherbourg for the bad weather that would promise a fast run at the race, but *Wildtrack* was not among them. Rita brought me the magazines and a selection of the daily papers. There had been reports of a shooting incident off the Devon coast, a report that received neither confirmation nor amplification and so the story faded away. Bannister's name was not mentioned, nor was mine. The *Daily Telegraph* said that a man was being sought in connection with the shooting, but though the police knew his identity he was not being named. The police did not believe the man posed any danger to the general public. England was being hammered at cricket. Unemployment was rising. The City pages reported that Kassouli UK's half-yearly report showed record profits, despite which, about a week after I'd reached George's yard, there was a story that Yassir Kassouli was planning to pull all his operations out of Britain. I smelt Micky Harding behind the tale, but after a day or two Kassouli issued a strong denial and the story, like the tale of gunfire off the Devon coast, faded to nothing.

I worked for George Cullen. I mended engines, scarfed in gunwales, repaired gelcoats, and sanded decks. I was paid in beer, sandwiches, and credit. The credit bought three Plastimo compasses. I mounted one over the chart table, one on the for'ard cockpit bulkhead, and one just aft of the mizzen's step. I bought the two big anchors off George and stowed them on board. I nagged George to find me a good chronometer and barometer. And every day I tried to phone Angela.

I did not leave messages on the answering machine in Bannister's house, for I did not want him to suspect that I had reason to trust Angela. I left messages on her home answering machine, and I left messages at the office. The messages told her to phone me at Cullen's yard. Rita, whose skirts became shorter as the weather became hotter, listened sympathetically to my insistent message-leaving. She thought it was like something out of her magazines of romance.

The messages achieved nothing. Angela was never at her flat, and she never returned the calls. I tried the television company and had myself put through to Matthew Cooper.

"Jesus, Nick! You've caused some trouble."

"I've done nothing!"

"Just aborted one good film." He sounded aggrieved.

"Wasn't my fault, Matthew. How's Angela?"

He paused. "She's not exactly top of the pops here."

"I can imagine."

"She keeps saying that the film is salvageable. But Bannister won't have anything to do with you. He's issued a possession order for *Sycorax*."

"Fuck him," I said. Rita, pretending not to listen as she buffed her fingernails, giggled. "Will you give Angela a message for me?" I asked.

"She's stopped working, Nick. She's with Bannister all the time now."

"For Christ's sake, Matthew! Use your imagination! Aren't good directors supposed to be bursting with imagination? Write her a letter on your headed notepaper. She won't ignore that."

"OK." He sounded reluctant.

"Tell her to find a guy called Micky Harding. He's probably out of hospital by now." I gave him Micky's home and work numbers. "She's to tell Micky that he can trust her. She can prove it by calling him Mouse and by saying she knows that Terry was with me on the night. He'll understand that."

Matthew wrote it all down.

"And tell her," I said, "that Bannister's not to try the St Pierre."

"You're joking," Matthew said. "We're being sent to film him turning the corner at Newfoundland!"

"When are you going?"

He paused again. "I'm not allowed to say, Nick."

"Jesus wept. OK. Just give her my message, Matthew."

"I'll try, Nick."

"And tell her something else."

I didn't need to tell him what else; he understood. "I'll tell her, Nick." He sounded sorry for me.

I rattled the phone rest, then tried to phone Micky Harding, but he was not at the paper and there was no answer at his home. I put the phone down. Rita unlocked the petty cash box and put my IOU inside. George charged me fifty pence a call and fifty pence a minute thereafter. Rita scaled the charges down for me, but I still owed the old crook over ten pounds. "He wants you to go out tonight, Nick," she said.

"Out?"

"His usual bloke's got a broken arm. George wants you to take the 52-footer. He says you're to fill her up with diesel. He'll go with you."

So that night I joined the distinguished roster of Devon

smugglers. I helmed the 52-footer twenty miles offshore where we met a French trawler. The Frenchman swung three crates across to our boat. They contained radios stolen from harbours and marinas up and down the Brittany coast. George paid them off with a wad of cash, accepted a glass of brandy, and added a bottle of his lousy Scotch to the payment. Then I took him home again. There were no waterguards to disturb us as we chugged into the Hamoaze in a perfect dawn. George puffed his pipe in the cabin. "Got a very sweet little MF set there, Nick. You could do with an MF, couldn't you?"

"I'll take a VHF as my fee for tonight."

He sucked air between his teeth. "You haven't paid your berthage fees, Nick."

"You call that bloody rubbish dump of a dock a berth?"

He chuckled, but before he drove home he dropped a battered VHF set on to a sailbag in *Sycorax*'s cockpit. I spent the next Sunday fitting it and, to my astonishment, it worked.

I spent the Sunday after that salvaging a galley stove from a wrecked Westerly that George had bought for scrap. I manhandled the stove across the deserted yard. I'd already rigged the gaff as a derrick and only had to attach the whip to the stove, but as I reached the quay above the boat I saw I had company. Inspector Harry Abbott was sitting in *Sycorax*'s cockpit. He was wearing his check golfer's trousers, had a bottle of beer and a packet of sandwiches in his lap, and my Colt .45 in his right hand.

"Afternoon, Nick." He aimed the Colt at my head and, before I could move, pulled the trigger.

It was unloaded. He chuckled. "Naughty, Nick, very! You know what the penalty is for possession of an unlicensed firearm?"

"A golfing weekend with you, Harry?"

He tutted. "Ungrateful, aren't you, Nick? I save your mangy hide and all you do is insult me. What's George bringing in these days?"

"Nothing much. A few radios, mostly French." I tied the whip into place and climbed down to the deck. By using the peak halliard I had a perfectly good crane that swung the stove dangerously close to Abbott's head. He deigned to steer it down to the cockpit floor.

"I thought you'd like to know," he said, "that there is no longer a warrant out for your arrest."

"I didn't know there ever was one."

"A hue and cry, Nick, that's what there was. We searched for you high and low! Do you know what you have cost Her Majesty's Government in police overtime?"

"Is that what you're on now, Harry? Overtime?" I saw it was my beer he was drinking. He courteously offered me a bottle, which I took, then I sat opposite him. "Cheers, Harry."

"Cheers, Nick." He drained the bottle and opened another. "The funny boys are in on this one, Nick."

"Funny boys?"

"Very funny boys. They're not kind and gentle like me, Nick. They're full of self-importance and they talk impressively about the safety of the realm. They have nevertheless decided that your life should be spared."

"Why?"

"How would I know?" He lit a cigarette and flipped the dead match over the side to float among the other garbage in George's dock. "But there is a condition, Nick."

I put my legs up on the opposite thwart. I was wearing old shorts and the scars at the backs of my thighs looked pink and horrid. Abbott glanced at them and grimaced. "Phosphorus?"

"Yes."

"I thought you were shot?"

"Bullet hit a phosphorus grenade hanging on my belt. The phosphorus caught fire, and the bullet split in two. One lump went down the right thigh, and the bigger lump up my spine."

"Nasty." He said it with genuine sympathy.

"I've had better days than that," I agreed.

"It's because of that, you see, that they trust you. Wounded war hero and all that, Nick. I mean, it's unthinkable that one of Her Majesty's VCs would be carrying an illegal shooter or helping Georgie Cullen bring in dicky radios from the French coast, isn't it?"

"Quite unthinkable," I agreed.

"So you're going to piss off, Nick. You're going to sail this heap of garbage round the world and you are not going to try and stop Mr Bannister sailing on the St Pierre."

I finished the beer and opened another. The day was blisteringly hot. "Is that the condition, Harry? That I bugger off and leave Bannister alone?"

"Took a lot of my time to fix it." He spoke warningly. "If the Chief Clown had his way, Nick, you'd be roasting in prison now. And not in some nice open prison like your dad, but a real Victorian horror story."

"Thanks, Harry."

Inspector Abbott had surrendered to the day's heat far enough to discard his blazer, but no more. He wiped his face with a rag. "Mr Bannister lodged a complaint about you. He says you dismasted his boat, cut its warps, and all in practice for the day when you were going to sink it at sea. Do you know he's even got a tape-recording?"

"That tape's a –"

"I know, Nick!" Abbott held up a weary hand. "We've spoken to Mr Harding, haven't we? And Mr Harding has seen the error of his wicked ways. He hasn't got any proof now, so there can't be a scandalous little story which will upset our American cousins. We don't want to upset them, because they've got all the money these days. We are a client state, Nick."

"I understand."

"I don't suppose you do, Nick. Who was the little bloke with you on the night you put nasty holes in nice Mr Bannister's speedboat?"

"I can't remember, Harry."

"Make sure he forgets, too. Sleeping dogs should be left slumbering, Nick, and you were in danger of waking them up."

I offered him another beer. He took it. "Mind you," Abbott went on, "Mr Bannister had a mind to aggravate things. He was unleashing the lawyers on you, but we pointed out that if they found you, and if he pressed charges, then we'd naturally insist that he and his Boer would have to stay in England and give evidence."

"Which he didn't want to do ..." I was beginning to understand some things now "... because it might jeopardize his timing for the St Pierre?"

"Exactly."

I tipped my head back and rested it on *Sycorax*'s guardrails. I wondered if I was understanding too much. "You want Bannister to die, don't you?"

Harry tutted. "You mustn't talk about death, Nick."

"You want to keep Kassouli's jobs?"

"I imagine the Chief Clown wants to, yes."

My head was still tipped back. "Are you a funny boy, Harry?"

"I'm just the dogsbody, Nick."

I brought my head forward. This policeman liked to play the genial fool, but his eyes were very shrewd.

"So Yassir Kassouli gets what he wants?" I said.

"The rich usually do, Nick." He paused. "And between you and me, and no one else, Mr Kassouli wanted you arrested. He wanted the bloody book thrown at you. But we've persuaded him that we can look after our own. That's what I'm doing now, Nick. Looking after you."

"This comes from the bloody Government, doesn't it?"

He heard my anger. "Now, Nick!"

"Jesus wept!" I drank some beer. "Suppose Bannister's innocent?"

Abbott shook his head. "Why confuse the issue?" He laughed at me. "Bloody hell, Nick, since when were you the white knight?" I said nothing, and he sighed. "You're a bloody fool, Nick. Why did you go to the press?"

"I wanted out."

"You should have talked to me." Abbott looked at me in silence for a few seconds, then shook his head sadly. "Nick, it comes from the top, and you're powerless to do anything. So forget it."

I made a non-committal noise.

Abbott drank beer. "I saw your dad last week."

"How was he?"

"He misses you. When are you going to see him?"

"I wasn't planning on it."

"I think you should, Nick. In fact I think I'll make that another condition of not arresting you."

"I thought you said there was no warrant for me any more?"

Abbott hefted the gun. "Three years?"

"How did you find it?"

He smiled. "Did George tell you I threatened to use a metal detector?"

I smiled back, remembering the charade. "Yes."

"Which meant that you'd hide the gun near a piece of metal, so as to confuse your Uncle Harry. So I just had a look at your engine, and hey presto."

"It's a souvenir, Harry."

He looked at the barrel. "*Ejercito Argentina*. Didn't do the silly buggers a lot of good, did it? So, are you going to try and warn Mr Bannister?" I hesitated. Abbott shook his head at my foolishness. "It won't do you any good, Nick. Do you think he'll listen to you?"

"No."

"So I'll take it you won't try, which answer will please the Chief Clown. Are you going to stay away from Bannister's house, his television studio, his mistress's house, and everybody else's bloody house?"

"Yes."

"Are you going to see your father?"

"Probably."

"I'll take that as yes." He fished in his jacket pocket and brought out two Monte Cristo cigars in their tin cases. "Give him these from me, Nick."

"I will."

"And, having seen him, are you then going to bugger off in this floating junkyard?"

"Yes."

"Welcome back to the human race, Nick Sandman." He dangled the gun by its trigger guard. "I assume this is an arcane piece of yacht safety equipment?"

I smiled. "Yes, Harry, it is."

"Then bleeding well hide it where a middle-aged copper

doesn't trip over it." He tossed it into my lap. "How much did George offer you for it?"

"He didn't name a price."

Abbott laughed, then stood and stretched his long arms. "That's it then, job done. I did try to warn you in the spring."

"What was the job, Harry?"

He ignored that question. "I've brought you some sandwiches and I'll leave you the newspapers. They're full of lies, but you might enjoy the comic strips."

"Thank you, Harry."

He climbed to the quayside. "You're an awkward bugger, Nick, and you're probably a lazy sod who should get a proper job, but I don't dislike you. And I do like your old man. Tell him I sent my regards."

"I will."

"*Bon voyage*, Nick."

I fitted the stove after Harry had gone. I gimballed it, connected it up to a gas cylinder, then celebrated the achievement by making myself a cup of tea. The dock stank in the heat. I sat on *Sycorax*'s stern, drank the tea, and read the papers.

In Northern Ireland a man's kneecaps had been shot away. Iraq and Iran were slagging each other in the desert. The Russians were slagging the peasants in Afghanistan. The miners were slagging everyone. A disease called Aids was threatening to achieve what a millennia of Puritans had failed to do. Unemployment was still rising. England was still being hammered at cricket. Angela's photograph stared at me from an outside page devoted to gossip.

I stared back at the photograph. For a second I didn't believe it was Angela, but it was. Bannister sat beside her in the picture. There was a story alongside the photograph. 'Almost a year since the tragic death of his first wife, the American heiress Nadeznha Kassouli, Mr Tony Bannister, 46, has announced his engagement to Miss Angela Westmacott. Miss Westmacott, who has never been married before, is a producer on Mr Bannister's programme.' There was more. The wedding would take place very soon, most likely in Paris, and certainly before Bannister set off on his St Pierre attempt. The bride was giving up her job in television, but would probably work for Bannister's production company which made rock videos and advertisements.

She looked so very beautiful in the photograph. She sat on a sofa in Bannister's Richmond house. In the foreground was a brand new glass-topped table which must have replaced the one I'd broken. Bannister sat beside her with a smile like the cat that had got the cream. Angela's long slim legs were crossed. She wore a hesitant smile that I'd come to know so well, though her eyes were cool. She was in a light dress that hinted at her body's supple elegance. Her right hand rested lightly on Bannister's shoulder, while her left, hanging over the sofa's arm, bore a big shining diamond. She looked like a thoroughbred; leggy and beautiful, a girl fit for a handsome celebrity. A girl it was ludicrous for a broken sailor in a broken boat in a stinking dock to want. But the photograph told me that I did still want her, and I suddenly felt forlorn and bereft and miserable. God damn her, but she had surrendered to safety, and I was alone.

The county's police force were playing the inmates of the open prison. The police had been bowled out for 134, while the prisoners' team had so far scored 42 for the loss of just one wicket. I was in the Midlands and my father, because I had at last come to visit, seemed to be in a private heaven. I'd seen his garden, the workshop where he made ship models, his room, and now he walked round the cricket field with me. It was like a boarding school, only the pupils were middle-aged men rather than boys. It was quite unlike my idea of a prison, but only the trusted felons were sent there; those who were not violent and who would not try to escape. The warders called my father 'Mr Sandman', and he had clearly charmed them all. He asked after their wives, sympathized over their children's exam results, and promised them herbs from his garden. "They're good fellows," he said happily.

He looked so damned well. He'd lost weight, which suited his six-foot four-inch frame. His black hair was touched with grey at his temples, he was suntanned, and he was fit. "The gardening helps, of course. I play a bit of tennis, quite a lot of badminton. I swim a fair bit, but they keep the pool damned chilly. I get a bit of the other, too."

"Don't be ridiculous, Father. You're in prison."

"An open prison, my dear Nick. I do recommend one if you're ever in need of a rest. Admittedly the admission procedure is tiresome, but after that it's a very decent life. We do work on the local farms, you see, and the girls know where to find us. They're mostly professionals, of course, but a chap has to stay in practice. Are you in practice?"

"Not really."

He laughed. "I thought you were looking decidedly doggish. Won't Melissa lay it out for you?"

"I've never asked."

"My exes always did," he said, as if it was the most normal thing in the world. "Just because a woman can't bear to live with a fellow doesn't mean she won't bed him. Did you find another?"

"For a time."

"Lost her, eh? Not to worry, Nick. There are, thank God, so many women in this world. God was very good to us in that regard. Oh, well done!" This was for a fine late cut that left a policeman running vainly towards the boundary. "The batsman" – my father pointed with his cigar – "is doing three years for computer fraud. Not very clever to be caught, was it?"

"Wasn't clever of you," I said.

"Bloody stupid of me." He smiled at me. He was delighted I had come and had not once mentioned all the unanswered letters. I felt awkward, ashamed, and inadequate. He had always made me feel that way, though never intentionally. "My trouble," he said, "is that I think too big."

"True."

He laughed. He'd been arrested for fraud and God alone knows what else. He had been running an insurance company and there had been no money to pay the claims, and over half the policies – which he had been selling off to other companies as a bookmaker lays off his bets – turned out to be false. "Another year," he said wistfully, "and I'd have been solvent. Had a very tasty scheme going in Switzerland with Iranian money. In fact, Nick, if you fancy a trip to Berne . . ."

"No, Father."

"Of course, Nick. Money never was your thing, was it?" He sounded contrite. We paused in our stroll and I was proudly introduced to a warder and his family. My father made a great point of mentioning the VC. The warder's family seemed really grateful that my father had taken notice of them, just as if he was from the local gentry and they his tenants. They said how pleased they were to have met me.

"Decent people," my father said as we strolled on. We found two deckchairs in the shade of a fine oak tree and we sat. "So what have you been doing, Nick?"

"Recovering, mainly." I told him about *Sycorax*.

He thought it was a wonderful jest that I'd found a refuge with George Cullen, and I had to give a detailed description of our night trip to rendezvous with the French trawler. "I thought the old rogue would have died years ago. Drinks like a bloody judge! He's making you pay for all this gear?"

"Through the nose."

"Nick, Nick!" I had disappointed my father who had the haggling skills of the bazaar. He frowned in thought. "Ask him about Montagu Dawson."

"The artist?" I was puzzled, but that was nothing new when I was with my father. I did remember, though, how he used to have two classic Dawsons hanging in his London offices; both paintings showed tall ships driving through foam-flecked seas.

"George sold a few Dawsons," my father said. "They were as bent as a snake's wedding tackle, of course, but George used to find American yachtsmen in the Barbican pubs, and he'd spin this yarn about Dawson having been a friend of the family." My father chuckled. "The paintings were done by a fellow at Okehampton. He's the same chap who painted that Matisse your mother's so very fond of. Talented fellow, but a piss-artist, I fear. Anyway, point of it all, one of George's bent Dawsons ended up in the wrong hands, the police were tumbled out of bed, and officially the case has never been closed. It isn't a major threat to George, of course, but he won't like to be reminded of it, and he certainly wouldn't like it if you suggested you might drop a line to Scotland Yard. Do they still have a fine-art squad? I don't know, but George has certainly got a couple of those fake Dawsons still hanging in his home. Have you ever been to his house?"

"No."

My father shuddered. "Ghastly place. Plastic furniture and music-box cocktail cabinets. The old bastard's as rich as Croesus, but he's got the taste of a camel. Oh, good shot!" The ball flicked across the grass straight towards our chairs. I fielded it with my foot, then flinched as I bent to pick the ball up. I threw it to the nearest fielder and my father watched me sadly. "Is it bad, Nick?"

"It's all right. I can sail a boat."

"Round the world?" he asked dubiously.

"Round the world," I said stubbornly.

He was quiet for a moment or two. His cigar smoke drifted up into the oak leaves. He'd been pleased with Harry Abbott's gift, and I wished I had brought him something. He looked very relaxed and confident despite the blue prison clothes. He gave me one of his shrewd, amused glances. "Harry Abbott came to see me a week or so back. He gave me some news of you."

I was watching the cricket and said nothing.

"Been in the wars again, have you, Nick?"

"Harry should keep his mouth shut."

"You know Kassouli was setting you up, don't you?"

For a second I didn't react, then I turned to look into his eyes. "What the hell do you know about it, Dad?"

He sighed. "Nick! Do me a small favour. I might not be able to sail a small boat through a hurricane, but I do know what makes the wicked world go round. I did some business with Kassouli once. He's a tough bugger. Still got the stink of the souk about him, despite his Boston wife and Savile Row suitings."

"Setting me up?"

He drew on his cigar. "Tell me about it, Nick."

"I thought you knew the answers already." I was defensive.

"Just tell me, Nick." He spoke gently. "Please."

So I told him. I hadn't planned to tell him about Angela, but I did in the end, because I wanted to tell somebody. I missed her horribly. I kept telling myself that she was not for me, that she was too urbanized and ambitious, too elegant and difficult, but I could not persuade myself that I would be better off without her. I missed her, and so I found myself telling my father about the visits to London, the nights in her small bedroom, the weekend in Norfolk, and then the recent news of her engagement and forthcoming wedding. The date had been announced in the papers. Angela would marry Bannister in the English Church in Paris after the coming weekend.

I told my father more. I told him about Mulder and Jill-Beth and Bannister and Kassouli. He listened in silence. He finished the cigar, threw it away, and its stub smoked in the grass like a newly fallen fragment of shrapnel. He rubbed his face. "This Kirov girl. You say she phoned you at Angela's flat?"

"Yes."

"Why would she do that?"

"She wanted to reach me, of course."

He shook his head. "Ostensibly she wanted you to be Kassouli's man in Tony Bannister's crew, yes? The whole essence of that, Nick, is that Bannister wouldn't know that you were Kassouli's man. So why risk alerting him by leaving a message on his girlfriend's answering machine? There's only one answer to that, Nick. They wanted Bannister to know you were dodgy. They gave you a high profile, didn't they? She makes sure you rescued her from Mulder, she flies you to the States, and she smudges a damn great fingerprint on Angela's answering machine. Why?"

A ribald cheer went up as one of the prison batsmen was run out. The prison needed fifty-three runs to win and still had eight wickets left. "And someone sent Mulder a picture of me, too." I spoke slowly. It was like a moment after an awful storm when the clouds rend, sunlight touches an angry but settling sea, and the storm damage at last becomes visible. Seeing the sense of my father's words, I felt foolish. "It was a photograph taken at Kassouli's Cape Cod house. He didn't say who the sender was."

My father gave me a pitying look. "It was the Kirov girl. Or Kassouli. They wanted Bannister to know you were tied up with them. And who do you think told this Mulder fellow where to find you and Jill-Beth Kirov on Dartmoor?"

"She did?" I said it hesitantly, not wanting to believe it.

"Of course! They want Bannister to feel safe. They want Bannister to believe that he's found the fly in his ointment: you. So they set you up to be the threat. You just happened to be convenient, Nick, so they pointed a damned great finger at you. They did some clumsy sabotage, but only when the boat was where you could get at it. And all the time the real man was lying very low."

"Mulder." It was obvious.

"Bingo. How did Bannister meet Mulder?"

"His wife found him."

"Who took the tape-recording?"

"Mulder."

"That was just a happy accident, of course," my father said. "He probably had a camera with him, and planned to take a snap of you and the Kirov girl together, instead of which he lumbers on your mate with his tape-recorder. So who, my dear Nick, do you think Mulder works for?"

"Kassouli." I sat there, feeling very foolish. "And Mulder beat me up because he had to prove his loyalty to Bannister?"

"I would imagine so, wouldn't you?"

"But the rumour says Mulder helped with the murder!"

"Who's spreading the rumours?" my father asked patiently.

"Kassouli?"

"And who has convinced Kassouli that his daughter was murdered?" my father asked, then answered it himself. "Mulder. And why? Because a rich man's gratitude can be very bankable. Mind you, I'd have smelt a rat the moment Kassouli offered four hundred thousand! The going rate for a killing can't be much over twenty grand, but people like you always think that a big sum only increases the seriousness of something."

"But Jill-Beth brought it with her!" I protested. "I saw it. A hundred thousand dollars."

"Which Mulder would have taken from you as proof that you were betraying Bannister." My father spoke gently. "Why do you think he followed you in the boat that night? He probably thought you had the hundred grand in *Sycorax*. My dear Nick, they were stitching you up. Kassouli probably hoped you might help him by being a back-up to Mulder, which is why he laid it all out for you in America, but once he saw you were going to be boring and honourable he danced you like a puppet to distract Bannister." He saw my face. "Don't blame yourself, Nick. Kassouli's played for higher stakes than this and against some of the slimiest creatures that capitalism ever spawned. You musn't feel bad at being beaten by one of the best."

But I did feel bad. I'd never been clever, not as my father and brother and sister were clever. When we'd been growing up they had always competed to win the word games, while I would sit silent and lost. I lack subtlety. Only a bloody fool would have charged straight up that damned hill when there was another company working their hard way round the flank. Still, I'd saved that company from some casualties. "Damn it," I said now. My father did not reply, and I tried one last and despairing protest. "But Kassouli doesn't even know if his daughter was murdered!"

"Perhaps he does. Perhaps Mulder has the proof. Perhaps Mulder has been blackmailing Bannister and taking money off Kassouli. Whatever" – my father shrugged – "Yassir Kassouli will get his perfect revenge. You can kiss Bannister goodbye."

"At sea," I said bitterly.

"Far from any jurisdiction," my father agreed. "There'll be no messy body, no police dogs, no forensic scientists, no murder weapon, no witnesses who aren't Kassouli's men, nothing."

"But I'll know about it," I said stubbornly.

"And who would believe you? And if you made a fuss, Nick, just how long do you think Yassir Kassouli would tolerate you?" He touched my arm. "No, Nick. It's over now as far as you're concerned."

I stared at the cricket, but saw nothing. So the night that Jill-Beth had screamed, and I had thought Mulder was raping her, had all been a part of the careful construction to trap me? And I, believing myself to be full of honour, had fallen for it. I swore softly. I knew my father was right. He'd always been so good at explaining things. The truth had been there for me to see, but I'd been blind to it. Now, according to the yachting magazines, Fanny Mulder was to be the navigator on Bannister's boat. Bannister himself would skipper *Wildtrack*, but Mulder would be the boat's tactician and navigator. From Kassouli's point of view it was perfect, just as it was always meant to be; perfect.

"What time's your bus?" my father asked.

"Five."

We strolled slowly round the boundary together. "The world's a tough place," my father said softly. "It isn't moved by honesty and justice and love, Nick. That's just the pabulum that the rulers feed the people to keep them quiet. The world is run by very ruthless men who know that the cake is very small and the number of hungry mouths is growing all the time. If you want to stop the revolution then you have to feed those mouths, and you do it by being very tough with the cake. Kassouli means jobs and investment."

"And Bannister?"

"He married the wrong woman, and he carelessly lost her. At the very least he'll be sacrificed for carelessness. You think that's unfair?"

"Of course it is."

"Good old Nick." He rested a hand on my shoulder for an instant. "Seen your brother or sister lately?"

"No."

He smiled. "I can't blame you. They're not very nice, are they? I made life too easy for them."

"You made life too easy for me as well."

"But you're different, Nick. You believed all that claptrap they fed you in the Sea Scouts, didn't you? You still do, probably." He said it affectionately. "So what, my favourite son, will you do about Angela?"

"There's nothing to do. They get married on Monday."

"There's everything to do!" my father said energetically. "I'd start by buying every orchid in Paris and drenching them with the most expensive perfume, then laying them at her feet. Like all beautiful women, Nick, she is there for the taking, so take her."

"I've got *Sycorax*. I'm sailing south."

He shrugged. "Will Angela sail on the St Pierre?"

I shook my head. "She gets seasick."

"If I were you, then, I'd wait till she's a rich widow, which can't take very long, then marry her." He was being quite serious.

I laughed. That was vintage Tommy Sandman.

"Why ever not?" he asked, offended.

"I'm sailing south," I said stubbornly. "I want to get to New Zealand."

"What about Piers and Amanda?"

We stopped at the prison entrance. There were no guards, not even a locked gate, but only a long drive that stretched between pea fields. "I'll fly back and see them," I said.

"That takes money, Nick."

I held up my hands that were calloused again from the weeks of good work. "I can earn a living."

"I've got some cash. The buggers didn't get it all."

"I never thought they did."

"If you're ever in trouble, Nick . . ."

"No." I said it too hastily. "If I've learned one thing these last months, it's to pay my own way in life."

"That's a mistake." He smiled. "With full remission, Nick, I'll be out in a year. You'll let me know where you are?"

"Of course."

"Perhaps I'll come and see you. We can sail warm seas together?"

"I'd like that." I could see the bus coming up the long drive. Dust plumed from its wheels on to the pea plants. I fished in my pocket and brought out the flat box. "I thought you might like to keep this for me," I said awkwardly. I told myself that the gesture was spontaneous, but I knew it wasn't because I'd taken the trouble to bring the box with me. I might not have brought my father cigars or wine, but I had fetched him the one thing I knew would give him the most pleasure.

He opened it and I saw the tears come to his eyes. He was holding my medal. He smoothed the claret ribbon on his palm. "Are you sure?"

"I'll probably lose it." I tried to avert any expressions of emotion. "Things get lost on small boats."

"They do, yes."

"Look after it for me, will you?" I asked, trying to make it a casual request.

"I will." He turned it over and saw my name engraved in the dull bronze. "I'll have it put in the governor's safe."

"The bronze is supposed to come from Russian cannons we captured at Sevastopol," I said.

"I think I read that somewhere." He blinked the tears away and put the medal into his pocket. The bus turned in the wide circle in front of the gate, then stopped in a shuddering haze of diesel fumes.

"I'll see you, Dad," I said.

"Sure, Nick."

There was a hesitation, then we embraced. It felt awkward and lumpy. I walked to the bus, paid my fare, and sat at the back. My father stood beneath the window. A few more returning visitors climbed in, then the door hissed shut and the bus lurched forward. My father walked alongside for a few paces. "Nick!" I could just hear him over the engine's noise. "Nick! Paris! Orchids! Scent! Seduction! Who dares wins!"

The bus pulled away. He waved. The gears clashed as we accelerated, and then I lost him in the cloud of dust.

Duty was done.

I insisted on two bilge pumps, both manual. One was worked from the cockpit, the other from inside the cabin. George grumbled, but provided them. "Tommy shouldn't have told you about the Dawsons," he said.

I wondered why such a small crime worried him, but later realized it was because the London police were still searching for the forger. George would not have cared about the local force, for he had his understanding with them, but he was leery of London.

There was a letter from London waiting for me on Rita's desk. I eagerly tore it open, half expecting it to be from Angela, but of course she was in Paris. The letter was from Micky Harding. He was recovering. He apologized for messing up. He was sorry that the story had died. There was no evidence to support it, and such a story couldn't run without proof. He'd floated the Kassouli withdrawal rumour to a city editor of another paper, but I'd probably seen how that story had rolled over and died. If I was ever in London, he said, I should call on him. I owed him a pint or two.

On Tuesday *The Times* had a photograph of Bannister's Paris wedding. The bride wore oyster-coloured silk and had flowers in her hair. Her Baptist minister father had pronounced a blessing over the happy couple. Angela was smiling. I cut the photograph out, kept it for an hour, then screwed it up and tossed it into the dock.

I spent the next few days finishing *Sycorax*. I installed extra water tanks, two bunk mattresses and electric cabin lights. I also had oil-lamps, which I preferred using, just as I had oil navigation lights as well as electric ones. George found me a short-wave radio which I installed on the shelves above the starboard bunk. I screwed a barometer to the bulkhead over the chart table and bought a second-hand clockwork chronometer that went alongside it. I began stowing spare gear and equipment in the lockers, and took pride in buying a brand new Red Ensign that would fray on my jackstaff in faraway oceans. I found an old solid-fuel stove to heat the cabin. There had been a time when every cruising yacht carried such a stove, and *Sycorax* had always been so equipped, and I took a peculiar delight in installing the cast-iron monster. I caulked and capped the chimney in seething rain. The hot weather had gone. Cyclones were bringing squalls and cold air that made the channel choppy and promised a tumultuous wind in the far north Atlantic.

The first hopefuls set off from Cherbourg to take advantage of the Atlantic gales. An Italian crew went first and made an astonishing time to the Grand Banks, but their boat was rolled over somewhere east of Cape Race and lost its mast. Two French boats followed. I read that Bannister was honeymooning in Cherbourg while he waited for even stronger winds.

It was the wrong weather for compass-swinging, which demanded smooth water so that the delicate measurements were not joggled, but I took advantage of one sullen, drizzly day to sail between carefully plotted buoys and landmarks in Plymouth Sound. I had roughly compensated the compasses with tiny magnets that corrected the attraction of the metal in the engine and stove, but I still needed to know what other errors the needles contained, so I sailed *Sycorax* north and south, east and west, and courses in between, noting the compass variations on each heading. Some were big enough to demand more fiddly work with the tiny magnetic shims, which then meant that every course had to be sailed again, but I finished the job by sundown and pinned a clingfilm-wrapped correction card over my navigation table. That night I took my dirty washing to a launderette and reflected that, with a little luck, my next wash would be on shipboard where I'd use a garbage bag filled with two quarts of water and washing powder. It works as well as any electric machine.

I went to London the next day and took the children to

Holland Park where we played hide and seek among the wet bushes. Afterwards I insisted on seeing Melissa. "They're going to kill Bannister," I told her.

"I'm sure that's not true, Nick."

"He won't listen to me," I said.

"It's hardly surprising, is it? I gather you declared war on him! Are you sure you're recovered from the Falklands? One keeps reading these tedious stories about Vietnam veterans who seem to be perfectly normal until they open fire in a crowded supermarket. I do hope you won't go berserk in the frozen-food section, Nick. It would be jolly hard for Mands and Pip to have a mass-murderer for a father."

"Wouldn't it," I agreed. "But would you phone Bannister? He'll listen to you. Tell him he mustn't trust Mulder. Just convince him of that. I've written to him, but . . ." I shrugged. I'd broken my promise to Abbott by writing to Bannister. I'd written to his Richmond house, the television studios, and to the offices of his production company. I'd written because there was no proof that he was guilty of the crime for which, I was certain, he was about to be punished. Doubtless my letters had been categorized with all the other nutcase letters that a man like Bannister attracted.

Melissa ran a finger round the rim of her wine glass. "Tony won't listen to me now, Nick. He's married that ghastly television creature. She's certainly done well for herself, hasn't she? And I'm quite sure Tony's in that post-marital bliss thing. You know, when you swear you'll never be unfaithful?" She laughed.

"I'm serious, Melissa."

"I'm sure you are, Nicholas, but if you think I'm going to make a fool of myself by telling Tony to give up his little boat race, you're wrong. Anyway, he wouldn't believe me! Fanny Mulder may not be everyone's cup of tea, but he's completely loyal to Tony." I'd told Melissa everything, including my new certainty that Mulder was Kassouli's man and would navigate *Wildtrack* to a death.

"Phone him!" I said.

"Don't be nasty, Nick."

"For God's sake, Melissa!" I closed my eyes for a second. "I'm not mad, Melissa, I'm not shell-shocked and I'm not having bad dreams. I don't even like Bannister. Would you believe it, my love, if I was to tell you that it could suit me hideously well if he were to die? But I just cannot stomach the thought of murder! Especially when it's in my power to prevent it." I shook my head. "I'm not being noble, I'm not being honourable, I just want to be able to sleep at nights."

"I do hate it when you get into a Galahad mood. I remember how it used to make me miserable when we were married."

"So phone him," I urged her. "You can find out which hotel he's in, can't you?"

She lit a cigarette. "His secretary might tell me," she allowed cautiously.

"Then phone him and say that you think it's all nonsense. Blame me, if you like. Say I'm mad. But say you promised to pass on the message. The message is that Mulder is Kassouli's man and always has been."

"I won't speak to that little television upstart."

"You want Bannister to die?"

She looked me up and down, noting my dirty trousers and creased shirt. "You're being very dramatic, Nick."

"I know. But please, my love, please?"

She havered, but plumped for safety. "I'm not going to make a fool of myself . . ."

"You want me to tell the Hon-John about you and Bannister?"

"Nick!"

"I'll do it!"

She considered me for a few seconds. "If you withdraw that very ungentlemanly threat," she said acidly, "then I will consider telephoning Tony for you. I won't promise it." She frowned. "On the other hand, it would be decent to congratulate him on his wedding, would it not? Even if it was to that vulgar little gold-digger."

I knew I would get no more from her. "I withdraw the threat," I said, "and I apologize for making it."

"Thank you, Nick. And I will promise to consider talking to

Tony." She looked pleased with her tactical victory. "So what are you going to do now?"

"I've got a job," I said, "working in the boat trade." I had no intention of telling Melissa that I was leaving England. If I had, then her lawyers would have been round my stern like sharks smelling blood. I fabricated my casual work for George Cullen into a fantasy of yacht-broking, which mildly pleased her.

"So you're not sailing into the sunset?"

"No," I said. "I'm not sure I'm physically up to it, you see."

"Quite right. So have you got a proper address now?"

I invented an address in Plymouth, which satisfied her. By the time she discovered there was no such place as 17b Institute Road, I would be long gone. I reckoned I would be ready in three or four days, after which I would slip my warps and head out past Drake Island, past the Breakwater, and thus into the Western Approaches. I would pass Ushant on the French coast, then go to the great emptiness.

I made Melissa promise once more that she would try to phone Bannister, or at least think about it, then I took the bus back to Plymouth. Buses were cheaper than trains, and I had no Angela now to tempt me into high-speed but expensive travel. Another bus took me to George's boatyard.

George, his workers gone for the weekend, was peering down at *Sycorax*. I saw he'd moored the fishing-boat outside *Sycorax* again. "You're not going this weekend, are you?" he asked me.

"Monday or Tuesday."

"I'll be glad to have the dock back," he said as though there were yachts lining up in the Hamoaze for his skilled attentions. "So you've got everything you need, Nick?"

"I still need fenders, a Dan buoy, jackstays, a rigid tender" – my old dinghy was still at Bannister's house, and somehow I did not think I would see her again – "fuel filters, radar-reflector, sail needles, courtesy flags, a couple of spare impellers, medicines . . ."

"All right!" He checked the flow. "I'm going home. Look after the yard."

It began to rain. I went into *Sycorax*'s cabin and made myself a cup of tea. I screwed a framed photograph of Piers and Amanda over the navigation table and tried not to think of how many months it would be before I saw them again. Instead I wondered whether Melissa would telephone Bannister, and decided she probably wouldn't.

Yet I had done all I could to preserve his life, save going to France and confronting him. Yet confrontation would do no good, for Bannister undoubtedly would not believe me. He doubtless would not believe Melissa either, but I had tried. Kassouli would win.

I told myself I had behaved decently in trying to save Bannister. Melissa had asked me why, and I'd given her the answers of truth and justice which she believed, for she knew how important those things were to me, yet the real truth was both simpler and far less noble. The real truth was that I cared very little whether Bannister lived or died, or whether he deserved punishment for his wife's death; the truth, however ignoble it might be, was that I had struggled to warn Bannister because that was my only way of staying in touch with Angela.

I had done it all for Angela. Each attempt to reach Bannister was a way of reminding Angela that I lived and loved. Each high-minded attempt to save his life was a pathetic protestation of my love. That was why I had tried so hard. It was unsubtle and demeaning, but also irresistible, for Angela had lodged in my desire, and life without her seemed flat.

I needed to go to sea. I needed winds and waves to blow that flatness clean away. I sipped my tea and jotted down what few items of equipment I still needed. I started a list of perishable supplies; the very last things I'd buy before I turned *Sycorax* towards the earth's end.

Through the rain outside, coming from George's locked offices above me, I heard a phone start ringing. I could not concentrate on the list of supplies, so instead I teased my anticipation by unfolding my chart of the Azores. The season would be ending by the time I reached Horta, which was good because berthing fees would be low. I could resupply with fresh food and renew friendships in the Café Sport. I smiled in anticipation, then noticed that the phone in the offices still rang. And rang. And rang.

I banged my right knee as I scrambled up the side of the wharf. The curved coping stones were wet, throwing me back down the wall, but I seized one of *Sycorax*'s warps and scraped my way over the top. My knee was numb and my back laced with pain as I limped across the yard. The rain had begun to fall harder so that it bounced in a fine spray from the cobbles.

The phone, dulled by the window and the rain, still rang.

I slipped in a puddle. I had the keys to the yard's outer gate in my pocket, but George never trusted me with the office keys in case I made phone calls that he could not monitor. I pulled at the door, but he'd remembered to lock it. I swore. The phone still rang.

I told myself it was probably only a customer asking about one of George's endlessly delayed jobs, but it was a bloody stubborn customer who'd phone at this time of the evening. I found an abandoned stanchion and swung it to shatter the door's pebbled glass. I reached through for the latch. The phone sounded louder now that I was inside the building.

I limped upstairs, thanking providence that there was no burglar alarm. I knew the phone would stop before I reached it. I smashed the glass in the door of Rita's office, then tripped on the frayed carpet as I lunged across the room. I stumbled and, as I fell headlong, my right hand grabbed the telephone's old-fashioned braided lead and the ancient Bakelite instrument slid off the desk to shatter its case on the floor. I fumbled for the fallen handset and prayed I had not cut off the connection. "Hello!"

There was silence. Except for the airy and echoing hiss that told me the line was not dead. I straightened the broken phone on the carpet and twisted myself round so that my back was against Rita's desk. "Hello?"

"Nick?" The voice was very small and unnaturally timid.

"Oh, God." I felt tears in my eyes. Then, stupidly, I really was crying with the relief of it. "Angela?"

"Nick."

"I'm crying," I said.

"So am I," she said, "for Tony."

I closed my eyes. "Where are you?" I asked.

"Cherbourg. Melissa telephoned."

I said a small prayer of thanks for Melissa's caring and compassionate soul. "I told her to."

"I know. I don't know what to do, Nick."

"Stop Tony sailing."

"He's already gone. They caught the afternoon's tide."

"Oh, Christ."

"Melissa called just afterwards and then I spoke to that journalist you told me to find and he said you'd been telling the truth. I should have believed you before, Nick, but . . ."

"It doesn't matter." I stared up at a calendar that Rita had hung on the wall. The calendar, which showed three kittens nestling in a pink blanket, was an incongruous advert for a firm that supplied VHF sets. "You must radio him," I said. "Get a taxi to the Chantereyne Marina. Go to the office there – "

"I've tried him on the radio telephone already. It wasn't any good. He says I'm being hysterical. He says it's newly-wed nerves. He says you're just trying to stop him winning the St Pierre because you work for Kassouli."

I scrambled to my feet to see if there was a clock on Rita's desk. There wasn't. "What time is it now?"

"Nearly seven o'clock." I subtracted one hour to get British Summer Time. "Nick?" Angela asked.

"I'm still here."

"Can you stop him, Nick?"

"Jesus." I thought for a few seconds. The answer had to be no, but I didn't want to be so bleak. "What time did he leave?"

"He crossed the start line at twenty past three exactly."

"Local time?" I asked. She confirmed that and I told her to wait.

I went into George's office and ripped pin-ups off his wall to reveal an ancient and faded chart of the Channel. I dragged open his desk drawer and, among the pipe reamers, corkscrews and patent medicines found an old pair of dividers. This year's tide table was in the other drawer. High Water at Dover had been ten minutes after mid-day, British Summer Time, which meant Bannister was sensibly using the fastest tidal current to launch his run.

I went to the window. The wind was southerly, gusting hard enough to slap the rain against the dirty panes. I picked up the phone on George's desk. "Are you still there?"

"Yes."

"Wait." I walked the rusty dividers across George's wretched chart. I knew that *Wildtrack* would be going like a bat out of hell to clear the Lizard before she swung up towards the Mizen on Ireland's south-west coast. After that she would go north-west, hunting for the backwash of the depression-born gales that arced their way eastwards across the North Atlantic, but the only place I could stop her was in my own back alley: the Channel. I added a divider's pace for the fair current and reckoned that, by three in the morning, and assuming *Wildtrack* had taken a slightly northerly course to clear the traffic-separation zone, Bannister would be in an area about twenty nautical miles south-south-west of Bolt Head. I drew a circle on the chart to limit the search area.

It's easy to posit such a search on a chart, but out in the Channel, amidst a squally darkness, it would be like trying to find a dying firefly in the Milky Way. I shortened the dividers to compensate for *Sycorax*'s pedestrian pace, then pricked them north from my circle to Plymouth. Eight hours of windward discomfort.

"I might intercept him if I leave now," I said dubiously.

"Please, Nick?" There was a pleading eagerness in her voice. "Will you stop him?"

The difficulty was not stopping *Wildtrack*. "Listen, Angela, I can't even promise to find him."

"But you'll try? Please?" The last word was said with all her old seething passion.

"I'll try. I promise." I thus volunteered for the madness. "What will you do now?"

"I don't know." She sounded helpless and frightened.

"Listen," I said. "Fly to Exeter. Hire a private plane if you have to. Meet me at Bannister's house tomorrow. I'll be there about mid-day."

"Why?"

Because I want to see you, I thought, but did not say it. Because I'm about to flog myself ragged in a bloody night for your rotten husband, and the least you can do is meet me afterwards and say thank you, but I didn't say that either. "Just be there, Angela. Please?"

She paused, and I thought she was going to refuse. "I'll try," she said guardedly.

"I'll try too." I put the phone down. The wind rattled George's window panes and blew damp litter in tumbling disarray across his yard. It was a south wind, and still rising, which meant that tonight's sail would be a windward slog to nowhere. The chances of finding Bannister were negligible, but that was no excuse to break the promise I'd just made to Angela. I closed the broken doors behind me, ducked my head to the wind, and limped to *Sycorax*.

I moved George's half-wrecked fishing-boat, primed my wretched engine, and hurt my back turning the flywheel. I needed a self-starter. I needed self-steering. I needed my head examining. I supposed that this was the manner in which knight errants had arranged their own disappointments; one bleat from the maiden and the fools galloped off into dragon land. The motor caught eventually and I let it get used to the idea of working while I dragged the foresails through the forehatch and hanked them on their halliards. I felt a moment's jealousy of the slick sailors who had roller-reefing and self-tailing winches, then forgot the self-pity as I took *Sycorax* stern first into the river where the waves scudded busily before the cold wind. I hammered the gear lever into forward and *Sycorax* bluffed her bows against wind and water.

I prayed that the engine would keep running. We were pushing past drab quays where even the gulls, perched to face the southerly wind, looked miserable. Once out of the river I hoisted all the sails, but left the engine running so I would not have to tack my way past the breakwater. The sky on this

English summer's evening was a low, grey and wintry murk through which two Wessex helicopters thumped towards a frigate moored in the sound. A landing craft, black and khaki, thumped evilly towards Mount Edgcumbe, and the brutal, squat lines of the ugly craft brought back memories of the time when I had two good legs and the belief that I was both invincible and immortal. A sudden percussive bang from the Wembury gunnery range brought the memories into sickeningly sharp focus, but then I forgot the past as my engine gave an ominous bang of its own. It stopped dead, but it had taken me safely to the searoom at the breakwater's western edge.

The open sea was raggedly high. *Sycorax* jarred at the first wave beyond the breakwater, then she seemed to realize what was expected of her and she tucked her head round and heeled to the wind that was flicking the tops off the waves into tails of white spume. I was sorting out the tangle of sheets in the cockpit. I was soaked through. Once clear of the Draystone I'd go below and find rough-weather clothes, but for now I knew I must stay with the tiller. A big Moody ran past me and the skipper waved and shouted something that got lost in the wind. He was probably calling that I had a nice boat. He was right, I did.

But that was small consolation tonight. I hunched low in the cockpit and knew that I was only making this gesture to impress Angela. I was meddling in her life because it gave me a chance to be close to her, but there had been no sign on the telephone that she reciprocated that wish. She had sounded desperate for her husband, while I had wanted her to be desperate for me. Such is pride.

I turned on to the starboard tack and hauled the sheets tight. I might have done this mainly for Angela, but there was a small part of me that was offended by what had happened. I'd been warned off by people who did not give a toss for the justice of their cause. No one knew how Nadeznha Bannister had died, but that ignorance had not prevented them planning a callous revenge. So tonight, despite the warnings, I would sail out of bloody-mindedness. I remembered another night when I'd been told, ordered, not to do something. There'd been a sniper, I remembered, and two bunkers with bloody great .50 machine-guns. The sniper was the real bastard, because he'd had a brand new American nightsight and had already hit a half-dozen of our men. The boss had radioed that we were to bug off out of there, but to do that would have been to jeopardize . . . I jerked back to the present as *Sycorax* crashed her bows into a steeper wave and the spray rattled harsh along her decks. I shivered, pegged the tiller, and went below for sweater, boots and oilies.

As it fell dark I saw the vaporous loom of the Eddystone's light sweeping its double flash through the pelting rain. *Sycorax* was holding her course beautifully as she pounded through a broken sea; she might not have slick self-tailing winches and roller-reefing, but her long deep keel made her a better sea boat than any of the modern plastic-fantastics that roamed the pleasure coasts of the world. I switched on my electric navigation lights and hoped the battery was properly charged. The engine smelt weird, so I just put the cover back on and hoped benign neglect would cure whatever had gone wrong. I tapped the barometer and found the glass was rising. I called the coastguard on the VHF and asked for a forecast. Strong winds tonight, but falling off towards dawn, then another depression following quickly.

I went topsides briefly and checked that no merchant ship was about to turn me into matchwood. None was, so I went below again and emptied two tins of baked beans into a saucepan. It was all the food I had, and tasted good. I filled a Thermos with tea and carried it to the cockpit. Now it was simply a question of letting the wet hours pass. The rain slackened as the full darkness came, and I wondered if the wind was already falling off. The sea was softer now, though the swell which slid under *Sycorax*'s counter was long and high. The waves had gone from silver-grey to grey to dark. Soon they would be jet black, but perhaps streaked with phosphorescence. Clouds drowned the moonlight.

Sycorax sailed herself. Her tiller was pegged and her sheets cleated tight. Sometimes, as the swell dropped her hard into a trough, the mainsail would shiver, but she picked herself up and drove on. I still had no radar-reflector and hoped that the big ships which were bashing down from Amsterdam and Hamburg and Felixstowe were keeping a proper watch. I could see the bright confusion of their lights all about me.

Midnight passed and the wind dropped and veered. I let out the sheets and felt *Sycorax*'s speed increase as she found herself on her favourite point of sail: a broad reach. I'd seen few other yachts, but just before one o'clock, and when I should still have been well north of *Wildtrack*'s course, I saw the lights of a vessel under sail. She was travelling west and, to intercept her, I unpegged the tiller and hardened *Sycorax* into the wind again. The big swell sometimes dropped the other yacht out of my sight, all but for her masthead's tri-coloured light which would flicker over the shredding wavetops. I tried to judge her size, but could not. I took bearings on her which told me she was sailing fast.

I opened the locker where my flares were stored. Bannister would not stop if I radioed him on the VHF, and if I tried to sail across his bow I invited a collision that, though it would stop him, could also sink *Sycorax*. Instead I planned to cross his stern and loose red emergency flares into the sky, because even a racing boat would have to stop and help a boat in distress. That was the law. Mulder and Bannister might curse, but they would have to gybe on to the new course and come to my rescue. Once they had come alongside I would play what cards I had. They were not many, but they included a Colt .45 which I had fetched up from its hiding place. I knew that if I fired the rocket flares I would cause chaos in the Channel. There would be lifeboats, radios and other ships all contributing to a rescue that wasn't needed, but I had promised Angela to stop her husband, and if that promise turned a busy sealane into chaos, then chaos it would be.

I saw I was heading the approaching yacht. He was on the port tack, I on a starboard, so it was his job to stay clear of me. He'd seen my lights, for he steered a point southerly to give me room. I hardened again, and he thought I had not seen him and shone a bright torch beam up on to his mainsail to make a splash of white light in the darkness. At the same time another of his crew called me on Channel 16; the VHF emergency channel. "Sailing boat approaching large yacht, do you read me, over."

It was not Mulder's voice, nor Bannister's. I thought I detected a French accent in the crackling speaker. I was close enough to see the sail number in the torchlight and, because it was not *Wildtrack*, I fell off the wind to go astern of him. The torch was switched off. A voice shouted a protest that was made indistinct by the spray and wind. The yacht's stern light showed me the name *Mariette* on the white raked transom. The port of registry was Étaples. I waved as I passed, then the wind tore us apart as I headed south again.

By three o'clock I knew I must be well inside the rough circle I'd sketched on George's chart. The night was black as pitch and the wind was still dropping. I turned westwards, heading against *Wildtrack*'s course. I searched for an hour. I saw two more Frenchmen, a Dutchman, but no *Wildtrack*. A bulk-carrier crashed past and *Sycorax*'s sails slatted as we were tossed on the great wake. Apart from the big ship the sea was empty. I had failed.

I turned north. There was already a lightening to the east as the false wolf-light of dawn edged the clouds. I was bone tired, cold, and hungry. I had failed, but I had always known how narrow was my chance of success. From *Sycorax*'s cockpit I could never see more than two miles and *Wildtrack* could have run past me at any time in the darkness. In truth I doubted whether I had ever sailed far enough south. Bannister was gone to the Lizard and death.

It began to rain again as I ran for home. The rain beaded the shrouds and dripped from the lacing on the boom. I made some more tea and found a wrinkled apple in the galley. I cut out the rotten bit and ate the rest.

Dawn showed the sea heaving in a greasy, slow swell. Patches of fog drifted above a sludge-like sea. If the fog lifted, it rained. The wind was west now, but negligible and sullen. The rudder, with no speed to give it bite, banged in its pintles. Another depression was meant to be racing towards the Channel, and *Wildtrack* would be praying for its arrival if she was to make a fast outwards run.

I was just praying to get home. Sailing isn't always fun in the sun. It isn't always happy friends on sparkling decks in a perfect force four on a glinting ocean. It can be misery incarnate. It can be rain and fog and cold and hunger. It can be a sulky sea and a listless sky. It can be failure, and then the only consolation is to remember that we volunteered for the misery.

So, in misery, I crawled north. I spent a quarter-hour working out the tidal currents to help my course, then tried to coax the engine into life. It was on strike, and the wind seemed to be in sympathy with its grudge. I stripped the fuel system, tried again, and still it wouldn't start, so, instead, I tidied up the cabin and washed the decks. I told myself time and time again that I would not be disappointed if Angela had not returned to Devon. I told myself that the two of us had no future. I told myself over and over that I really did not care whether she was waiting for me at Bannister's house or not.

At mid-morning, reluctant at first, a wind scoured the sea and creaked the port shrouds. I dropped the mop and seized the tiller. I listened to the growing sound of water running past the hull and felt my excitement increase because Angela might be waiting for me. I did care. I cared desperately.

It was mid-day before I passed the Calfstone Shoal. The bell-buoy clanged at me. The wind was fitful now, but strong enough to carry me up the river and round the point.

Where, on the terrace above the river, and in front of an empty house, Angela was waiting.

She had been crying. She was in jeans and sweater, her hair bound in a single plait that hung to her narrow waist. "It's a hell of a way to start a marriage."

Or to end one, I thought, but did not say as much.

She was distraught, but I was too cold and famished to be a gentle listener. I made myself eggs, bacon, coffee and toast that I ate at the kitchen table. Angela sat opposite me and I noticed the thick gold wedding ring on her finger beside her diamond. She shook her head despairingly. "I tried to talk to him . . ."

". . . but he wouldn't listen." I finished the sentence for her.

"He thinks you put me up to it. He thinks you want him to

fail." She stood and paced the floor. She was restless and confused, and I did not blame her. She only had my word, and that of Micky Harding, that her new husband was sailing to his death.

For a time she tried to convince herself that it was untrue. I let her talk while I ate. She talked of Bannister's belief that he could take the coveted St Pierre, and of his happiness because she had walked up an aisle with him. She spoke of the programmes Bannister would make in the new season; she spoke of the future they had discussed and, because that future was threatened, it only seemed the brighter and more blessed to her now. "Tell me it isn't true." She spoke of Kassouli's threat.

"As far as I know," I said carefully, "it is true."

She shook in sudden anger. "How dare they say he murdered Nadeznha?"

"Perhaps because they believe he did?"

"He didn't! He didn't!"

"You know that?" I poured myself more coffee.

"For Christ's sake!" She was still angry. "Do you think I'd have married him if he'd killed her?"

"Why did you marry him?"

She lit a cigarette. She had been chain-smoking ever since I'd come back. "Because I love him," she said defiantly.

"Good." I hid my disappointment.

"And because," she said, "we can make a decent life for each other. I give him the security he wants, and he gives me the security I want."

"Good," I said again.

"And," she said even more defiantly, "because I couldn't marry you."

I smiled. "I'm not a very good prospect."

She drew on her cigarette. "You've caught the sun." It sounded like an accusation.

"I've been working. Real work. Sawing and planing and getting paid for it. I didn't get much money, but I've finished the boat. All but for a radar-reflector. And some fenders. And one or two other things."

"Have you found a girl?"

The question surprised me, for it implied a jealousy that I had not expected. "No. I kept seeing your picture in the papers and I'd cut it out, keep it for ten minutes, then throw it away. I got drunk once or twice."

She smiled, the first smile she'd given me. "I watched you in the film rushes. I used to go to the cutting rooms and run loops of your ugly face." She shrugged. "You screwed up my lovely film, Nick Sandman."

"I'm sorry."

"No, you're not." She shrugged. "I've given up the business, though, haven't I? That was one of the promises I made to Tony. No more telly." She looked at her watch. "Where will he be by now? Off southern Ireland?"

"Yes."

She had begun to cry very softly. "He can't give up, can he? He's got cameras watching him, so he has to be a big, brave boy. Men are so bloody stupid." She blew her nose. "Including you, Nick Sandman. What are you going to do now?"

I shrugged. "I'm going to provision *Sycorax*. I shall go to town, visit the bank, and spend a fortune on supplies. After that, on tomorrow's tide, I shall sail away. I'll make a landfall at Ushant, then head for the Azores."

She frowned. "Just like that?"

"You think I should lay on brass bands and cheerleaders?"

She gave me a flicker of a smile. "I'd want seasick pills."

"Goldfish get seasick."

She laughed. "They don't!"

"No, it's true. If you take them to sea as pets, they get seasick." I poured the last of the coffee. "I wouldn't mind a cat."

"Truly?" She sounded surprised.

"I've always liked cats," I said. "You're a bit cat-like."

She stared down at the table. I'd thought our last few moments had been too relaxed and, sure enough, her mind was still with *Wildtrack*. "I've thought of phoning the coastguard. But it won't do any good."

"No. They'd just laugh at you."

"I've tried the radio-telephone again, but he just gets angry.

He thinks I'm trying to stop his moment of glory. And the last two times I tried, it was Fanny who answered."

"I'm sorry," I said. We'd been through this already, and there was nothing I could do. "Pray that he lives," I said.

She stared bleakly at me. "Perhaps I should go to Canada?"

I smiled. "What can you do there?"

"I can try and stop him. I could go with the film crew."

"What will you do?" I asked. "Ram him? And how do you know the film crew will even find him? I know they'll be in radio touch, but have you ever seen the fog in those waters? Or perhaps *Wildtrack* will make her turn at night. What will you do then? Crash the camera helicopter on the foredeck next day? Or do you think you can persuade him to give up there when you couldn't do it here?" I suddenly realized that my pessimism was doing her no good. "I'm sorry. Maybe you should try. Anything's better than doing nothing."

She sighed. "Tony may not even reach the turning point. God knows."

"He'll reach St Pierre," I said.

"He will?" She was puzzled by my certainty.

I stared in silence at her, thinking of something Kassouli had said to me. Jill-Beth had not been specific when I tape-recorded her words, but Kassouli, I now remembered, had wanted me to steer a certain course on the return leg. "Jesus wept," I said softly, "I've been so bloody stupid."

"What do you mean?"

"They're going to take him to the exact place where Nadeznha died! Don't you see? On the outward leg he'll have to go much too far north, but coming back he can run the great circle with the gales! That's why they'll let him turn, because the perfect revenge has to be at the same damn place!"

"What place?" Her voice was urgent.

I couldn't remember. The only places I'd seen the coordinates were on the frame of Nadeznha Bannister's portrait in *Wildtrack*'s after cabin and on the papers that Kassouli had shown me. "Forty something north," I said helplessly, then shrugged to show that my memory had failed me. Then I remembered the inquest transcript.

Angela ran from the kitchen, and I followed her. She went to Bannister's study where she pulled open drawers to spill old television scripts, letters and diaries across the carpet. She found the transcript at the back of a filing cabinet. She turned the pages quickly, then seemed to freeze when she came to the evidence she wanted. "Forty-nine, eighteen north," she read aloud, "and forty-one, thirty-six west." She turned to me. "Where is that?"

I used an atlas to show her. I took one of Bannister's pencils and I showed her how, on the mercator projection, *Wildtrack* would have to sail an arching parabola westwards, then a shallower curve back home. I put a cross on the point where Nadeznha Bannister had died. Angela used a ruler to work out the distances. I watched her thin fingers and I knew, in the room's silence, what would come next.

"Nick . . ."

I had gone to the window. "It's about three thousand nautical miles for *Wildtrack*," I said. That was the distance from Cherbourg to the turning point at St Pierre, then back to the pencil cross.

"And from here. By the fastest route?" I could hear hope in her voice.

"Seventeen hundred?" It was probably fractionally less, but there was no such thing as a 'fastest route'; not against headwinds and the North Atlantic current. "Say two thousand land miles."

"How long would it take . . .?" She did not finish the sentence, but she really did not need to. She wanted to ask me how long it would take *Sycorax* to reach that cross on the map.

I could see the trees on the far bank heaving in the rising wind. It was odd weather; a quick succession of winds and calm, but tonight would see another stiff blow. "Sixteen days," I guessed.

"Nick?" Her voice was tentative, even frightened, but she was pleading with me. She wanted me to go into the North Atlantic to save her husband.

"It would be faster," I said brutally, "if I had someone to crew for me."

She shook her head, but so abstractedly that I thought she had not heard properly. "But could you . . .?" she started, then seemed to think of something that drained the hope out of her face. "It's your leg, isn't it? You're frightened that it will collapse."

"It hasn't happened for weeks," I said truthfully, "and even if it had, it wouldn't stop me."

"So . . ." She could not bring herself to ask the favour directly.

"Yes," I said. *Wildtrack* had a day's start, but *Wildtrack* had much further to go. Yes, I could reach the killing place, and yes, I would try.

I've never victualled a boat so quickly, nor so well. Angela used her car and credit card to go to the town, while I raided Bannister's larder and boathouse.

"I can't let him die!" she said to me as she pushed a wheelbarrow of food down to the wharf. She said it as if to justify the insanity of what I did.

I didn't care to discuss the motives; it was enough that I'd agreed to go for her. "What's in the barrow?"

"Coffee, dried milk, eggs. Tins of everything."

"The eggs need to be dipped in boiling water for five seconds. It preserves them."

She took the eggs back to the house while I stored the tins in freezer bags to keep the bilge water from rusting the metal and obliterating the labels. I stored packet soup, fresh bread, fruit, vegetables, biscuits, baked beans, more baked beans, Irish whiskey, still more whiskey, margarine, tinned fruitcake, salt, sugar, tinned ham, and corned beef. I'd finished my rough list of perishable stores and hoped I'd forgotten nothing essential. Teabags, washing powder, compass alcohol, rice, oatmeal, disinfectant, multivitamins, cooking oil, lamp oil, soap. I wasn't victualling only for a North Atlantic run, but thinking of what would follow. My own suspicion, my own certainty, was that I would never find *Wildtrack*. I went on a quixotic search because I did not know how to say no to a blonde, but once I had failed I would turn *Sycorax*'s bows southwards, and so I provisioned for a long dog-leg voyage that would take me from England to the Canadian coast, then southwards to where the palms and slash pines grew. Fruit juice, nuts, stock cubes, more whiskey, spare light bulbs, lamp wicks, loo paper, washing-up liquid that could also serve as salt-water shampoo.

The wind was still rising, and the glass dropping. By nightfall there would be a half gale blowing. Bannister had what he wanted, a fast start, and I would share it.

Angela brought the parboiled eggs and I gave her more errands. "I want some coal or coke. Firelighters. I want sweaters, socks, warm weather gear. I want the best bloody oilskins in the house. I need a sextant, charts, the best sleeping bag you've got. I want an RDF and a self-steering vane."

"Whatever you want, Nick. Just look for it."

I ransacked the house for things I might need. I borrowed a set of Bannister's spare oilskins that were so much better than mine. I borrowed a sextant so I would have a spare. I found charts of the North Atlantic and the Canadian coast. I stole the battery from the Peugeot to supplement the two already on board *Sycorax*. From a drawer in Bannister's study I took a fancy hand-held radio-direction finder and a pack of spare batteries, then scooped an armful of paperbacks from his shelves. More whiskey. I took the fenders off *Wildtrack II*. I crammed provisions into *Sycorax*'s every locker. Angela helped, piling stores higgledy-piggledy on the cabin sole. Half the time I didn't know what she was stowing below, but I could sort out the whole mess on the voyage. I used the boathouse hose to top up with water, then craned three extra cans of diesel fuel on to the foredeck. I lashed the big cans down, though I doubted if the bloody engine would ever run long enough to need them. There was some broken self-steering gear in the boathouse and I put it all aboard. It could be mended and rigged at sea.

I still needed medical stores. Angela drove her Porsche into town and came back with bandages, butterfly clips, plasters, hypodermics and painkillers. I'd told her to go to the doctor and get a prescription for painkillers, local anaesthetics, tranquillizers, antibiotics and Benzedrine. I scribbled a note to the doctor explaining my need and Angela brought everything back. More whiskey. Potatoes, flour, crispbread, Newcastle Brown Ale, chocolate bars, razor-blades, bacon, fishing-lines, antiseptic cream, sunglasses.

By six o'clock it was almost done. The wind was blowing hard now, coming from the south-west. If the weather pattern held then I'd have a stiff beat out of the river and a wet blow down to the Lizard, and a rough sea to the Mizen Head, but after that, off the shelf waters, I'd be reaching fast into the high latitudes. From there I'd drop down to the rendezvous.

My tender was still in the boathouse. As Angela took the last two boxes down to the cabin I hoisted the dinghy on to *Sycorax*'s coachroof where I lashed it upside down. The dinghy was my only liferaft; there were not even lifejackets aboard. As I tied the last lashing to the starboard handrail it began to rain and suddenly there was no more to be done except to say goodbye.

I kissed Angela. We stood in the rain beside the river and I kissed her once more. I held her tight because a part of me did not want to leave. "I can't promise anything," I said.

"I know."

"You just have to wait now," I said.

"Yes." She was embarrassed that I was doing this for her, but it was the last desperate throw, and I could not deny it to her. I'd planned to sail away whatever happened, and all I did now was make a northerly detour to where the seas would be cold, grey and bleak.

"Time to go." I wanted to stay with her, but the falling tide beckoned. There were no bands or cheerleaders, just an overloaded boat on a river pecked by rain and squirled by wind. "I'll write," I said. "Some day."

"Please do." She spoke stiffly.

"I love you," I said.

"Don't say it, Nick."

It was a miserable parting; a miserable departure. The engine wouldn't start, but the jib tugged *Sycorax*'s bow away from the wharf. Angela let go my springs and warps as I hoisted the mainsail and mizzen. Water swirled between the hull and the bank as I coiled the ropes.

"There's a present for you in the cabin!" Angela shouted. *Sycorax* was moving fast now, snatched by the ebb and the river's turbid current. Angela thought I had not heard her, so cupped her hands and shouted again, "In the cabin, Nick! A present!"

I waved to show that I'd heard, but I couldn't go below to find the gift until I had *Sycorax* settled into the main channel. Once there I pegged the tiller, went down the companionway, and found the last two boxes that Angela had loaded. One was filled with catfood, the other contained a small black female kitten that, as soon as I opened the box lid, greeted me with needle-sharp claws.

I went topsides. I looked back, but the rain had already driven Angela away from the wharf. The kitten, astonished by its new home, glared at me from the cabin steps. "I'll call you Angel," I said.

Angel hissed at me. The hair on her back bristled. I hoped she was a sea cat. I hoped she'd bring me luck.

I passed the pub and wondered when I would see it again. Someone, recognizing the boat, waved from the window, and I waved back. I knew that in far-off seas I would remember that bar as a place of idle talk and lustrous beer, but then I had to tack in the village's narrow reach and the manoeuvre took my mind off the anticipated nostalgia. I saw faces watching me from the holidaymakers' cars which were parked on the riverside. The tourists saw a business-like boat loaded for a voyage. There was nothing glossy about *Sycorax* now; she was lashed tight in the evening's rain and her beauty was that of a functional craft ready for the ocean. The kitten scrambled up to the cockpit and bared its tiny teeth at me. I scratched her under the chin, then watched as she leaped up to the coachroof where she began to sharpen her claws on the dinghy's lashings. "Angel," I tried out the name. "Angel."

I hadn't filled in my Form C1328, Part One, to inform Her Majesty's Customs and Excise that I was travelling abroad. Bugger Form C1328. I didn't have *Sycorax*'s registration papers, the lack of which would mean bureaucratic aggravation in foreign ports. Then bugger the bureaucrats, too; the world had too many such dull killjoys and *Sycorax* would sail despite them. Ahead of me now were the town quays, then the river's entrance where the half-gale was smashing waves white across the bar. The clouds were bringing an early dusk beneath which the homely lights gleamed soft from windows in the town. The blue-neon cross on the gable of the Baptist church flickered like lightning and I said a prayer for my small ship that was going down to the big seas. Rain slashed down at us, and the kitten protested to me from inside the cabin's hatch.

Car lights flashed from the stone jetty by the town boatyard. As *Sycorax* drew closer I saw the blue Porsche parked there and knew that Angela had come to see us off. She ran down to the fuel pontoon and waved both arms at me. I waved back and I wondered why the farewell was suddenly so enthusiastic when, a half-hour before, it had been so cool. "I like the cat!" I shouted as loud as I could.

"Nick! Nick!" Then I saw she was beckoning. I pushed the tiller over, sheeted in on the new tack, and let the boat glide up towards the pontoon. Two big motor cruisers were moored there and I watched as Angela climbed over the poop of the larger boat. She stood outboard of its guardrails, holding on to a stanchion. She carried a bag.

I put *Sycorax*'s head to the wind and let the tide carry me alongside the cruiser. Angela threw the bag on to the foredeck, waited a second, then caught my hand and jumped into the cockpit.

I pushed the tiller to starboard and sheeted the jib across to turn our bows. I saw that Angela had left her car door open and its lights still burning.

"Are you sure?" I asked her.

"Of course I'm not sure, but . . ." She sounded oddly angry with me.

"But what?"

Her eyes were red-rimmed from crying. "It's your leg. You're going to kill yourself out there, Nick."

"I'll be fine, I promise."

"And you said it would be quicker with two people on board."

"That's true." I let the sails flap. "But not if one of them is seasick." I wanted her to come more than I could possibly say, yet I was using arguments to make her stay behind.

She bent back her left ear to show me an adhesive patch. "The chemist says they're infallible." She must have bought the patch when she had gone to fetch my pills and potions, which meant she must have been debating this action for hours.

"It's going to be rough out there," I warned her. I was letting *Sycorax* drift on the current in case Angela wanted me to take her back to the pontoon.

"If you give me a choice now," she said, "I might not stay."

I did not give her the choice. Instead I gave her the tiller and hauled in the sheets. "Hold this course. See the white pole on the headland? Aim for it."

I fetched her bag from the foredeck and hoisted the staysail. I was so happy I could have walked on water.

Then *Sycorax*'s bows hit the waves at the river's bar, the first cold spray shot back like shrapnel, and the three of us were going to sea.

PART FOUR

Part Four

Angela was seasick.

For hour after miserable hour, day after night, night after day, she lay shivering and helpless. I tried to make her spend time in the cockpit where the fresh air might have helped, but she shrank away from me. She stayed in the cabin's lee bunk, wrapped in blankets, and retching into a zinc bucket.

The kitten was fine.

The kitten seemed to think a world permanently tipped away from the wind and battered by a half-gale was a perfect place. It slept in Angela's lap, giving Angela the one small pleasure she could appreciate, while in the daylight it roamed the boat, performing daredevil acrobatics which made me think it was bound to be washed overboard, yet the little beast had an instinct for avoiding the rush of sea. Once I saw her leap up to the mainsail's tack. She clung to the cotton, legs splayed, as a sea thundered over the coachroof to shatter on the tethered dinghy. The kitten seemed to like the mainsail after that and would sometimes scamper up the sail as I bellowed hopelessly that she'd tear the cotton with her claws. She'd get stuck up by the gaff jaws, looking like a small black spider on a vast chalk wall, but somehow she always found her way down. Her other favourite place was the chart table and every time I opened a chart she would leap on to it and curl up by the dividers. Then she'd purr, defying me to throw her off. I navigated from cat hair to cat hair.

There was little else to steer *Sycorax* by. The sky stayed clouded, the nights dark, and, once we had left the Irish lights behind, we were blind. I could not make Bannister's fancy radio-direction finder work; all that happened when I pressed its trigger was that a small red light would glow, then nothing. Finally, in a fit of tired temper, I hurled the damn thing into the sea with a curse on all modern gadgets. I told myself, as I had told myself a million times before, that the *Mayflower* had reached America without a silicon chip, so I could too.

So, like the *Mayflower*, we thrashed north-west under a press of sails. Angela had the lee bunk, the bunk tipped away from the wind, which meant she could not fall out, so I used the weather bunk and snatched hours of sleep curled against the canvas straps that held me in place. I made Thermos flasks of soup that Angela pushed irritably away. I had never been seasick, but I knew well enough what it was like. For the first day she feared she was dying, and thereafter she feared she was not. So much for the chemist's adhesive patch.

Sycorax thrived. She seemed to be telling me that she had endured enough nonsense in the last months, and this was what she was born to do, and she did it well. There were the usual crop of small problems in the first days. The jib clew began to tear and I temporarily replaced it with the storm jib and spent an evening sewing the stiff cotton tight again. The caulking round my chimney lifted, which was my own fault, and I spent a wet two hours tamping it back. The short-wave radio gave up its ghost after just two days and no amount of coaxing, banging or cursing would bring it back to life. The lack of the radio was more serious than the loss of the radio-direction finder, for without the short wave I could not check the accuracy of my key-wound chronometer. We were sailing by God, by guess, and by the Traverse Tables until the sky cleared and I could take a sight in the hope that the chronometer was keeping good time. There was a deal of water in the bilges whenever I pumped her, but I'd expected that. The caulked seams would tighten soon enough.

My greatest problem was my own tiredness. Angela could not help, so I was having to sail both day and night. I still had not rigged the broken self-steering gear which was stowed under the tender, but *Sycorax* had always sailed well enough with shortened sail and a pegged tiller while I slept. Such a procedure presupposed a constant wind direction, and entailed frequent wakings to check the compass headings. The worst moment came eight nights after we'd put to sea when a cleat horn snapped clean off and I woke to the hammering panic of the staysail flapping. The boat was rolling like a drunk on the swells as I struggled on to deck.

Rain was seething in the darkness as I turned *Sycorax* into the wind, backed the jib, and sheeted the main across. Then, with my lifeline locked on, I went forward to find the lost sheet. It took me ten minutes to bring it back to the cockpit, belay it over the jib cleat, and settle the boat back on her compass heading. My nightlights flickered on the shrouds while, beyond them, ghostly and fretting, the crests were shattering white as they rolled towards us. I pumped the bilges, then, in my rain-soaked oilies, climbed back over the washboards. Angela woke and groaned. "What happened?"

"Cleat broke, nothing to worry about."

"Why don't you have proper winches like Tony?"

I thought the question showed a return of interest; perhaps even the first symptom of resurrection. "Because they're flashy nasty modern things that would look wrong on *Sycorax*, and because they cost over a hundred pounds apiece." I felt my back aching as I tugged off the stiff, wet oilskins. "Do you want something to eat?"

"God, no." She groaned again as the boat slammed into a wave. "Where are we?"

"West of Ireland, east of Canada."

"Are we sinking?"

"Not yet. But the wind's piped up a bit."

I woke an hour later to feel the boat pitching and corkscrewing. I oilied up, then went topsides again to find the weather was brewing trouble. I took down the main and hoisted my loose-footed storm trysail instead. I dropped the jib and reefed the mizzen. The boat was still unbalanced, trying to broach into the hissing seas, so I took down the trysail and re-rigged it as a mizzen staysail. That stiffened *Sycorax* nicely, and she needed stiffening for the sea was heaving like a landscape gone mad. We were far north now, so the night was light and short and I could see that the wind and heavy rain were creaming the wavetops smooth and covering the valleys with a fine sheet of white foam. *Sycorax* buried her bowsprit twice, staggered up, and the water came streaming back towards the cockpit to mix with the pelting rain. I had neither dodgers nor sprayhood, though the lashed tender offered some small forward protection from the sea. I pumped the bilges every few minutes.

For the rest of that night, all the next day, and into the following night, that wind and sea pounded and shivered us. I slept for an hour in the morning, woke to the madness, pumped for a half-hour, and slept again. I took Benzedrine. By the midnight of the gale's second night the wind was slackening and the sea's insistent blows were lessening, so I pegged the tiller, left the sails short, and crawled into my bunk. Angela was weeping in despair, but I had no energy to soothe her. I only wanted oblivion in sleep.

I slept five hours, mostly in half-wake dreaming, then crawled from the damp bunk to find the gale had passed. I forced myself out of the sleeping bag, pulled on a soaking sweater, and went topsides to see a long, long swell fretted with small and angry waves that were the remnants of the wind's passage. I took down the mizzen staysail, unlashed the boom and gaff, hoisted the main and jib, then unreefed the mizzen. I pumped the bilge till my back could take no more pain. I was hurting in every bone and muscle. This was called sailing, but the wind had dropped to force four and there were rents in the dawn clouds that promised sunshine. The sea glinted silver in the west and I leaned on the coachroof, too tired to move, and thanked *Sycorax* for all she had done. I patted her coachroof and spoke my thanks out loud.

The cat, hearing my voice, protested that she had not been fed for hours. I slid back the hatch and climbed down into the soaked cabin. The cat rubbed itself against my legs. I no longer called her Angel, for every time I did Angela answered. I opened a tin of cat food and was so hungry I was tempted to wolf it down myself. Instead I cleaned up the cabin sole, including the spilt contents of the zinc bucket, and tried to persuade myself that this was indeed the life that I had dreamed of in those long hospital nights.

An hour later a Russian Aurora Class missile-cruiser cleared the northern horizon. She was escorted by two destroyers that sniffed suspiciously towards *Sycorax*. I dutifully lowered and raised my Red Ensign. That courtesy over, and duly answered by the dipping of a destroyer's hammer and sickle, I switched on the VHF. "Yacht *Sycorax* to Russian naval vessel. Do you read me, over?"

"Good morning, little one. Over." The operator must have been expecting my call for he answered instantly. He sounded horribly cheerful, as though he had a bellyful of coffee and fried egg, or whatever else constituted a hearty Russian breakfast.

"Can you give me a position and time check?" We stayed on the emergency channel which was hardly likely to disturb anyone this far out to sea. "Over."

"I don't know if our American satellite equipment is working," he chuckled. "Wait. Over."

I smiled at his answer and felt the salt crack on my face. A minute later he gave me a position and a countdown to an exact second. He wished me luck, then the three grey warships slithered southwards through the fretting sea.

We'd done well. We'd cleared the tail of the Rockall Plateau, though I was further north than I'd wanted. If Bannister was doing half as well in his faster boat, then he'd take the St Pierre, so long as he lived to do it. My chronometer had stayed accurate to within a second, which was comforting.

"Who were you talking to?" Angela rolled over in her bunk.

"A Russian destroyer. He gave us our position."

"The Russians help you?" she sounded incredulous.

"Why on earth shouldn't they?" I gently pushed the cat off the Rockall Plateau and made a pencil cross on the chart. "Would you like some coffee?"

"Please."

Resurrection had definitely started. I made the coffee, then scrambled some eggs. Angela said she could not possibly eat any eggs, but five minutes later she tentatively tried a spoonful of mine, then stole the mug from me and wolfed the whole lot down.

"More?"

"Please." I made more. Resurrection was on course. She found her cigarettes and lit one. In the afternoon that we'd spent provisioning *Sycorax*, Angela had hidden twenty cartons of cigarettes in the forepeak, just as she'd stowed a second sleeping bag and a set of foul-weather gear on board. "Just in case I decided to come," she'd explained. Now she smoked her cigarette in the cockpit where she blinked at the misty grey light. She reached behind her ear and tore off the small patch. "So much for modern science." She tossed it overboard. She looked dreadful; pale as ash, stringy haired and red-eyed.

"Good morning, beautiful," I said.

"I hope you haven't got a mirror on this damned boat." She stared disconsolately around the horizon, seeing nothing but the long grey swells. Behind us the clouds were dark as sin, while ahead the sky was a sodden grey. She frowned at me. "Do you really like this life, Nick?"

"I love it."

The cat did its business on the windward scuppers where it had somehow learned that the sea cleaned up after it, then it stepped delicately down on to Angela's lap where it began its morning session of self-satisfied preening. "You can't call her Angel," Angela said.

"Why not?"

"Because I don't like it. Call her Pixie."

"I am not going to have a bloody cat called Pixie."

"All right." She scratched the cat's chin. "Vicky."

"Why Vicky?"

"After the Victoria Cross, of course."

"That's immodest."

"Who's to know if you don't tell them?"

"I'll know."

Angela growled at my intransigence. "She's called Vicky, and that's the end of it. Do I look really awful?"

"Absolutely hideous. Loathsome, in fact."

"Thank you, Nick."

"What you do now," I said, "is go below, undress, wash all over, dry all over, put on clean clothes, comb your hair, then come out singing."

"Aye, aye, sir."

"Then open the forehatch to air the boat. Then sit here and steer 289 while I sleep."

"On my own?" She sounded alarmed.

"You can have Cat for company."

"Vicky."

"You can have Vicky for company," I said.

She's been Vicky ever since.

That night the sky clouded again and I was woken in the short darkness to hear the water seething past the hull and I knew we were getting the spinning backlash of yet another gale.

Angela was sick again, but not so badly. She was becoming accustomed to the boat, even to its chemical loo. I'd assured her that constipation could not last clean across the Atlantic, and had been rewarded with a sour look.

But the next couple of days brought colour to her cheeks. She began to eat properly. I did all the cooking, for there is something about cooking on a boat that prompts seasickness.

We ran fast in those days. We saw no other sails, only a trawler steaming west and another warship heading north. The contrails of aircraft laced the sky; jumbo jets carrying their huddled masses between the world's great cities. The passengers, if they looked down at all, would have seen the wrinkles of a featureless sea, while we, leaning to the wind, watched a whale blow its vents. Angela stared like a child. "I never thought I'd see that," she said in wonder.

But most of the time she talked of her husband and I detected how desperately she needed to justify her presence on *Sycorax*. "He's more likely to believe the warning if he hears my voice on the radio," she would say. "He'll know it's serious if I go to these lengths to reach him, won't he?"

"Sure," I would say. I was treating her like porcelain. My own belief was that Bannister would be mad as hell when he discovered his new wife had sailed the Atlantic with another man, but Angela did not need that kind of truth.

"I can't believe he's really in danger," she said that evening.

"Danger's like that," I said. "It didn't seem real in the Falklands, either. War didn't seem real. We'd trained for it, but I don't think any of us really thought we'd end up fighting. I remember thinking how bloody daft it was. I shouldn't have been thinking at all. I was supposed to be counting the rounds

I'd fired, but I clean forgot to do it. That's what we were trained to do. Count the bloody rounds so you knew when to change magazines, you see, but I was just laughing! It wasn't real. I kept pulling the trigger and suddenly there were no more bullets up my spout and this bloody great bloke with a submachine-gun appeared in a bunker to my left and all I had . . ." I shrugged. "Sorry. Talking too much."

Angela was sitting next to me in the cockpit. "And all you had was what?"

"Did we bring any pickled onions?"

"Was that when you were wounded?" she insisted.

"Yes."

"So what happened?"

I mimed a bayonet stroke. "Mucky."

She frowned. "You were shot then?"

"Not for another minute. I was like a wet hen. I couldn't go back, because it would have looked as if I'd bottled out, so I kept on going. I remember shouting like a bloody maniac, though for the life of me I can't remember what I was shouting. It's stupid, really, but I'd like to remember that."

Angela frowned at me. "Why wouldn't you talk like that on the film?"

"I don't know . . ." I paused. "Because I'd made a balls of everything, if you really want the truth. I'd gone to the wrong place, I was frightened as hell, and I thought we were about to be worked over by a bunch of bloody Argies. I just panicked, nothing more."

"That's not what the citation says."

"It was dark. No one could see what was happening."

She mistook my tone, which was dismissive. "Do you regret the fighting now?"

"Christ, no!"

"No?"

"Queen and Country, my love."

She stared incredulously at me. "You really do mean that, don't you?"

Of course I meant it, but there wasn't time to say any more, for the sun had dropped and conditions were perfect for taking a sight. I fetched Bannister's expensive sextant with its built-in electronic stopwatch and brought a star sweetly down to the twilit horizon.

The wind dropped the next day. There was still a modicum of warmth in the mid-day sun, but by early afternoon we were both swathed in sweaters, scarves and oilskins. That night, after I'd plotted our position, I called Angela on deck to see the aurora borealis that was filling the northern sky with its great scrims of curving and shifting colours. She stared in enchantment. "I thought the Northern Lights only showed in winter?"

"All year round. You can see them from London sometimes."

"No!"

"Two or three nights a year," I said. "But you city-dwellers never look. Or else you've got so many neon lights on that you drown it out."

A great coral-coloured lightfall shimmered and faded in the twilight as *Sycorax*'s booms slatted across in an involuntary but slow gybe. If I had been racing in the St Pierre I would have been fretting because of this calm. The sea was flattening to a sheen of gun metal while Angela and I sat in the cockpit and watched the magic lights drape the northern sky.

"Do you know what I forgot?" Angela broke our silence.

"Tell me."

"A passport."

I smiled. "I shall tell the Canadians that I kidnapped you."

She turned on the thwart so that she could lean against me. It was the first intimate gesture that either of us had made since she had first stepped aboard. She gazed at a vast ripple of star-dusted blue light. "Do you know why I came, Nick?"

"Tell me."

"I wanted to be with you. It wasn't because of your leg, and I'm not really sure that Tony's in danger. I know I should believe it, but I don't." She lit herself a cigarette. "I was angry."

"Angry?"

"When he said I had newly-wed nerves. Because he didn't believe me." She had brought a bottle of Irish from the cabin and she poured us each a glass. "Is this what's called running away to sea?"

"Yes," I said. "So why don't you use the opportunity to give up smoking?"

"Why don't you shut up?" So I shut up and we sat in silence for a while. The surge and fade of the great lights shimmered their reflection on the sea. "I married Tony on the rebound," Angela said suddenly.

"Did you?"

"From you." She twisted her head to look at me. "I shouldn't be here, should I?"

"I wanted you to be here." I ducked her question.

She smiled. "Shall I light the cabin fire?"

"You want to be inside when God puts on this light show?"

"You want to make love in the cold?" she asked. I hesitated, and she scowled. "Nick?"

"You're married," I said awkwardly, not wanting to say it, and knowing that I wanted her to batter down my feeble moral stance.

She closed her eyes in exasperation. "I'm cold, I'm lonely, I'm frightened, and I'm on a bloody boat miles from bloody anywhere because I wanted to be with you, and you play the bloody Boy Scout." She twisted on the thwart and looked angrily at me. "Do you know when I last needed to ask a man to take me to bed?"

"I'm sorry," I said miserably.

She wrenched the rings off her left hand and thrust them into a pocket. "Does that help?"

Principles are fine things, but are soluble in lust, too. We lit the cabin stove.

"Do you really believe in God?" she asked me the next day.

"I don't know anyone who sails deep waters in small boats who doesn't," I said.

"I don't believe." Her voice came down from the coachroof where she was catching the sun's small ration of mid-day warmth. I was in the cabin with bits of the engine spread around me. If we were to reach the place of Nadeznha Bannister's death and intercept *Wildtrack*'s return, then I would need the bloody engine.

Because in the night a flat calm had quietened the sea and by dawn the smoke from our chimney was drifting with the boat. The sails hung like washing. The glass was steady and the sky was palely and innocently veined with high wispy cloud.

"I can't believe in God." Angela had evidently been thinking about it.

"Stay on a boat long enough, and you'll believe." I wondered if prayer would help the engine.

"Ouch," Angela said.

"What?"

"Vicky's claws."

"Throw her overboard." The damned cat had spent the whole night in the sleeping bag with us. Every time I turfed it out it would come back, purring like a two-stroke and burrowing down for warmth.

"If you think sailing encourages belief in God," Angela said pedantically, "then do you think Fanny Mulder believes?"

"Deep in his dim soul," I said, "I expect he does. I agree that Fanny's not a very good advertisement for God's workmanship, but there you are; I have my theological problems just like you." I decided I also had a problem with the engine's wiring system. I began spraying silicon everywhere.

"What are you doing?" Angela heard the aerosol's hiss.

"Debugging the electrics."

"Do you want to debug me of this cat?"

"Why can't you do it yourself?"

"Because I want you to do it."

I pulled myself up to the cockpit and laughed. I'd been invited topsides, not because of the cat, but because Angela was lying naked on the port coaming. I threw the cat up on to the slack mainsail where she did her spider performance, then I leaned over and kissed Angela. "Do you feel like a debauched man?" she asked.

"I feel happy."

"Poor Nick." She stared out at the glassy sea. "Was Melissa unfaithful to you?"

"All the time."

She turned her face back to mine. We were upside down to each other. "Did it hurt?"

"Of course."

She stroked my face. "This won't hurt anyone, Nick."

"No."

"You are an ugly sod, Nick, but I love you."

It was the first time she had said it, and I kissed her. "I love you."

"But . . ." she began.

"No buts," I said quickly, "not yet."

We floated on an empty sea. The glass stayed steady. The North Atlantic had calmed.

More things are wrought by prayer than this world dreams of. The motor started.

We went west under the engine, leaving a trace as straight as a plough-furrow in the sea behind. So long as the engine was charging the batteries I left the VHF switched on to Channel 16. Its range was no more than fifty or sixty miles, but if any boats were talking within that circle I would hear them, and then I could ask if they had news of *Wildtrack*. I heard nothing. I took the short-wave to pieces and discovered that water had somehow penetrated the case. The intricate circuits were now a mess of rust and mould. I gave up on the wretched thing. I lost my trailing log when it snagged on a piece of flotsam and tore itself free and, though I turned the boat upside down, I could not find either of the spares which I was certain I had stored on board.

The sea was no longer smooth. A tiny wind rippled it and a long swell stirred beneath the hull. I tapped the glass again and saw the needle sink a trifle. The clouds thickened. I took running sights of the sun and, logless now, measured our progress between the sights with chips of wood. Angela timed the chips with a stopwatch as they floated past the twenty-five measured feet I'd marked on *Sycorax*'s starboard gunwale. The chips averaged three and a half seconds which, multiplied by a hundred, then divided into the twenty-five feet times sixty, meant that the motor was pushing us along at just over 4.2

knots. We were running against a half-knot current, so our progress was slow.

"Why, great mariner," Angela asked icily, "do you not have a speedometer?"

"You mean an electronic log?"

"I mean a speedometer, you jerk."

"Because it's a nasty modern thing that can go wrong."

"Stopwatches can go wrong."

"Put it back in its bag," I said, "while I think of an answer."

It was in those middle days of the voyage that Angela learned to sail *Sycorax*. She stood her own watches while I slept below. Life eased for me. And for her. The seasickness was gone and she seemed like a new woman. The strains of London and ambition were washed out by a healthier life. She looked good, she laughed, and her sinewy body grew stronger. The winds also strengthened until we were under sail alone, beating stiffly westwards, close-hauled all the way, but I knew we must soon turn south to run down on the place where a girl had died. Day by day we could see the pencil line closing on the cross, yet it still did not seem real that we sailed to a place of revenge.

What seemed real was the two of us. It was a child's game that we played, only we called it love and, like all lovers, we thought it could never end. We had run away together for an adventure, but the adventure now had little to do with Kassouli or Bannister; Angela's naked finger on her left hand showed the truth of that. We were happy, but I suppose neither of us forgot the cloud that waited beyond the western horizon. We just stopped talking of it.

We were busy too. A small boat made of wood and powered by cotton generates work. I repaired the broken cleat, sewed sails, and touched up worn varnish. Our lives depended on the boat, and there was a simple, life-saving rule that no job should ever be deferred. The smallest gap in a sail seam had to be repaired before it ripped into useless shreds. It was a life that imposed its own discipline, and thus enjoyment. "But for ever?" Angela asked.

I was caulking the bridge deck where the mizzen had strained a timber. "For as long as it takes."

"For as long as what takes?"

"I don't know."

"Nick!"

I leaned back on the thwart. "I remember waking up in the helicopter after I was wounded. I knew I was hurt bad. The morphine was wearing off and I was suddenly very frightened of dying. But I promised myself that if I lived I'd give myself to the sea. Just like this." I nodded towards the monotony of the grey-green waves. "That stuff," I said, "is the most dangerous thing in the world. If you're lazy with it, or dishonest with it, or try to cheat it, it will kill you. Is that an answer?"

Angela stared at the sea. We were under full sail, close-hauled and making good progress. *Sycorax* felt good; tight and disciplined and purposeful. "What about your children?" she asked suddenly. "Are you abandoning them?"

She touched a nerve, and knew it. I bent again to the caulking. "They don't need me."

"Nick!" she chided.

"They need me as I am. Hell, they've got Hon-John, and Mumsy, and the bloody Brigadier, and the floppy great nanny, and their ponies, and Melissa. I'm just the poor relation now."

"You're running away from them," Angela accused me.

"I'll fly back and see them." The words were inadequate, and I knew it, but I did not have a proper answer. Some things just have to wait on time.

We turned south the next day and our mood changed with the new course. We were thinking of Bannister now, and I saw that very same night how the two rings appeared again on Angela's hand. She shrugged when she saw that I'd noticed.

We spoke of Bannister again. Now, though, Angela spoke of his innocence, telling me again and again how she had insisted on hearing the truth before they married. Nadeznha, she said, had been killed when a wave swamped *Wildtrack*'s aft cockpit. The grounds of her belief, I thought, were as shifting as those of Yassir Kassouli's, but I said nothing.

"If we don't find him," she said, "and he's all right, then I can fly home from Canada before he reaches Cherbourg?"

"Yes," I promised her. She was planning her departure from

me and there was nothing I could do to stop it. My immediate worry was the glass. It had begun to fall fast, and I knew we were in for a bad blow and that, by sailing south, we sailed towards the depression's vortex.

We won that race by hours. We reached our destination before the gale reached us. We reached the blank and featureless place where, a year before, a girl had died. The clouds were low, dark and hurrying. The sea was ragged and flecked. I hove to at mid-day as a kind of tribute, but neither of us spoke. There was no ship in sight, nor any crackle on the radio. I wished I had a flower to throw into the sea, then decided such a tribute would have been maudlin.

"Are you in the right place?" Angela asked.

"As near as I can make it, yes." I knew we could be miles away, but I had done my best.

"We don't even know that Kassouli planned to meet him here," Angela said. "We only guessed it."

"Here, or nowhere," I said. But the truth was that we did not know. We had sailed into nothing because that had seemed better than doing nothing, but now that we had arrived there was still nothing we could do.

Angela, her face hardened by the sea and her hair made wild by the wind, pointed *Sycorax*'s bows to the west. I let her choose the course, and watched as she sheeted home the foresails and pegged the tiller. The cat sharpened its claws on a sailbag.

"Perhaps," Angela said after a few minutes, "they haven't reached here yet?"

"Perhaps." On my Atlantic chart I had marked *Wildtrack*'s presumed progress, and if my guesses were right then our meeting would have been a close-run thing, but the growing seas made any chance of a sighting unlikely.

Angela stared around the empty sea. "Perhaps they didn't even come this way?"

"Perhaps."

The seas were growing and the visibility was obscured by a spume that was being whipped off the wavetops. Angela, without asking me, but with the new confidence born of the days we had shared, reefed the mainsail and stowed the staysail. The waves were running towards us; some of them smashed white on our stem and under their pounding Angela's confidence began to shred like the wavecrests. "Are we in for a storm, Nick?"

"Only a gale. That isn't so bad. I don't like storms."

By twilight we were under the heavy canvas of storm jib and mizzen staysail alone. Both sails were tiny, yet they kept the heavy hull moving in the churning water. Angela and I were both oilskinned and harnessed, while the cat was imprisoned below as *Sycorax* staggered in troughs of green-black waves that were scribbled with white foam. The sky was smeared with low quick clouds and the wind was loud in the rigging. Angela was shivering beside me. "Where are the lifebelts?" she shouted.

"I don't have any. If you go over in this, you're dead anyway. Why don't you join Vicky?"

She was tempted, but shook her head. "I want to see a gale."

She would have her gale, and was lucky she was not in a full-blooded storm. Yet even so that night was like an echo of creation's chaos.

The noise is numbing. The wind's noise is everything from a knife-sharp keening to a hollow roar like an explosion which lasts forever. The sea is the percussion to that mad music, hammering through the boat so that the timbers judder and it seems a miracle that anything made by man can live.

The noise is bad, but the sight of a gale-ripped sea is worse. It's a confusion of air and water, with foam stinging like whips in the sky, and through that chaos of white and black and grey the great seas have to be spotted and the boat must be steered by or through them. After dark the wind veered to set up cross-seas. The main swell still roared from the west in big seas, but now the crests were saw-edged by the crossing waves, yet still *Sycorax* rode the waters like the witch that she is. We staggered up the sides of ocean mountains and spilt at heart-stopping speed down to their foam-scummed pits. I felt the tug of the tons of cold water on her keel, and once I heard Angela scream like the wind's own eldritch shriek as *Sycorax* laid over on her side and the mainmast threatened to bury itself in a skirl of grey-white water.

Sycorax was upright, hauled there by the metal in her keel, the same metal that would take her like a stone to the ocean's bed if the sea won this night's battle. Except it was no battle. The sea had no enmity, it was blind to us and deaf to us, and there comes a moment when the fear goes because there seems no hope any more, just submission.

Water boiled over the decks, ran down the scuppers, and swamped the cockpit drains. I made Angela pump; forcing her to do it when she wanted to stop, for the exercise made her warm. The cold would kill us before the sea did. The sea might flog, claw and tear at us, but the cold would lull us to death. I made her go down to the cabin to get warm and to fetch the Thermos and sandwiches we'd made ready. She brought me the food, then went below and stayed there, and I imagined her huddled in her bunk with the cat clutched in her arms. I pumped as *Sycorax* climbed the crests and I steered as we careened madly down the wind-crazed slopes. The wind was making my eyes sore. It was a wind born somewhere in the heartland of North America, brewed in the heat of the wheat fields and twisted into a depression that would race round the ocean's rim to take rain to the barley fields in England. Yet, despite the steepness of the seas, I sensed that this was not one of the great ship-breaking storms that could rack the Atlantic for days, but merely a snarling wildcat of a low that would skir across the water and be gone. On a weather chart this gale would look no bigger than the one in which Nadeznha Bannister had died.

Even before the night was out the wind was lessening. It still seethed in the rigging and flicked the water off the crests, but I could feel the boat's motion easing. The gale was passing, though there was still a sickening wind and a cross-sea confusing the threatening swell. I opened the cabin hatch once and saw that Angela slept.

I hardened the boat into the wind, took down the aft staysail and hoisted reefed mizzen and main. The wavetops slashed across *Sycorax* and rattled on her sails. Angela still slept, but I stayed awake, searching for a yacht running fast towards Europe.

My search was merely dutiful, for I believed we had missed *Wildtrack*. The odds of finding Bannister's boat had always been astronomical, and so I expected to see nothing, and when, in the shredding dawn, I did see something, I did not at first believe my salt-stung eyes.

I was tired and cold, and I thought I'd seen a lightning flash. Then I thought it was a mirage, and then I saw the reflected glow of the flare on the clouds above and I knew I'd seen that pale sheen before. It was a red distress flare that cried for help in the middle of nowhere. It flickered out, then another seared to burst against a dirty sky made ragged by the gale's wake and I knew that, either by ill-luck or by God's loving mercy, we had come to the killing place.

I pushed back the hatch and switched on the radio, but there was only the crackling hiss of the heavens. *Sycorax* was juddering to the short steep waves that ran across the grain of the surging swell. Angela was still curled in a corner of the bunk. "I've just seen flares," I said.

It took her a sleepy moment to understand. "*Wildtrack*?"

"I don't know." I tried not to sound hopeful, but the look on Angela's face told me I'd failed.

She struggled into her oilskins and came up to the cockpit. She closed the hatch to keep the seas from swamping the cabin, then hooked her lifeline to a jackstay and I saw her shudder at the height of the great green swell that was running down on us. *Sycorax* soared her way up the slopes and slalomed down again. At each crest I stared ahead, but saw no more flares.

I began to think I had hallucinated. I stood in the scuppers, holding on to the port mizzen shrouds, and searched the broken sea. Nothing. The wind was slowing and veering. I was tempted to let go a reef in the mainsail, but, just as I was plucking up the energy to make the effort, Angela shouted.

"Nick!" Her voice was snatched by a wind gust. "Nick!"

I looked where she was pointing. For a second I saw nothing but the jumbles of foam on the waves' glassy flanks, then, a half-mile off, I saw the yacht.

A yacht. It had to be *Wildtrack*.

But not the *Wildtrack* we both remembered; not the great and gleaming rich man's toy, so sleek and proud and towering. Instead we saw a dismasted yacht, half-swamped, with warps cascading from decks awash with water. She rolled to each sea like a waterlogged cask. We had arrived, and we had failed, for she was nothing but an abandoned hulk. For a second I dared to hope that this wreck was of some other dismasted yacht, but then a heave of swell momentarily bared the hull's flank and I saw the distinctive bold blue flash. It was *Wildtrack*. We had sailed over seventeen hundred nautical miles and by a miracle we had found her, and by a cruel fate we had found her too late.

I stepped down into *Sycorax*'s cockpit and unpegged the tiller.

"Nick! Nick!" Angela's voice held a new urgency and I saw, in *Wildtrack*'s aft cockpit, a moving splash of orange. At first I thought it was a seat cushion, or some other flotsam, then I saw it was a man in oilskins. Alive. It had to be Bannister, and he was alive, unless the sea just stirred a corpse.

I scrambled down to the cabin sole. I threatened the engine with death if it did not start and cursed that I had no self-starter. I staggered as the boat pitched, swung the handle, and to my amazement the cold engine banged straight into life. I bolted the companionway steps back over the motor compartment and climbed to the cockpit. *Wildtrack* had vanished in a wave valley, but as I kicked the motor into gear I saw her bows sluggishly rise on a wind-fretted ridge.

I turned head to wind, arrowing into the seas, and let the engine push us. Our sails banged like guns. Angela was staring, her mouth open. I did not want to know what she was thinking, or what hopes, hers or mine, might be on the verge of tragedy.

The wind slewed viciously, heeling and thrusting us. We pitched on a crest and the motor raced like a banshee before the stern sank underwater again. But as we were on the wavecrest I saw that the orange figure in *Wildtrack*'s stern was alive, for he waved, then fell back. He was either hurt or so tired that he could hardly shift himself.

"It's going to be bloody hard to fetch him off!" I shouted at Angela.

She hardly needed me to explain the difficulties. Going alongside a flooded boat in a high sea and in a shifting wind would be a piece of seamanship that needed a Jimmy Nicholls or a lifeboat's coxswain. Worse, if Anthony Bannister was injured, he would not be able to help himself which meant that one of us would have to board *Wildtrack* to give him aid. It would have to be me, and I did not want to do it, but it was one of those moments when it was really best not to think too deeply about the advantages of prudence over God-damned bloody stupidity. "You're going to have to steer the boat!" I called to Angela. "You'll have to lay us alongside, then sheer off once I'm aboard *Wildtrack*, understand? I don't want that hulk stoving us in!"

She nodded. She was staring at the figure in the hull-down *Wildtrack*. His hood was up and his collar buttoned across his mouth.

"When I've got him," I went on, "you're going to have to come alongside again!" Christ alone knew how. She'd become a good sailor, but this manoeuvre was like asking a passenger to land a jumbo.

I left her on the tiller while I tied all the fenders I'd taken from Bannister's boathouse on to *Sycorax*'s guardrail stanchions. I hung the fenders more in hope than with any expectation that they would save my boat. *Wildtrack* and *Sycorax* would be pitching as they met and I feared I would crash my bows down on her deck or, worse, rip off my rudder and propellor with the force of the collision. I was scared of *Wildtrack*. She was a floating battering ram that could disable us or even crush in our bilges.

I let the mainsail fall and roughly lashed gaff and sail to the boom which I then secured to the gallows. I did not want Angela distracted by hammering sails as she tried to manoeuvre the boat. I stowed the staysail and mizzen, but left the storm jib sheeted taut to stiffen *Sycorax* and to give some leverage to the bows at the moment when Angela needed to sheer away. I took the tiller. "Are you hooked on?"

She showed me her lifeline. I accelerated. We were close enough to *Wildtrack* now to share the same valleys of sea. I wanted to circle the crippled boat and approach from the lee so that the wind would be pushing *Sycorax* away from that treacherous hull once I was aboard her. In choosing that course I risked *Wildtrack*'s trailing ropes tangling in *Sycorax*'s propellor, and I told a worried Angela that, once I was aboard, she was to put the motor in neutral and let the storm jib carry her clear of the warps. "Let the sheet run a bit, OK?"

It was clearly not OK. "Should I go across to him?" Angela shouted.

I'd thought of that, but I knew she did not have the physical strength to lift a helpless man. And Bannister was helpless. He was hardly moving except to follow our progress with his orange-hooded face. There was also another reason for me to go; if anything went wrong then Angela would be left on the safer of the two boats. I explained that I would clear the trailing ropes once I was aboard *Wildtrack* so that she need not worry about fouling the propellor on her second approach. "But if you can't get us off," I shouted, "then stay close if you can! If you can't, good luck! Go west! You'll find trawlers on the Grand Banks. And don't forget to feed Vicky!"

She gave me a frightened look. I grinned, trying to reassure her, then gunned the engine to spin *Sycorax* up into *Wildtrack*'s lee. I noticed that *Wildtrack*'s flooded hull gave us some small shelter. "Take the tiller! Remember, tiller hard over and motor into neutral as soon as I'm on her!"

Angela took the tiller and I staggered forward to *Sycorax*'s starboard shrouds. I unclipped my lifeline from the jackstay and coiled it into a pocket. I put my good left foot over the guardrail and held on for grim life as we rolled our gunwale under. We were six feet from the swamped boat, five feet, closing to three, two, and I put my right foot over the rail and was about to leap across the churning gap into *Wildtrack*'s flooded central cockpit when the sea heaved between the boats and *Sycorax* slewed away. I clung to the shroud with my left hand as the green water churned up my boots. "Closer!" I shouted, though I doubt if Angela heard me. She turned the tiller too far and we came surging back towards the other boat. The lurching movement had driven us far up *Wildtrack*'s hull; almost to her bows. In another second it would be too late to jump.

Then the sea heaved the hulls together and I heard the crashing grind of wood on fibreglass. I jumped.

I pushed off with my left leg, which meant I landed on my right, and, for the first time in weeks, my knee buckled. I must have cried aloud, though I could hear nothing but the turmoil of water and wind. The leg was numb, it crumpled, and I sprawled heavily on *Wildtrack*'s slippery foredeck. Pain speared out from my back. I heard *Sycorax*'s engine falter as Angela rammed the lever into neutral and I had a terrifying glimpse of *Sycorax*'s bowsprit arcing above my head, then a new terror swamped me as a sea broke over *Wildtrack*'s foredeck and swept me towards the side. I grabbed a guardrail stanchion with my right hand

and held on as the water shattered about me. The rush of cold sea slewed me around, but my left boot found a purchase on *Wildtrack*'s forehatch and somehow I held fast in the bubbling and seething thunder of the sea. I couldn't think, except, over and over again, to repeat a refrain in my head: "You must be fucking mad, you must be fucking mad", and I suddenly remembered those were the very words I'd screamed aloud as I'd charged uphill with an SLR in my hands. I'd been scared witless then, and I was scared now. The sea began to stream off *Wildtrack*'s deck and I lifted my head to see blood spewing into the flooded scuppers. It seemed to come from my left hand, but I could not see how bad the cut was. I tried to move my right leg, but there was no feeling there. I watched *Sycorax* sheering off, plunging her bowsprit into the wavecrests.

Wildtrack's hulk lurched up, freeing me from the water and letting me pull myself down the scuppers. I saw that I had slashed my left hand on a stub of metal shroud that had been sheared clean and astonishingly bright with bolt-cutters. The cut was across the fleshy base of my thumb and, though it was pulsing blood, there was nothing I could do about it now. I was cursing my leg as I pulled myself forward. My oilskins snagged on an empty jib-sheet track and, in my fear and rage, I ripped the jacket savagely to free myself before the next wave hammered over the rolling hulk.

I slithered over the coaming into the flooded central cockpit. I was soaked through, but adrenalin was warming me. The wind was lashing spray across the boat, but there was some small shelter in the cockpit, though it was frightening to be so low and unprotected in the water. The great swells loomed steep above me, their sides like crinkling slopes of bottle glass up which the swamped boat rose sluggishly but never quite made the tops so that the waves would break over her and, for an instant, she would be awash. The truth was that *Wildtrack* was sinking, and I was suddenly gripped with a terrible fear that she would go down before Angela could bring *Sycorax* back. I looked around for a lifebelt or raft, but when the crew had abandoned *Wildtrack* they had taken all such equipment. Yet, even if she did succeed in coming back, I did not know how I would transfer myself, let alone Bannister. My leg was useless. I sat half underwater and clawed fingers into my thigh and knee in an attempt to feel something.

I tried to stand, fell again, and pulled myself to the cockpit's edge. The leg would have to look after itself while I dragged trailing ropes from the water and jammed them into cave lockers. As I pulled the last line aboard, a swell rolled the boat's stern up and the water in the cockpit surged forward. I saw the horror then.

I wasn't ready for it, and I puked.

The door to the rear cabin was open and the body floated forward with the ship's sluggish motion. It floated out of the door until its shoulders stuck. When I first saw the corpse I was stowing the last treacherous rope and summoning the courage to cross the rear coachroof to where Bannister sheltered, but suddenly I knew it was not Bannister who waited for me in *Wildtrack*'s stern.

It was not Bannister, because I was looking at Bannister now, and he at me. Or rather his dead eyes were gaping at me from the companionway that spilt yet more water into the cockpit. He was wearing a lifejacket that should have kept his head above water, but his throat had been cut almost to the spine so that his head lolled back and his fish-white eyes were alternately above and under the rush of seawater. There was no blood. All the blood had been pumped and washed out of him. He must have been dead for hours for he was nothing but a bleached and bloodless thing that floated in the mass of cabin flotsam. The throat had been cut clean by a blade, then washed cleaner by the salt water. The sight of that wound made me vomit.

Wildtrack's bows rose and the body mercifully washed back out of sight. I scrambled aft and, using my arms, dragged myself onto the coachroof and hung on to the handrails as another sea bubbled and spilt around me. It was then that the man in the stern cockpit turned his hooded gaze on me.

It was Mulder.

Wildtrack shuddered under me as the sea poured off her topsides. I scrabbled towards Mulder and fell into the small after cockpit. "Can you stand?"

He shook his head, then pointed to his left leg that was bent unnaturally. He shouted something, and I had to cup my hand to my ear to show him I could not hear his words. He pulled open the flap that had covered his mouth. "Fucking fell." He shouted it bitterly, as though fate had been peculiarly unkind to him. "My leg's broken!"

That made two one-legged men in a doomed boat. "Where's the rest of the crew?" I was trying to stand, holding on to the rail beside the aft cabin door. I was searching for *Sycorax* and saw her, hull down, two hundred yards off, and still going away from me. I saw the storm jib's sheet had come loose and the sail was flogging itself into shreds, then a heave of green water hid her from me. I tried to put my weight on my right leg and felt it shivering with the strain. "Where's your crew?" I shouted.

"Taken off!" Mulder shouted back. "They're safe."

So another boat had stood by and rescued the crew? Mulder had clearly stayed on board to try and salvage the damaged ship and had then been marooned when the gale blew up. I wondered where the rescuing boat was, and why it had not steered for the flares. "Is that who you were signalling?" I asked. "The rescue ship?"

"Get me the fuck off here, Sandman! She's sinking!"

"I should bloody leave you, Fanny." I ducked as we reared up the side of a green cliff and as the tons of water smashed across us. "Why did you cut his throat?" I shouted the question again as we heaved up from the cold waves.

"Accident." He shouted the word vehemently.

He looked so damned smug in his expensive foul-weather gear and lifejacket. I hated him then, and tried to kick him, but my damned leg folded so that I fell awkwardly in the cockpit. I fell over his broken leg and I heard Mulder's odd falsetto scream. I rolled off him and pulled myself into a sitting position. "Why did you cut his throat?" I shouted again.

He just stared his hatred at me, so I lifted my left leg to kick his broken bone and the threat made him babble in a desperate attempt to avoid the pain. "Because I couldn't push him overboard!"

"Did you kill his wife?"

He stared at me as if I was mad. "Get me off here! The boat's sinking!"

"Did you kill his wife?"

"No!"

"You are a bastard, Fanny." I managed to kneel upright and unshackle his lifeline from a D-ring. He watched me, not sure whether I intended to push him overboard or save his life. I grabbed a braidline rope out of the tangle of wreckage in the cockpit and pulled forty or fifty feet free before the line jammed. "Knife!" I shouted over the sound of wind and sea. "Give me your knife!"

He handed me a sheath knife which I supposed had been the murder weapon. I used the heavy blade to slash off the length of braidline, then clung to the handrail as another sea hissed about us.

I tied a small bowline, then shackled the line of Mulder's safety harness to the bowline's loop. The other end of the rope went round my waist. Once Angela returned I would scramble on board *Sycorax*, then haul Mulder to safety. I explained that to him. "It's going to hurt you," I added, "but if you want to drown, then cut yourself loose." I tossed the knife back to him, then pulled myself to the lee rail.

I stood there, clinging for dear life to the guardrail stanchion, and willed my right leg to take my weight. I searched the broken sea for a glimpse of *Sycorax*. *Wildtrack* rolled slow as we were washed by a wavecrest, then we dropped again and I thought, just as I lurched with the downwards roll, that I saw a mast's tip beyond a saw-edged crest. I waited, I prayed, and a moment later, as once more we heaved slowly upwards, I saw *Sycorax*'s stern with its bright flash of the frayed Red Ensign. I knew Angela must be struggling to turn the old boat. She was already a quarter-mile off and I hoped to God she did not lose sight of us. I looked for a boathook, or oar, or anything that I could jam upright as a signal for her, but anything of use had long been swept overboard.

I crouched back into the small shelter of the aft cockpit. "You're going to have to wait, Fanny."

"Who's sailing your boat?"

"A friend," I said.

Mulder shrugged. He looked worn down to his last reserves; grey-faced, red-rimmed eyes, and with pain creasing his cheeks. "They lost us in the night," he said.

"Who lost you?"

"Kassouli. Who do you think?"

Who else? I should have known that Yassir Kassouli would be here at the kill. I clung to the handrail as a sea thundered and crashed over the coaming. I thought for a second that the waterlogged hull was sinking, dragged down by the weight of her engine and ballast, but somehow the sleek hull came up again. I found a length of rope that I wrapped as a crude bandage around my cut hand.

"If Kassouli finds you here," Mulder said, "he'll bloody sink you, Sandman."

"He's deserted you, Fanny. He's left you here to die." Down in the wave troughs the wind's noise was lessened, though I still had to shout if Mulder was to hear my words. "He's left you, Fanny, but I'm going to save your miserable life. I'm taking you to where I can stand up in a courtroom and tell them about Bannister and his cut throat."

The South African stared at me with loathing, then shook his head. "Kassouli won't desert me."

"He already has." I flinched from another tumble of water, then pulled myself upright to search the southern horizon. *Sycorax* had turned, but she was still far off and I prayed that Angela was not having trouble with the engine. There were no other boats in sight.

A gasp of pain made me turn. Mulder, the knife in his hand, had tried to lunge towards me, but a combination of his broken leg and the obstruction of his inflated lifejacket had stopped the murderous thrust. It seemed he really did believe that Kassouli would return for him, and that it was better to risk waiting for that salvation than to be turned over to justice. In that hope he had lunged at me, and now I kicked at the knife in his hand to stop him trying again.

My kick missed, and once again the effort toppled me. My bandaged left hand slipped off the handrail so that I fell forward towards Mulder. I tried to regain my balance, but only managed to drop my right knee on to the thigh of Mulder's broken leg.

He screamed, and the sound was whipped away by the wind and searing foam. *Wildtrack* heaved up as I collapsed. Mulder was still moaning with the pain, but the strength of the man was extraordinary. He wrapped his left arm round my neck, and I knew he was reversing the knife in his right hand and that any second the blade would be in my ribs. Water sloshed up about us.

I rammed my head forward, smashing the bridge of his nose with my forehead, then I screamed myself from the pain that clawed at my back as I twisted away from him. I glimpsed the knife against a background of water and I reached for it with both hands and my right caught his wrist as my left was slashed by the blade. I jerked his knife hand towards me, then sank my teeth into the ball of his thumb and bit down until I could taste his blood in the back of my throat.

His hand tried to jerk away, but I clung to him. He hit me with his free hand, then tried to loop his lifeline about my neck. I was kicking with my left foot; not in any attempt to hurt him, but rather to gain a purchase in the flooded cockpit. The lifeline rope was around my eyes and he hauled it back, making me let go with my teeth. Then my left foot rammed against the coaming and I used all my strength to force myself up, dripping and bleeding. I let go of his knife hand and drove my bunched fists down, falling with all my weight on them, down on to the broken bone in his shin.

I hit him like a pile-driver, and the force of my blow was made worse by an upward lurch of the boat. I fancied I felt the broken bone grate as I hit him.

He screamed and twitched, the knife forgotten. I plucked it from his nerveless fingers. I could never have disarmed him if he had not been so weakened, but now, because of his leg, and because he was half dead with exposure and thirst, he could not fight properly. I saw blood on his face, then the sea washed it away and I was scrambling desperately backwards, the knife in my hand, and I jammed myself in the corner of the cockpit by the wheel and held my breath to let the pain ebb away.

Mulder had given up. He lay exhausted and hopeless. I struggled upright, still holding the knife, and saw the spray bursting apart from *Sycorax*'s bows. Angela was fighting towards us, still four hundred yards off, and still struggling against wind and sea. The storm jib was now nothing but tattered streamers.

I put my left foot against Mulder's broken leg. "Now," I said, "you're going to tell me what happened."

"Piss off." He would be defiant to the end, stubborn as a cornered and wounded boar.

I felt no remorse for the pain I would give him. He'd tried to kill me, now I would take the truth from him and one day give it back in a court of law. I slammed my heel forward.

When he stopped screaming I asked him again, and this time, because I still threatened and had proved that I would use pain, he told me of Kassouli's revenge. The story came slowly, and I had to tease it out of him between the slashing assaults of the breaking waves.

Mulder, obedient to his paymaster, had brought *Wildtrack* to this waste place in the ocean where, two nights before and under the cover of the night watch, Mulder had sheared a port shroud. He had sabotaged a shroud before, trying to cast suspicion on me, and he had known that as soon as he put weight on the shroud the mast would bend and break. He had gone aft, tacked ship, and let the chaos overtake the long hull. The crew had tumbled up from their bunks to find disaster and salvation.

The salvation was *Kerak*, the supertanker. A Kassouli ship that had loomed with blazing lights from the darkness, and I imagined the terror Bannister must have felt when he heard, on the radio, the identity of the ship that had so fortuitously appeared.

The crew had been taken off, Mulder said, leaving only himself and Bannister on *Wildtrack*. "Bannister wouldn't leave."

That was a clever touch, I thought sourly. Bannister would have chosen to stay with the one man he could trust; his own assassin.

Bannister and Mulder had cleared the mast's wreckage then ran westwards under the engine. That was when the gale had blown up. Mulder steered to the tanker's lights, but some time in the darkness *Wildtrack* had broached, or else had been struck by a cross-sea, and an open hatch had swamped the boat. *Wildtrack*'s electrics had died, and the motor had coughed into silence. Mulder had clambered forward to start the engine by hand, but had slipped on the companionway and broken his leg.

They had drifted in the darkness then, the tanker lost, and some time in that next long day Mulder had ripped his blade across Bannister's throat and thus fulfilled his contract. Then he had waited for Kassouli, but the swamped hull would not have shown on the tanker's radar and Mulder had waited in vain. He had slept for a time, waking to the darkness into which, at long intervals, he had sent his few flares. I had seen the last three fired.

Now, huddled and cold, battered and shivering, I listened to Mulder's tale. I massaged my leg, feeling the slow return of life to the cold flesh. At times, struggling up in the streaming cockpit, I would see Angela's painfully slow progress towards us. I waved once, and saw her wave back. All I could do now was pray that *Wildtrack* did not sink before *Sycorax* reached us. I wondered if I should go into the after cabin and strip the lifejacket from the dead man, but I could not face those empty eyes and flayed throat.

"What happened," I shouted at Mulder, "to Nadeznha?"

He had thought my interrogation was over, and I had to raise my left foot to encourage him. "I don't know!" he shouted.

"You do bloody know!" I put my heel against his broken leg.

"I wasn't on deck." Mulder seemed hypnotized by my threat. "Bannister relieved me."

"You didn't say that at the inquest."

"Bannister didn't want me to! He paid me to say that I was on watch!"

"Why?" I shouted. The wind was shrieking at us, snatching our voices, and tumbling cold water about our two hunched figures. "Why?" I shouted again.

"He didn't want anyone to know he wasn't a watch captain. Me and Nadeznha, we sailed the boat, not him! But if anyone had known his wife was skippering and he was just crewing, he'd have lost face."

I stared at the shivering man. Good God, I thought, but it made such sense. Bannister had not been half the sailor his wife had been, nor that Mulder was, yet his vanity would have insisted that he was seen as the expert.

Mulder mistook my silence for disbelief. "As God is my witness" – he was shaking with fright and cold – "that's all I lied about. I swear it! I don't know what happened. I wouldn't have killed her, I loved her!" I still said nothing, and Mulder still construed my silence as a threat. "I loved her, man! We were lovers! She and I!"

"Lovers?" I was incredulous; gaping at him. It made sense, if I had bothered to think about it, yet the conjunction of Nadeznha Bannister's beauty and Mulder's bestiality seemed so very astonishing. "Did Bannister ever find out?"

"He never found out." There was a curious sort of pride in Mulder's voice; the boast of a man who had made a notable sexual conquest. Poor Bannister, I thought, cuckolded by so many sailors.

But if Bannister had known about Mulder and Nadeznha, I thought, then his pride might have made him kill both. "Did Bannister kill his wife?" I asked.

"I don't know." Mulder's voice was a whimper that barely carried over the hiss of sea and air. "In God's name, Mr Sandman, I don't know."

"But you told Kassouli that he killed her."

"I told him I'd lied for Bannister at the inquest." Mulder was desperate to be believed. "It was Mr Kassouli's idea that Bannister killed Nadeznha, not mine!"

"But you encouraged the idea?"

"I told him the truth. I told him Bannister hated Nadeznha. Behind her back he called her a spoilt wog bitch." Mulder babbled at me. "He was terrified of her!"

"But you don't know that he murdered her, do you?"

"Who else?"

"You bastard," I said. This whole God-damned, star-crossed, bloody mess was because Kassouli had misinterpreted Mulder's lie at the inquest. And all along the bloody Boer had known nothing, but his venality had led to this killing place. He had taken money for one lie, then seen that he could make more money by betraying Bannister to Kassouli. Now he lay shivering and broken in a sinking boat and, if I could save him, it would only be for a courtroom and a prison.

That fate suddenly seemed closer as *Sycorax* thrust her bows through the crest of the neighbouring swell. I hurled the knife overboard and struggled to the lee rail. *Sycorax* surged down the wave slope, then a rolling crest came between us and all I could see was her topmast above the frantic water. I held on to the guardrail for grim life as another crest slammed over *Wildtrack*, and when the water seethed away I saw that *Sycorax* was foully close, too close. She was rearing above us, her chain bobstay dripping weed and water that was whipped horizontally by the wind. *Wildtrack*'s hulk was falling down the wave, but *Sycorax* was coming faster and higher on the churning slope. I could see the copper sheathing at her stem. "Sheer off! Sheer off!" I shouted it vainly as I felt *Wildtrack* rising beneath me, heaving slowly up, then *Sycorax* seemed to dip towards me as Angela saw the danger. She was too late. I flinched away from *Wildtrack*'s gunwale as *Sycorax*'s bows crashed into the hulk. I seemed to be drowning in the savage churn of water and I heard, rather than saw, the slamming of the two boats. I forced myself upright to see *Sycorax*'s timber scraping and gouging away from me. I'd put the fenders too far aft.

"Nick!" I heard Angela scream and I knew she would never manage to make the run a second time. I took a breath, willed my legs to push me up, then lunged to seize *Sycorax*'s pulpit rails. My left leg thrust me upwards as the two boats banged and thumped each other. If I fell between the hulls now my legs would be crushed to mincemeat. I hooked an arm over the rail, swung my left leg up to the toerail, and suddenly I was clinging to the outside of *Sycorax*'s bows. I was choking with water, and being deafened by the bellow of wind and the grating of wood and the seething anger of the sea.

Angela thrust the tiller over to sheer off as I'd told her, and suddenly I knew she would accelerate the boat and she would not know that I was tied to Mulder. When the braidline jerked taut it would be me who was plucked into the sea, not Mulder. He was a great weight in a waterlogged cockpit, while I was just clinging by weakened arms to *Sycorax*'s gunwales. I screamed for Angela to slow down, but the wind snatched my voice into nothing. I had thrown the knife away, and all I could do was grab the trailing braidline with my right hand and reach under *Sycorax*'s guardrails to loop it round a berthing cleat. I looped it once, twice, then it snatched taut and I heard the shout of pain as Mulder was plucked out of *Wildtrack*'s cockpit. The loops on the cleat had held, but were slipping now and I let them slip so that the rope's tension helped to pull me inboard.

I dragged myself to safety. I was sobbing with pain and cold, dripping with blood, but there was no time to catch breath. *Sycorax* dipped in a trough and water smashed me back towards the mainmast where I was stopped short by the braidline's tension. I kept that tension hard as I undid the bowline about my waist, then knelt up to lash the braidline to a belaying pin on the fiferail. Angela was staring at me, her eyes wide in terror, but she had done all I had asked her to do, and done it well. The pain was all over me. Blood was dripping from my left hand from which the crude rope bandage had washed free.

I crawled down the scuppers. "Hard to starboard! Engine out of gear!"

Angela had turned to stare at the figure who was being towed in the water behind us. "Is that Tony?"

"Starboard the tiller now! Out of gear!" The foam was breaking and boiling around Mulder.

Angela pushed the tiller over, kicked the throttle lever into neutral, and the strain vanished from Mulder's taut rope. I had to go forward again, this time taking a coil of rope from a locker in *Sycorax*'s cockpit. My right leg was shaking, but holding me. I harnessed myself, then leaned over the guardrails and tied my new rope to Mulder's with a rolling hitch. The knot was stained with blood by the time it was fast. I released the braidline from the fiferail and berthing cleat, then went back to the cockpit. The wind was screaming, or perhaps I screamed, for the pain was making me sob. I was moving like a horror-film monster and muttering instructions to myself. *Sycorax* was broaching, rolling and pitching, snatching like a tethered wild colt.

I pulled the braidline inboard, undid the rolling hitch, and fed

Mulder's line through a block that hung from the boom gallows. Then I began to haul him alongside.

"Is that Tony?" Angela helped me pull.

"It's Mulder!"

"Where's Tony?"

"He's dead." I could not soften the blow. I spoke too curtly, but I was at the end of my strength and I did not know how, in this welter of sea and wind, to break the news gently.

Mulder was too heavy for us. We brought him to the gunwale, and there he stuck. I thought at first it was the clumsiness of his inflated lifejacket that was blocking our efforts and I told Angela to fetch a knife and slash the jacket. Mulder, who must have recognized Angela with astonishment, then fear, flinched from the blade, then subsided as he saw that she posed no threat. She stabbed and stabbed through the tough material until the jacket went limp.

"Pull!" I said to her, and we pulled, but Mulder's weight and the weight of his soaked clothing was too great and we still could not hoist him over the guardrails. *Sycorax* rolled her gunwale under and Mulder tried to pull himself up, but he was as weak as we were. "Hold on!" I shouted at him. He nodded and gripped a guardrail stanchion. I cleated the braidline, then fetched my bolt-cutters from a locker. If I cut the guardrails away then a surge of sea would probably roll the South African on to our scuppers.

I cut the wires and was just loosening the braidline from the cleat when Angela screamed.

I thought it was because Mulder had died, but it was for quite another reason.

"Nick! Nick!" Her voice held pure terror. I turned and saw, coming out of the grey-white murk, the bows of a giant ship.

It was a supertanker. A great black, dripping, slab-sided, bulbous-bowed monster of the sea, and I saw she had the yellow kestrel-painted funnel of the Kassouli Line. The tanker slammed through the ocean like a great sea-beast; like a Leviathan come for its revenge. It was the *Kerak*. She was in ballast, showing her red paint, while the great bulb at her stem seemed like a ramming prow that was heading straight for *Sycorax*. I remembered Mulder's threat – that Kassouli would sink us – and it seemed only too real as the vast bows splintered the seas aside.

"Nick!" Angela screamed again.

"Hold fast!" I shouted at Mulder, then I banged the tiller across and throttled up. It was all a sudden panic in cold horror. The great ship was closing at what seemed her full speed and I could do nothing but shout in impotent rage at her streaked bows.

Kerak must have seen us as I shouted, for she seemed to turn, or else *Sycorax* found a twist of speed I'd never known in her. Whatever, we would not be rammed, but we still risked being swamped and I instinctively wrenched my tiller to port so that our bows would meet the great tanker's wash head on.

I turned and, by doing it, I killed Mulder.

I had not meant to, I did not know I was doing it, but I killed him. Or perhaps, mercifully, he was already dead before I pulled the tiller across.

I had released the two locking turns on the cleated braidline after I'd cut the guardrails away. I'd done it so I could pull Mulder inboard, but my alarm at the *Kerak*'s threat had made me abandon the cleat. It still had three turns on it, but the braidline was made of a slick synthetic fibre that, without the locking turns, slipped on the cleat's horns. The surge of our acceleration must have loosened Mulder's grip on the stanchion, he had let go, and his weight had dragged the braidline's loops inch by deadly inch, and with each lurch he had fallen further from safety. As I turned to port a wave had lifted our stern and he must have been thrust under the boat.

The first I knew of it was a chopping judder in *Sycorax*'s timbers, a quivering in the hull, and then I snatched the engine out of gear, but the blood was already spreading in our wake. Blood and horror surfaced, churned up by the spinning blades, and then Mulder's tethered body bobbed up on the surface, a mess of red, and I jerked the rest of the braidline loose and throttled hard forward so we would leave him astern and Angela would not see the butcher's mess on the sea behind. Mulder's skull had taken the propellor's blows. He was dead.

Then the *Kerak*'s streaked and cliff-like hull smashed past to block out the eastern sky. Faces, made tiny by height and distance, stared from behind the bridge windows. A single figure, standing on the jutting wing of the bridge, hurled what I thought was a lifebuoy towards *Sycorax*. The thing twisted in the air, was snatched by the wind, and red flowers shredded from the wreath as it dropped to the sea. Flowers for a dead girl.

The wake of the tanker was like a storm wave, breaking and running white. I pushed *Sycorax* hard round, under full throttle again, then snatched the lever back to slow as we met the first wave head on. We pounded into the sea, rearing and plunging, and water exploded from our hull as we crashed down from its peak. The second wave tossed us up again and the boom shook and I thought the topping lift would snap. I hurled useless curses at the receding tanker.

"What happened?" Angela was staring at the cut guardrails where Mulder had been.

"He died," I said. "My fault." Our bows pitched into what seemed like a black hole in the sea. We crashed into the next wave, Angela staggered, then *Sycorax* clawed her way back up.

"Who died?" Angela asked, and I realized that she was in shock.

"Mulder died!"

Her eyes were vacant. "And Tony?"

"I'm sorry," I said. I didn't know what else to say, except that I was sorry. I was sorry for her, for her husband, even for the man who had died because I had undone the locking turns of his safety line. I would dream about those turns. A life had gone because I'd pulled a rope free. It was a foul dream to add to the one about the man who'd cried "*Mama!*" as my bayonet twisted in his gut.

Kerak had disappeared in the spume, leaving *Sycorax* in lesser waves. I turned her to face the swells when the squawk of the radio startled me. I forced Angela to take the tiller, then pushed open the cabin hatch and leaned down to the set. Vicky mewed at me from the chart table and I muttered something soothing as I pulled the microphone towards me. The call sounded again from the speaker. "This is merchant vessel *Kerak* to yacht *Sycorax*, over."

"*Sycorax*," I responded. A sea shattered on our bows and slashed down to sting my face.

"Is that Captain Sandman? Over." It was Yassir Kassouli's voice.

"Who else?" I snapped back.

There was a pause. "I could not see anyone on board *Wildtrack*. Did you get close enough to see anyone aboard? Over."

"I got on board *Wildtrack*," I said. I was too tired, too hurt, and too cold to be bothered with radio courtesies.

The radio hissed. Angela was watching me, but so dully that I did not think she could hear what I was saying. "You were on board? Over," Kassouli asked, and I could hear the incredulity in his voice.

"Why don't you just piss off?" Except I hadn't pressed the microphone button so he did not hear me. Now I did press it. "I was on board," I confirmed, "and there was no one there alive. No one. Bannister's dead. So is Mulder."

Kassouli's metallic voice sounded after another pause. "Who was the body being towed behind your yacht, Captain? Over."

"That was Mulder. I tried to save him. I couldn't."

"What happened? Over," Kassouli persisted.

"Mulder died," I said. "He just died." I raised my head to look for *Kerak*, but the tanker was still lost in the whirl of windborne spray. She'd be watching me on her radar, though, and I feared that she would turn and come back. "It was an accident," I said into the microphone.

"And Bannister's death? Over."

I hesitated. I wanted to vent my anger at Kassouli over the air, I wanted to accuse him of murder, I wanted to tell him that I did not think his daughter had been murdered, I wanted to tell him that his perfect American Princess had chosen a Boer brute for her lover, but somehow, in this stinging ocean, the truth seemed out of place. There had been too much killing, too much anger, and it was time for it all to end. Revenge breeds revenge, and I had the chance to end it now. So I hesitated.

"Are you receiving me, *Sycorax*? Over."

"Bannister's death was an accident," I lied, and only after I'd told the lie did I wonder whether my motive was simply to stay alive for, if I'd accused Kassouli of murder, then the great Leviathan might have returned from the north and crushed me like matchwood. I pressed the button again. "All three deaths were accidents, Kassouli, all three."

Kassouli ignored my protestation that his daughter's death had been an accident. He was silent. There was nothing but the wind and the sea and the hollow emptiness of the gale's dying throes. *Kerak* had vanished and the radio only hissed. I watched for a few minutes, but nothing appeared in the north. Kassouli, I thought, had succeeded and his daughter's soul could fly free. It was over.

I killed the engine, took down the shredded storm jib, stowed the gallows, and set the reefed mainsail while Angela hoisted the mizzen. She pegged the tiller, then helped me down to the cabin where, before I could put butterfly sutures on my cut hand, I first peeled off my wet, stiff, torn oilskins. I was shaking with cold and fatigue. Angela found the strength to make oxtail soup, to wrap me in a blanket, and then to hold me tight as though she could pour her own body warmth into me.

"Tony was dead?" she asked at last.

"He was dead."

"And it was an accident?" she asked, and I realized she must have heard my words on the radio.

"It was an accident." I shivered suddenly, remembering the slit throat, then the image of the blood boiling up from *Sycorax*'s stern drove the memory of Bannister's body from my mind. I closed my eyes for a second.

"Tell me the truth, Nick, please." Angela was staring very gravely into my eyes. But I did not know what cause the truth would serve now. If I told Angela the truth there was no saying where her intense nature might take her. It was over and she would live better in ignorance. I tried to move off the bunk, but Angela pressed me back. "Nick!"

"I need to set a course for St John's," I said.

"What happened to Tony, Nick?" Angela asked. The seas were hammering our hull, shaking us.

"The boat was knocked down." I made the story up as I went along. "Mulder broke his leg. Tony was struck on the head. I don't think Mulder tried very hard to save his life, but it was an accident. He was unconscious. I think he died of exposure in the end. It's the cold that does it. It can be so bloody cold." I was shivering as I spoke.

"Mulder told you that?" Angela asked suspiciously.

"I saw the body." I closed my eyes. "It was an accident."

I think Angela believed me. It was better that way. If I'd told her the truth about her husband then I do not think she could have resisted using it. She would have mocked Kassouli for his daughter's choice of lover, she might even have tried to take Kassouli to court. Wherever her life went now, I thought, she did not need Yassir Kassouli's enmity to haunt her. Thus, at least, I justified my untruths to myself.

Angela sat back on the other bunk and dragged a thin hand through her lank hair. "I need a bath. God, I need a bath."

The metallic squawk of the VHF startled us both. "Yacht *Sycorax*. This is merchant vessel *Kerak*, over." I did not recognize the man's voice that had an American accent.

Angela picked up the microphone. "*Kerak*. This is *Sycorax*, over."

The voice betrayed no surprise that a woman had answered his call. "Our determination is that *Wildtrack*'s hull is a danger to shipping. Can you confirm that there's no one aboard? Over."

Angela looked at me, I nodded, and she pressed the microphone button. "There's no one alive," she said curtly.

"Thank you, *Sycorax*. Over and out."

I could feel Kassouli's brooding presence like a threat. I slid back the coachroof and climbed to the bridge deck. Angela joined me. Neither of us spoke, but we both wondered whether the great tanker would come back to crush us for being inconvenient witnesses to a rich man's anger. We waited two minutes, then the vast shape appeared from the grey north. *Kerak* had turned and come back to us.

She had come back to finish her rotten task. I saw the swollen bow wave pushing ahead of her, evidence that the engines drove the tanker at full speed. She was not coming towards *Sycorax*. I looked for *Wildtrack*, but could not see her among the broken waters. The tanker could see her, though, and was aiming all her weight at the half-sunk yacht. Angela's face was expressionless. "Is Tony's body still on board?"

I took her hand. "Yes."

Then the *Kerak* struck the floating hulk. I doubt if a shudder went through the hundred thousand tons. She hit the floating hull and I saw *Wildtrack* ride up the bulb at the *Kerak*'s prow and she seemed to be caught there like a piece of driftwood trapped by the steel bows.

The *Kerak* ploughed on. The spinning windscreens on the bridge looked like the malevolent eyes of a machine. There were lights behind the windows, and figures moving there in the soft comfort of the huge boat.

Angela cried then. She had loved Bannister enough to marry him. She had put flowers in her hair for a handsome man, and now she watched his dream being sunk into two thousand fathoms of water.

Wildtrack freed itself of the tanker's bows. For a second the yacht's handsome, blue-streaked hull reared up, a toy boat against the steel wall that broke it, then, sliding and crumpled, *Wildtrack* was sinking down to where Nadeznha Bannister's bones lay, down to where there are no storms, and no light, and only silence.

"Oh, Jesus," Angela said, and it sounded like a prayer. I said nothing, but just watched the tanker recede into the grey nothingness of the ocean. Only when it had at last disappeared did either of us speak again. "Is there an airport at St John's?" Angela asked in a small voice.

I nodded.

"Nick?"

"It's all right," I said, "I understand." I'd always known that she was no girl for a small boat in a great sea, but I had dared to hope. Now I knew she would go home and so I set *Sycorax*'s bows towards the west. West towards Canada, west towards parting, and west away from the unmarked place where the dead would lie in silence while the corroding salt dissipated their bones so they would drift as a nebulous part of the very sea itself until the dying sun would one day boil the oceans dry.

Sycorax dipped her bows to the sea and sluiced green water down her scuppers. She at least had come home, while we sailed on, in silence.

EPILOGUE

It was a hard winter. Frosts, fog and a cold to pierce the very soul. Yet it was a hard winter in a good place. I liked Newfoundland; it had the virtues of a place where honest folk did decent work.

Sycorax's stem had been undamaged by the collision with *Wildtrack*. One copper sheet had ripped loose, but it took just a few minutes' work at low tide to nail it back into place. I re-rigged the guardrails and had a new storm jib made from heavy cotton. The sail took the last of my savings, but Vicky and I did not starve. I found work, illegally, in a boatyard.

Vicky grew. A rat came aboard and lived just long enough to regret the transgression. Vicky, blooded at last, disdained my congratulations and instead stalked along the frost-rimed scuppers with her tail aloft in victory. She was my company now; she and the photograph of Angela that I'd screwed to the bulkhead above the portside bunk.

I stripped the engine down and rebuilt it. I welded a radar-reflector from scrap metal and fastened it below the spreaders. I made my boat ready.

In the early spring I took *Sycorax* north; not on a voyage, but to test the engine and new jib. We sailed till the sky was brilliant with the reflected sun from the ice-fields. There was a stiff cold breeze coming from the north-west and, well short of the treacherous ice, and beneath a sky rinsed of colour and cloud, I backed the staysails and eased the main so that *Sycorax*, tractable and steady, lay hove-to.

I had read Angela's letter a dozen times, now read it one last time. The inquest had blamed the deaths of Bannister and Mulder on the pressures of modern ocean-racing. Neither Kassouli's name, nor his presence at *Wildtrack*'s end, had been mentioned, and my notarized and sanitized affidavit had been given scarcely a glance. The verdict was that the deaths were accidental. Angela thought the film about me could be cut into a fifty-minute programme and would I consider taking *Sycorax* to England so she could shoot an end sequence? But she did not want me to go home just for that sequence. She had taken over Bannister's production company and she knew I could help her. Please, Nick, she wrote, come home.

I sat there getting cold, and staring into the shimmer above the brilliant ice. There was a temptation to go home; to trade a medal for comfort and friendship and safety; but it was a temptation to avoid. I was one of life's plodders; no match for the glittering people who made television and money. Back home I would have to compete with bright, sharp minds. Back home was a world that Kassouli and his likes ruled.

But I had said I would sail to New Zealand. There was no reason for New Zealand; it might have been Utopia or La-la land for all that it mattered, it was just a goal to keep me in the cockpit of my boat and beholden to no one. I'd gazed, one year ago, out of a hospital window and found a star to snare in a sextant's mirror, and now I was where the star had fetched me. I was lonely, alone with a sea cat, and happy. I competed with no one, felt no jealousy, and wished no man ill. Here, at sea, I could be honest, for to be anything less was to risk the sea's power. Here there were no bad dreams, no nights riven with tracer or seared by phosphorus, and my leg, like my rebuilt engine, worked most of the time.

So here I would stay. I released the foresail sheets and *Sycorax* dipped her bows as we turned and as Vicky pounced on the fluttering sheets of Angela's letter. I picked her up and scratched under her chin as *Sycorax* caught the wind and drove forward.

"So now that we've arrived," I said to Vicky, "where shall we go?"

BOOKS BY BERNARD CORNWELL

THE SAXON TALES

THE LAST KINGDOM
Available in Paperback and eBook

Set during the reign of King Alfred the Great, *The Last Kingdom* depicts a time when law and order were ripped violently apart by a pagan assault on Christian England.

THE PALE HORSEMAN: A Novel
Available in Paperback and eBook

As England is reduced to nothing but a small patch of marshland, a beguiling sorceress and fearful Danish warrior complicate Alfred's desperate plans.

LORDS OF THE NORTH: A Novel
Available in Paperback, eBook, and Large Print

After achieving victory at King Alfred's side, Uhtred of Bebbanburg returns to his home in the North, finally free of his allegiance to the king—or so he believes.

SWORD SONG: The Battle for London
Available in Paperback, eBook, and Large Print

Alfred survived the Danish invasions, but fresh Viking ships are arriving to plunder and enslave the Saxons.

THE BURNING LAND: A Novel
Available in Paperback, eBook, and Large Print

The epic story of the birth of England and the legendary king who made it possible.

DEATH OF KINGS: A Novel
Available in Paperback, eBook, and Large Print

The sixth volume in the Saxon Tales series resumes the saga of the birth of a nation.

THE RICHARD SHARPE SERIES

SHARPE'S TIGER: Richard Sharpe and the Siege of Seringapatam, 1799
Available in Paperback, Mass Market, and eBook

The first of Richard Sharpe's India trilogy, in which young Private Sharpe must battle both man and beast behind enemy lines as the British army fights its way through India.

SHARPE'S TRIUMPH:
Richard Sharpe and the Battle of Assaye, September 1803

Available in Paperback and eBook

Richard Sharpe must defeat the plans of a British traitor and a native Indian mercenary army in this second volume of the India trilogy.

SHARPE'S FORTRESS
Richard Sharpe and the Siege of Gawilghur, December 1803

Available in Paperback and eBook

In this explosive conclusion to the India trilogy, Sharpe and Sir Arthur Wellesley's army try to conquer an impregnable fort in a battle with stakes both personal and professional.

SHARPE'S TRAFALGAR
Richard Sharpe and the Battle of Trafalgar, October 21, 1805

Available in Paperback and eBook

Having secured a reputation as a fighting soldier in India, Ensign Richard Sharpe returns to England and gets caught up in one of the most spectacular naval battles in history.

SHARPE'S PREY: Richard Sharpe and the Expedition to Denmark, 1807
Available in Paperback and eBook
Sharpe fights once again to keep the treacherous French troops at bay in Denmark.

SHARPE'S HAVOC
Richard Sharpe and the Campaign in Northern Portugal, Spring 1809
Available in Paperback and eBook
Sharpe finds himself in Portugal, fighting the savage armies of Napoleon Bonaparte, as they try to bring the Iberian Peninsula under their control.

SHARPE'S ESCAPE: Richard Sharpe and the Bussaco Campaign, 1810
Available in Paperback and eBook
Sharpe has made enemies among the Portuguese, and when the British army falls back through Coimbra, he and Sergeant Harper are lured into a trap designed to kill them.

SHARPE'S FURY: Richard Sharpe and the Battle of Barrosa, March 1811
Available in Paperback, eBook, and Audio CD
Richard Sharpe has been sent by Wellington on a mission to Cadiz, now the capital of Spain, to rescue the British ambassador from a spot of undiplomatic trouble.

SHARPE'S BATTLE
Richard Sharpe and the Battle of Fuentes de Oñoro, May 1811
Available in Paperback and eBook
As Napoleon threatens to crush Britain on the battlefield, Lt. Col. Richard Sharpe leads a ragtag army to exact personal revenge.

SHARPE'S DEVIL: Richard Sharpe and Napoleon and South America, 1820-1821
Available in Paperback and eBook
An honored veteran of the Napoleonic Wars, Lt. Col. Richard Sharpe is drawn into a deadly battle, both on land and on the high seas.

THE NATHANIEL STARBUCK CHRONICLES

REBEL: The Nathaniel Starbuck Chronicles: Book One • Bull Run, 1861
Available in Paperback and eBook
When a Richmond landowner snatches young Nate Starbuck from the grip of a Yankee-hating mob, Nate turns his back forever on his life in Boston to fight against his native North in this powerful and evocative story of the Civil War's first battle and the men who fought it.

COPPERHEAD
The Nathaniel Starbuck Chronicles: Book Two • Ball's Bluff, 1862
Available in Paperback and eBook
Nate Starbuck is accused of being a Yankee spy. In order to prove his innocence and prevent the fall of Richmond, he must test his endurance and seek out the real spy.

BATTLE FLAG
The Nathaniel Starbuck Chronicles: Book Three • Second Manassas, 1862
Available in Paperback and eBook
The acclaimed Civil War series continues as Confederate Captain Nate Starbuck takes part in the war's most extraordinary scenes.

THE BLOODY GROUND
The Nathaniel Starbuck Chronicles: Book Four • The Battle of Antietam, 1862
Available in Paperback and eBook
Nate serves under General Robert E. Lee during the famous battle at Antietam Creek.

THE GRAIL QUEST SERIES

THE ARCHER'S TALE • Available in Paperback and eBook
Determined to avenge his family, Thomas embarks on a quest for the Holy Grail.

VAGABOND • Available in Paperback and eBook
Thomas continues his quest as he weaves through the battlefields of the Hundred Years War.

HERETIC • Available in Paperback, eBook, and Large Print
To reclaim what's rightfully his, Thomas finds himself in a murderous race with a black rider.

THE SAILING NOVELS

SCOUNDREL: A Novel of Suspense
Available in Paperback and eBook
A relentlessly suspenseful contemporary thriller set in the lethal world of international terror.

STORMCHILD: A Novel of Suspense
Available in Paperback and eBook
A man must save his daughter from Genesis, a shadowy environmental activist group.

WILDTRACK: A Novel of Suspense
Available in Paperback and eBook
Nick Sandman dreams of sailing away from his troubled life. But to keep afloat, he strikes a devil's bargain with another sailor...

CRACKDOWN: A Novel of Suspense
Available in Paperback and eBook
After accepting a job on a yacht, Nick is lured into a web of cocaine, cash . . . and killings.

STANDALONE NOVELS

1356: A Novel
Available in Paperback, eBook, Large Print, and Audio CD
A thrilling tale of danger and conquest at the Battle of Poitiers.

THE FORT: A Novel of the Revolutionary War
Available in Paperback and eBook
The story of the Penobscot Expedition, the largest American naval expedition of the Revolutionary War, a story largely untold—until now.

AGINCOURT: A Novel
Available in Paperback, eBook, Large Print, and Audio CD
The inspiring story of that "band of brothers" who survives devastating hunger and disease only to face the horrors of the field of Agincourt.

GALLOWS THIEF: A Novel
Available in Paperback and eBook
A private investigator in 1820s London explores a murder case that may rescue an innocent man from the gallows.

STONEHENGE: A Novel
Available in Paperback and eBook
An epic historical saga about the building of Stonehenge.

REDCOAT • Available in Paperback
A mesmerizing saga of a family, a city, and a soldier, torn apart on the battlefields of the American Revolution for independence.